CANDY
APPLE
RED

CANDY APPLE RED

NANCY BUSH

KENSINGTON BOOKS
www.kensingtonbooks.com

KENSINGTON BOOKS are published by

Kensington Publishing Corp.
850 Third Avenue
New York, NY 10022

All Kensington titles, imprints, and distributed lines are available at special quantity discounts for bulk purchases for sales promotion, premiums, fund-raising, educational, or institutional use.

Special book excerpts or customized printings can also be created to fit specific needs. For details, write or phone the office of the Kensington Special Sales Manager: Attn. Special Sales Department. Kensington Publishing Corp., 850 Third Avenue, New York, NY 10022. Phone: 1-800-221-2647.

Kensington and the K logo Reg. U.S. Pat. & TM Off.

Library of Congress Card Catalogue Number: 2004113886
ISBN 0-7582-0905-3

First Printing: October 2005
10 9 8 7 6 5 4 3 2 1

Printed in the United States of America

CANDY
APPLE
RED

Chapter One

If I'd known they were about to find a body at the bottom of Lake Chinook, I never would have gotten myself into the whole mess. The lake's deep in places and the Lake Corporation only drains it every couple of years to check the sewer lines running along its muddy bottom. The thought of the little fishy things trolling the waters, chewing off teensy nibbles of human flesh, would have been enough for me to say, "*Hasta la vista*, baby" and I would have exerted great haste in making tracks.

But I didn't know. And I also didn't know my whole life was about to change. The day I spoke with *uber*-bitch/lawyer Marta Cornell I was blissfully ignorant of the events in store for me which was just as well. Don't ever tell yourself you're happy with the way things are because that's when everything changes in seconds flat. And not necessarily for the better.

That particular morning—let's call it The Day Jane Kelly's Life Changed, Not Necessarily For The Better—I walked through the front door of the Coffee Nook, breathing hard from the two-and-a-half mile run from my bungalow. I had nothing more in mind than a cup of coffee and maybe a little conversation with friends. I slid onto my usual stool and Billy Leonard sat down next to me.

He said, "How ya doin'?"

I nodded. "Good."

"Me, too."

"Good."

We both ordered basic black coffee. Billy, an ex-I.R.S. man and current C.P.A. whom I turn to for advice about my modest finances, seemed a bit preoccupied. I assumed it was over his kids. Billy has this theory about why there seems to be less ambition and direction among young people in general, and his boys in particular.

As I blew across the top of my cup, Billy said, "I'm a fisherman, y'know? I mean, I fish." He pretended to cast out a line with an imaginary fishing pole.

Maybe I was wrong as Billy appeared to be heading onto a new topic. I carefully tested my drink. Steaming coffee. Sometimes the damn stuff is so hot it burns off the taste buds and a few layers of tongue underneath.

"When you've got a wild salmon, a Coho, on your line, it's like *zziinnnggg!*" He cast again, this time with more body English.

I watched his invisible line grab an equally invisible Coho. Billy rocked and twisted and generally acted as if Moby Dick himself had swallowed the bait.

My eye traveled past him to a newcomer to the Nook, a woman I didn't recognize. She was thin and small and her hair was completely wrapped in a virulent pink scarf. Wide, round sunglasses covered much of her face which was perched upon a long, white neck. She was a passable Audrey Hepburn. She stood to one side and pretended interest in the glass case of pastries, but I could tell her mind was on something else. I could swear she was playacting, pretending to be thinking over a purchase.

Billy continued, "I mean you *know* it, y'know? It's fightin' and fightin' and you're rockin' and rollin'." He twisted to and fro and nearly fell off his stool. "Those fish are tough. Really tough. But sometimes you cast out . . ." He reeled in again. Actually reeled in. And for just a moment I almost forgot it was all illusion. Once more the imaginary line sailed toward the heads of the other customers whose blank oblivion said more about the hour of the morning than any disinterest in Billy's story. "You get a bite and it's kinda like . . . ugh." His shoulders drooped. He jiggled the line with a slack wrist. "He's on, y'know? Grabbed it big time. But there's just no *zzziinnnggg*." He grimaced and nodded. "Hatchery fish."

Julie, the Coffee Nook's proprietress, asked "Audrey" what she would like. I realized with a jolt that Audrey seemed to be staring across the room at *me*. She saw that I noticed and quickly murmured something to Julie, then hurriedly walked out of the Nook. Julie shrugged.

I sipped my black coffee. It's a shame, but I struggle with both caffeine and lactose. I'm determined to give up neither. If I ever have to give up alcohol I'll start smoking or doing drugs or indulging in weird sex acts. If I can't have a vice I just don't want to live.

Billy continued, "They don't quite have that survival instinct, y'know?" He sighed and wagged his head slowly, side to side. "Just can't really make it out there. And that's the problem with our kids. They're hatchery fish."

Aha . . . he'd managed to pull the allegory back to his favorite subject. Billy's boys were in college, taking a jumble of courses with no clear career path in sight. Most of their friends were in the same boat. I grimaced. Even though I hit the big 3-0 this year and consider myself long finished with higher education, I'm not convinced that I won't be tossed in with these shiftless souls Billy seems to know so much about. My job situation alone might drop me into the loser bin.

"But they'll—they'll figure it out," Billy added. He nodded jerkily as if to convince himself, then ran his hands through his hair, making it stand straight off his head. Billy always looks like he just woke up after a two-week bender. He's so *not* the three-piece-suit type that his choice of profession almost awes me. But then, I've changed professions so many times that sometimes I think I should tack Misc. after my name. Jane Kelly, Misc.

I asked Julie, "Do you know who that woman was? The one dressed like Audrey Hepburn?"

She shook her head. "Never seen her before. She didn't want anything."

I decided to forget about her. If I started thinking people were watching me, I would become as paranoid as the rest of the world. I turned to Billy and said with conviction, "My brother's a hatchery fish."

"Booth?"

"Yep." I hoped this deflection would take the light off me since I definitely preferred the idea of being a wild Coho to a hatchery fish.

Billy considered. "Booth's all right."

I snorted. My twin was a source of irritation to me. Path of least resistance, that was Booth. Christened Richard Booth Kelly, Junior after my shiftless, deadbeat father. Mom, in a moment of belated clarity, decided she couldn't have her children be Dick and Jane and so Booth became Booth.

"Hey, the guy's got a job," Billy remarked.

Yes, Booth was part of the Portland Police Department. I, on the other hand, felt like a poser. I pointed out dampeningly, "The L.A.P.D. breathed a sigh of relief when he left."

"Nah . . ." Billy smiled and clapped me on the shoulder. He loves it when I'm grumpy.

My brother did choose a career path while I've seesawed around the whole issue for years. But Booth's reasons are so wily that I can't trust anything he does. During his stint in L.A. I'm sure he spent most of his time patrolling the area around the University of Southern California and hitting on the sorority chicks on 28th Street. I don't think he ever got lucky, but it wasn't for lack of trying. I suppose I should look on his following me out of So-Cal north to Portland, Oregon, as a move in the right direction, but with Booth, you just never know. This isn't to say I don't love him. Family is just a pain in the ass. Ask anyone.

Billy said, "You're a process server, Jane."

I just managed to keep myself from saying, "You call that a job?"

Billy shrugged. A friend of mine Dwayne Durbin, an "information specialist" (current buzzwords for private investigator) fervently believes I have all the earmarks of a top investigator, which means he thinks I'm a snoop. He wants me to hone these skills while learning the biz through him. The idea makes a certain amount of sense as I took criminology courses at a Southern California community college with just that thought in mind. Well, okay, there were other reasons, too—reasons that had everything to do with blindly following after a guy who had a serious interest in police work and whom I was nuts over and who subsequently dumped me. But regardless, I've done a fair amount of classroom training.

As I sat at the counter, I truly believed—at least in that moment—that I could become an information specialist. I had training and a mentor who would guide me into that world. Why not just go for it? I'd been resisting the full-on private investigator gig all the while I'd been in Portland. I'm not sure why. Self-preservation, I guess.

However, for the last six months I'd been working as general dogsbody to Dwayne who sometimes needs to be in two places at the same time. The fact that Dwayne thinks I have the makings of a first-class information specialist worries—and yes, flatters—me. Dwayne's cute in that kind of slow-talkin' cowboy way, but I'm not sure he's really on the level sometimes. Half the time I get the feeling he's putting me on. Sometimes he's enough to make me want to rip out my hair, scream and stamp my feet. (I also have a problem with a name that begins with *Dw*. I mean . . . *Dwayne, dwindle, dweeb* . . . None of those words conjure up an image of a guy I want to hook up with, even professionally.)

But between doing background checks for Dwayne and process serving for some of the people he knows—mainly landlords—I've kept my head above water financially speaking. I keep toying with the idea of selling the Venice four-unit I own with my mother, but that would mean dealing with her in close contact and I've already voiced my feelings on family. Mom lives in one of the upstairs units, and though I love her dearly she's not exactly on my wavelength about a lot of things. Sometimes we struggle just getting through to each other. She's talked about selling the units, but selling entails moving, and she's dropped more than a few hints about making a move from So-Cal to Portland, and I'm damn sure I don't want her to be the next member of my family to follow me north. Booth's bad enough. I'm just not good with either of them. (I'm very self-aware, especially about my failings. Not that this has helped me much, but if pushed to the wall, I'll pull it out as some kind of badge of honor.) I've reminded my mother of this fact many a time. She always looks at me half-puzzled, as if she can't understand how she could have given birth to me. Luckily, she seems to feel the same way about Booth so I've never worried that he was her favorite.

"You were a bartender in Santa Monica, right?" Billy said on a note of discovery. "What was the name of that place?"

"Sting Ray's. Ray being the owner."

"My old man owned a bar. Did I tell you?"

I nodded. On numerous occasions. About as many times as I've told him I used to bartend. Neither Billy nor I worry that we recycle conversations. I also never have to worry that he'll get pissy over my inherent lack of attentiveness. Hey, I was ADD before it was even popular.

"Evict anyone I know lately?" he asked, grinning.

"Probably."

This was a long-standing joke between us. The scary part was that his question might one day become reality as Billy knew a wide, wide range of people around the greater Portland area.

He slid off the stool and turned toward the door. At the last moment he said, "Hey, I ran into Marta last night at Millennium Park. She wants you to do some work for her."

"What kind of work?"

Billy shrugged. "Said she had a job that required tact. You any good at tact?"

"About as good as you are," I said.

"You hear about that kid fell in the lake? He's in a coma in the hospital."

Billy's good at shifting subjects faster than warp speed. I may
be ADD but he takes the cake. "What happened?"

"Buncha kids screwing around in a boat." He shrugged. "He
fell somewhere and was trying to get back in the boat. Think it
happened on the island."

There is one island in Lake Chinook. Circling it is a footpath
and guarding this footpath is a black chain-link fence. Enter-
prising teenagers make a habit of leaping the fence and racing
the perimeter, trying to speed all the way around before the island's Dobermans catch their scent.

"He was running around the island?"

"Probably. Mighta tried to jump in the boat from the island.
There are a lot of big rocks around that one side. But kids are
tough. Don't know what his name is. Julie . . . you know?"

"What?" Julie was deep into the whir of a latte, staring into a
fat silver cylinder where foam lifted and fell in white waves.

"What the Coma Kid's name is?"

She shook her head. "Everyone's been talking about it this
morning. I hope he's okay."

Billy nodded, then waved a good-bye as he headed out. I sent
a silent wish that the Coma Kid would be all right. Hadn't we all
done something dangerous and stupid in our youth that might
have killed us?

I drank some more coffee and my thoughts turned to Marta
Cornell. She was the best and baddest divorce lawyer in the city
of Portland and probably the entire state. Come to that, she
could probably rival anyone in the region. Dwayne was her information specialist of choice, and I'd done a bit of work for her
through him. Not pretty stuff. Divorces were messy and ugly
and, personally, I'd rather be a process server and evict crack
dealers armed with semiautomatic weapons than deal with one of
Marta's jobs. (This is a lie as guns generally worry me, but you
get the idea.)

But Marta pays well. Dwayne says he'd put her first for money
alone. This makes him sound mercenary and maybe he is a little,
but you'd never be able to tell by his minuscule cabana off North

Shore which makes my bungalow on West Bay look like a palace. Dwayne wants me to move my business to his cabana, but I fear for my independence and my soul. Not to mention I can't see myself working cheek-to-jowl inside Dwayne's living space. This is where the guy resides, after all, and Dwayne just doesn't strike me as the kind of guy I want to get that close to. I have this sneaking suspicion I will turn into his cleaning woman/coffee maker/receptionist and God knows what else.

I finished the rest of my coffee. Every muscle felt stretched out of whack from my run. I don't think exercise can seriously be good for you, but I sure as hell have to keep up with it. The last time I process-served, the woman opened her door, reluctantly accepted the eviction notice I thrust into her hands, gave it one look and howled as if I'd hit her. She then grabbed a broom and whacked me once, hard. I left with one shin smarting and my pride bruised even worse. Talk about killing the messenger. I don't plan on being taken by surprise again.

I wondered what Marta had in store for me. Her jobs tend to be a little more involved than mere process serving. I'd once been asked to drive to Baker—a city plopped way off in eastern Oregon and miles and miles from *anything* else—and question the locals about the habits of a Portland businessman who'd suddenly grown a hankering for ranch life out in this remote wind-blown part of the state. His wife wanted to know whom he was ranching with and what she looked like. It turned out the lady in question was surprisingly plump, sweet and homegrown, and I didn't blame the guy one bit when I met the real wife, Marta's client, who was thin, grim, long-nailed and tense. It sorta bothered me to be on her side, so to speak. But, once again, it paid well.

With a last gulp of now cold coffee I gathered up my energy and jogged the three miles back to my rundown 1930s bungalow on West Bay, the small body of water on Lake Chinook's westernmost tip. Once upon a time wealthy Portlanders owned summer homes on the man-made lake. Lake Chinook was created by Chinese laborers who dug a canal in the late 1800s and connected the sluggish nearby river to what was by all accounts little more than a large pond, beautifully named Sucker Lake. Now the town thinks it's beyond upscale, and though Lake Chinook is a nice community, I think it's good to remember one's roots.

My cottage is a ramshackle remnant, built a few decades after the lake became a desirable locale for summering. It's Craftsman style, which means there's a lot of wood trim, a wraparound porch and the exterior is composed of shingles. The inside must have been utter crap because my landlord, Mr. Ogilvy, updated the place before I moved in. Ogilvy's known for his pecuniary ways, so the improvements—new kitchen appliances and a low-water pressure toilet which requires two or three good flushes to work properly—are a complete and utter gift. The cottage sits on a flag lot, encroached on each side by huge new homes whose builders fought city ordinances against the setbacks and succeeded. Ogilvy is about sixty-five and hates government, especially city government, so he cheerfully okays every variance sent his way. Along the way he's chopped off chunks of his own property and sold them for a premium price so now I have a teensy line of sight and strip of land that leads to the water. Still, there's enough room for a boathouse, also ramshackle, which matches the taupe, shingle siding of the cottage. This matching color scheme exists because last year I talked Ogilvy into painting the place. This is saying a lot for my skills of persuasion as Ogilvy bitched, moaned and side-stepped until we were both beyond exasperation. Eventually, he just bellowed, "Fine!" and signed on the painters. Now the place looks semi-presentable and if I had any serious cash I'd try to buy it. On my own dime I'd cleaned out everything on the inside— some of the items in the storage shed had been left over since the cottage was built, I swear—ripped up the carpet and had the old hardwood floors stripped, sanded and generally redone. I possess a modicum of furniture, all of it castoffs that, for some reason or other, I can't seem to cast off as well. Except my bed, which is new, springy and a double—nothing bigger fits in the bedroom— and covered with a solid red, quilted cover—a splurge at Pottery Barn.

As I jogged up to my front door, catching my breath and slipping the key in the lock, I mentally congratulated myself on my industrious fitness program. Self-affirmation is all that stands between me and the depression of reality so I keep a steady "Atta, girl!" going in my head at every given opportunity.

Stripping off my In-N-Out Burger T-shirt (which I brought back with me from my last trip to California) I walked into the bathroom and reminded myself I had to buy groceries or die. My desktop computer—years old and a real electronic grinder—sits cold, blank and silent in the little desk/nook I've arranged next to my bed. Though mainly used for writing up short reports for Dwayne, invoices for my process serving services, e-mail, and the occasional resume, I worry its life is close to ending and whenever I hit the switch, I fear its little green "on" light might sputter and slowly fade out forever. I'm not only afraid of the cost of replacing it, I'm afraid of new technology, period. I keep a laptop in a case nearby, just in case. It's far newer, though given how quickly computers grow obsolete, it's definitely in its twilight years. I'm attached to both of them in a way that defies description, especially for a loner like myself. And what's really amazing is although they both have this nagging quality about them— their very silence a stern reminder for me to get to work—I would be completely bereft without them.

I took a quick shower, toweled off, threw on a robe, then pushed the play button on my answering machine. Marta's voice loudly told me to phone her A.S.A.P. I made a face, sensing I should avoid the call. Then Billy's hatchery fish comment skimmed across my mind and propelled me into action.

"Jane Kelly returning Marta's call," I snapped out to the receptionist. This particular woman has one of the snottiest voices on record and I always try to cut her off as fast as possible.

She smoothly responded, "Ms. Cornell's in a meeting."

Though I should have felt relief that I could delay my talk with Marta, I was consumed with impatience. There's a whiff of smugness to the receptionist's tone which calls me to battle in spite of myself. "Tell her I'm on my cell phone," I said, then reeled off the number as fast as humanly possible.

"Could you repeat that, please?" she asked, not bothering to hide her scorn.

"Oh, sure." This time I spoke clearly and slowly. Even while I was running through this mini-drama I asked myself why I do such things. Call it my low tolerance for frosty self-importance.

"I'll give her the message," she said and abruptly clicked off.

I sat back in my chair and surveyed my domain. Pretty much a desk, chair, phone, notepad, pen and stapler. And computer, of course. I switched it on and waited while it went through its beeps, whirs and flashing screens. I know others grow annoyed if their computer doesn't jump to attention like a military cadet but I don't mind the wait. It's like a cat stretching awake.

Sometimes, there's a moment of perfect synergy when what you're thinking suddenly comes into the moment of your life. As I waited for my computer to finish its wake-up routine, my mind drifted to thoughts of Murphy. Tim Murphy, to be exact, though no one called him by his first name. He was the guy who'd walked into Sting Ray's one night and bowled me over with quick repartee, wicked sarcasm, innate politeness and one dimple in an otherwise masculine jaw. I'd fallen in lust with him right there and then. When I learned he was taking criminology courses, I'd signed up at the first opportunity. And when he'd finally left L.A. for his native Oregon, I'd followed him blindly to Lake Chinook as soon as I could. I'd wanted to live with him, soak him into my system, wrap our lives together, but Murphy had resisted. He'd sworn he loved me, but it turned out his love hadn't been quite as real as mine. His was the kind that disappeared like fairy dust as soon as I grabbed for it. And though it lasted a while, it had already faded some by the time a horrific tragedy involving his best friend from high school placed us on opposite sides of the law. Murphy never forgave me for believing the worst of his friend, despite overwhelming evidence. He chose to run away from me and all things related to Lake Chinook. I, however, have remained. A part of me I don't often face knows that although Murphy was devastated by his friend's tragedy, he also used that event as an excuse to end our faltering relationship.

These thoughts flashed across my mind in quick succession, about three seconds in real time. At the end of those three seconds my cell phone buzzed, splintering the images and memories.

"Hello?"

"Jane!" Marta boomed over the phone. The woman was over six-feet-tall with a voice to match. She could deafen with one word. I yanked the phone from my ear and hoped I still possessed my hearing.

"Jane?" Marta demanded, her voice now tinny and faraway as my arm was stretched straight out from my torso. I carefully placed the receiver to my ear.

"I hear you."

"I have a client who has an unusual request and I think you're just the person to help."

I opened and closed my mouth several times, seeing if I could pop my ears. They seemed okay but there was an alarming little creaking sound at the corner of my jaw. I thought about TMJ. Temporal . . . mandibular . . . jaw thing. Whatever. It was bad and sometimes it takes an operation where your jaw's wired shut for six weeks. I don't normally worry about such things, but the thought of all food coming through a straw for six weeks was enough to scare me straight. No more caramels? No more Red Vines? I'd *never* be able to eat beef jerky again?

"What unusual request?" I asked.

"It's about Cotton Reynolds."

My heart leapt. Christ, I thought a bit shakily. Had thoughts of Murphy actually triggered the past? "What about him?" I asked, trying to hold my voice steady.

"My client wants some follow-up on . . . Bobby Reynolds." Marta hesitated, unlike her to the extreme. "She wants you to interview Cotton."

I stared at my office door and instead of its scarred, paneled wood saw the white-haired man who happened to be one of the wealthiest in the state of Oregon. Cotton Reynolds lived on the island—the site of the Coma Kid's accident—and it was less than a mile from my bungalow. By boat, I could be there in ten minutes, if I wanted to. By car, it would be trickier. The island was private and Cotton's was the only house on its three acres. If I dropped in to say hello, I wouldn't get past the huge wrought iron gate nor the Dobermans.

But interviewing Cotton wasn't what was on my mind. Following up on Bobby Reynolds was. Murphy's close, high school friend. His best buddy. The cause of the horrific tragedy my mind had briefly touched on.

I almost hung up right then. I probably should have. A shiver slid coldly down my spine; someone walking on my grave.

Bobby Reynolds had murdered his family and left their bodies lined up in a row—wife, Laura; Aaron, 8; Jenny, 3; and infant, Kit—somewhere in the Tillamook State Forest, just off the Oregon coast. Bobby Reynolds was a "family annihilator": a man apparently overwhelmed with the responsibility of his family so he chose to send them to a "better place." He shot them each once in the back of the head, then drove away. He dumped his Dodge Caravan on a turnout off Highway 101 which meanders along the West Coast throughout Washington, Oregon and into California, then disappeared without a trace, though he'd been rumored to have been seen as far north as the Canadian border, and as far south as Puerto Vallarta. To date, after four years, he was still very much a fugitive. The murders—disputed by Murphy who simply could not believe his friend capable of cold-blooded homicide—had driven Murphy away from Lake Chinook, the tragedy and me.

I cleared my throat and asked, "Who is this client?"

"Tess Reynolds Bradbury."

"Bobby's *mother?*"

"Cotton won't talk to her about Bobby or anything else. They haven't spoken civilly in years. When it was all over the news they had words, but it wasn't exactly what I would call communication."

"I remember," I said, recalling how Cotton's ex, with her blond bob, hard eyes and angry mouth had been bleeped out by the local news, time and again. Cotton had been silent and stony, although my impression was that it was a mask for deep, deep pain and shock. I'd tried to talk to Murphy but he'd gone to a place inside himself, as distant as a cold moon, before he'd left for good.

"Why does she want me to talk to him?" I asked, baffled. "The police and F.B.I. and every news channel around has been on this since it happened. What could I learn? I don't even know Cotton."

"You've met. You were Tim Murphy's girlfriend."

"I wouldn't call myself his girlfriend," I said succinctly. "I knew him." Not as well as I thought I did, as it turned out.

"Murphy was close to Bobby and Cotton. Tess thinks you can use that connection—"

"*No*," I said again, with more force. "I'm outta this. I'd be useless."

"She stopped by my office the other day, and we started talking about Bobby a little. She never could before. But it's like she's suddenly gotta get it out."

"You're a divorce attorney," I reminded Marta tonelessly. I couldn't keep up with this. My head reeled. I felt ill.

"I'm her divorce attorney," Marta agreed. "But I'm also a friend. After she started talking, your name came up. She remembered you."

If I hadn't been so overwhelmed I would have been surprised. Tess had barely seen me. She'd been divorced from Cotton in those few months before Bobby's deadly deed was discovered. I hadn't known Bobby very well, as he and his family had moved to Astoria. I mostly knew about them through Murphy. I'd only met Bobby and his wife Laura a few times, so when their pictures were in the papers they'd looked like the strangers they were to me. I said, "It would be a miracle if Cotton remembered me."

"He knows Murphy. That's all that matters."

I didn't like it. It was sneaky and wrong. Oh, sure, I can be a snoop, but this tragedy was epic. I felt small and mean even talking about it with Marta. "What kind of information does she expect?" I asked. "I don't get it."

"Whether she's right or wrong, she thinks Cotton's been in touch with Bobby. I know the police and F.B.I. have wrung him dry, and he's been more than cooperative. I'm just telling you what she wants. And she's willing to pay well."

"I'm not a private investigator." *Or information services specialist.*

"As good as," Marta dismissed, but then she was always saying things like that when she wanted something.

"How much is she willing to pay?" I asked cautiously, lured in spite of myself. I inwardly shuddered. It was like dipping a toe in cold, cold water.

"An initial five hundred dollars and then whatever you work out. She wants you to develop some kind of relationship, Jane," Marta went on. "She says Cotton always admired you when you were there with Murphy. She thinks you could . . . have some sway."

"I doubt it."

"Are you saying you won't do it?"

I didn't know what I was saying. I was out of my depth and I knew it. I'm not all that hot at self-delusion. If I were really thinking about taking the jump to information specialist, I'd sure as hell like to start with something smaller. Like grand larceny. Or . . . corporate tax fraud. Or that Erin Brockovich deadly chemical thing. I did not want to be personally involved in the investigation, no matter how distantly, as I was in this one.

"Cotton remembers you," Marta insisted. "Bobby told Tess how his dad liked you."

"Bobby told his mother that his dad liked me? That's just great. When was that, Marta? I was only here for a few months before it happened."

Marta sighed at my obstinance. "Are you going to do it, or not?"

"All signs point to *not*." I paused, belatedly hearing some innuendo between the lines. Why did Tess want me to get close to Cotton? My thoughts took a turn toward the salacious. "I'm not going to sleep with him."

"Oh, for God's sake, Jane. Tess just wants you to suck up to him a little, show some interest in the guy. He's been living like a hermit with his young wife ever since Bobby slaughtered his family and ran." I cringed at her words. "Tess thinks this is the perfect time to lend a sympathetic ear."

"I won't get any results the police haven't."

"Five hundred dollars plus, whether you learn anything or not," Marta coerced.

Five hundred dollars plus. My brain started calculating, taking a trip of its own, as I wondered how many "sessions" I could squeeze out of the deal. It's hard to turn down pure, cold cash. Dwayne would be proud of my way of thinking.

"Cotton's having a party next Saturday night." Marta sweetened the pot. "I can get you an invitation."

"How?"

"Well . . . Murphy's been invited. He's coming into town this week."

I swore beneath my breath, loud enough for Marta to hear. *Murphy?* "What a setup. I'm not interested, Marta. Not one little bit."

"He knows you might be there. He wants to see you."

"Not a chance." Marta knows what she's doing at all times. She's an operator, someone who sees what she wants and goes after it, no matter how many souls she grinds into the pavement along the way. I almost admired her.

"Murphy still talks to Tess," Marta went on. "He mentioned you the other day. That's what got Tess thinking."

"Murphy and I don't talk."

"Jane, Tess is going to be in my office at three today. She'd really like to meet you."

"You're railroading me. I can hear the train whistle."

"I thought you might want to see him."

"Bullshit. You thought of a new way to squeeze money out of a client. How much is Tess paying you for this setup?"

"Plenty," was her equable answer. "Tess is a grateful client."

I almost laughed. I could imagine how well Marta had put the squeeze on Cotton as Tess's representative in the divorce. Her unabashed greed appealed to me, maybe because deep inside I'm a kindred spirit. Okay, maybe it's just that I'm not that deep inside.

She seemed to sense my lessening fury. "Is that a yes?"

Distantly, I heard the sound of a buzzing boat's engine. I walked toward the rear windows for my peek-a-boo view of the water. It was a beautiful, 75-ish afternoon in late July. The weatherman had said the temperatures were going to rise through the weekend, peaking at about 88 degrees late afternoon Saturday. The night of Cotton's party. Great boating weather.

I had an instant memory of a hot midnight on Murphy's boat, illegally docked in the shelter of Phantom's Cove, two hundred feet beneath the houses perched on the bluff above, hidden by the canopies of oaks and firs which kept the cove under shadow most of the time. I remembered fevered bodies wrapped tightly together, sweat and silent laughter that remained caught in the back of my throat. And pleasure.

An ache filled me inside. I'd fallen in love once in college, but Murphy was the next, and last, man who'd ever filled my senses so completely. I half-believed now that it would never happen to me again. Maybe it would, but right now it felt impossible.

The thought that he might actually be at this party was enough to send me into the kind of female panic I loathed seeing in others. I couldn't go. Even if I met with Cotton, I couldn't go to this party if Murphy was going to be there.

I said as much to Marta. At least I think did. But she responded with a quick overview of how much income this could provide me. I turned her down over and over again, I swear. Yes, dollar signs danced in front of my eyes, but the thought of clapping eyes on Tim Murphy again was something my system couldn't take. I told myself I would rather live in destitution for a thousand lifetimes than go another round with Murphy.

". . . we'll see you at three, then," Marta said happily and hung up.

I was left staring into space, my jaw hanging open. Slowly, I brought my lips together again and clicked off my cell phone. There was no memory in my mind of an agreement to meet with Tess, but somehow I'd managed to say yes.

Chapter Two

I had hours before my date with Marta but that didn't mean I didn't have things to do. I yanked on a pair of black jeans that had shrunk, making me look as if I were wearing capri pants. I coupled this with a once black, now gray, sleeveless T-shirt and quickly tied on my gray and black Nikes without socks. I gave another cursory glance in the mirror. My light brown hair lay in a shoulder-length tangle. I'm beyond stylish, no doubt. The Nikes were my good shoes, not my running shoes. I also own a pair of flip-flops and that about says it all for my entire shoe selection. There are a few dresses in my closet, left over from college when I used to care what I wore. I save them for weddings and funerals. One of these days I'm going to have to learn how to shop, but it hasn't happened yet.

I dragged a brush through my hair, hoping for a miracle. No use. The gods of coif gifted me with straight, forgettable hair that firmly defies any kind of style. I used to complain about it until I listened to the woes of those cursed with serious curls/frizz whose taming time at least tripled my alloted five minutes for hair. Now, I keep my mouth shut. As I scraped my hair into a ponytail I remembered things could be worse.

Locking the door behind me I thought about lipstick and settled for Chapstick. I skimmed a wax coating on my mouth, inhaled deeply and smacked my lips. Tropical fruit. Who needs breakfast?

My car is a dark blue Volvo wagon which my mother purchased years earlier and donated to me. Actually, I think she just forgot she owned it, which is fine by me. I drove it out of California a little over four years ago and never looked back. Well, okay, I've looked back, but though I grew up in the land of southern California sunshine, I don't mind the Oregon rain . . . too much.

With a supreme effort of will I pushed thoughts of Murphy and Cotton and Bobby Reynolds aside. At least I managed to push them to a distant corner of my mind for the time being. As I climbed into the car I called Dwayne on my cell phone to see if any of the property owners he deals with needed someone (me) to post 72-hour eviction notices. These same property owners then pay me a fee for chasing all over the greater Portland area and potentially facing enraged evictees like the howler.

"Hullo," Dwayne drawled, sounding as if I'd interrupted him.

"Hi, it's me."

I could hear papers being shuffled. Dwayne's in love with hard copy. He relies on the hunt-and-peck method, and therefore he runs off pages and reams and cargo loads of paper. It's a form of compensation, or maybe Dwayne's a belt-and-suspender kind of guy—an inverse reaction to his line of work. "What's up?" he asked without any real interest.

I wanted to blab about Marta's call and my pending meeting with Tess Reynolds but I also wanted to gauge Dwayne's reaction to the news when we saw each other in person. I asked instead, "Have you got any work?"

"Hayden needs some 72's posted," Dwayne said.

"Great. I'll stop by his office."

"Bring me a Standish burger, would'ja?"

"No," I responded without a second thought. Standish's was known for its burgers the size of a large dinner plate. The place was a Portland institution, the original tavern located out Sunset Highway, past Hillsboro, which in my mind, is halfway to the beach. Its satellite offshoot is on Macadam Avenue which runs north from Lake Chinook proper to Portland, right across from Hayden's office.

"Be a good girl. I'll give you an extra buck or two for delivery."

"Oh, yeah, sure. Sweet-talk me. Where do these notices need to be posted? I'll bring you a burger if it's on the way."

"I don't know where the hell they're supposed to go. You're not gonna make me wait." He sounded disbelieving.

"Yes, I am," I stated succinctly and clicked off.

The Volvo started right up but it was warm inside, the worn black leather seats infused with heat. I flipped on the air-conditioning and left my house on West Bay, heading into Lake Chinook proper so that I could drive the road which runs alongside the Willamette River straight up to Greg Hayden's office and Standish's.

Greg needed to alert several defaulting renters that they had 72 hours in which to vacate their premises. Usually by the time Greg decides to pay me to post the notices, these deadbeats are way past due. For a few extra dollars I will also traipse to the county courthouse to file the paperwork. When I'm low on cash I start looking for work as a process server. My friends see this as a personal flaw. Maybe it is, but the real jobs I've tried haven't worked out all that well. Even my bartending gig had its drawbacks. I need flexibility and mobility or I'm doomed.

Greg's office is an older house off Macadam that has resisted the commercial development surrounding it on all sides. It looks cute on the outside, smells like dog on the inside and is a death-trap of sloping floors and haphazard furniture. When I walked in Greg was rummaging through his desk, talking on the phone and tossing around loose papers. He makes Dwayne look like a man of the 22nd century as Greg still doesn't use a computer at all. When I entered he motioned to an untidy stack of stapled papers. I scooped up the forms, sent him a high sign and headed back to the Volvo, breathing deeply as soon as I stepped onto the porch. There is no dog any longer. The cotenant with the back office and his Basset hound are gone, thank God. Dogs are fine,

but they smell. And shed. And dig. And bark. Not to mention the
fact that they do not have designated indoor toilet facilities. My
idea of pets is the geese and ducks that paddle around on the
lake. However, if they flap onto my property in a group, as
they're wont to do, I'll shoo them off faster than you can say
"group duck poop."

Glancing at the addresses, I realized one of the soon-to-be
evictees wasn't that far outside my neighborhood. I had just
enough time to grab Dwayne's burger, speed over to his place,
tack up the notice, then buzz downtown to meet Marta and Tess.
Maybe I even had time for a quick stop at the grocery store. I
could head home later and make myself a sandwich, thereby saving myself a few bucks on lunch/dinner. As soon as this thought
crossed my mind, I nixed it. Better to buy a Standish burger for
myself and charge that to Dwayne, too.

Standish's was packed. I edged to the bar and placed a take-
out order. As much as I love those huge burgers, I settled for a
more moderate size. The bag smelled of juicy beef, onions and
grease. I paid with some crumpled dollars and coins and was on
my way within fifteen minutes.

I ate in the car. I covered my lap with extra napkins and
chowed into the burger, one handed. In New York it's against the
law to hold a cell phone while driving. Other states may soon follow. But as yet you can still eat a burger. I know a woman who ap-
plies eyeliner on her way to work each morning while driving. I
call it multi-tasking.

By the time I pulled up to Dwayne's place and parked behind
his car I was finished with my burger. Dwayne lives in a cabana
on Lakewood Bay. The cabana is still pretty close to its original
style which is basically one-story shotgun. At one time there
were a row of like cabanas sitting side by side, two-bedroom
homes built on stilts over the water, but most of the others have
long since been purchased and redone. Now Dwayne's looks like
a stunted step-cousin surrounded by towering heirs to the throne.
Its pebbled roof is faintly mossy; its gray paint blistering and
peeling. Still, its waterfront location means it's worth a mint.

Dwayne's neglect is more part of his style than a matter of his pocketbook, though you'd never know it by his cheapness.

Hurrying up the cracked concrete walk, I pounded loudly on his dark-stained front door which is weather-worn and splotchy.

Dwayne answered. He was wearing a pair of low-riding faded denim jeans, a straw cowboy hat and not much else. My eyes were level with an expanse of hard flesh. I could make out the muscles sliding beneath his taut skin as he threw open the door without giving me much notice. He was on his cell phone and he turned his back to me almost instantly, heading the way he'd come.

"Don't bother," he said to the caller. "It'll work itself out."

Dwayne has this slow way of talking that other women seem to find irresistible. Me, it just bugs. "It'll work itself out" is "It all wook itsalf aut" rolling off Dwayne's tongue. He sounds all western or Texan or just plain cowboy. I have this sneaking suspicion he's from somewhere like Philadelphia or Columbus. One of these days I'm going to find out.

Tentatively, I followed after him into the condo. His long strides had already placed him at the far side of the room but I stepped inside more carefully. Instantly my sensitive nose picked up the faint scent of someone's lilac, and decidedly feminine, perfume. A female visitor? I glanced over Dwayne's chunky tan leather sofa and chair, his boxy coffee table, end tables and massive desk, currently masked under a mound of papers. Not a sign of any visitor.

My curiosity meter rose into the red. I've never known Dwayne to be with a member of my gender. Not that he isn't interested; hell, no! I've seen his eyes wander over a lovely set of breasts, legs, etc. more than a time or two. But to date he's been very, very circumspect about letting me inside his dating world. I've got to say I was hoping to run straight into her, whoever she was, so it was with a degree of impatience that I waited for someone to appear from the short hallway that led to Dwayne's bedroom and bath—not that I dared head down that way myself, I mean, God knows what you'll discover lurking inside a bachelor's abode. Whatever it is, I just don't want to know it about Dwayne, potential girlfriend or no.

Cradling the cell phone on his bare shoulder, he swept off his hat, raked his fingers through his hair, jammed the hat back on and said succinctly, "We're done." He clicked off and threw the phone on the leather chair. "Got my burger?" He gave me his full attention for the first time.

"Hello to you, too," I said, tossing the sack at him. Dwayne's jeans have to be decades old and he doesn't give a damn. It kinda bothers me how good they look, low slung on his hips. No sign of undershorts. I wondered briefly if he went commando style.

"You owe me twenty-one fifty," I said. "You bought mine, too."

Dwayne grunted in disbelief. He still thinks a burger should cost $1.95 on all occasions. Muttering something about highway robbery, he jammed his hand inside the bag. "Where's yours?" he demanded, pulling out one burger.

"Ate it on the way."

He took a healthy bite, the kind that makes any woman marvel. It looked like he swept in a pound of ground beef, I swear. Like a chaw in his cheek, he moved it to one side and mumbled, "Need something to drink?"

"A little early for me."

I was standing by the desk which was pressed up against the sliding glass door, making it possible only to open the door about twelve inches. Dwayne squeezes himself in and out of the door when necessary to stand on his deck/dock. Beyond lies the lake—dark green and gently restless. You can literally step off his dock and sink into the water.

I could see a .38 peeking out from the teetering stack of papers. I know he's licensed, and given his profession he probably needs the handgun, but the sight of a firearm just lying around unsettles me. He swears he only loads it when he's on a job, but it still gives me the willies.

"I mean a soda," he said, digging into his pockets for money. The jeans dipped precariously lower. I watched in fascination, wondering if I was about to see more than I'd bargained for, but he managed to haul out twenty-five dollars. Dropping it into my palm, he said magnanimously, "Keep the change," then turned and took one giant step into his tiny U-shaped kitchen, yanking open the refrigerator door in one fluid move. "Diet A&W?"

"Sure. I'll take it for the road."

Juggling the burger, he pulled out two cans of root beer. I took them from him and opened his—hey, I can be truly helpful when I want—then perched on one of the two suspect bar stools which crowd against a small, jutting counter that divides Dwayne's kitchen and dining area. This dining area is now used as Dwayne's den; the desk takes up the whole expanse. Dwayne hooked a leg over the other stool but continued to stand as he took another bite of his burger.

"Would love to stay, but I have miles to go before I sleep," I said, twisting my unopened soda can on the counter, my thoughts on my upcoming meeting with Tess Bradbury.

Dwayne said around a mouthful of onions and beef, "Did you hear about Cotton Reynolds?"

I nearly fell off my stool but Dwayne was regarding the catsup running down the side of his hand and didn't notice. I couldn't think of any response. Dwayne seemed way ahead of me anyway.

He licked the catsup before it dripped to the floor. "There's a benefit at his house this Saturday for the Historical Society. Saw it in the papers. First time he's opened the house since it happened."

It was Cotton's son's quadruple homicide, and now I understood how Marta had wangled me an invitation to Cotton's party. She'd merely bought tickets to the benefit. I opened my mouth to inform Dwayne about my meeting with Tess when his cell phone rang loudly. He snatched it up, examined the caller ID and grunted, "Been waitin' for this all day."

As he barked a hello, I climbed off the stool. I wondered if the island's latest tragedy, the Coma Kid, would affect all the "ladies who lunch" who would be at the benefit. Or, would the original horror be enough to absorb everyone's mind? The property itself was incredible, but I had a feeling attending might be more like being witness to a car wreck than marveling over the width and breadth of the massive Douglas firs surrounding the property. The island and therefore Cotton were already infamous.

I glanced at Dwayne. Full disclosure would have to be later when I had his complete attention. Besides, I didn't have time to waste. Dwayne crumpled his leftover wrapper into a ball with one hand, listening hard to whomever was on the other end of the line. I gave him a high-sign good-bye, popped open my soda and headed out. The answer to Dwayne's mystery woman would have to wait.

Sucking down the ice-cold root beer, I whipped the Volvo up Taylor's Ferry Road and curved through neighborhoods perched on hills. The house where I was to deliver the 72-hour notice was a seedy little ranch style with a cracked driveway near the I-5 freeway. I suspected the land value alone would soon make it worthwhile to initiate a complete demolition; the residence wasn't much to write home about.

But my thoughts were on Bobby Reynolds as I pulled to a stop in the driveway, my wheels in ruts, the Volvo's undercarriage tickled by a foot-high swatch of weeds and grass. For four years there had been relative silence about Bobby's homicides. Now, suddenly, the tragedy was right in front of my face. Was Bobby still alive? I wondered. And if so, where was he?

Stowing the empty can in my cup holder, I climbed from the car and trudged through more knee-high weeds to the front door. Knocking on the screen door, I automatically held tight to my small purse. Its strap was slung over my shoulder. I was poised. If I saw even one whisker of a broom I was out of there. After waiting a few moments I rapped again, hoping against hope that she wasn't home and I could just post the notice. Greg could mail the 72-hour notice but because of the extra mailing time the tenant was allowed six days' leeway instead of three. When rent was late, sometimes that just didn't pan out, especially for Greg who wasn't known for his patience anyway.

Relieved that no one was there, I dug in my pocket for my

Scotch tape. As soon as I stuck the tape on the paper and reached for the screen door handle I heard shuffling footsteps on the other side. I dropped my hand and waited. A woman with a tired face and a well-smoked cigarette dangling from her lips swam into view from the darkness beyond. The screen door was still between us. There was a big rip in the mesh down by my knees but I didn't think I could hand her the notice from that angle. It just didn't seem polite. I could drop it through the hole, but it was always better to actually see the notice in their hands. No questions later. If she took it, then the deed was done. I've always liked things wrapped up neat and tidy.

"Gail Mortibund?" I asked.

"Yeah?" She waited as if expecting bad news. I got the feeling she'd received a lot of it in her life, and I hesitated.

One moment I was debating whether to even give her the notice, the next a pit bull was charging toward the door at full bellow, heading straight for the rip in the screen. I pivoted and ran before my brain even locked into gear. The woman screamed at the dog to no avail. I pounded toward the Volvo. The beast was barking its head off and sounded right at my heels. The eviction notice flew from my hands. I leapt for the car. The dog snapped at my jeans, brushed my ankle and caught a piece of my left Nike as I hurled myself atop the hood of my car. Arms flailing, I landed in full sail. My stomach hit with an *oof* and all the wind burst from my lungs. I sprawled in classic starfish position for one heartbeat, then yanked up my legs at the knees while the monster snapped and snarled beneath me. With an effort I pulled myself to safety on the center of my hood.

My heart hammered like a woodpecker on steroids.

So, where was Gail The Tired now?

I glared at the house. The front door was solidly closed. She'd left Woofers out here to bark and lunge and bare his nasty teeth. I snarled back at him, and that sent him in paroxysms of dancing around and clawing at my paint job.

"Stop that!" I yelled in fury.

His wrinkled mouth revealed canines that sent visions of

ripped, bloody tissue across the screen of my brain. I shivered, hugged my knees tighter and considered.

Five seconds of intense thought ensued. A lightning bolt of remembrance. That hard pain against my hip bone was my cell phone. Jammed into the pocket of my black pants. I pulled it out and examined its LCD, tracking the battery life. Only one little miniature battery icon was left. I had enough time for one, maybe two, calls. I mentally castigated myself, telling myself to plug the damn thing into the portable charger as soon as I was back inside my car.

First I called Marta's office. Her receptionist snottily told me she was, as ever, in a meeting. I sighed inwardly, wondering what drives me to piss people off. Certain personalities just beg me to annoy them. I told her that I wanted to leave a message and was snottily told to go ahead. Meanwhile, Woofers prowled and growled somewhere along the edge of the car. My heart still thundered in my ears.

"Tell Marta I can't make the three o'clock with her today. Something's come up."

"Could you be more specific?" she asked in a tone that held a world of judgment.

"Why won't 'I'm busy' just cover it?"

Woofers began barking furiously again, having trotted back a few feet to spot me on top of the hood. The receptionist couldn't help but hear. "Is that a dog?" she asked.

"Could be."

"Just a moment."

I was clicked off for a second. Woofers was really going to town. I was going to have a headache before this ordeal was over and the hood was blistering hot. I shaded my eyes, glancing toward the door again. Gail was back. Her figure stood like a wraith in the deepened shadows behind the screen door. I waved at her, but it was more an acknowledgment. She had me treed with her miserable, vicious dog.

Marta snapped on. "I'm in a meeting, Jane." She sounded totally irritated.

"I didn't ask to be put through. I was just leaving a message."

"Yes?" she said tensely.

"I'm sitting on the roof of my car. There's a vicious beast barking its head off—"

"I can hear."

"—and until its owner decides to CALL IT OFF!" I yelled, "I'm stuck."

"Fine. I'll tell the client you can't make it. That's what you want, right?"

"As soon as I'm free, I'll be there," I said, growing irritated myself. "Trust me. I'd much rather be with you than here."

"You need to be here on time, Jane."

"Do you get that I'm in a bind?"

"Well, figure it out," she ordered and hung up. I clicked off with a certain amount of righteous indignation, pushing a few extra buttons in the process. The phone beeped at me as if in distress before the deed was done. I sat cross-legged, debating what to do next. Should I call someone else? There was still some battery life left.

The only person who came to mind . . . the only friend I knew who would really drop everything and help me out . . . was Cynthia Beaumont. Cynthia worked in an art gallery in the Pearl District in northwest Portland. She was a sometime artist, specializing in watercolors of evil cats peeking through dense forests thick with red, blue, mustard yellow and violent purple flowers and fanglike hovering grass. I considered it a plus, given my current situation, that she seemed to understand the animal mind.

"Cynthia! It's Jane. I need some help."

"Jane?" Her voice came in stuttered cell phone static.

"Yes! It's Jane! Can you hear me? I'm stuck on top of my car and I need you to come help me escape."

"What?"

I repeated my words, debating on whether to mention the dog at this juncture. Despite her drawings Cynthia wasn't exactly the model of heroism when it came to ferocious animals. Neither was I, come to that. Muzzles were invented for a reason and this slavering monster now lying in silent wait somewhere over the edge of my car sure needed one.

"I can't hear you," Cynthia said in fits and starts. I heard more static. There was a bit of whining in her tone so I had to get stern.

"I need your help!" I yelled directions into the phone, praying she'd hear them. "And don't get out of the car. Just pull up beside me."

"Okay . . ."

I sighed and turned off the phone. Woofers was challenging my paint job again. "Call off your dog!" I yelled to the front door but Gail The Tired seemed to have blended back into the house. Probably having one hell of a belly laugh at my expense. I could picture her doubled-over, struggling for breath, the stub of the cigarette dropping to the floor in her fit of hilarity.

Three-quarters of an hour later Cynthia's battered Honda pulled into the rutted driveway and slowly bumped its way toward me. As soon as she stopped she opened her door and I screamed at her as the Pit Bull charged her car. She yanked her foot back inside and slammed the door. Woofers leapt upward, jaws snapping at Cynthia's surprised white face behind the window.

I should have warned her about the dog.

Motioning her to edge her car next to mine so that they would be side by side, making it possible for me to jump from one to the other, I stood up on the top of my hood and glared at the closed front door. There was a twitch of ragged curtains at Gail's front window.

Cynthia aligned her car with my Volvo. I leapt to her hood, trying not to make too much of a dent as I landed. Woofers also leapt and spun but could make no purchase against the Honda's slick exterior . . . except for a few nicks that is. Actually, it was a couple of rather deep scratches. Luckily, her car was hardly the latest model. Luckier still, I'd managed to keep from dishing in her hood with my weight although my ribs felt bruised.

I turned over and lay spread-eagled on my back, staring upward into the dusty blue heavens. Why was I so determined to stay out of the information specialist business and keep up with process serving? Today hadn't been exactly good for my health.

Cynthia rolled down her window. Her mouth was set. "Want me to back up?" she bit out.

"Hell, no. I want you to move forward. Right through her front door!"

Cynthia took me at my word, although mostly I was just railing at the sky. As the Honda jerked forward, Woofers trotted along beside us, barking so hard that I wondered if he might actually tear a lung or something. When Cynthia stopped just short of the porch Woofers gave up the call. His tongue lolled out and he glanced at the door of the house. He seemed lost in indecision. Apparently this was as far as his little pea brain could take him. Gail The Tired stepped outside—still with the cigarette between her lips—and made a shooing motion. Woofers suddenly scurried inside the house. I slid off the top of the car, found the 72-hour notice which was marked with a dog paw print and slapped it into her hand. She just looked at me and smoked.

I slammed into the passenger side of Cynthia's car. She turned to me, her spiky short dark hair standing straight up, as if in surprise. As this was her normal hairstyle I couldn't blame it on the events with Woofers. She said dryly, "You forgot to mention the dog?"

"I'm just sorry we didn't get a good run at him."

She snorted, knowing me too well. She wore a black suit coat over a black camisole and one of the shortest skirts on record. I have to admire a woman with that kind of moxie; I'd be showing the world things not meant to be seen in the light of day even if you gave me a couple of extra inches. She shot me a look that could curdle milk.

I would pay for my omission about Woofers.

We backed down the drive to where I'd parked my car. Climbing out of Cynthia's Honda, I checked the paint job on mine, swore, then opened the driver's door and slid inside. Examining my watch, I swore again, and then I saw the small tear in my right Nike and I swore a third time.

Cynthia gave me a look that warned the issue wasn't finished as she drove away. I mouthed, "Thanks." I would thank her more concretely later—with food and alcohol.

As soon as I was behind the wheel I drove straight to Marta's office, punched the elevator number to her floor, then burned into her outer office. The receptionist raised an eyebrow at me, but I sailed by as if I owned the place. I realized belatedly that my black top and pants were covered with dust, so I steered myself to the bathroom for a quick once over. "Shit." I looked as if I'd been treed by a wild animal, which wasn't that far from the truth.

A few moments later I was knocking on Marta's door. I heard her call for me to come in. When I entered she was sitting at her desk, hands behind her head. Though her expression was neutral, I could tell she was grinning to herself. Bobby Reynolds had single-handedly delivered Tess to her, no matter what his crimes, and Marta was counting greenbacks in her head. Marta, it now appeared, had become a full-service divorce lawyer. Need someone to chat up your husband in case he's been secretly aiding and abetting your murderous son? Just ask Marta. She could find you an information specialist, or a facsimile thereof. And payment to Marta Cornell did not hinge on Jane Kelly—said information specialist's—success. Marta simply delivered someone to help— and her clients paid her for her trouble.

I sat down in one of the two cream, faux-suede client seats on the opposite side of Marta's Brazilian cherry desk; Tess Reynolds Bradbury sat in the other. I recognized the tight lips and blue eyes from her pictures in the paper and television interviews. I also recognized the pink scarf, now lying across her shoulders and down the front of her suit. She'd had it on this morning in the Coffee Nook. Wrapped around her blond hair. I hadn't recognized her behind the Audrey Hepburn sunglasses.

The hairs on my arms lifted. Had she come to the Nook in search of *me*?

She pretended this was our first meeting, her smile of welcome brittle and tight.

She still possessed the hardness I'd first seen on TV, and she had a tense, nervous quality about her that rattled my equilibrium. I inhaled and exhaled slowly. Tess fit right into Marta's decor: all taste and money. If she was anything like Marta in determination she was a force to be reckoned with. In Marta's opinion: rain forest be damned. Marta would cut down every tree herself if it meant the good life. It was only a first impression, but I would bet my bottom dollar Cotton Reynolds' ex-wife felt the same.

The question was: what did she really want?

"Tess Bradbury, Jane Kelly," Marta introduced. "Jane, Tess . . ." I reached out a hand. Tess held hers as if I should kiss it, but I clasped it and gave it a quick shake instead. A small line dug between her brows, but then it smoothed away a moment later. She withdrew her hand, folded both of them demurely in her lap, and said, "I'm so glad you decided to help me."

She had a faint southern twang. Texan, I believed, though I'm no expert. I really didn't know what to say to her. Her son had been accused of multiple homicide. He'd killed his own family and bolted to escape prosecution. From what I'd read in the newspaper accounts, there was no doubt that he'd committed the act. Though no crime scene investigator had revealed any of the little forensic tidbits that so interest the scandal-hungry public, clearly the authorities had Bobby dead to rights.

Still, I knew his mother wouldn't want to believe it. I cleared my throat, my curiosity growing in spite of myself.

"What exactly would you like me to do, Ms. Bradbury?"

Chapter
Three

It felt like I waited an inordinately long time for Tess to answer. She shot me a look, glanced away, then gave me another cool, blue-eyed stare. In the end she turned to Marta who assumed command like the general she was.

"Bobby's been missing for nearly four years," Marta started in. "The Tillamook County Sheriff's Department and F.B.I. and God knows who else haven't been able to turn him up. They're beginning to think he headed out to sea. A small boat was stolen during those same two days. Capsized, apparently. Pieces floated back along the coast about ten days later."

"But no body," I put in, remembering.

"But no body." Marta nodded.

"One theory is that he set it up to look as if he drowned," I pointed out, "but that he's living large and free."

"If he's dead, I need to know." Tess's voice was flat, nearly emotionless. I gave her a careful look while trying to appear as if I were merely waiting for direction. Her hair was obviously bleached but done so expertly that it could almost be natural. It was cut in a short bob that curved in at the edge of her chin. She was probably in her late forties, but she could have passed for ten years younger. Her nails were lacquered a pastel pink shade, and she wore a pair of cream-colored slacks and matching jacket. I admired the suit's lack of wrinkles. If I'd been wearing it, it would have looked like I'd pulled it from the bottom of the laundry basket. The pink scarf added the right touch, making her look like a confection. Hard candy, I thought, if the set of her mouth were anything to go by.

Marta continued, "The authorities believe he killed his family, each with a shot to the back of the head, then left them on state forestry land outside Tillamook. There's been precedent for this. Two other alleged family annihilators: Edward Morris and Christian Longo have been arrested for committing similar crimes in this state. Morris left his family in the Tillamook State Forest like Bobby, Longo dropped the bodies in coastal inlets off Newport and Waldport. Maybe they gave him the idea." At this point Tess tried to interrupt, but Marta, once engaged, hates losing the floor, so she threw Tess a quelling look and added in an aside, "I'm just filling in background. Bobby may have been a victim as well, but this is what the authorities are thinking, I guarantee it."

Tess settled back in her chair but her body remained tense. I felt tense, too. Fighting off Woofers seemed like child's play compared to this. I was already out of my league.

"Familicide is fairly rare. Nationally, maybe 50 cases a year. For some reason, Oregon's got more than its share. Usually these guys are white, in their 30's or 40's, and they feel intense responsibility for their families. Meanwhile, their lives are falling apart, usually financially. Oh, and they generally have a strong faith. Most often, once they've killed their families, they take their own lives. That happened with our third local family annihilator, Robert Bryant, who shot his family in his home then turned the shotgun on himself."

I threw another glance at Tess to see how she was taking this. The pink nails were digging into the arms of her chair. With an effort, she folded her hands back in her lap. Hands are betrayers, I thought. Tess Bradbury looked as if she wanted to claw herself out of this life.

Marta pulled a slim folder from a drawer and laid it out in front

of her, consulting her notes. "The perpetrators are usually depressed, often paranoid, men. They can't face failure, so they see
killing their families as their only option." She put a finger to the
page and looked up, studying Tess. "There's a lot more, but
you've heard all this before."

"Over and over again," Tess gritted.

"Do you mind if I give Jane this file? She can read up on it later."

Tess didn't immediately respond. Finally realizing Marta was
waiting for an answer, she flapped a hand at the file which meant
"yes." Marta slid the blue folder my way. I flipped open the edge
and saw several reports off the Internet and copies of newspaper
articles from the *Oregonian*.

Switching gears, Marta said, "I handled Tess and Cotton's divorce five years ago. Bobby was married to his wife, Laura, and
they'd just had Kit. Their other two children were Aaron and
Jenny. Tess, would you like to fill Jane in on what your thoughts
are, what you'd like her to do?"

Tess drew a long breath, then exhaled delicately. "My husband was seeing another woman. Dolly Smathers."

It was curious she went to her divorce first. I was having trouble keeping my mind off anything but Bobby and the deaths of
his children. With an effort I pulled my thoughts to Tess herself,
and her ex, Cotton. Let's face it. Any man involved with both a
Dolly and a Tess has got to have a country western fetish, big
time. But then with a nickname like Cotton, you had to figure
Reynolds was a man full of boots and bonhomie. I thought about
voicing this opinion, but now didn't seem the time.

"I sued him for every dime I could get," Tess went on. "I put
the money in an art gallery in the Pearl District, the Black Swan."

My ears perked up. Cynthia had shown some of her art at the
Black Swan. It was a trendy, spacious gallery in an area where the
floor space went for mucho-grando-buckos per square foot. "I've
been there," I said.

She smiled faintly. "I hardly made a dent in his fortune, but it
was enough to get me going. He got the house, the boat, three of
the cars. I went back to my maiden name."

Owen Bradbury . . . the name of Tess's other son, Bobby's older half-brother, crossed my mind. From the way we were talking, Bobby could have been Tess's one and only. But Owen wasn't Cotton's son and since he went by Bradbury, Tess's maiden name, it didn't appear as if his real father counted for much. Maybe in Tess's mind Owen didn't count for much, either. Again, I kept my mouth shut and just listened.

"Tess, we did well by you in the divorce," Marta reminded her dryly.

Tess raised a hand in agreement. "But Cotton still has a lot of assets, and the bastard told Bobby that he wasn't worth one thin dime. His *only* child. That's why Bobby was in financial trouble. And Cotton wouldn't help him. At the time I was all tied up in legalities. I gave Bobby as much as I could, of course, but he'd made these investments . . ."

I nodded, remembering. Bobby Reynolds had been floundering in a sea of debt. And some of his "investors" were purported to be out-and-out crooks looking for a way to tap into Cotton's mega-assets. But Cotton had cut that off quick. He'd let Bobby deal with his own problems and apparently those problems had fast become insurmountable, at least in Bobby's mind, hence the exit from reality. I wondered if Bobby were still alive if he was now horrified at his own actions. With an act so heinous, could anyone really accept his own responsibility, culpability?

"I've had the F.B.I. all over me," Tess went on bitterly. "Every cent I make, or lose, is examined by the goddamn government! They want to know if I'm helping Bobby. Because it's a murder investigation, they seem to have the right to harass me forever!"

Marta said, "The I.R.S. has been particularly diligent about fine-tooth-combing Tess's income and assets."

I nodded again. The government was marshaling their resources, determined to find Bobby and anyone who might be helping him out. They wanted to know if Tess was sloughing off money to her fugitive son.

"Are you under active surveillance?" I asked.

Tess straightened her spine, clearly jolted by the idea. "After all this time? I don't think so. Not anymore, anyway. I think they're finally realizing that I've got nothing to do with Bobby. I don't even know if he's alive."

"Why do you want me to talk to Cotton?" I finally got back to the only part of the issue I was really involved with at this point.

"If Bobby is alive . . ." She stopped, swallowed, drew another breath. "If Bobby's alive, Cotton knows it. And I think he could be helping him."

That caught my attention. "Back up. If Cotton wouldn't help him before . . . why would he now that Bobby's on the run? That's aiding and abetting a wanted felon."

"His guilt. Finally." She practically spit the words. Her fury at her ex-husband was deep and real, maybe even more so with the passing of time. "Cotton never treated Bobby right. And I think it's rotted his soul."

"Have you thought about talking to the police about any of this?" I asked cautiously.

"It's all supposition," Marta interjected smoothly. The last thing she wanted was to lose a client's money.

"I don't know anything for sure. It's just a feeling I have, and frankly, if Bobby's alive, and Cotton's been helping him . . . I don't want the police to know."

A knot of discomfort tightened in my lower back. Like someone twisting a screw into my spine. "You know, if by some long shot, I found out where Bobby was, I would have to go to the police myself. He is wanted for murder."

"I understand," Tess said quickly. "All I'm asking is for you to go to the benefit on Saturday, have fun, get some kind of impression. Do you see?"

· For the first time I read the desperation in her eyes. True, naked desperation. A mother's need to know. "So, what is this benefit?" I asked, already knowing.

Tess relaxed. "It's part of the Lake Chinook Historical Society's annual showing of homes. Cotton had to lobby like crazy because he's a pariah now. He's been quietly shunned by some of the more prominent Lake Chinook and Portland snobs."

She sniffed. "They come into the gallery sometimes, but it's mostly to get a look at me."

I saw how much she hated being the monkey in the zoo. Famous was one thing; infamous something else.

"Tickets for the event are in the file, too," Marta said.

"I'll go," I said to Tess. "But I honestly don't see what I can do."

"Cotton loves Tim Murphy. Just mention Murphy's name and he'll love you, too."

I never mention Murphy's name, I thought. I try not to think about him too much. With a stab of honesty, I said, "This may be a waste of your money."

"It's mine to waste," she said.

"Just meet with Cotton," Marta inserted quickly. "See what you think. See if you can get to meet him again."

"If he's really helping Bobby, he's hardly likely to talk to anyone," I pointed out.

"I need to know if my son's alive," Tess insisted, her curiously flat voice taking on an edge of determination . . . or hysteria. "I'm at my wit's end. Cotton won't speak to me. And his wife's even worse."

I'd forgotten that he'd remarried. "Dolly?" I guessed.

She shook her head. "Heavens, no. She was trash. This one's more sophisticated. A real snake in the grass. Heather." Her mouth recoiled around the word. "Younger than my son. Cotton seems to be having a second midlife crisis. Sixty-two, going on seventeen."

There was something about the way she was looking at me. She thought Cotton would like me. Maybe that's why she'd come to check me out this morning, incognito. "Is there some reason this has all cropped up right now?" I asked. "Bobby's been missing a while."

Marta cleared her throat. "There's a rumor," she said slowly, her eyes on Tess. "One we can't substantiate."

I waited.

"Cotton's ill," she said. Rumor or no, she'd made up her mind.

"I think he's got a pre-nup with Heather, and if so, his estate will go to . . ." She shrugged her small shoulders lightly. "Bobby, I'd imagine."

"But if he's cut out of the will . . ."

"I think he's back in. I just have the feeling that if Cotton's dying, he's making amends."

I looked from her to Marta and back again. So, this was where the big money supposedly was. Cotton's fortune might be earmarked for Bobby. If Bobby was still alive, that is. And if Bobby were found and arrested, and Cotton was gone, Bobby might put his mother in charge of his finances.

A lot of "ifs" to bank on, but then we were talking about a lot of money.

I wondered what the terms of Cotton's will were. Was Bobby back in? And was he Cotton's designated heir? What about Heather, his wife? Or Owen, who might not be his own flesh and blood but was someone Cotton had taken care of for the greater part of Owen's life? Who else would Cotton Reynolds want to leave his fortune to?

Murphy . . .

The thought came unbidden and once in my head, couldn't be dislodged. Murphy had been *very* close to Bobby. They'd gone through school together: little league, Pop Warner football, high school athletics . . . From all accounts Murphy could "whup Bobby's ass" in sports, but they'd remained friends. When I'd followed Murphy back to Oregon, he'd taken me around to the usual haunts. The Pisces Pub was the hangout for all the legal (and under-aged kids with good fake IDs) graduates from both Lakeshore and Lake Chinook High Schools. Murphy had barely begun to reacquaint himself with old friends when Bobby disappeared. Tess called Murphy, looking for Bobby. I'd never hung out with either Bobby or Laura all that much. If I'd had any inkling about what was to come, I would have paid closer attention, believe me. As it was, my impression of Bobby hadn't been all that flattering, but neither was it criminal. He'd seemed like a typical red-blooded American boy who'd outgrown high school and therefore the height of his popularity. He'd married Laura, a high school sweetheart, who probably had been a beauty in her day but whose figure after three kids was well on the way to matronly. She was also quite religious. It was clear she didn't feel comfortable having a beer with Bobby, his good buddy Murphy, and Murphy's sometime girlfriend, me. She carried a small worn book in one hand, a prayer book I later learned, and I came out of the Pisces feeling like I didn't quite fit in.

Murphy was quiet afterwards. We didn't talk much about either one of them. Bobby, Laura and the kids went back to Astoria the next day. They lived near members of his wife's family and were apparently pretty locked in with Laura's family's small, local church. Murphy and Bobby's friendship clearly wasn't what it once was, but it was still the deepest of either of their lives.

But when the familicide story broke, Murphy was frantic. He fell instantly back into "best friend" role, ardently decrying the outrage of the media, law enforcement officials, anyone who even entertained the idea. Like Tess, Murphy would not believe Bobby was responsible. The whole thing consumed him. I just figured Bobby did it. I also figured that Murphy might be using his absorption to not only come to grips with the depths of Bobby's crimes, but also as a means to slowly pull away from me.

Marta got up from her desk, shaking hands all around, acting as if we'd just signed some kind of Nobel Peace pact. I certainly felt a pact had been formed, but I wasn't convinced of its positive nature. But there was the matter of the money . . . five hundred per visit with Cotton. Tess was ready to pay and though I sorely wanted to take a check in advance, I kept my mouth shut on the subject. I would go to Cotton's benefit and see what I thought. I was firmly convinced it would be a one-time-only event. I wasn't sure I wanted more than that anyway.

And it seemed to me that Tess was counting her chickens before they were hatched. She seemed to believe that Bobby would inherit and that she would be a side beneficiary. Where that left Heather, I don't know.

"Did I see you in the Coffee Nook this morning?" I asked her as I picked up the file and trailed after her and Marta. Tess stopped short at the door, clearly surprised by my question. For a moment she was going to deny me; it was in her eyes, her body language. But then she must have known I wouldn't be convinced because she muttered, "I sometimes get my coffee there. Yes, I stopped by this morning."

"Small world," I said.

The snotty receptionist gave me the elevator eyes, a silent comment on my dust-grimed clothes. I rewarded her with a brilliant smile while calling her all kinds of names in my head. She wrinkled her nose and got back to work.

"Call me after the benefit," Tess ordered. She started to hold out her hand in that same princess-like manner, then thought better of it, shaking my hand in the customary way instead. A frisson of fear shivered down my back. A vision of someone sticking pins in a voodoo doll with my likeness came to mind.

Have I mentioned I have a very active imagination? I can be overly dramatic at times.

Unfortunately, I was going to learn that this time wasn't one of them.

I spent the remainder of the afternoon lost in thought while posting the rest of Greg Hayden's 72-hour notices. Easily accomplished, it reminded me that process serving was more my speed. Apart from an occasional Woofers, it was fairly benign. I headed home a couple hours later, feeling unclean and anxious in a way I didn't want to analyze too closely. With an effort I shoved thoughts of Bobby Reynolds and Tim Murphy aside and concentrated on food, or my lack of it.

Foster's On The Lake is the one and only restaurant actually on Lake Chinook, and therefore the only restaurant-bar with boat docks. I don't own a boat myself. I firmly believe in the definition that a boat is a hole in the water in which to throw money away. That said, I love to be invited on someone else's boat and it's convenient that my boat dock is still in working order in case that someone wants to pick me up.

I called Cynthia, asking her to meet me for a drink, leaving a message on her cell phone. She sent a text message back on my cell, telling me she was unavailable. I am going to *have* to figure out how to do that, I reminded myself, marveling at the tiny typing on my LCD screen. I may fear technology but I also admire it.

The idea of driving to Foster's held no attraction. Patrons of Foster's On The Lake take up the parking spots early and it's an overall pain in the ass to find anywhere else to leave a car.

I debated on whom to call. Reluctantly, I settled on Dwayne. He's perfect for two reasons: (1) he's someone I can share information with, and (2) he owns a boat. Another plus is that he doesn't blather. He's the strong, silent type a lot of the time, and when he does speak it's not wasted small talk. And though he's physically attractive, he's not for me, which is just as well, since thoughts of Murphy circling my brain make me unstable and unreliable when it comes to sex. I can make a *huge* mistake, if I'm not careful. After all, I was nuts over Murphy. Much as I would like to believe differently, I'm not sure I've learned resistance over the years. Luckily Dwayne's name alone puts me off.

His answering machine picked up on the fourth ring. "Dwayne?" I called, knowing he was probably there and ignoring the beep. "Dwayne, pick up. Let's go to Foster's and have a drink. Get your boat and come get me."

I waited. Dwayne has a derelict boathouse attached to his cabana which is in need of serious work. He also is a proud owner of a broken boat lift which is meant to keep the boat out of the water and save the hull, but is pretty much a hunk of twisted metal in need of excising. One of his professed long-term projects is fixing the boathouse/lift, but while he tinkers away Dwayne pays for an easement. There are several such easements dotted along the shores of Lake Chinook. Depending on where you reside, you might have easement access. However, there are only so many boat slips within the easement and you have to put your name on a waiting list if they are all full, which they generally are. Dwayne was lucky enough to pick one up the third year of owning his cabana. He bought a well-used boat with worn seats and suspiciously squishy floorboards, but he keeps the engine running like a top. "Dwayne?" I yelled again.

The line clicked on. "Quit belly-aching," he complained. "I was finishing up some notes."

"What are you working on?"

"You throwing in with me, darlin'?"

"Not yet."

There was a hint of equivocation in my response that I tried, and failed, to suppress. I could tell he heard it. "Not yet" was far better than plain "no."

"I'll be there in thirty minutes."

I hung up. Dwayne wanted an intern, a protege, an acolyte. He wanted me to be that person, but I wasn't sure I wanted the job. Bartender, process server . . . hatchery fish . . . that was me. Damn Billy Leonard for labeling me so accurately. Yes, I was unfocused and undisciplined and at a loss to find a serious career path, but so what? Couldn't I bump along as I'd been doing? Did I have to make some kind of choice?

Dwayne was true to his word, putt-putting at six miles per hour as he came into West Bay—lake requirements—and smoothly drifting up to my dock, his hull kissing the once white bumpers Mr. Ogilvy had installed several seasons earlier. I was waiting in khaki shorts and a white tank over a blue two-piece swimsuit. Not that I intended swimming. Good lord, no. But being prepared came naturally to me. A fact Dwayne had pointed out on more than one occasion which added to my inherent gifts as an information specialist.

"Hey," he grunted as I stepped into the boat.

"Hey, there," I responded, and we took off.

I saw a bottle of wine nestled in a spot beside the throttle, ready for consumption as soon as we reached Foster's. By unspoken understanding Dwayne and I would share the wine after he docked the boat and before we walked into the restaurant. This meant we would sit in our boat and drink, viewing the restaurant diners as if they were a kind of open theater. Believe it or not this was

considered okay behavior even though we would be docked at
On The Lake's pier. It's all part of Lake Chinook's summer cus-
toms. It's perfectly okay to pull up next to someone else's boat
and examine what they'd brought to drink or possibly eat as sometimes people didn't even bother walking into the restaurant at all.

On The Lake's owner, Jeffrey Foster—known simply as
Foster to anyone who's acquainted with him—allowed this behavior because when the weather is nice enough for boating the
place is already spilling over its edges with customers. This is
amazing in itself since the prices at On The Lake are astronomi-
cal. The rest of the cheapies and myself generally sway in our
boats, listen to the live music and refuse to open our wallets.
Foster doesn't have time to pay attention to us. Every chance I
get I complain to him about the prices, but he just shrugs his
shoulders and tells me to go somewhere else. Like, oh sure, there
is nowhere else on Lake Chinook. So, I have to limit my nights of
food buying. To this end I sometimes go beyond the limits of
cheap into downright miserly by circumventing the restaurant altogether. I trek along the sidewalk which is squeezed next to the
teensy movie house which is part of On The Lake's building and
which boasts excellent popcorn and a fireplace in the lobby, then
I cross State Street and sneak into Johnny's Market to buy
Doritos and a jar of salsa. Affordable, and a few notches closer to
real food than Chapstick.

I used to cadge rides to the restaurant with Murphy, but since
that broke up I've been forced to rely on Dwayne and sometimes
my neighbors, two houses down, who are screechingly, unhappily
married at the best of times; sullen, boiling fury at the worst. Not
exactly a laugh-fest are the Mooneys. They're in their late for-
ties/early fifties and haven't experienced a moment of joy in their
quarter-century of marriage, I'm sure. Whenever they get a no-
tion in their heads to go boating, they always invite me. I guess
they need a referee. Whether I accept or not depends on my own
phase of boredom. Luckily, I hadn't resorted to their company
yet this summer.

Foster's was rocking and rolling as we pulled up. Blue flags fluttered at the top of poles attached to each boat slip. Luckily, we were able to nab a docking space, one made available as a boat was just pulling out. It was a Master Craft with a pole jutting out of the center, constructed for waterskiing and wakeboarding. I *can* wake-board and water-ski, but it's so much work I pretty much just don't do it. Anyway, I just had alcohol on the brain, and food, if I could afford some. If not, just alcohol. I'm pretty sure this is a bad sign, but I didn't much care.

There were two seats open at the outdoor bar, a curving wooden structure nestled beneath the boughs of an oak tree which was arranged for a perfect view of the water. Dwayne grunted that he was going across the street to Johnny's Market but I bee-lined for the chairs. I settled myself down with a sigh of content-ment and ran my repertoire of mixed drinks through my head.

Manny, On The Lake's best bartender, looked over at me.

Even though I've done my share of bartending I buckled, turning toward the all-time female standard. "Could I have a glass of Chardonnay?"

"Any particular kind?"

"The cheapest."

I used to make all kinds of fancy concoctions at Sting Ray's. Once in a great while I still manage to whip something up. I spent a lot of hours at Sting Ray's trying to create a drinkable drink that includes blue curacao. Personally, I feel the stuff is damn near toxic but its electric blue shimmer is inviting as hell. My best answer to date: cut its godawful taste with Sprite or Seven-Up or some other lemon-lime soda.

I wasn't sure whether I cared that Dwayne had left me to my own devices. Two weeks ago I'd been forced to drive over and sit by myself at the bar as, once again, I'd been looking for friends and everyone was busy. It had been one of the few, rare, lovely nights like this one, the kind where it stays warm way past dusk and beyond. I'd actually struck up a conversation with a guy who'd just arrived in Lake Chinook and was surprised by the good weather.

"I thought it rained all the time here," he said.

I warned ominously, "Don't let this fool you. Once or twice a year. Maybe three times tops. That's all the really fabulous weather you can count on. Some years, not even that."

"Lived here long?" he asked, then proceeded to look me over in a way that made my inner voice go, "Uh-oh."

"Awhile," I allowed.

He gazed speculatively over the water. "I'm traveling through, though I'm really thinking about making a move."

Our small talk dwindled from that point, mainly because I bowed out of the conversation. After a while he went and stood on one of the docks, his back to me. My last vision of him was in silhouette, the flags dancing above him in a quirky little breeze. Now, I glanced automatically to where he'd stood. I wondered idly if he'd made the move from wherever it was he'd come.

Manny brought me my Chardonnay and I managed to down most of it by the time Dwayne reappeared from across the street with a bag which he hefted into the boat. I watched him from my perch, aware that he was debating whether to open up his cache and munch away in the boat, or join me at the bar. While he considered, Manny poured me a second glass and slid it my way without asking.

I said, "I hope you're trying to get me drunk, and if you are, great. But I warn you, I have limited resources."

"It's on the house," he said.

"And what if Foster finds out?"

"He doesn't get worked up over a few 'on the house' glasses of wine."

I sent Manny a knowing look. "I bet those specials are supposed to be for the paying customers."

Manny shrugged and smiled to himself. He wasn't a serious conversationalist but he looked damn good in Hawaiian shirts and shorts, Foster's summer employee uniforms.

My cell phone buzzed at that moment. I hate people who get calls in crowded restaurants and then proceed to yak loudly on and on about nothing. But I was curious because this was my second unexpected cell call of the day. Unheard of.

Squinting at the LCD display I saw my mother's phone number pop into view. I grimaced. I wasn't sure I was ready for the kind of convoluted conversations that were as much a part of my mother as her Thursday hair appointments. But guilt won out, as it most often does, and I answered cautiously, "Hey, there, Mom."

"Jane?"

It confuses my mother when I answer already knowing the caller. Mom doesn't understand caller ID, and I don't think there's any power in the universe able to explain it to her in a way that makes sense. Her call was unusual as she generally phones on weekends, claiming to be too busy during the week. I'm almost afraid to ask "doing what?" because the explanation will no doubt be long and involved and never be a true explanation. Most often I'm left struggling to decipher half of what she says, but she never fails to be entertaining.

"Hi, Mom. Yeah, it's me," I said.

Once assured she'd called the right number, Mom didn't waste time on preliminaries. "Your Aunt Eugenie died and left you her dog."

"What? A *dog*?" The events with the pit bull and the image of Dobermans flashed across the screen of my mind. "I can't have a dog, Mom! I'm not around to take care of it. Dogs need—people—don't they?" I paused. "Who's Aunt Eugenie?"

"You don't remember Eugenie? Shirttail relative who lives around Portland . . . ? Well . . . lived. She's been sick an awful long time. We started calling kind of regularly after she found out she was sick. It is just still a shock, though."

My brain felt like it was on stall. I could feel things already spiraling out of control. "But . . . I can't have a dog. I don't want a dog. You didn't tell her I'd take the thing, did you?"

"Well, yes, I did, as a matter of fact. I knew you'd be happy to help. She'd been worrying so much. You know, I really thought Eugenie would give the dog to her daughter, but they haven't been close for a long time. Years. What's that daughter's name . . . Diana? No, Donna? Maybe it's just Dawn. Anyway, she has children and a husband with allergies, I think. Oh, he might be in a nursing home. Not sure . . ." My mother's voice wandered off.

"I can't have a dog," I reiterated.

"You *can* have a dog, Jane. You said Mr. Ogilvy allows pets."

I pulled back the receiver and stared at it. How can my mother draw these obscure factoids out of her brain when she has difficulty remembering the name of the city where I live? And how can she remember Ogilvy's name? I may have mentioned him once to her, but the owner of my bungalow isn't generally a hot topic between us.

"Aunt Eugenie has a friend who'll be bringing it by," my mother went on. "I gave her your number."

I seriously doubted whether I ever had a shirttail relative named Eugenie. My mother meets new "best friends" faster than I can blow through a twenty and invariably these new buddies enter my life as well. Leaving it all behind had felt like a side benefit in following Murphy to a new state, but it appeared now that my mother's incessant friend-gathering had followed me to Portland as well.

"Well, I'm not going to take it. I don't have room for a dog. I'll send it to the humane society."

"You need a dog. You need something around to keep you safe."

I almost asked "What kind of dog?" but stopped myself at the last second. No good encouraging my mother. "Aunt Eugenie should have made other provisions for Fido 'cause it's not going to be with me."

"You'll have to tell the girl who's bringing it over, then," my mother said with a sigh. "I hope it's not going to be a problem. I promised Eugenie I'd take care of things. If you really can't take the dog, maybe the girl can talk to Eugenie's daughter."

"Who is this girl?"

"I'm not sure. Someone Eugenie knew. Maybe she can push Eugenie's daughter . . . Dawn, I think . . . to take the poor thing in. I hope it all works out." Her message delivered, Mom then abruptly changed the subject. "Have you seen your brother lately?"

"Booth? No."

"He has a new girlfriend. I think it's serious this time. I'd like you to check her out."

"What do you mean check her out? Like, check her out by *looking* at her, or are you saying you want me to dig into her background?" My mother was cagey this way. You had to be really certain what she was asking at all times.

"I just think you should meet her."

The last time I'd met one of Booth's dates I'd been unable to drag my eyes from the tattoo she had inked around her neck, one of those choke chain designs meant for feral animals. I really felt this particular female should have been sporting the real thing. She looked like she ate human flesh on a regular basis, and she had a habit of staring straight through you that was meant to be intimidating. It was.

"I'll . . . meet her whenever I can."

"Booth's free right now. I just talked to him."

"Well, I'm not." On that I was firm. "I'm with friends now. And I've got a benefit to attend Saturday night."

"With a date?" My mother was completely blown away.

This irked me and sent me into a riff of lying. "Yes."

"With a man?"

Well, hell. "Yes. A real live man." I embellished. "Wealthy, too. Owns an island."

"Oh, Jane."

Clearly, I'd pushed it too far. "Gotta go," I said. "I'm getting beeped and I'm expecting a call. I'll check in with Booth and let you know what I find."

"And the dog, Jane? Remember the dog. Please think about it."

I ground my teeth. I wanted to scream that there wasn't an ice cube's chance in hell of me taking on an orphaned canine, but I managed to keep my cool. I then rushed into a passel of more excuses and hung up before she could say anything more.

"Sheesh," I said, reaching for my wine.

Dwayne appeared at that time. "I'll have a Bud," he told

Manny who brought him the sweating beer *tout de suite*. Then Dwayne, who'd been nice on the boat ride over, asked, "Evict anyone today?" before sucking down half of his long neck in one swallow. On the heels of my mother's call, his remark really pissed me off. Billy Leonard can get away with that kind of banter, but it doesn't work with Dwayne. And the way my mother just assumes I'll be perennially dateless . . .

I said, bristling, "That really pisses me off."

"Everything pisses you off," he responded without a care.

Because that pissed me off as well, I felt compelled to defend myself. "I never tack up eviction notices unless it's three days before Christmas and the family has six children and an unemployed handicapped father." I sipped at Chardonnay number two, determining I wasn't going to guzzle it as quickly as number one. There were a lot of hours left before bedtime and I didn't want to flame out too quickly.

"You should take on a real case," he said.

I said, baldly, "I have."

Dwayne's brows lifted with real interest. And at that same moment another boat docked in a newly vacated boat slip. I looked at the captain of the craft and recognized the glowing white mane of Cotton Reynolds.

Chapter
Four

I watched as Cotton guided a young woman ahead of him through the short gate into Foster's On The Lake, one big hand touching the small of her back. I took this to be Cotton's wife. She looked past me, smiled, and waved fingers at a couple already seated at one of the tables. My head turned as if pulled by a string. Of the couple, I recognized the woman as one of the most successful real estate agents in the area though I couldn't immediately come up with her name. The man looked like either her son, or a very young, very buff companion. Cotton's wife sailed past me, clad in blue culottes, white Polo shirt and a red sweater draped across her shoulders Martha Stewart style. The straw hat atop her reddish-blond hair was encircled by a red, white and blue ribbon. Heather, I remembered. She looked as if she were playacting.

Cotton, his distinctive white hair like a beacon, followed after her and shook hands all around. Waiters hovered and Jeff Foster made an obligatory appearance. Several expensive bottles of wine were deposited on the table with a flourish and everyone looked ready to settle in for a long evening. Cotton hugged his wife and she smiled and turned her face up to his. It was all very loving.

"What about this case?" Dwayne asked.

I had been prepared to tell him about Tess Bradbury's request but faced with Cotton Reynolds in the flesh I found myself suddenly unable to go there. I needed time to think, so I said as a means to collect my thoughts, "I gave a lady a 72-hour notice and her pit bull chased me to my car."

"I asked you if you'd evicted anyone today and you got pissy."

"So sue me." I surreptitiously kept an eye on Cotton's group. Dwayne, who was turned toward me, twisted on one thigh to see what had captured my attention. I asked quickly, "What are you working on?"

He turned back and lifted his bottle. "A beer. Some R&R." He squinted through the branches of the oak at the lowering sun. "Maybe a tan."

"You were waiting for the call that came in this afternoon."

He grunted. "It's all about scamming insurance money. Bastards. That's what the world's come to. Everybody cheating everybody."

"Hmmm . . ." I said. I was miles away but luckily Dwayne wasn't picking up on my social signals. Either that, or he was simply ready to talk and he'd be damned if I were listening or not.

"Northwest Beneficial Life comes to me. They want me to check up on this potential scam artist. Think he's falsified some life insurance claims. I start digging and it turns out this guy's rounded up a crew of alcoholic, drug addict, derelict types who are at death's door. He buys 'em policies in their names through an independent insurance agent who's listed at the bottom of every policy. Clarkson. He's the broker. In on the deal. This Clarkson goes out and hunts for policies through lots of insurance companies, not just Northwest Beneficial."

I managed to pick up the fragments and condense his report. "Scam artist buys life insurance policies for derelicts through an agent named Clarkson."

Dwayne nodded. I knew he thought I was paying a hell of a lot more attention than I was. A master trick from one of life's perpetually distracted. Sometimes I even impress myself. He went on: "Scam artist plans to benefit by the derelicts' deaths. Figures the derelicts have got one, maybe two years left on this planet. So, he takes out a bunch of policies on them, making himself the beneficiary, then waits for them to kick off."

"That's not illegal, is it?" I asked.

"Not as long as they have health exams and are proven to be hardy individuals who should have years ahead of them. But these guys couldn't pass a health exam to well . . . save their life."

I surfaced for a moment. I couldn't hear the conversation at Cotton's table but it was clear they were just ordering from the menu. "Why does this sound familiar?"

"Because a story like this has been on TV," Dwayne said with one of those "can you believe it?" shrugs. "One of those real crime programs. Our scam artist happened to come up with the same idea—or maybe he *gets* the idea from TV." Dwayne signaled Manny for another beer and a glass of wine for me. I tried to stop the order as I was feeling remarkably giddy and flushed, but the Chardonnay materialized in front of me. "He's in cahoots with Clarkson who takes a fat commission on all the policies he writes, and probably a kickback from our perpetrator. Clarkson writes up a bunch of smaller payoff policies, say under twenty-five thousand, because you can get by without the physical under a certain limit. Of course, these derelict guys have terrible, checkered medical histories and any honest agent—if there is such a thing—wouldn't write policies for any of them. Sometimes Clarkson pencils in false social security numbers, too. He doesn't want there to be any way to fully trace back to these derelicts. So, scam artist pays the small premiums and hopes the derelicts kick off within two years of the policies to make it worth his while. When they die, he collects. The more policies on each guy, the better."

"Why aren't the false social security numbers a dead giveaway, so to speak? They should be checked out."

"Should they? Why?"

"I don't know. Isn't there someone following up?"

Dwayne pointed a finger at me, underscoring his point. "This is why identity theft is becoming such a problem. Somebody could be using your number and you wouldn't know it until something came up wrong, all of a sudden. Like on your credit report."

This gave me a bad feeling. I vowed to never give out my social security number again unless I was damn sure it was for the purpose it was intended. "What if the guy doesn't kick the bucket within two years?" I asked.

"Ahh . . ." Dwayne smiled without humor. "That's where our perp turns into a monster. He invites the derelicts to live with him in utter squalor, then pours alcohol down the poor losers' throats, speeding up the process as best he can. Their bodies are in deep shit already. They're time bombs. Scam artist helps them along, all under the guise of being a buddy, y'know? Let's party. Let's drink! They don't last long."

I pushed my third glass away. "Are you trying to get me on the wagon?"

"You don't get it," Dwayne said with a shake of his head. I stole another glance at Cotton's table. They were deep into their entrees. "It's not about alcohol. It's about taking advantage, y'-know? Hurting someone else for your own gain. I hate those bastards."

I gave him a long look. Dwayne is a decent guy. An attractive, decent guy. I recognized the danger of too much wine a wee bit late, but at least I recognized it. I reminded myself sternly that Dwayne was off limits.

The guy next to Dwayne suddenly let out a loud belch. The woman seated next to him hunched her shoulder and tightened her lips. I didn't blame her. The incident caused Dwayne to swallow a smile. His attractiveness grew.

I reminded myself of the feminine scent lingering in his condo and pushed dangerous impressions aside. Leaning toward him, I said, "How do you feel about family annihilators?"

Dwayne zeroed in on me as if I'd answered the riddle of the sphinx. "You're talking Bobby Reynolds."

I nodded. "I was called into Marta's office today. One of her divorce clients is Tess Bradbury, formerly Reynolds. Tess apparently asked for me. Wants me to interview Cotton." I spoke softly, practically in Dwayne's ear, bringing him swiftly up-to-date. "I made it clear I thought it was a waste of time."

"How much is she paying you?"

"Five hundred dollars per interview."

"She expects more than one?" Dwayne asked, surprised.

"Well, she's hoping, I guess."

"Jesus."

"And FYI, Cotton Reynolds, his latest wife and a few friends are seated about four tables from the bar."

Dwayne tapped his fingers on the bar but never turned around to look. Tiny white lights wound around the tree in the center of the bar shimmered in the fading light and threw shadows across Dwayne's face.

He said, "Go for it. Take Tess for all she's got."

"I don't even know if I want to do it at all. What do I know? The only reason she asked for me was because of Murphy."

Dwayne gave me a long look. "You seen Murphy recently?"

"How?" I demanded, annoyed. "He left the state, remember?" I was touchy on the subject.

"He's your connection to Bobby. I figure he's in there somewhere."

"So Murphy's the only reason Tess would call me?"

"What do you think?"

I tried not to let it bug me that Dwayne was right. Of course it was the only reason. Marta Cornell be damned. Tess went to her to make sure she connected with me because I once had a thing for Murphy and that put me inside Cotton's circle.

"You aren't going to learn anything new, so you might as well take the money," he pronounced.

"You're really full of encouragement."

He was unperturbed. "I don't know what Tess thinks she's doing. The F.B.I.'s been hunting Bobby like the vermin he is. If they can't get him, nobody can. Personally, I think he's dead."

His attitude pissed me off some more. Not that he wasn't

right; I suspected he was. I just wanted some encouragement. "So, Bobby Reynolds is vermin?"

"He shot and killed his whole family and ran away. What do you call him?" At this Dwayne checked his watch, reached across the bar for a bowl of nuts and shot a sideways glance toward Cotton's table.

"Sick. Twisted. Desperate. He's definitely not at the top of my Mr. Nice Guy list."

"You know what I think?" Dwayne dropped his voice to whisper level. "Bobby was mollycoddled. Treated like a prince by both Cotton and his mom. Never had to be responsible for anything. Entitlement. So, he marries this gal who's all wrapped up in her religion. Her family moves away and Bobby goes with 'em. They all belong to this fundamentalist church. The money gets tight. And she keeps popping out the babies and he gets scared. Then Big Daddy Cotton cuts him off and he's got money troubles. Suddenly has to do something about wifey and the screaming kids. So, he blows 'em away. That's his solution."

"I met Bobby. He didn't seem the type."

"What type is that? The type whose dreams never materialize? The type who suddenly looks around at the old ball-and-chain and the ankle-biters and says to himself, 'If it weren't for them I'd be fine'? Can't you just see that idea taking hold, Jane? Eating away at him. Can't you just see him in church, watching the plate being passed and wishing he could steal the cash?"

"Lovely," I observed.

"Think I'm wrong? Bobby was born and raised in Lake Chinook, on a private island, the only private island on the lake. He had everything his shriveled little heart desired. During the investigation people had a way of calling him a red-blooded American boy. Shaking their heads, wringing their hands, asking, How could it have happened? How could it have happened?"

"Murphy called him that, too," I admitted.

"Everybody did."

"Except you, obviously," I pointed out.

"I met Bobby a few times," Dwayne admitted. "When he

used to run that Master Craft around the lake, breaking all the rules. I can remember him laughing his ass off at some friends he ditched in the water. Lucky they didn't drown or get killed by another boat."

I absorbed that. "Murphy never believed Bobby was guilty."

"Oh, yes, he did," Dwayne said sagely. "Just couldn't face it, but I bet he knew."

I turned away. Hearing Dwayne's assessment pounded the thought home. Maybe he was right. "Murphy never wanted to believe Bobby was capable of killing his family," I said.

"Who can blame him?"

"You're right though," I said, capitulating even though I wanted to keep arguing. "Murphy had to know. The evidence was overwhelming. Law enforcement was crawling all over him. He just couldn't accept the truth about someone he loved, so he moved away."

"Durango ain't so far away, darlin'," Dwayne pointed out, turning all cowboy on me all of a sudden.

"Santa Fe," I corrected, to which he faintly smiled. I realized belatedly that he'd set me up on that one. I ignored him and mentioned instead the benefit at Cotton's on Saturday.

Dwayne grunted. "Take Tess's money. Have a little bit of fun. Be glad their problems aren't yours."

I was absorbing this when Jeff Foster saw me and came over. "Why aren't you eating?" he demanded, as if I'd personally maligned the food.

Afraid his arrival might cause people to notice us, I turned a shoulder toward Cotton's group and responded to Jeff in my usual fashion, "Because I could buy a small country with the amount I would spend on a steak here."

"For you, Jane, it's on the house."

This was utter bullshit and we both knew it. I pretended to dig through my purse—a stylish burlap-type sack that I saved for boat trips as it was deep enough to hide a bottle of wine—and thereby kept myself further averted from Cotton's view. "One of these days, I'm going to call you on that, Foster," I threatened. I caught Manny's eye. I wasn't going to rat him out about the free beverages. Foster grinned, waved me away and returned to the kitchen.

Dwayne said, "You ready to go?"

"Just about."

Sensing that I wasn't quite steady I carefully put one foot on the ground. Dwayne finished his beer, ignored my thrust-out hand full of crumpled dollars, settled the bill with Manny and slid off his stool.

"Here's my pizza," he said as a server handed him a cardboard box. I looked up in surprise. I hadn't even known he'd ordered. On The Lake's menu is diverse; its mainstay steak and seafood. But it has a killer array of gourmet pizza listed on the backside of the menu, and I could smell the blue cheese and garlic as if that cartoon aroma finger were beckoning me near. In that vein I stumbled after Dwayne through the maze of small tables, embarrassed at the way my mouth watered, and damn near ran straight into Cotton as he pushed open the knee-high gate from the patio to the boat dock. Cotton, Dwayne and I stepped outside the eating area toward the boats. Dwayne threw an arm around me and pulled my head into his chest as we walked, giving the impression we were lovers. It was his way of hiding me from Cotton. I appreciated it, but my gut tightened for reasons I didn't want to examine too closely.

We turned toward our boat slip and I risked a glance toward Cotton. He'd pulled out a cigar and was absorbed in the ritual of cutting off the end. He didn't know I was alive.

Dwayne stepped into the boat, pizza box held aloft. I followed a bit unsteadily and he held a hand out to me.

I clambered inside with a lack of grace attributed to alcohol. "I haven't seen Cotton out in ages. He's been like a hermit. What happened all of a sudden? Has the limit on Bobby's disappearance expired and no one bothered to tell me?"

He handed me a piece of pizza. "There's no expiration on murder."

"That's not what I meant."

I gave Cotton a long look from beneath my lashes. It had to be a struggle to keep up appearances. Bobby's crimes had taken a real bite out of Cotton's social calendar. Snap judgements being my specialty, I decided I didn't like either Cotton or his wife.

I bit into the pizza slice and nearly fell over with delight. Not just blue cheese, several other combos of the stuff as well lay a half-inch thick on the crust. And garlic. Tons of garlic. It was certain to clog up my arteries. I munched away with gusto. We ate in silence for a moment. I tried not to make too much noise but food had been scarce around the apartment and I was certain I'd lost five pounds in the last three days. All I wanted to do was scarf it down with as much haste as possible and damn the lactose intolerance.

Note to self: go grocery shopping.

After a second large piece of pizza my stomach suddenly seized up. I visualized an influx of cheese comprised of not only milk sugar but thirty percent fat. I could picture my overloaded stomach pushing the food through as quickly as possible in an effort to keep me from exploding. And then I could see the little villae in my small intestine sucking up that fat and shooting it straight to my bloodstream.

"You don't look so good," Dwayne pointed out, working on his third piece. He, apparently, doesn't suffer from anything beyond suffocating good humor. I shook my head when he silently offered me another slice. He chewed away in silence while I tried to pull myself together. Just as I was feeling better he closed the pizza box and started the engine.

Ducks had gathered outside the low fence which opened from the patio to the boat dock and they looked eager for a crumb. A furry creature I first thought was a beaver stood on its hind legs, equally eager. A second glance had me realizing there was no paddle tail on the rodent. A muskrat. He twitched his nose at me, hoping for a handout. I leaned over said, "Sorry, buddy. No can do."

The critter actually placed a paw on the gunwale and looked for all the world as if he were about to jump inside.

"Do it and die," Dwayne growled. The muskrat took him at his word and moved back. Dwayne gently guided the boat into the bay. Ignoring the signs posted to not feed the wildlife, I tossed the muskrat a piece of crust. He raced over, sniffed it a few times and waddled off.

"Did you see that?" I demanded, incensed. The flapping ducks appeared more appreciative but Foster, who'd happened to walk by at my moment of generosity, glared at me. I waved sheepishly and grimaced to myself. I wasn't going to get that free meal unless I changed my ways.

Dwayne hit the accelerator, trying to outrun the fading light. It wasn't that you couldn't boat after dark; it was that you couldn't go fast. Lake Chinook was only a few miles from end to end, but it seemed like forever at six miles per hour—night speed. We had to slow down as we went beneath the bridge and through the tight curves of Half Moon Bay, a narrow inlet that connected Lakewood Bay to the main lake. As soon as he was able, he punched it up again and we were hurtling across the water.

"Wait!" I screamed as we neared the looming tree-shrouded cliffs of Cotton's island, his fortress completely surrounded by the moat of Lake Chinook.

Dwayne ignored me.

"Damn it, Dwayne! Slow down! Circle the island!"

Swearing under his breath, Dwayne did as I requested and we knifed slowly through the restricted speed areas that surrounded all the shoreline. The boat cut beneath the private road that led from North Shore Road to the island and through the fading purple light I glimpsed the path that circled the Reynolds' private compound. There was the black chain-link fence and I could faintly make out the trail just on its other side.

I glanced around automatically for the Lake Patrol. They weren't bad; an offshoot of the sheriff's office. The Lake Chinook Police Department was another story altogether. Their motto was: no call too small. And they meant it. There was relatively little crime in Lake Chinook, and officers had nothing to do but dispense speeding tickets and M.I.P.'s, Minors in Possession, to underage drinkers and pot smokers. Once in a while they saved a cat in a tree. Their dedication worried me and I steered clear of them on general purposes. Having Booth as a policeman probably contributed to my overall paranoia.

"We haven't done anything illegal," Dwayne pointed out, interpreting my glance around for what it was.

"Yet," I said.

Dwayne smiled to himself. He thought he had me; I could tell. Maybe he did.

Pulling back on the throttle, he coaxed the boat around the island at the regulation six miles per hour. Neither of us said anything as we both examined the fence, the oaks and Douglas firs with low sweeping boughs, the faint outline of the path, and the glimpses of rooftops: Cotton's house and garage and outbuildings. The two Dobermans came to the fence and eyed our slowly motoring boat suspiciously.

I said, "I bet the Coma Kid was running from the dogs."

"Wouldn't you be?"

"I'm not a fan of dogs."

"What's that kid's name?" Dwayne asked.

I shook my head. There was a side of the island that was faced with basalt rock walls. Shivering, I pictured a body falling over that edge, possibly knocking himself out cold on the way, way down to the water.

Light had faded to a thin glimmer on the western horizon when Dwayne suddenly swung the boat toward the main lake and turned up the gas. We roared across the water, just ahead of complete nightfall. He delivered me back to my place, cutting the engine and letting the hull slap softly on little incoming waves toward the dock. I climbed to the gunwale, expecting to lithely leap ashore but the rocking vessel coupled with my two-and-a-half glasses of wine caused my equilibrium to fail. I stumbled, stubbed my toe on a cleat, cried out, and watched my plastic flip-flop teeter on the edge of my bruised toe. I desperately tried to squinch onto it, but it slid off to slip gently into the murky, algae-furred depths of the lake.

I stared down in disbelief. "It sank!"

"It's only three feet deep here. You can probably find it."

Like, oh sure. I'm going to walk along the muddy, duck-poop-slimed bottom of the bay. I silently mourned the loss. The pair had cost me $5.89 at the pharmacy and they didn't even float.

"They looked cheap," Dwayne observed, which pissed me off anew.

"They're irreplaceable. I ordered them special."

"Yeah, right. Give me a push."

My toe was still hurting so I knelt down and shoved his hull away with my hands. When Dwayne's bow had drifted clear of the shore he began putt-putting toward the West Bay Bridge in the direction of the main lake and eventually his cabana.

"Want me to come with you Saturday?" he called, his voice clear and loud with the amplification of the water.

"I have a feeling I'd better go alone. Thanks for the surveillance tour."

"Be careful."

He switched on his running lights and I watched the red and green and white lights move toward the bridge. I shivered and glanced around. I'd forgotten to leave any interior lights on in the bungalow. Carefully, I picked my way up the moss-surrounded flagstone steps to the back door. It was locked, but it was the same key as the front door and I let myself in and stood silently for a moment, listening hard. Dwayne had spooked me with his warning.

I counted my heartbeats in my throbbing toe, strained my ears, called myself a fool, an idiot and a hatchery fish. Taking off my remaining sandal, I hobbled across the floor and switched on the lights. The living room burst into view. Not a shadow out of place.

The file lay on the coffee table where I'd left it. I opened it and shuffled through a few of the papers. Marta had been thorough in collecting the information. Maybe Tess had supplied it. I thought about taking the file to bed and poring over it closely but then I suddenly found pictures of Bobby's three kids. Faxed copies of grade school close-ups complete with goofy smiles, missing teeth and rooster tufts of hair. The nine-month-old was sitting in one of those baby chairs looking rather surprised.

I felt a surge of rage directed at Bobby Reynolds. Was I seriously considering delving into this family tragedy? Even peripherally? I thought about Murphy. His acquaintanceship had brought me to this point. It was because of him that I knew anything about Bobby, Cotton and Tess. It was also because of him that I'd first flirted with this kind of work. He was the reason I'd taken criminology classes, the reason I'd come to Oregon, the reason I'd become a process server, the reason I was introduced to information specialist Dwayne Durbin.

This wasn't a "take the money and run" case, to quote Dwayne. It was so much more. But I'd promised I'd go to Cotton's benefit. I could do that much. Then I would wash my hands of the whole sorry affair and let the authorities take over.

I closed the file almost reverently. I made sure all the locks on my doors and windows were shut tight. Then I checked again.

For a while I stood looking out my back window at the rippling sliver of moon-striped water, the length and breadth of my view.

A long, long time after that I managed to fall asleep.

Chapter
Five

Saturday dawned an ominous gray and I pulled my red comforter over my head and groaned aloud. It never failed in the greater Portland area. Party = Rain. The equation was etched in stone. After weeks of beautiful sunshine, now the heavens would open and drench everyone at Cotton's benefit. Fantastic.

But acting like an ostrich wasn't going to help, so I threw back the covers and climbed out of bed. Yawning, I padded barefoot to the kitchen and opened my refrigerator. As soon as the door was in motion I inwardly asked myself, "Why?" I already knew there was nothing inside. It's sort of like when the power goes out and you hit the light switch anyway because it's dark. Pure habit. Peering inside I was faced with a half-empty carton of skim milk, a tub of margarine, a jar of tartar sauce that may have been left over from the ice age, a couple of dehydrated carrots and one lone diet cola. I don't know why I expect anything else. The grocery elves hadn't shown up during the night and stocked my shelves.

Picking up one of the pathetically shriveled carrots, I waved its limp form several times before I dumped them all into the garbage disposal and ground them up. I hung on the refrigerator door for a while just because I can. That's the great thing about living alone; no one to warn you about the electric bill.

It occurred to me there might be something to eat in the pantry—the pantry being the cupboard above my microwave. To my delight and astonishment I discovered behind the cans of Stagg Chili and Campbell's soup a miniature box of Krusteaz pancake/waffle mix and an equally tiny bottle of boysenberry syrup wearing a bright red bow, both part of a Christmas gift package. My eye had passed over this bounty for months but now I zeroed in on it like a sniper, aware there was probably just enough milk left to whip together breakfast, as long as I didn't mind teaming it with water or . . .

"Aha!" I declared triumphantly, pulling out the instant Folgers.

With that I clattered through my pots and pans, outdated dregs from my mother's cabinets which I'd managed to wrest away from her, until I found the piece of equipment I was really looking for: a waffle iron. The occupants before me had left this little housewarming gift. Upon discovering it, I'd pulled it out and examined it thoroughly. It seemed passable, so I'd scoured the waffle-iron-squares by hand, then run them through the dishwasher about five times to make sure there were no leftover cooties. Now I read the Krusteaz directions and realized I was short an egg. I asked myself how important an egg might be. If I threw in a few teaspoons of water to make up for the egg liquid, wouldn't that cover it? I shrugged and went ahead. No question: I'm a gourmet.

Ten minutes later I poured the batter onto the griddle and let my eye move back to the file I'd closed so carefully several nights before. But my mind shied away from Bobby Reynolds and turned instead to thoughts of the party itself. I tried to remind myself of all the reasons I might have a good time. There would be tiny, mouthwatering hors d'oeuvres and all the liquor anyone could drink. There would be music and people dressed in cool, expensive summer clothes. There would be Cotton Reynolds and his wife Heather, and there would be Murphy.

Shutting my mind, I flipped a lightly toasted waffle onto a plate and drenched it in boysenberry syrup. I tried to concentrate on food, either my current waffle or the luscious array sure to be awaiting me at Cotton's. Just because I'm eating one meal doesn't mean I can't think ahead. My motto's like the Girl Scouts': Be prepared. You never can be too sure where, or when, you'll eat again. In my life, this is painfully, painfully true.

The waffle turned out to be exceptionally good. Either that, or my standards have sunk exceptionally low. But it didn't matter because I couldn't keep my mind on anything but the benefit. Tonight loomed like the proverbial black cloud. I was filled with a low-level dread that infected everything I did. I don't know if other people are this way, but I tend to instantly regret every serious new responsibility I take on. I always want to take it back. I certainly wanted to back out of my obligation to Tess Bradbury.

I cleaned up slowly, taking my time. Not that I'm this terrific housekeeper, or anything, but there were still loads of hours ahead of me. I had oodles of time to regret being so eager to get my hands on five hundred dollars. Of course, rent would be due in a couple of weeks and the money would be nice. Still . . .

I wiggled my toes. The injured one had recovered. I reminded myself to pick up another pair of flip-flops as my eyes traveled to the telephone. My mother's request sounded in my ears and before I could think about it, and therefore stop myself, I was calling my brother. He had a new girlfriend. Mom wanted to know about her. My mission, should I choose to accept it, was learn all I could about her.

I reminded myself that Booth could be at work; I had no idea what his rotation was. Being a cop means working different shifts. I could never count on him being on the same schedule more than a couple of weeks at a time, though I've never really tried all that hard to keep track. As the receiver rang in my ear, I began to hope that my mission was accomplished. Duty fulfilled. I'd made the phone call. I was free to go.

I was just about to hang up when Booth suddenly picked up. "Hello," he greeted, his voice sleep-drugged, his tone a few degrees short of welcoming.

"Hey, Booth," I said.

"Oh. Hi, Jane."

"You work late last night? Sorry to call so early."

"Just catching up on sleep." He yawned loudly.

"Okay."

The conversation, such as it was, stalled. I wasn't sure how to proceed from here. It wasn't like me to just check in with no reason.

"You want something?" he asked, sounding more awake.

"No. Not really."

"Mom tell you to call?"

His perception caught me up short. I debated on a lie and decided, why bother? "She says you have a new girlfriend and she wants me to find out all about her."

"I have a new fiancée," he reported with a hint of self-satisfaction.

Fiancée?

"Good God," I said. "You're getting married?"

"Not right away. But, yeah."

"And we haven't even met her? Who is she? What's her name?"

"Sharona."

"Sharona?" I repeated. "Like 'My Sharona'?" I felt mildly hysterical and attempted to hide it. My twin was getting *married*? And he hadn't even bothered to inform me? "Is this a joke?"

"Nope."

"You haven't told Mom yet," I accused.

"Nor Dad."

I snorted. I *knew* he hadn't told our father because Dear Old Dad departed when we were both still wee tots. And he departed into the arms of another woman, his secretary at work. The scandal pretty much kicked them both out of the law firm where they were employed. Dear Old Dad was now in private practice and our lovely stepmother had popped out three more children, my half brothers and sister, at an alarming rate. They all still lived somewhere in southern California. No wonder Booth and I both left the state for good, and Mom occasionally makes noise to that effect.

"Mom wants me to meet her," I informed him. "She wants information. But I'm not going to tell her you're engaged. That's for you, Bucko."

"She can call me."

"Pick up a phone."

"I'll call her in a while. I just don't want to, yet."

I could understand. When I have big news I sometimes have to pick my time to share it with anyone. It's like I need to almost believe it myself. But I didn't want Mom calling me every two hours and demanding information while I sat on this powder keg.

"Come on, Booth."

"Why don't you meet Sharona?" he suggested. "Come by tonight."

"The one night I have plans."

"Tomorrow?"

"Will you call Mom before I come?"

"Sure."

"I won't walk in the door unless I know she's talked to you."

"I'll call her later today."

"I'm holding you to it," I warned.

"Jesus, Jane."

"Should we meet for dinner?" I suggested. "I'll order pizza."

"Sharona's a vegetarian."

Well, of course she was. I was getting the sneaking suspicion she might be too cool for me. Probably lived in the Pearl District, currently the most chi-chi, wildly growing part of Portland. "I'll order gourmet veggie pizza. Will that work? I haven't been struck by a miracle and suddenly learned to want to cook."

"Any chance we could invite ourselves boating with some of your friends?"

Trust Booth to push the envelope. "My scintillating company won't be enough?"

"Just thought I'd ask."

I thought of Dwayne and his boat and immediately dismissed him. I hadn't gotten over my fleeting attraction to him the other night. I next considered my neighbors, the Mooneys, remembered their constant bickering, dismissed them as well and returned to Dwayne. "Possibly." I was cautious.

"Great. See you around four?" he asked, then hung up after my grunt of agreement.

I hoped this didn't mean I was going to have to seriously play hostess. I'm not good at it. Playing hostess means serving food, smiling and welcoming practical strangers into your home. I wrinkled my nose. This was my twin's fiancée. I had my Costco card. If worse came to worst, I could rush over and buy some frozen hors d'oeuvres—those little quiches, or chicken wings, or something.

Groaning to myself, I stripped out of the T-shirt and sweats I used for sleeping, and stepped into the T-shirt and sweats I use for running. Within two minutes I was out the door and making for the Coffee Nook and a way to waste more hours until evening.

I stayed at the Nook until my butt muscles were numb from sitting on the bar stools too long. Then I half-ran, half-power-walked home. At four o'clock I asked myself what I was going to wear, why it mattered, and, once again, what the hell I thought I was doing. I was no private dick. I was no dick at all, which was a good thing as far as I could see. But I was in need of cash and this seemed an easy way to earn some.

I glanced outside. The clouds still hung low in the sky. No rain had fallen, as yet, but the air was sticky and close. I pulled on a white T-shirt, a pair of khaki capri pants—real, this time—and my Nikes without socks. Since I'd lost my flip-flops I was pretty much down to sneakers. I might look a little out of place but if, and when, the rain came, no one was going to care. I glanced down at the Nikes. Woofers' bite marks still infuriated me. I was definitely going to have to buy new shoes.

Dragging my hair into a loose ponytail, I corralled it at the nape of my neck into a funky bun thing. Stray hairs jutting out kept me from looking too coiffed. Can't stand that super slick look on myself. It's just not natural. I next did a makeup job in pink and peach that made me look like a washed-out imitation of myself. I wanted to fit in with the benefit crowd—mostly members of the Lake Oswego Historical Society whose mean age was probably fifty—as best as I could. Pastels felt like the answer. Maybe if they saw my face, they'd forgive me my sneakers.

There was an anxious little humming going on beneath my skin. Nerves. I snatched up my keys and headed out.

Less than ten minutes later I pulled to a stop behind a blue Ford sedan already parked on the access road near the bridge which crossed to Cotton's property. Drawing a breath, I stepped into evening air choked with battling barbecue scents from the island and homes along the shore. Lamb, chicken, beef, grilled onions and hot dogs were a heady concoction. I walked across the bridge. The gates were open and I could see people already dotting the property. Tiki torchlights flickered invitingly against the charcoal sky and restless water. Barbecue smoke wafted behind the house, a wispy gray curtain. I circled along a brick path with little ankle-high signs pointing the way to a greeter's booth. I gave my ticket to a woman wearing a straw hat covered with fake cherries. She could have given Carmen Miranda a run for her money in fruity-style points.

A waiter dressed in all black swung a silver platter with crab-stuffed mushroom canapes under my nose. My mouth watered instantly. Things were looking up.

I wandered around the back of the house. Tables were scattered across a manicured lawn which stretched over a rise toward the lake. I followed a flagstone path and stood at a low wall. Tiered below me was an in-ground swimming pool, its aqua surface faintly dark beneath the clouds. The pool was surrounded by flagstones rather than cement and tiered to more flagstone steps and eventually the lake which lay green and dark beneath crowding fir trees.

I caught a glimpse of the path, just inside the chain-link fence. There was a certain amount of overgrowth but it was clear enter-

prising youths were still vaulting over the barrier and running
around the edge. Something was keeping the ground clear, and
dollars to doughnuts it wasn't Cotton.

Shimmering glasses of champagne passed by me, tiny raspberries nestled in the V of the bottom. I snagged one and smiled
at the cute waiter. He looked about eighteen. He said, "It's Dom
Perignon."

"Uh-huh." Like I believed that. Cotton might be wealthy, but
he wasn't stupid.

The waiter inclined his head toward a long table covered in
white cloth. In the center stood a regiment of champagne bottles,
all Dom Perignon. I strode over to get a closer look and saw the
boxes of a cheaper brand tucked beneath a corner of the table.

I snagged another glass of Dom. Might as well knock back the
good stuff before it ran out or it rained.

I sipped out of one drink and held the other as if I were waiting for my date to appear. A middle-aged woman with a huge
purse nearly backed into me. I did a quick sidestep out of harm's
way.

"Oh, I'm sorry," she said. "I didn't see you." She was going to
stick out her hand to greet me but realized my hands were full.
"What a beautiful setting," she said, almost on a sigh. "This is
the most unique property on the lake. I'm glad Mr. Reynolds allowed this benefit before he sells it."

"He's selling the property?"

"That's the rumor. I'm Lorraine Bluebell," she introduced.
"I'm a Realtor with Lakeside Realty."

"You're Cotton—Mr. Reynolds'—agent?"

"No . . ." She wrinkled her nose. Lorraine was about fifty-five,
a shade plump, with a whitish streak of bangs against an otherwise dark blond bob. She was stylishly dressed in a taupe linen
jacket and straight skirt. Her purse was an iridescent lilac shade
and looked big enough to carry a bowling ball. A leaf-shaped
brooch of amethyst-like stones sparkled on one lapel. Catching
my look, she said, "They're fake. Pretty though. I think Paula

Shepherd's got the lock as Cotton's real estate agent, but that doesn't mean I can't find the buyer."

So, Cotton was selling. What did that mean? Anything? Or were he and his wife just ready to move on? "Why is he leaving?" I asked Lorraine.

"I'm not sure. Lot of grounds to maintain, although he does a beautiful job." She glanced around with admiration.

"How much is he selling for, do you know?"

"It's all speculation at this point. If and when Paula gets the listing, she'll put it in the RMLS for some exorbitant amount. Everyone will gasp and it will sell at a couple of hundred thousand less than what they're asking. But it's bound to be in the ten million plus range."

"Wow."

Lorraine slid me a sideways glance full of suppressed humor. "It would be a nice sale."

"Yeah," I said with feeling. "What's the RMLS?"

"Realty Multiple Listing Service."

She signaled one of the waiters. I finished my first glass of champagne and started on my second. In tacit agreement Lorraine and I became "benefit buddies" and we toured the house and the grounds as the crowd around us grew larger and louder.

"You remind me of my daughter," Lorraine said, her hand hovering over the canapes. These were tiny rolls of roast beef, sour cream and some kind of green leaf. Possibly basil. "Her name's Virginia but she goes by Ginny. She lives in Santa Monica. Works as a production manager on commercials. I don't really know what that is, but she organizes everyone involved in the shoot." She cocked her head. "What do you do?"

Good question. I wasn't sure how to answer her. I was saved from a response by the roar of a motor boat engine. We were standing on the grassy level above the pool. Both Lorraine and I looked toward the water where a deluxe Ski Nautique in mustard yellow was docking. Waves from the boat's wake lashed the stone wall, rocking the boat violently. I winced, half expecting it

to smash into smithereens, but a couple of party employees scurried over and managed to find safe mooring in a sheltered cove
behind a wall of large screening rock. The new guest stepped
onto a slippery rock step, half inundated with slapping water and
made his way around the pool and up to the party. I was surprised
to see I recognized him: my acquaintance from my night at
Foster's some weeks ago. The one who was thinking of moving
here; it looked as if he had.

Lorraine's gaze followed mine. She seemed about to say something, just as a thin, forty-something woman with blond, spiky
hair and a tense walk strode up to her. I recognized her immediately as half of the couple sharing a table with Cotton and Heather
at Foster's On The Lake.

My curiosity was all but choking me. I couldn't believe I knew
not one, but two people, both of whom I'd met at Lake
Chinook's one hot dining spot on the lake.

"Hello, Lorraine," she greeted tautly. Her eyes swept past
both of us to the man arriving below.

"Hello, Paula," Lorraine answered. There was cool reserve in
her voice, one I hadn't heard in our hour spent together.

Paula Shepherd. Aha. I guessed Lorraine's detachment was a
form of professional rivalry. And to be honest, on first impression
Paula Shepherd was not the warmest and fuzziest person on the
planet. She seemed pent-up and tense, her eyes following the
newcomer with laser-like intensity.

"Do you know him?" I asked.

She turned to look at me, frowning. "Have we met?"

I stuck out my hand. "Jane Kelly."

"Paula Shepherd. Are you with Lakeside?"

"She's not a real estate agent," Lorraine informed her.

"I'm just another Lake Chinook resident," I said.

"That's Craig Cuddahy." She jerked her head in the direction
of Cotton's latest guest. "We're not supposed to arrive by boat.
Since the accident last weekend Cotton specifically requested all
guests come by car. The moorage isn't safe and Cotton doesn't
want uninvited gawkers to just show up."

"The accident with the teenagers?" I asked.

She nodded. "But the dogs are locked up, so no one's going to stop him." Her tone was full of contempt. She smiled at the end, as if negating everything she'd just said, but her feelings about Cuddahy were clear.

"I didn't think he lived here," I said.

"He doesn't. He's staying at the Shoreline." Her lip curled. Hearing herself, she laughed. "He's a developer. From somewhere in the Southwest. He wants to buy this property for a song. I'm sure he hopes the accident will work in his favor."

And he's not using you as his real estate agent, I thought. "He's made an offer?"

"There are always tacit offers, Miss Kelly." She left abruptly and I looked around to realize that Lorraine had moved away to mingle with others. I couldn't blame her. Paula Shepherd might be an effective real estate agent, but she wasn't someone you could happily sip champagne with. Not when you were standing on a piece of property that had anyone involved with real estate salivating over it.

I meandered toward the three-piece-string combo, strumming softly on a buried section of lawn away from the action. A few drops of rain fell on my head and I looked up anxiously. The fir trees rustled in warning, but the deluge held off for the moment.

I'd caught glimpses of Cotton and Heather on my tour with Lorraine. They were always surrounded by a small crowd. I'd learned more about the dynamics of the house than what my host was all about. I'd even seen Heather's and Cotton's bedrooms, separate, but with a shared bath, and I'd been shown the closed door to Cotton's den, situated at the far eastern corner of the house.

In my head I was totting up the five hundred dollars Tess was going to pay and feeling a little self-satisfied. As long as no one wanted serious results, this kind of work was easy. I had to manage a few words with Cotton to make my job legit, but that was duck soup.

Craig Cuddahy caught up with me as he was knocking back a

glass of the cheaper champagne, reaching for another, knocking it back as well. The waiter tried to turn away but he stopped him and swept another glass off the tray, dropping off his dead soldiers with an alarming clink of glass against glass. I imagined there was "chippage" involved. Cuddahy didn't even notice.

He did, however, notice me. A line drew between his brows. I could tell he was trying to place me. I debated on ending his struggle, but his demeanor wasn't exactly warming me to him, either. He'd seemed thoughtful and pleasant that night at Foster's, staring over the water, but tonight he was impatient and bordering on rude. I glanced at my watch. At this rate, he'd be drunk by eight o'clock.

"We've met," he said.

I should have grabbed another glass of champagne while I had the chance, cheap or no, but it was too late: the waiters were avoiding Cuddahy like the proverbial plague. Since I was currently talking with him, they were avoiding me by default.

Great. Where was Lorraine when I needed her? Someone benign and helpful? I determined right there that I was going to become Lorraine's friend. I liked her. And she knew people in the area. If I were to become an information specialist, I needed friends.

And it would be nice to have friends I actually liked.

"I saw you at Foster's," I said, offering Cuddahy a clue.

"The restaurant?"

"A few weeks ago."

"Oh . . ." Remembrance flashed over his face. "You were wearing that red shirt."

Actually, I was wearing a skimpy red skirt, way outside of my usual attire. The need for femininity—something that rarely attacks me—had taken hold that night and I'd actually curled my hair and made myself look pretty okay. The disappointment Cuddahy showed as he viewed me now really gave my ego a beating. Okay, so I wasn't dolled up. I was all right, wasn't I? It took all I had not to self-consciously touch my hair or look down at my clothes.

"Well," he said, lifting his now empty glass. "Let me see if I can get us a refill."

"Let me," I said, jumping at the chance to vamoose.

I had no real interest in hanging around with Cuddahy, but I'd spied Cotton in a heated conversation with a young man whose back was toward me. I had a strangled moment when I thought it was Murphy, but this guy's physique wasn't even close. I'm just paranoid that way. Murphy is tall and lean and serious with eyes that seem to look right through you. It's his smile that does me in: wide and bright in true Hollywood style. And his dimples . . . and his developed sense of humor. Whoever was bending Cotton's ear was far shorter and his hair was darker. As I glanced at him, he half-turned. I realized he was the other half of the couple who'd joined Cotton and Heather at Foster's the other night. I'd overheard Paula say she'd brought her partner, Brad Gilles. This must be the man.

"Well, we're all accounted for," I murmured to myself as I tracked down a waiter and pulled off two more glasses of champagne. These were now sans raspberries and of some brand far less lofty than Dom. The night was wearing on.

I turned and just missed face-planting myself into a broad, male chest.

"Is one of those for me?"

A sudden shift in air pressure. The hairs on my arms lifted and I shivered.

My smile felt stilted. I stepped back and said, "Hi, Murphy."

Chapter Six

Well, I knew he was going to be here, didn't I? It was just a matter of time until I ran into him. I'd worried and fretted and wondered about him, and he'd finally materialized. No need for histrionics. It was what it was. Still, I had to struggle really, really hard to look merely glad to see him, not sweating and tremoring from emotion.

Murphy accepted a glass of champagne from one of my nerveless hands. His gray eyes searched my face. I don't know what he saw but it felt like my skin had turned to thick rubber. Nothing moved apart from my heartbeat, racing light and fast.

"How's Santa Fe?" I asked, congratulating myself on my faintly interested, not overwhelmed, tone. There was a funny little thrumming beneath my skin. My legs seemed to be shaking. I was half afraid my right knee was going to break out into a can-can.

"It's all right."

"Been involved in criminology somehow?" He'd been far keener on his studies when we were at college than I had. I'd been merely keen on him.

"Not much." He was abrupt, glancing around as if he were looking for a way to escape. He didn't have to explain that

Bobby's murdered family had spun him off the investigation track. I didn't explain that the same had not happened to me. "I didn't expect to see you here," he said.

"I, um, heard that Cotton was selling." I broke smoothly into the lie. No sense in telling him the truth. We had enough to wade through without me breaking into an explanation of why I'd come to the benefit. "This seemed like my one chance to see the island. Whoever buys it might not be as interested in opening its gates."

"He's selling?" Murphy was clearly surprised.

"That's the rumor."

"I'd never sell."

I looked past him, past the crowds of people, toward the lake. In the distance a red and white boat skimmed by, pulling a water skier under threatening skies. Another day you would be able to hear the dim roar of the motor; today there was too much chatter, laughter, music and overall noise.

"It's a lot to keep up," I pointed out. Landscaping and grounds maintenance, so important, but areas where I stumble, fall and die. Housekeeping nearly does me in. I can't imagine the world beyond my front door expecting me to take care of it. Not that Ogilvy does such a hot-shot job. Once in a while I sweep my flagstone steps, but hey, that usually requires libations and plenty of rest. I'm not really lazy, but I'm intimidated and just plain disinterested in outdoor labor.

"What are you doing now?" he asked.

I liked the timbre of his voice. It just reminded me of so many pleasant memories. When you're in love—obsessively in the first blush of that nearly fatal emotion—everything is so damn wonderful it hurts. I was being assailed by those haunting moments when Murphy and I were buried inside each other's self, as if there was nothing else.

"I'm process serving. And working with Dwayne. You know him."

He nodded but his brows knit. I could tell he was faintly disappointed. I felt the urge to tell him what my real mission was, but I bit my tongue. There was no point in defeating my purpose so early in the game. Lots of hours left for that.

With Murphy, I didn't trust myself. Far worse than the way I didn't trust myself with Dwayne. Far, far worse . . .

I snagged a coiled cocktail shrimp drenched in melted butter from a passing tray. The waiter stopped, somewhat impatiently, giving me time to grab a second. Murphy shook his head at the waiter, then downed his champagne in one shot. He swiped the back of his hand across his mouth in a thoroughly sexy "I don't give a damn what others think" sort of way. I chomped down both my shrimp, barely tasting them. I wanted to kiss him. I wanted to throw him down on the ground and writhe on top of him. My thoughts shot down a thoroughly pornographic path that left me feeling breathless and vulnerable. I had to look away.

Inhaling unsteadily, I hazarded a sideways glance at him. He was tapping the edge of his empty glass with one finger, gazing around for another waiter. I should have been relieved that he couldn't discern—or didn't care about—my feelings, but the realization made me mildly hysterical. I wanted to laugh. I didn't know *what* I wanted. I desperately glanced around for help. I was in big, big trouble. God knew what would happen if I were left alone with him for too long.

It was at that moment that Craig Cuddahy rediscovered me. "Hey," he said, sounding put out. "Thought you were bringing me a drink."

"I think we could all use another." I marched away on that, heart beating painfully, glad for the escape.

I never went back. Call it an attack of the "junior-highs." I couldn't face Murphy and act as if everything was okay between us. I just couldn't. And after a couple of more glasses of champagne which seemed to have no effect whatsoever, I decided I didn't have to. Screw it. I didn't need to play nice-nice. I could display bad behavior with the best of 'em.

But I couldn't get Murph out of my mind, and my peripheral vision was on a constant search for his whereabouts. I saw him standing amid a group of young people, women mostly, though they were doing all the talking—and heavy flirting—while Murphy was quiet, distracted and apparently not the least bit interested. This did my jealous heart good.

"Welcome," a gravelly male voice intoned. I looked over my right shoulder and there was Cotton Reynolds, a beefy hand outstretched in my direction, a smile on his rather large face. There were creases around his droopy brown eyes, as if he spent a lot of time in the sun. Even so, his pallor beneath seemed pale. The tanning appeared to be a cover-up, which I guess it is for most of us. Tess had said he wasn't well; maybe she was right. Against the tan, his white hair had a neon effect. I'd met him before but it had been a few years. Up close and personal I could see the way the flesh around his face had loosened. Cotton may have a new, young wife, but the march of years—or illness—was upon him.

He was holding a martini in his left hand, the glass sweating, fine ice crystals floating in the fluid, a fat green olive stuffed with pimento settled in the V of the glass as if embraced. He tossed back a healthy slurp. "Can't stand champagne," he said. "Give me gin anytime." He held out his right hand.

I shook hands with him, uncertain whether to mention that we'd met before. He seemed to be regarding me quizzically, trying to place me. I wondered if he would. I'd only been Murphy's girlfriend, nameless and easily forgotten. I had a feeling guys like Cotton thought all young, semi-attractive women looked the same. My Nikes might give him something to think about later, but maybe not. Lovely as this benefit was, there was a barbecue feel to the event this evening, whether the Hysterical Society had meant for it or not. If I'd shown up in red-checks and chaps I would have caused only mild interest, unless, of course, the chaps were all that stood between me and the outside air.

"I'm Jane Kelly," I introduced.

"Glad to have you come. This is my wife, Heather."

He practically plucked her from a conversation she was involved with directly behind him. She'd been talking with the two real estate agents, Paula and Brad. Paula shot me a venomous look when she realized it was I who'd stolen Heather and Cotton's attention. I wanted to tell her that she had nothing to worry about, but I decided I didn't care. I'm past the point of wanting people to like me. This may be a serious flaw, something that should go on my permanent record, but it's made life a whole lot easier from my point of view.

"Hello," I said, shaking hands with Heather.

"Hi there." She smiled a question at me and I introduced myself again.

"I'm Heather," she answered, enthusiastically pumping my hand.

Heather's hair was a shade between blond and orange. If it had been short and spiked she would have been labeled "alternative" but since it was shoulder length and softly curled, she looked only mildly interesting. Her eyes were blue and large and she had a way of holding them open that suggested a wide-eyed, blinking innocence. As an affectation it distracted me. That, and the fact that she thrust her breasts forward as if they were the first line of attack. I had trouble keeping my mind on our conversation. Luckily, it wasn't exactly snapping and popping.

"Isn't it a beautiful night?" she said with a little lift of her shoulders.

Well, yeah, if you liked the idea of gathering storm clouds and the threat of serious rain.

Cotton dropped his empty glass on a passing tray, then slipped an arm around Heather's shoulders, but I could feel him sizing me up. He hadn't tumbled to my identity and I was reluctant to jump right in with it. I wasn't sure exactly what Tess expected. Was I supposed to glean information about Bobby by mere conversation? Like, oh, sure . . . if I started grilling Cotton he wouldn't catch on that I was the fox in the henhouse.

"You a part of the Historical Society?" he queried.

"I'm just here for the event." I lifted my champagne glass to the surroundings.

"Didn't think you looked blue-haired enough to belong to

that crowd." He grinned. I figured he might be right in there—age-wise—with a large section of the Historical Society's members but I kept my mouth shut.

Heather glanced skywards. "The weatherman assured us the liquid sunshine wouldn't ruin our party. It's supposed to rain later."

"So far, so good," I said.

We all smiled at each other. I racked my brain for some pithy thing to add.

Cotton said suddenly, "We've met before. You're . . . Murphy's girl!"

"Murphy and I once dated. That's all."

"Murphy?" Heather's blue eyes widened even further. I was afraid the skin might stretch far enough to allow a view inside her skull. She glanced past me. I automatically turned and we both watched as Murphy, standing under a branch of Douglas fir, shook his head to the waiter's tray of further champagne.

Cotton insisted, "You were together, though. I saw you with him several times, with Bobby . . . my son . . ."

"That's right."

Cotton ran his tongue over his teeth. I felt he wanted to say something more. I struggled to come up with something to keep the conversation going. I could practically hear Tess screaming at me to find out everything I could about Bobby.

A waiter hurried over with another martini for him. He took it carefully, as if maybe he were feeling the effects. I suspected the martini he'd just finished wasn't his first.

"I only met Bobby three times," I said, feeling my heart start to pound. "I liked him."

This wasn't exactly the God's honest truth. I'd been introduced to Bobby having already been colored by Murphy's opinion that he was a great guy. I'd never really formed my own opinion one way or the other. Since Bobby was Murphy's best friend I determined I would like him. This just made good dating sense. Like the boyfriend, like the boyfriend's best friend. Otherwise one risked banishment from the clan.

Cotton stared at me. Then he gazed past me, upward toward the trees. We were both thinking about Bobby. He drank from his glass. I could practically feel his emotion.

"I'm sorry," I said, meaning it.

Now he was staring toward the water. I followed his gaze, watching the sun-dappled water turn dark as a cloud scudded quickly overhead. He said with an effort, "It's been hard."

Now there was an understatement. I wanted to toss out all kinds of platitudes, but nothing came to mind. I had a sudden remembrance of Bobby. He'd been intense. He'd been nice to me, but I'd felt on guard. I'd put that feeling down to my own churning insecurity over Murphy, but in retrospect I realized it might have been because of him as well, his presence, his tautly coiled tension. Saying I liked him was definitely pushing it.

Heather appeared to be only half-listening. While we talked she fussed with the fabric flower on the bottom edge of her striped pink and yellow top. The flower was the color of Creamsicles, made out of a netting and seemed to be near her hem, and in a place that constantly struck her arm. Her goggly eyes were covered in eyeliner and mascara. She was young, but gave off the appearance of an older woman trying to appear young. Hip, she wasn't. She was cute, not beautiful, and I suspected her bobbed nose might have been fixed. She was uncomfortable with the turn of our conversation and who could blame her.

Cotton released her and to my surprise he cupped the back of my elbow and led me a few steps away, near a white trellised archway nearly buckling under the weight of a deep, purple clematis, the blossoms so huge and loppy there was something vaguely sexual about them. Or maybe it was just Cotton's touching me. I was feeling a tad grossed out for some reason but I put a look of interest on my face.

"Bobby . . . you met him . . . you know him."

"Well, yes . . ." I was vague. As far as I was concerned nobody knew Bobby. If they had they might have had some inkling about what he'd been contemplating. But I was working for Tess and having Cotton think I was some long-lost bosom buddy might work for me.

"You know he wasn't that way. What he was accused of doing . . . it wouldn't happen."

I deepened my look of interest. I just couldn't make myself nod and agree. Cotton was searching for a friend, an ally, someone to bolster his view on Bobby. Still, it was damned hard to side with him when I knew Bobby had murdered his family in cold blood.

His hand tightened on my elbow. "I'm glad you're here." His voice had grown thick, from emotion or alcohol or a combination of both. "You and Murphy. It's nice to see people who remember him the way he was instead of dwelling on all that terrible shit. It's damn slander, if you ask me."

He was giving me way too much credit. I was an utter fraud. But I didn't want to derail him at this juncture. If he wanted to reminisce I was all for it. "Bobby was an incredible athlete," I prompted lightly.

"Yes! Yes, he was." Cotton's expression lightened. "He could beat anybody. He was a good kid. You know, he was tagged by his senior class as most likely to succeed? He loved Laura and the kids. There was no reason for it."

"No."

"Someone else did those killings. Someone sick."

"It would take a sick person to kill children, babies," I agreed cautiously. I didn't want him to think I was accusing Bobby.

But Cotton was on his own track. "Whoever did it wants Bobby to take the blame. That's all. That's why it looks like Bobby took off."

"So, you think this person attacked Bobby, too? That's why he never came back?" I was trying to figure out if Cotton really believed this theory or if he was just trying it out on me.

"Yeah." He nodded several times. "Bobby didn't hurt them. He couldn't have. Not my son."

"Cotton . . ." We both turned to find Paula Shepherd hovering nearby. Her smile was about as real as my belief in Cotton's theory. Cotton frowned at her. Clearly he was having a bit of trouble focusing and I suspected he wanted to keep spinning his yarn, hoping someone would buy it. I was more than willing to listen. This was what Tess was paying me for, after all. Spying, listening, and then reporting back.

"When you have a moment? I'd like to run some thoughts by you?"

He flapped a hand at her. "Not today, Paula."

She studiously avoided looking at me. She was on a mission, as unrelenting as a heat-seeking missile. "But it's summer. This is the time to market. The most value is right now. Pretty as this is in winter, it's not the same."

"Not . . . now . . ." There was a definite chill in Cotton's voice.

Paula's crimson lips tightened, but she inclined her head and scurried back to a conference with her buddy Brad. They both kept popping up their heads and looking over at us. "You're selling the island?" I asked.

"Oh, who the hell knows."

He'd never taken his hand from my elbow and the continued contact began to nettle me. I'm not good with touchy-feely stuff. It makes me feel sticky and uncomfortable no matter what the reason. And even through his pain, I felt something from Cotton, some kind of sexual message. Maybe I was making it up, but I didn't think so. My mind flitted suddenly to what it would mean to have Murphy's hand against my skin and my heart lurched.

As if reading my thoughts, Cotton's fingers squeezed me. "Seen Murphy yet?"

"Uh-huh."

"Something still there?"

"Nope." I wondered if I would kill any chance of learning more if I suddenly jerked my arm free.

Cotton moved in closer. His breath heated my cheek. *Good God*, I thought in alarm, *is he going to kiss me?*

"It means something, that you like Bobby. It means something to me."

"It does?" I pulled back as much as humanly possible without shifting the position of my feet.

"A lot of people just blamed him, y'know? The cops . . . just about everyone. I'm not even sure what Heather thinks. But Bobby was a good kid."

Say it enough times and you might just believe it. I pretended to see someone I knew. Waving gently at this mirage, I eased myself away from Cotton's grip.

"That Murphy?" Cotton twisted around.

"No, someone else." Heather was standing by, her gaze lasered on me. I pantomimed that I needed to catch up with my unseen friend and headed down one of the pathways away from both Mr. and Mrs. Reynolds.

My rather abrupt strides ended me near the detached garage which was obscured by a circular mound cut into the stone driveway. The mound was thick with several large pine trees and some sorry-looking rhododendrons. Even those like me, who know next to nothing about gardening, could have pointed out the soil wouldn't be worth shit beneath the pines. The rhodies weren't suddenly going to get healthier.

The gabled and paned windowed garage jutted at an angle to the rest of the house. If the massive house were to suddenly disappear, the garage would look like a cottage with six vehicle bays. I wondered if there were a guest room inside, but as I cruised near the building I heard distinct canine growling. The hairs on my forearms lifted as well as on the back of my neck. Whatever the building's purpose, it currently housed the Dobermans. I hoped to hell they wore steel collars and were chained to iron girders. I glanced toward the crowd and viewed a lot of bare, exposed limbs. These were watchdogs. Imagining the scene through their eyes, I saw a feast to be had.

I wasn't alone by the garage. An older man wearing a pair of pants that rode halfway up his chest and whose weather-beaten skin was brick red nodded to me then cocked his head where the low rumble of warning came from behind the garage bays. "Sound mean, don't they?" he said.

"I wouldn't want to test them."

He looked me up and down. He didn't seem like he belonged at this high-falutin' Lake Chinook event, but then neither, probably, did I.

There was an untidy pile of slate to one side of the garage next to an upturned rowboat. He pushed a toe at the slate pieces, frowning. "I had a mean dog once," he revealed. "His name was Beezlebub. We called him Beez. He bit the postman clean through the back of his leg. Had to put him down. He was no good."

"Hmmm . . ." I glanced down at the ground, wondering if my destiny was to bounce from one unwanted tete-a-tete to another.

"I'm Grant Wemberly," he said, holding out a heavily veined hand. His grip was surprisingly strong. "Guess you'd call me the caretaker around here. Or groundskeeper. I just do whatever needs to be done." He eyed me harshly from beneath a pair of bushy gray-white brows. He could have been anywhere from sixty to eighty-five, maybe older. "You buy a ticket to come see the place?"

I nodded.

"Well, you don't look like the others. Guess you came to see where he lived."

"Who?" I asked automatically.

"Cotton's son."

"Oh . . . well . . ." I didn't really know how to respond. Maybe I should have dressed up more. Grant Wemberly seemed to think we were compadres or something.

"When someone's no good, you put 'em down. That's what they oughtta do with that Reynolds boy when they find him, but you know he'll go to trial with some hoity-toity lawyer and plead insanity and gum up the whole procedure." He grimaced and ran a hand through thinning, but still healthy-looking grayish hair. "Years'll go by. His daddy'll spend all his money trying to save him, but he's unsaveable. Tomcats kill kittens. It's a law of nature, but it don't mean they're likable. They're mean. Shriveled up little hearts. They're killers."

I stood by in disbelief. I was pretty sure I could count him out as a representative for PETA. "What about the Dobermans?"

"Oh, them's watchdogs. Been trained to run off trespassers." He shook his head. "Kids know they're here, but they just keep comin'. Running around the island. Damn fools."

"Like the Coma Kid?" I put in. He grated on me and I found myself wanting to argue with him.

Grant snorted. "If he was here, the dogs sure didn't chase him off. Betty was at the vet overnight. Surgery on her leg. Benny's no good without her. Told the police the same when they asked."

"The police were here?"

He said darkly, "Easy to blame someone else for your own kid's stupidity, but whatever happened to that boy, he wasn't chased by the dogs. Family wanted to sue is my bet."

Grant was just loads of fun. I glanced over at Cotton. Heather's arm was linked tightly through his while he chatted up a member of the catering staff. I wondered if I should feel jealous that he'd moved from me to someone else so quickly. I could see Heather's tension. The Creamsicle net rose was quivering.

Grant Wemberly followed my gaze. "What do you think about what he done?"

"Cotton? Oh. Bobby. It's beyond reprehensible. Unthinkable."

"Against nature," he agreed with a slow nod. "Men kill men. Sometimes they kill women or women kill men. But men and women don't kill their own kids. That's for tomcats and the psychos."

The Dobermans broke into more deep-chested growls which caught me up short. I glanced behind me and saw Craig Cuddahy coming around the backside of a huge lavender hydrangea bush that nearly touched the roof of the garage on the west end. He stopped short at the sound, looking alarmed.

Grant said nothing, but I assured Craig, "They're inside the building."

"It sounds like a death pack of 'em," he said, sidling up to me as if for protection.

"Just two," Grant grumbled as he ambled off. He stayed on the periphery of the grounds, not the party, a member of the team that made up Estate Reynolds.

Cuddahy had dipped into the champagne far more than I had. His face was red, his tie disheveled and he spoke very clearly, enunciating each word carefully as only an accomplished drunk can manage. I thought about when I'd first seen him at Foster's. He'd seemed so different, so in control of himself and delighted in finding this little corner of the world. But tonight he'd crossed into another level of alcohol consumption. Hey, I've been there. It's not a complete crime. I just sensed he might be doing it on a much more regular basis than was healthy.

It took all my wiles to rid myself of him. I tried to walk away but he dogged me, whining all the way. The hours had passed and the trio of musicians were packing their instruments into cases. The waiters were spending more time clearing up leftover dishes than offering more champagne and goodies.

The rain suddenly fell in a curtain, sending the surprised guests scurrying for cover. I used the time to escape from Cuddahy, slipping inside the house and zigzagging through several rooms. My antennae caught the sound of Murphy's voice saying his good-byes. I turned in time to see him shaking hands with Cotton. From my point of view I couldn't tell how they felt about each other. For one blinding moment Murphy looked my way. He lifted a hand in good-bye. I did the same. After he was gone I realized my mouth was spit dry and I felt like I'd been put through the wringer.

Cuddahy managed to catch up with Paula Shepherd's partner, Brad, who also seemed to be trying to ease himself away. Cuddahy had barely noticed the silent encounter, so intent was he on his own path. "This isn't the only property in Lake Chinook. It's the only one that matters," Cuddahy practically yelled at him.

Lorraine Bluebell's white-streaked hair came into my line of vision. Brad answered as he was backing away, "If you divided it up, you could put four, five houses on it easily. Maybe more."

"Are you kidding?" Lorraine's back stiffened. "There aren't many pieces like this. I'd never break it up."

Cuddahy regarded her pityingly. "You don't really know about development."

"I know about arrested development," she leveled at him, and I silently cheered her as I slipped further inside the house. I was tiptoeing like a thief for some reason. Catching myself, I walked with more purpose. Small clusters of people, in twos and threes, were roaming the rooms and hallways. I kept to myself and was almost home free when I ran straight into Heather.

"Hey," she said breathlessly. "The damn rain showed up early!"

"But it was a nice party," I said. "Really a beautiful setting."

She looked me up and down. I'd sensed earlier that she was bugged with the attention Cotton had given me, but my sincere words melted her. "Thank you. I'm so glad you came."

She made me feel like a heel.

"Maybe I'll see you around . . . like at Foster's?" she said.

"Maybe," I agreed. Female bonding . . . who knew?

The rain began to taper off and the crowd surged toward the door. I snuck away, wanting a last look around the house. I'm not sure why. But if Tess wanted information on Cotton, I figured I might as well push this until the end.

I found myself in Cotton's study. The bookshelves were natural cherry and the massive desk was painted black and then antiqued to make it look much older than it undoubtedly was. There was an equally massive black leather surface protector covering its surface. No errant papers littered the area. A phone in a dull pewter color sat beside a framed photo. I looked, expecting exactly what I saw: a photo of Bobby. There were no pictures of Laura or the children. Bobby was staring at the camera. He had Cotton's dark brown eyes and his hair was a thick mahogany, possibly Cotton's original color. Or maybe Tess's. Who knew how long she'd been a blonde. There were lines beside Bobby's mouth. He looked like a guy who might have a temper.

But maybe I was just making Bobby the villain. He could laugh, too, I remembered. I'd seen him throw back his head and holler with amusement. It took me a moment to pick through the rubble of my brain but I finally came up with the source of his amusement. Murphy had stepped in dog shit and the smelly stuff had collected in all the little crevices of his waffled hiking boot. Murphy had been good-natured about it, but I knew Bobby's laughter bugged him. The smell of dog feces was in the car with us on the way home and it took Murphy a long, long while over the utility sink to rid himself of the stinky glop.

Bobby hadn't been the greatest guy even before the murder of his family, despite his father's recollections. I shook my head. I just didn't get him. Sure, he wasn't great, but heinous? I wouldn't have believed it once. Now, I accepted it as fact.

There was a desk calendar opened to today's date opposite the phone. I perched on a corner of the desk and idly flipped through it, keeping one eye on the door. If I heard footsteps coming my way I'd be trapped. There was only one way out. I'd have a lot of explaining to do, and I didn't even know what I was trying to do.

I saw Cotton had an appointment for the following week with one Jerome Neusmeyer. I wasn't sure who he was though I felt I should know the name. A good one to ask Dwayne about.

Putting the calendar back, I peeked through the slatted blinds toward the roadway. I realized no cars were in view on the other side of the bridge, that damn near everyone had left. All that was left were a couple of stragglers standing on the bridge, apparently reluctant to leave the lovely site. The rain was now a fine mist, turning the outdoor lights to yellow halos. I watched that last couple head for their cars.

Time to go.

My purse was tucked under my arm and I was at the door when I heard Heather's bright voice calling to her husband, just outside the panels. I glanced around, panicked. There was a narrow closet behind the desk. I opened the door, sure it would be filled with shelves but to my relief the bottom half was open, leaving a space large enough for me to squeeze into as long as my chin was on my knees. I slid inside but couldn't quite close the door before Heather's voice sounded inside the room, near enough to make me jump.

"Come in here. Don't, don't don't, take so long. Nothing else needs to be done. You were perfect, honey." Her voice was a low coo. I couldn't tell if Cotton was with her or not. My field of vision was limited to a tiny slit, just enough to see the center of the desk. Heather's Creamsicle rose seemed suddenly to float in front of my eyes and I shrank back. She was directly on the other side of the door from me.

"Come on, Daddy," she said in a singsong voice.

Daddy? I didn't like the sound of that. It was way too potentially icky.

"Where's my baby?" Cotton suddenly asked.

Heather's answer was something between a giggle and a squeal.

My hands were covering my nose and mouth. My eyes were glued to the slit of light from the den. Heather had wriggled out of her dress and stood buck naked and proud in front of "Daddy," apparently. She had a lot to be proud of. Her skin was taut, her body lean where it should be, ditto where it was rounded. "Daddy" came into view and buried his face in her breasts. He, too, was as he'd come into the world. I saw to my mild surprise that he wasn't as excited as I'd have expected. But "Baby" went to work with the kind of systematic intent reserved for those with lots of practice and pretty soon "Daddy" was ready.

What followed was a lot of panting, humping, grinding and squirming across the leather protective pad atop the desk. I closed my eyes and ears. As a voyeur, I'm just fair. I would have thought I'd be better at it than I was, but you learn something new about yourself every day if you're not careful.

As soon as playtime was over, "Baby" disappeared and Heather was back full force. "I don't like the way you make me feel," she said flatly.

"Daddy" had a little more trouble coming back to himself. "You didn't seem to mind just now."

"I mean at the benefit," she hissed. "You could barely keep your hands off that blond girl's boobs."

"Oh, Heather." He was tired and bugged.

"And that one with the caterers? . . . Misty something . . . the smiling slut? Just don't make me feel bad in public, okay? If you're going to fuck her, just do it, but stop embarrassing me."

"I'm not having sex with anyone but you."

"Yeah?" She was spoiling for a fight.

"I don't want anyone but you."

"Even Tess?"

My closed ears opened a bit. Tess?

He groaned. "Oh, God, don't do this again."

"Even *Tess?*"

"I don't see Tess. I don't talk to her."

"Yeah? I heard you on the phone."

"I don't talk to Tess." Cotton was clear.

I peered out at the happy couple. Cotton was still lying on the desk. Heather stood in front of him, a beautiful virago. No wide eyes now. They were narrowed on him as if to probe for the truth of his feelings.

"Fuck me," Heather said in a low voice.

Cotton half-laughed. "I don't think it's in me."

"Come on, Daddy," she cooed. "Come on . . . come on . . ."

"No, Heather."

"Yes!" She was nothing if not insistent and despite his protests, I was treated to another Daddy/Baby intimate moment. I hoped Daddy was being helped out chemically, as Heather was really putting him to the test. At this rate, she could kill him with sex alone.

My cramped position was playing havoc with the back of my neck. And my whole head was feeling the aftermath of my champagne slugging.

I counted the seconds and they were *long* . . . as Cotton gave his lovely wife a few half-hearted thrusts and she dug her nails into his pale, wispy haired back. I wondered who was going to be hurting more later, me or Cotton.

It took another twenty minutes for them to gather themselves together and head out. It took another ten minutes for me to gather the courage to let myself out. Heather's Creamsicle rose lay on the floor, detached from her top whether by design or the throes of passion I wasn't sure.

I tiptoed down the hallway, my heart so loud it practically deafened me. But I made it out the front door, still unlocked, and was free! Skulking around the house, I sprinted as soon as I was near the bridge. The loud howl I heard behind me sent the hair up the back of my neck. I risked a look back. Two black, racing wraiths were charging full speed in my direction. No more barking. Just pure evil.

Jesus . . . Joseph . . . and Mary! I suddenly saw Grant Wemberly's point of view.

I ran as if my life depended on it, which I believe it did. In horror I saw the gate was closed. With barely a pause I launched myself at the iron bars, hauling my dangling ass over the top just as snapping jaws reached up at me. My arm wrenched. I bit back a yelp of pain, settling instead for some soft, terse swear words, the worst I could think of. I managed to get myself over the fence and out of reach. As soon as they saw they couldn't get to me the dogs yowled in frustration and threw themselves at the bars. A light came on above the front door.

I ran on, keeping to the shadows. By the time I got to my car I was shaking all over. I could scarcely get the key in the ignition.

I drove away and wound around Lake Chinook back to my little corner of West Bay. Tumbling into bed, sore and charged with adrenalin, I thought it might be in my best interests to reconsider this information specialist gig.

I was going to have to have a serious talk with Dwayne Durbin.

Chapter
Seven

Champagne . . . oh, champagne . . . it isn't how much I consume that affects me—anything counts. I can be quite drunk or stone-cold sober the whole night but as long as I drink champagne I'm bound to feel it. As I lay in bed on Sunday morning, gradually waking to the heat of a July scorcher, I could feel the aftereffects: the faint misery in my gut, the dull head, the niggling worry that I was going to have to give up alcohol along with dairy products and anything else that was fun.

I simply was not going to do it.

I turned over and that's when the alarm bells went off inside my left arm. A stinging pain reminded me that I'd gotten tangled on the fence. I'd barely escaped the damn dogs. Those Dobermans' bared teeth and snouts and frenzied barking had scared me so badly I would have gladly given my left arm to get away. I was grateful it was still with me, however, despite the screaming, tortured muscles that made me groan.

"Good . . . God . . ." My mental screen jumped to another scene. Burying my face in my pillow, I attempted to blot out unseemly pictures—like a series of snapshots complete with sound effects—of Heather and Cotton, humping, thrusting, faintly squealing and panting.

Oh, yeah. This is how I wanted to wake up.

And had I learned anything? Anything useful? I seriously doubted it and I was all for taking my five hundred bucks and running. What did Tess need me for anyway? I had another mental picture of her in her Audrey Hepburn disguise and I wondered again what the hell she thought she was doing.

Testing my arm, I was relieved to realize it wasn't seriously injured. Sore, yes, but working. My clothes were in a jumble on the floor. The dogs had missed me, but the fence . . . ? I examined them, found a few tiny rips, moaned over the loss, then decided it was simply a week meant for losing clothes.

In my T-shirt and board shorts, I moseyed out to my back patio, squinting through the pounding in my head, to stare out at the green waters of the lake. There was a cheap lounger with white plastic strips sitting in the morning sun. I eased myself onto it. It was Sunday. I could phone Tess and report my progress—whatever that was—as she was probably expecting a call.

It was going to be hot today. It was too bright to open my eyes. I climbed to my feet again, moving carefully as my bargain-basement lounge chair has a penchant for suddenly collapsing if you act too quickly. The phone started ringing and I squinted at my watch. Way too early for callers. I walked without enthusiasm to pick it up. Only family called this early on Sunday. It was either Mom or Booth. As soon as that thought struck me it sizzled along a nerve. Oh, shit. Booth was coming over with Sharona tonight.

My head throbbed like it was beaten inside by a hammer. "Hi there," I said into the receiver. No caller ID. I probably pay for the damn service but the phone in the kitchen's about a hundred years old and clunky as hell. Dwayne has cursed my slow conversion to everything electronic, but hey, he's not exactly a poster child for moving with the times himself. What's with that cowboy gear? Didn't that go out with the '80s?

"Hello?" a female voice greeted me back. The seesawing sound of fuzzy reception indicated she was on a cell phone. "Is this Jane—er—Kelly?"

"Uh-huh."

"Hi, this is Megan Adair. Um, y'know I have Binky with me? I was supposed to drop her off?"

"Who's Binky?"

"Aunt Eugenie's dog?" She faded out for a moment.

Another jolt like electricity. My eyes felt like they did not belong in my skull. "I'm not taking that dog."

"What?" Her voice was scratchy and faraway. I could scarcely hear her.

"I'm not taking the dog!" I yelled.

"Are you there? I can't hear you. Listen, if you're there, I'm just down the street. I'll be at your place in a few minutes . . ."

"I'm not taking the dog!" I practically screamed into the receiver but the phone was dead. I hung up and looked blankly around the kitchen. "Binky?" I repeated, dazed.

Coffee . . . and aspirin . . . or acetaminophen . . . stuff . . .

I dug through my cupboards and found some baby aspirin. Little tiny yellow pills with mini milligrams. Still, I'm a chicken when it comes to drugs. I swallowed four, which I suspected wasn't half of my normal dosage, but it pays to be careful. My shoulder sent little pain signals along my left arm. Just a reminder that last night hadn't been without its dangers.

Nothing helped and I was lying on my couch, arms cradled against my chest when my guest arrived. Megan Adair was true to her word. She knocked on my door so hard I thought she might break through the panel.

With an effort I climbed off the couch and opened the door. She was tall with a spiky cap of blond hair. She wore tan shorts, a red tank top and in her arms was the ugliest dog on record—a walleyed pug with a snorting habit that made me wonder if sticking the nozzle of a bottle of nose spray up its snout might be in order.

"This is—Binky?" I asked.

"Mind if I put her on the ground?" She didn't wait for a response as she set the dog on my hardwood floor and dusted her hands on her shorts. The pug snorted rapidly a few more times, turned a quick circle, then propped its tiny front paws on my leg and looked up at me. Its pink tongue lolled out of its mouth and it panted furiously.

"She could use a drink," Megan said.

Couldn't we all. "I can't have a dog named Binky," I said. But I dutifully walked to the kitchen, took down my grandmother's blue-flowered bowl and filled it with tap water.

"Eugenie was pretty specific." Megan followed after me, glancing around my small bungalow with interest. "How do you know her?"

"I *don't* know Aunt Eugenie." I paused. "How do you know Aunt Eugenie?"

"She's my aunt."

We stared at each other for several seconds. "You want a drink?" I asked, automatically pulling open the refrigerator door even though I knew better.

"What have you got?"

I leaned on the door. Without the shriveled carrots and milk there was nothing to commend it. "Tap water," I offered.

"Terrific."

I poured her a glass. Oregon water is not only drinkable, it's good. Having lived in southern California most of my life and dealing with water that tastes as if it's been fortified with soap, I sometimes forget that I can drink right out of the faucet. Right now it was all I had on tap, so to speak, so I poured myself a glass as well.

Binky squeezed between me and the refrigerator, propping her little paws against the lowest shelf. "Hey!" I yelled, to which she smacked her lips several times and panted some more.

"I've got her things in the car," Megan said, setting down her glass.

I watched her head outside. Her things? I glanced down at the dog who was sitting in a kind of odd sidesaddle position and gazing up at me as if ready for me to make a decision of some kind. "What things?" I asked. Binky closed her mouth and tilted her head, listening hard. I half expected her to respond, but all she did was resume panting.

The "things" proved to be a little furry bed, a leash, a half-full bag of dry dog food and a metal food bowl stamped with BINKY in big, raised letters. I was going to be able to save my grandmother's bowl for better things, apparently. Megan left this stuff in a pile in the middle of the living room and Binky ran over and snuffled everything before jumping in the bed and curling up, happy.

Megan glanced at her watch. "Gotta run."

"I really can't take this dog. I know my mother said I would, but it's a responsibility I can't handle."

Megan looked a bit crushed. She pulled out a pack of Players and turned them around in her fingers. "Can you keep her for a while? I don't have a place right now. I'm kind of in between living arrangements. I love the dog, but . . ."

"Sure," I said quickly, seeing my out. "Hey, for a while, no problem."

"Great," she said, heading for the door. She pulled out a cigarette as soon as she was on my porch. I followed her to her ancient Land Rover and watched her light up. The sharp smoke wafted my way as she waved out the match. Don't ask me why, but sometimes I like the first scent of a lit cigarette. It's a guilty pleasure most people don't understand, myself included. I've never been a smoker but sometimes that first whiff of tobacco is aromatherapy at its finest. Maybe I'm a latent pyromaniac. I inhaled a lungful of secondhand smoke as Binky shot through the door and came over to us, weaving between our legs.

"Does she understand about the road?" I asked. I lived on West Bay Road, a small connecting street between Bryant and South Shore, but it had its share of traffic. Twenty-five miles an hour be damned. People drove like maniacs.

"I don't think so. You'll have to watch her." Binks settled at Megan's feet, staring up at her. "I couldn't hand her over to Deirdre. Her husband's a complete ass and those kids don't look fully evolved. They're from the Pleistocene era, or something. They didn't want Binky and I didn't want them to have her."

It was interesting she was so averse to Deirdre—the correct

name for Aunt Eugenie's daughter, apparently. Deirdre must be spurious indeed, if Megan were more interested in handing the pooch over to a complete stranger. What did that say about relatives?

"Deirdre would be Aunt Eugenie's daughter?" I said, to clarify.

Megan snorted. Binky, watching and listening, snorted, too. I hoped to hear additional dirt on Deirdre, so to speak, but Megan had the good grace to keep her thoughts to herself, more's the pity. "You're lucky you're not related to her," was her final pronouncement. She reached into a Velcro pocket on the side of her shorts, withdrew a pen and piece of paper and wrote down a number. "That's my cell. If you need me, call."

"What do you do?" I asked.

"I'm a bartender."

"Really? I used to be a bartender in California. You're at a bar in Portland?"

"The Crock, short for Crocodile. You know it?"

"I've heard of it."

"Good Mojitos. Lousy tips. Young crowd." She shrugged. "On the east side. Not too far from Twin Peaks."

Twin Peaks was the name dubbed to the two bluish-green glass pyramids that rose above the convention center. The structure, with its glowing red lights crowning the tip of each pyramid, had been built around the time of the popular TV show and though the show was long defunct, its moniker lived on in Portland.

I found myself warming to her in a way I generally reserved for only a few close, twisted individuals.

"She's been spayed. And she's house-trained," Megan said, returning to Binky. "Her vet was down the street from my aunt. I don't have the number but I'll get it. They'll fax over her medical info."

I was overwhelmed. I didn't think I was ready to assume responsibility over another living creature. "My friend Dwayne has a fax machine." I reluctantly gave Megan the number and she promised the vet would send over all the medical information.

Megan finished her cigarette, ground it underfoot, then conscientiously picked up the butt and carried it to her car's ashtray. "Oh, and here are her papers. She's registered with the AKC."

I had an immediate vision of Binky wearing a white sheet with cutout eyeholes and carrying an automatic weapon before I realized I'd mixed KKK with AK-47. "What's the AKC?" I asked cautiously.

Megan was digging through the stuff thrown on the passenger seat of the Land Rover. She pulled out an envelope and put it in my hands. "American Kennel Club."

She fired up the Land Rover, sketched me a wave, then backed expertly out of my drive. Certain I was in over my head, I turned toward the house, Binky dogging my heels. We headed into the living room and I closed the door.

"Okay," I said, gazing down at the dog. She was one sorry-looking creature. Her eyes were so far apart I wondered if she really possessed stereoscopic vision. She looked more like a bird or a fish than a predatory mammal who relied on its eyes working together to hunt prey. It was doubtful Binky would hunt anything, for that matter, just based on shape alone. She was built like a wide, torpedo-shaped footstool, broad back and short legs. Her face and tail were black; her body light tan. She was like a Siamese cat on steroids who'd undergone a species-change and then taken up chasing parked cars.

I opened the papers. Binky's full name was THE BINKSTER. How cute. Aunt Eugenie had shortened it to Binky. Like something you'd stick in a baby's mouth. Or maybe some minor indiscretion, like a fart. I could see someone saying, "Oh, my. That was me. I just let loose with a binky."

The name had to go.

"Anyone tell you you look a lot like Ernest Borgnine?" I asked her seriously. "Maybe I'll call you Borg. How's that? Hello there, BORG!"

Binky turned around, faced the front door and started barking furiously. Her barking was close to hilarious. About as far down the scary scale from the Dobermans as one could get. She glanced back at me. My shouting had convinced her someone was here. "Not exactly swift on the uptake, are you?" I suggested.

She collapsed into her sidesaddle lounge and began panting anew.

"I don't understand how dogs can just accept that they're somewhere else and someone else is taking care of them," I complained into the phone later to Dwayne.

"What do you think they should do?"

"I don't know. Howl. Whine. Run away."

"Some dogs do."

"Not this dog," I said darkly. "It's made itself at home on my couch. And I've got the fan going full blast because all it does is pant and drink water."

"Have you fed it?"

"I've only had it an hour," I responded a tad testily. "I'm going to feed it tonight."

"What's its name again?"

I clamped my teeth together and counted to five. "Binky," I said evenly. Dwayne wasn't listening. He hadn't been listening throughout my diatribe, though he'd accepted that a fax would be appearing on behalf of the dog. Why I'd felt he could somehow help, or commiserate, escaped me now. "I've got to change it. I can't live with it. Even though this dog's going away at the first—"

"Did you go to the benefit?" he cut in.

Well, how rude. "Yes." I had half a mind to say nothing else. Name, rank, and serial number. That's all you get, buddy. But I had another bone to pick. "And I damn near got myself killed in the process!"

"Yeah?"

He seemed only mildly interested as I regaled him with the previous night's escapades, and he had the colossal nerve to respond with merely, "Write it down. All of it. Your impressions."

"Thanks for caring. You want me to put down the sight of Cotton's bare ass pumping up and down? Tess'll love that."

"When did you turn into such a prude?"

"That's such a . . . *wrong* thing to say. I do not do voyeurism well."

"Maybe you need some lessons."

I nearly bit out a response before I realized he was teasing me. Good old Dwayne, always trying to get my goat. "What kind of mother names her child Dwayne?" I said, jumping into battle.

"The kind who's in love with his father, Dwayne the dad."

"Oh. God. Seriously? Dwayne's your dad's name? Are you a *junior?*"

"Different middle names."

"What's yours?" I asked curiously.

"Austin."

"Dwayne Austin Durbin?" Much as I hated to admit it, I kind of liked the sound of that.

Dwayne got back to the subject. "Put your notes together. Put 'em on a file on your computer, or better yet, a disk or flash drive. You can write up a report for Tess and make her feel she's gotten her money's worth. Clients like hard copy."

"Flash drive?"

"An external piece you stick into a USB port. Mine's silver, about the size of my little finger but flat. Comes in all different storage amounts. Mine's 512 K. The size of the storage affects the price. Don't be cheap."

"I'm not cheap," I protested, lying through my teeth.

"They're also called flash hoppers, grasshoppers, a bunch of stuff. I know you don't have a zip drive, so we can forget that. You do have a USB port on that dinosaur, right?"

"Of course." I was pretty sure I did. He meant that little rectangular opening, didn't he? I wasn't about to ask.

"Get a flash drive. Better yet, get a new computer. It's past time, Jane."

"I love my computer."

"No, you don't. You're just afraid to upgrade."

"Fine, fine." I just wanted to get off the phone. Dwayne's relentless dragging of me into the current millennium tried my patience to the extreme. I practically slammed the phone down, then called Tess. My headache had diminished to a tiny throb and my shoulder felt stiff but okay. I wondered if I had time for a run, or if the heat was too unbearable.

Tess's answering machine picked up; a relief to me. In a cheery voice I told her I'd spoken to Cotton at the benefit about nothing important. I let her know I was awaiting further instructions. I did not mention the five hundred dollars I was now owed, but it took all my mother's hard-fought years of discipline to keep me from screaming the reminder to her.

I headed outside. My route to the Coffee Nook is shaded ninety percent of the way. I tested the air and thought I could make it. I hadn't had the nerve to call Booth yet. I knew I was running away from the phone.

Back inside I changed into sweats and Nikes. I was heading for the door when I saw the dog staring at the front door panels. Another tinkle trip, apparently, or else Binky was merely contemplating the value of oak versus maple.

Hmmmm . . .

"Come on, you," I said, wondering if this were a fool's errand. I found the leash Megan had left. The dog regarded me blankly. "I'm not going to call you Binky," I said sternly to which the dog raced over and started furiously licking my hand. I jerked back, wiped my hand on my pants, clipped the leash on Binky's collar and we were out the door. I wondered if this show of affection was because I'd mentioned its name. I was hoping it had understood me and was consumed with delight over the thought of being called something other than Binky. It made sense to me.

Silently daring the dog to keep up with me, I took off at a slow lope. My challenge was a joke. Binky was fairly swift on her stumpy little legs. Of course, she nearly ripped my arm off every time she stopped to sniff, which was often. We ended up walking most of the route which was just as well because the weather was turning beastly.

By the time we reached the Coffee Nook, my right arm was practically numb and this was my good one! The dog just kept yanking me to a stop. I was drenched in sweat and Binky, panting furiously, definitely showed signs of wear. I clipped the leash to a metal loop screwed into the building siding. The Coffee Nook was pet friendly. Not only were the metal loops ready for leashes, there was a large bowl full of water sitting invitingly under the roof overhang. Binky slurped noisily then flopped down beneath one of the outdoor chairs. She didn't seem to mind cement.

I wandered inside. Binky's walleyes watched me enter. I waved at her and was surprised and a little thrilled to see her curly tail wag. The weekend employees smiled at me, high school or college-age girls who all are blond and bordering on anorexia. Not my usual crowd. I felt them watching me as I poured myself a cup of black coffee from the help-yourself counter. I loved that about the Nook. If it's plain coffee you want, you can help yourself. The exotics have to line up for their caramel-mocha-frappe-what-the-hells. One of the coffee girls, Kate, the only one I truly know, caught my eye. I lifted my paper coffee cup and she nodded. I have a coffee card which is good for ten cups. They just mark me off until the card's done. The eleventh one is free.

I sat down on my usual stool but the weekend crowd didn't contain anyone I knew. Finishing my coffee, I drank a paper cup of water for the return trip, then somewhat deflated, headed back outside. Binky barked in greeting. She'd recovered her stamina and was on her feet. She'd also garnered a small group of children while I was gone. They all wanted to pet her but were afraid.

"Mad dog," I whispered to them as I unclipped the leash. I felt glaring eyes digging into the back of my neck. Soccer moms. Lake Chinook was rife with them. And the two soccer moms standing behind me didn't find me funny in the least. I often ask myself why I live in an area that is not single-woman friendly, and the answer continually escapes me. Murphy had introduced me to Lake Chinook and so I stayed.

"Charity, Julianne . . ." Soccer mom number one waved two of the little girls over. Reluctantly they turned away from the Pug.

"Whitney!" the other, shriller mom cried to the remaining girl.

"What's his name?" Whitney asked me, ignoring mom.

"She doesn't have a name yet," I said.

She gazed at Binky critically. "When does he get one?"

"She," I repeated.

"He looks like a boy."

I silently agreed. That face . . . I finally buckled, "She responds to Binky."

"Binky?" Whitney brightened and Binks yelped and jerked eagerly against her leash as the little girl bent down to pet her.

"Whitney!" The mother screeched as Whitney's fingers reached toward Binky's grinning, sloppy mouth. Binky promptly licked the girl's whole arm, sending her into fits of laughter and turning mom's face a brick red. Mom yanked on Whitney's free arm, and the little girl nearly tumbled off her feet. She glanced back as mom dragged her to the car, waving forlornly to me and Binky. The dog gazed after her as if she'd just lost a best friend. Or, maybe she just wanted a ride.

I suddenly thought of Kit, Bobby's youngest, and realized she would have been around Whitney's age if she'd lived. It hit me in the gut. Sobered, I pulled on Binky's leash and we started the slow walk home.

"Your real name is The Binkster," I said, "which is okay by me but I don't think I'm going to be using it all the time. I really will not be able to handle Binky. How about Binks?" For that I got a desultory wag of the curlicue. At least it was something. And for as long as I was going to have this dog, it was good enough.

Booth called just as we entered the cabin. I told him I'd phone back as both Binks and I were done in from the heat. I checked to see Binks had enough water then poured a glass for myself. We both drank thirstily.

A bit reluctantly I called Booth back. There were mere hours left before he and Sharona appeared.

"I've got to cancel," he said abruptly. "Work."

"Oh." I sounded appropriately crestfallen—at least I think I did—until he insisted that we meet on Monday. He had Tuesday off, but then Sharona was leaving for a few days, so Monday was both the perfect—and only—opportunity for us to get together.

I really, really wanted to postpone. I had enough on my plate right now. But visions of my mother's inquisition had me rolling over and saying yes. At least it left Sunday night free. I had thoughts of going to Foster's On The Lake . . . maybe in Dwayne's boat. We settled on Monday, both glad duty had been dispensed with, at least for the moment.

Thinking of Dwayne, I fired up my computer, planning my report for Tess. I started by writing down my impressions from the night before. I tried to remember everything Cotton had said about Bobby. After I wrote down his words, I added my own impressions.

I typed in: DOES HE KNOW WHERE BOBBY IS?

Staring at the words, I examined my feelings, struggling for some kind of thoughts on that. Finally I typed: NO, HE DOESN'T. I put a little *jk* after this, indicating this was a Jane Kelly thought rather than a fact. When I was finished I was rather proud of my follow-up skills.

Tess called around noon, just about the time I'd remembered to feed Binks who was practically eating the baseboard by this time. I'd managed to run out and buy myself a slice of pepperoni pizza and a Diet Coke, so I was fed and once that happens, hey, everybody else can just get their own.

Except now I owned a pet. Temporarily.

So, while Binks plowed through her food, I reached for the ringing phone and encountered Tess.

"Well?" she asked. "How did it go?"

"It went," I said.

"Did you talk to Cotton about Bobby?"

"It's not exactly a subject you can raise at a first meeting."

"What am I paying you for?"

I bit my tongue. "Cotton mentioned Bobby when he realized who I was," I said in a flat voice. "He seemed sad and heartbroken, which you'd expect."

"Did he say anything about where Bobby is?"

Like, oh, sure, that's what he'd blurt out to me, a virtual stranger. "We didn't discuss it."

"He has to know," she insisted.

"That's kind of a leap," I pointed out carefully. "If Cotton knows where Bobby is, he might feel compelled to tell the police."

"Bobby's his son," she said with an edge. "He'd want to protect him at all costs. I know he knows where Bobby is. He's my son, too!"

"I don't know how I can help you any further," I said honestly. "I met Cotton. He seemed to want to talk about Bobby but it caused him pain."

"Pain? How?"

"Considering what Bobby's accused of, I'd say it's the pain of a parent whose child hasn't . . . lived up to what's expected." That was putting it mildly.

"Did you talk to Heather?"

"Briefly."

"She thinks she's getting Bobby's money."

"Bobby's money?" I questioned. "You mean Cotton's?"

"Bobby should inherit everything. It should be his."

I made a face, something I'm prone to do when something just plain smells bad. But then Cotton's appointment with Jerome Neusmeyer crossed my mind and I suddenly remembered that Neusmeyer was an estate attorney, one of the more flamboyant ones. He might help you take care of your inheritance, but he spent his personal time with pretty young things. I think there was even a rumor of paid escorts. I would have to ask Dwayne, but I was fairly certain my memory was dead-on. "You want me to learn if Cotton's still leaving it all to Bobby?"

"That would be great!" she said in a rush, as if she'd just thought of it.

"I'm not sure I can accomplish that," I said.

"Oh, sure you can. Scrape up a deeper acquaintance with Cotton. Or, better yet, Heather. She's close to your age. I'll pay you an appropriate rate."

Heather *had* seemed interested in furthering our acquaintanceship. I said to Tess, "Even if I don't get results?" *And where's that first check, lady?*

"Find out any little bit you can about Bobby. I want to see my son again. I want to know he's okay," she said with a little catch in her voice. Bitch that I am, I wondered if she faked it.

"I'll do what I can," I said in a tone that suggested she was throwing her money away, hand over fist.

"Good. Time is of the essence. I hate to be so pushy, but we've got to get on this thing."

I wondered if Tess knew about Cotton's appointment with Neusmeyer.

"Why don't you call up Heather and invite her to dinner?" she suggested. "Just a girl thing. I bet she jumps on it."

"Great idea," I said cheerily, crossing my eyes. Maybe I should have Tess just plan an itinerary for me and send me merrily on my way.

I hung up wondering if I should have asked to see some greenbacks up front. I'm not good about demanding money. It always feels like begging, even if I've worked for it. I'm sure this is a flaw in my character. Tess didn't seem to have qualm one about going after Cotton's money, however. Her worries over Bobby were tied to his inheritance, or what she perceived his inheritance should be. I wondered if she expected some of that money to find its way to her pocket. Tess had stated that Cotton was ill and I had a mental image of circling vultures above his estate.

I dug Heather's card from my purse and dialed her cell. In a totally perky voice, I said, "Heather? It's Jane Kelly. I was heading over to Foster's tonight for a little R&R and wondered if you and Cotton, or just you if he's busy, would like to join me. The weather's just beastly but it's perfect for a Mojito or two, don't you think? I'll be there around seven. Hope to see you. Bye!"

I hung up and promptly bent over and made retching noises. Lying is easy for me, pretending I'm cute something else again.

Binks eyed me worriedly then curled up in her bed and began studiously licking one paw.

Chapter
Eight

I couldn't reach Dwayne for a ride in his boat, so I had to climb into the Volvo and drive around the lake to the restaurant. Lake Chinook is girded by a couple of main drags, but close to the water myriads of lanes wind aimlessly through tree-shaded neighborhoods. Once you've learned these byways, you can cut through and knock off some time. Many times the residents post signs that read: NEIGHBORHOOD TRAFFIC ONLY. I do my damnedest to drive on those roads whenever I can. I'm in the neighborhood, therefore I'm neighborhood traffic. Their asphalt; my asphalt.

Before I left the cottage Binky woofed and frantically guided me to her empty bowl. I scooped out a helping of dog chow from the Ziploc bag and refilled the bowl with the tiny kiblets. Binks ate so fast that the bowl hopped around the linoleum floor, bumped into the cupboards and chipped out a healthy chunk of wood from the corner cabinet. I looked on in dismay. I was glimpsing a whole new world—the world of dog ownership—and it was frightening.

"You have got to go," I said to the smushed-faced animal. She cocked her head and panted and we went out for another bathroom break before I took off.

* * *

Foster's was hot and crowded and thick with the scents of mesquite and hickory. The patio grills were going full blast. My mouth started watering before I crossed from the inside restaurant to the outside deck. I was so hungry I'd actually eyed Binks' kibbles. How bad can it be? I'd read once that if you were stranded on a desert island, the best, most complete, food to have with you is dog food.

Manny was at the bar and I squeezed up to place an order. This consisted of me elbowing out a guy wearing a white dress shirt, open to his navel, blue slacks with one hand deep into the pocket, making me suspect he was fighting a very frisky woody, and a godawful toupee that left a line horizontally across the back of his head. Always a good look.

"Hey," he said, not affronted, interested.

Since I wore my black capris and a loose green top that quite possibly has a teeny tiny stain near the hem that I fear I'll never get out, I wondered why he wasn't hitting on the other women around the bar, the ones dressed to kill and cradling glittering glasses of Chardonnay. The slowly setting sun seemed to shoot rays right off the glasses, fracturing the light, sending dazzling spots over all the patrons. Hair-Piece must be pretty hard up to be turning toward me.

"A Mojito," I told Manny. "When you get a chance."

He winked at me. I turned to find Hair-Piece planted in front of me, his right hand digging away in his pants pocket. Maybe he was just looking for change, I thought hopefully.

"I like a girl in a ponytail."

I gazed at him. Ponytails work for me. It's true. I don't look like I'm trying to be too young; I don't look like I came from the Fifties. I appear mostly athletic. Kind of the girl-next-door thing. Also, it gets the hair out of my face. The only problem is sometimes it gets in the way of the Volvo headrest.

I was pretty sure I was sorry I hadn't tried harder with my appearance. If I fit in better, maybe I wouldn't be garnering his unwanted attention.

To my surprise Heather walked onto the patio at that moment.

Had she accepted my invitation, or was she merely making the scene? She looked up, saw me, smiled a bit hesitantly and waved. That decided it. I scooted away from Hair-Piece and made my way toward her, fighting through the growing crush of Sunday evening diners and drinkers.

"You came," I said.

"Oh, yeah. I couldn't wait! I love my husband to death, but today . . ." She shook her head.

I was mildly surprised that Tess had been so right on the money about Heather wanting a night out with the girls. "I don't think we're going to find somewhere to sit. I've got a Mojito ordered at the waterfront bar."

"Oh, we'll get a table." She glanced around imperiously. As if by magic, Foster appeared, all smiles and solicitude upon seeing Mrs. Cotton Reynolds. His eyebrows shot up in surprise when he realized I was with her. I gave him the cute little fingertip wave practiced by flirtatious females everywhere. He found us a table at once, pissing off other customers, I was sure, but he paid no attention. I think he might have been uncomfortable having me dining with one of his most notorious and wealthy customers. Oh, the damage I could wreak.

Heather didn't wait for us to get to know each other better. "You can't believe the hell that's gone on today."

"Yeah?"

She ran her fingers through her hair, her goggly eyes rolling around in their sockets in remembered dismay. "You just won't believe what happened!"

"I'm all ears."

"Cotton got hit in the face. Not that he didn't ask for it. But I'm so worried about him," she launched in. "I don't know if you've heard . . . this town's so small there are no secrets. Cotton has a heart condition and the stress over Bobby's aggravated it. I'm just sick with worry." She stopped long enough to wave down a waiter. "Could we get served some drinks, here? She's got a Mojito at the bar and bring me a glass of Chardonnay." She snatched up the wine list and pointed to a label that made me want to put a hand over my wallet in protection. As soon as he was gone, she said, "I don't know what I'd do if anything happened to him. He's my rock."

"What do you mean, 'Cotton got hit in the face'?"

"He tried to punch out one of the developers. Craig Cuddahy." She glanced at the appetizers. "Let's get some coconut shrimp."

"And Cuddahy hit him?" I asked in disbelief.

"It was just kind of *pow pow*, y'know? But they both connected. I was screaming. I was just so mad. And scared," she added as an afterthought.

"And Cotton has a heart condition?" Here was loads of information, but it was almost more than I could handle all at once.

"For years and years, I think. Started before me, anyway. Probably brought on by living with that bitch, Tess." She sniffed. "And it worsened with Dolly. Poor guy. Men are so dumb sometimes. He finally gets rid of Tess, then goes out and dates a woman just like her! He was so miserable when I met him, and his heart was acting up. If he hadn't met me, I don't know what he would have done."

I tried to picture Cuddahy and Cotton Reynolds in a fist fight and failed. The waiter brought us our drinks. I said lightly, tasting mine, "So, you saved him from Dolly?"

"Yes . . . well . . ." She gave a pretty little shrug. "All this business with Bobby was starting. I helped him through some really bad days, and then we fell in love and got married. Dolly was just all concerned about her image, as was Tess. God, they're awful." She threw back a slug of Chardonnay that would have left me gasping. "Cotton was just devastated. Our marriage has really been a tonic. He says so all the time." She dimpled in remembrance of something. I could feel heat steal up my neck at *my* remembrance of something. I looked away to give myself a moment and it was then that I saw Murphy stroll onto the patio.

Heather's eyes followed mine. "You still love him?" she asked.

"Who? Murph? Love? No." I found myself speaking in monosyllables. "It wasn't ever like that."

"What was it like?"

I sipped some more. Heather's blue eyes were now watching me closely. There was a slight smile hovering around her lips. It worried me. Whatever she was thinking, I wanted to squelch it right now. "It was four years ago. Long over now. We've all moved on."

"I didn't really know him until he came back. He seems like a really great guy. Cotton just loves him. I probably should be jealous."

I murmured something inconsequential. Murphy spotted the two of us. For a moment I thought he was going to be downright rude and ignore us, but he reluctantly made his way to our table. Our view of him was crotch level, as we were seated and he was standing. Heather wasn't abashed in the least. She stared at his zipper and gushed, "Sit down with us! We were just catching up on old times."

"Not really," I said automatically, horrified.

He shook his head. "I'm sorry, I can't. I just stopped in for a minute between appointments."

"Appointments?" Heather slid him a sideways look. "What kind of appointments?"

He shrugged and looked around. I could feel how anxious he was to leave. He shot me a look. "What's that?" he asked, pointing to my drink.

"A Mojito," Heather jumped in.

"How are they?" His blue eyes were on me.

He still had the power to make my pulse leap, which pissed me off to no end. "Good."

"Sit down and have one with us," Heather insisted.

He gave her his full attention for the first time, smiling faintly. "I can't, Heather. Maybe next time."

Whatever he'd planned on doing, he changed his mind, because he strode back across the patio and out through the restaurant. Heather signaled for another Chardonnay. "I wonder what he's up to," she said, clearly annoyed. "I swear, everybody's got an agenda."

"Mmmmmm," I said.

"Oh, God . . ."

Her tone was full of repugnance. I looked around to see what was up. Craig Cuddahy had just appeared. His gaze passed over the guests at the restaurant, pausing momentarily on us before moving on. Whomever he'd come to see wasn't here, apparently, as he frowned and made his way toward us.

"What was the fight about?" I asked.

"The island, what else? Cuddahy wants it but won't pay the price. I don't want to sell it, but what are you gonna do? It got heated, to say the least. They were drinking and suddenly *bam, bam*. Stupid idiots."

"Cotton really wants to sell?"

"Oh, you know . . ." She swivelled in her chair. "Hi!" she greeted Craig, looking both pissed and amused at the same time.

Craig's bottom lip was thicker than normal. I tried not to stare.

"Sit down," Heather invited, scooching her chair over. I turned to her in surprise but I guess she held no grudges. Craig cautiously perched across from me. I hadn't known he was involved in real estate when we'd first met, but with additional information my perception of him had changed. He'd been a pain at the benefit, half-drunk and sticky. Sober now, I sensed in him a hunger—a money hunger, no doubt—that was ravenous and needed to be fed.

"I'm surprised you'll even talk to me," he said diffidently.

She slapped a hand at him. "Oh, for God's sake. He threw the first punch. You were just automatic. They say men have better control of their emotions," she added, leaning toward me, conspiratorially, just girl-to-girl. "Their emotions just don't leak out of their eyes, they're in their fists."

Then Heather began chatting on about real estate as if nothing untoward had taken place. Cuddahy was definitely having trouble keeping up with her, as was I. But eventually Craig joined in the real estate discussion, animatedly going on about other homes on the lake, a topic Heather seemed to know a lot about.

"They tore down that cottage on Lakeview," Craig said. "It was a piece of shit."

"Worse than," Heather agreed. "The foundation was crumbling. When you walked inside? It like sloped to one side. Scary! I told Cotton to buy it and redo it. You just can't get that kind of property these days."

"Well, you're on the property that counts." Craig smiled easily. I detected some covetousness there. Heather just smiled at him.

A waitress came by and took our dinner order and Jeff Foster cruised by to offer some more welcoming words to Heather, Craig and myself. I got up to find the ladies' room and Jeff was right on my heels.

"What's going on?"

"Oh, you mean because I'm here with my dear friend, Heather?"

"Uh-huh." Foster wanted answers. No game-playing tonight.

"I'm an urban scavenger. I go with people who feed me."

"Who's the guy?"

"Craig Cuddahy. Into buying property."

"The island?" Foster was interested.

"He's salivating over it. Got his nose pressed to the window. Cotton's kind of drawing the curtains though."

"So, no sale."

I shrugged. "I don't know that much about it."

"How's Cotton doing?"

I wasn't surprised Foster knew that Cotton was ill; Heather was like a sports announcer, spreading the news. "I don't really know," I admitted, my eye catching sight of one of the young waitresses. She was carrying a tray of drinks and something about her looked familiar. "Does that girl moonlight with a catering company?"

Foster looked around. "Who? Misty?"

Question answered. "Heather seems to think Cotton's got a thing for her."

Foster choked on a laugh. "Cotton likes attention. He's a big tipper so maybe he and Misty flirt a little. I don't know. Heather's married to him and by her own account, she's all he needs."

"I'm surprised you're leveling with me."

"I like Cotton and Heather's a good customer. I don't know what you're doing with her and I don't want to. Just don't screw things up, Jane."

"Hey, I'm one of your best customers these days. Show some respect," I called after him as Foster turned back to his managerial duties which involved directing a visibly inebriated customer to a waiting taxi.

I returned to the table to excuse myself and offer to help on the bill. This hurts me, the need to be fair and polite when it comes to money. My pecuniary side actually rolls on the ground and wails. But, cheap as I am, I cannot bear to be thought of as such.

I dug through my purse, an ancient over-the-shoulder model that had seen better days by 1985. I'd picked it up on a thrift table at one of those weekend outdoor marts. Initially I'd worried that it might come with cooties, but I made myself get over that. I've had the lining replaced twice. Can't bear to give the dinosaur up, though Cynthia despairs of my fashion sense. She feels my purse is the worst, but it's distressed black leather and I believe that makes it "today."

"Oh, put that away," Heather said with a wave of her hand. She fished for her credit card and slapped it down. I murmured a relieved thanks and Craig added a few appreciative words as well. Heather signed the slip with a flourish and a healthy tip that made me briefly consider asking Foster for a job as a waiter. This thought made me worry that I hadn't gotten enough for Tess's money. Maybe I needed to stick it out with Heather a little longer, just to log the hours. I was trying to figure out how to prolong the already torturous evening when Heather said, "Come back to the island for a nightcap. I make a mean Bailey's and coffee."

Craig instantly demurred. "Don't think your husband's ready to see me again."

"You'll never get the island by being coy," Heather said.

"Coy?" Cuddahy shook his head.

"What about you?" Heather asked me.

"Love to," I said and we all left at once.

I didn't quite get Heather. Sometimes I thought she'd emerged directly from the shallow end of the pool: no depth at all. But she possessed more savvy than I'd originally appreciated. She knew the score.

I was hoping to catch up with Cotton as soon as we got to the island and was disappointed to learn he was already in bed. It was nine o'clock and darkness had just settled over the lake. There were streaks of indigo and cobalt blue in the sky, vying with the stars. The water rippled beneath the faint light of a pale crescent moon as Heather, having snagged two mugs and a bottle of Bailey's, zapping leftover coffee in the microwave, then transferring it to a thermos, led the way down the slate path past the pool to deck chairs with thick white cushions which glowed in the dark night.

We sat down and Heather poured us a couple of mugfuls. I sipped the hot liquid. I decided right then and there that I love Irish cream liquor. Yummy.

It was still hot. The summer had been one of the warmest on record. Normally, seated by the water at night or in a boat on the lake, you're required to wear a light jacket. But not this summer. I could actually feel myself sweating a little. Or, maybe that was because I was here with Heather.

I was already writing up my report for Tess in my head. Heather had said a few notable things about the island and Cotton's frame of mind. The fight about the potential sale of the island said a lot. Cuddahy apparently wanted to buy, but Cotton wasn't having it. I couldn't get a read on where Heather stood in the negotiations. She minimized the fistfight, putting it down to boys will be boys.

She sighed and closed her eyes, her thin body dark against the white cushion of the chair next to mine. "I love Cotton," she mused. "It's been a tough four years for all of us."

"I don't want to be judgmental, Heather, but I'd think after today—the fight—that you wouldn't want to associate with Craig Cuddahy at all."

"Oh, that was so dumb!"

"Well, maybe . . . but you said Cotton has a heart condition. Fighting doesn't sound like it's on his health regimen."

Heather squinched down in her seat. "Cotton shouldn't drink, but he does. What am I, his keeper? He just makes me so mad sometimes."

"What made him swing at Craig Cuddahy? Specifically, I mean."

"Oh, I don't know. They were talking about the island and Cotton said something about Bobby, about how this was his sanctuary. And then that idiot Craig tried to say it was time Cotton stopped living in the past. It was time to move on. To sell . . . because Bobby was gone. He made it sound like there was no question that Bobby was dead and gone, so all of a sudden, Cotton just smacked him."

"Do you think Bobby's alive?"

"I don't know." She sounded like she was sick of thinking about it.

"You think he did it?"

"Of course he did!" she declared. "Cotton doesn't want to believe it, and I'm sure Tess the Wicked doesn't, but c'mon. He killed 'em. He left their bodies all over that Tillamook forest area. He probably killed himself, too, if there's any justice in this world."

Idly I wondered what the timing was on this thing. Why had Tess called me now? After four years? What was the driving impetus? Cotton's illness?

"Hey . . ."

The male voice coming from the darkness caused a little hiccup of fear to escape my lips. Heather, her movements heavy, turned to look for the newcomer. "Hey, yourself," she said.

Murphy materialized from the shadows. "Is this a private party, or is anyone invited?" He was looking directly at me, his eyes hooded by the darkness.

My jolt of fear now became an uncomfortable lurch of my heart. "Come one, come all," I said lightly.

He pulled up a chair. His knee was close to the end of my lounge chair. I'd taken off my shoes and my bare toes seemed mere inches from his flesh. Goosebumps rose on my arms.

"If it isn't the favored one," Heather said. "Wanna share my drink? I don't have another cup."

"I'm okay."

"Did you talk to Cotton?"

"Isn't he asleep?" Murphy asked. His gaze swept over our heads toward the house.

"So, you stopped by to see little old me?"

"Actually, I stopped by to see Jane." He turned to me. "I saw your car at the end of the bridge."

"Ah," I said, for lack of anything better. He stopped by to see *me*? I didn't want to put too much weight on it, but . . . he stopped by to see *me*?

"We didn't get a chance to really catch up the other day. I thought maybe we could do that."

"We could do that, I guess."

"Well, I guess I'm the third wheel." Heather got up from the lounge chair. The cushion made a funky little fart sound but no one laughed as our hostess was definitely miffed.

"I really should get going anyway," I said, to ease through the moment.

"I'll walk you out." Murphy got to his feet.

Silently we traipsed up the stone stairs and down the path toward the house. Heather peeled off one way, and I headed around the outbuilding side.

"Where're you going?" Murphy asked a bit sharply.

I'd wanted to circle the garage rather than leave by the direct route—a bit of a renewed reconnaissance of the area. I wanted to give Tess something, and I had a niggling interest in the property itself engendered by all the talk about what would become of it. I guess you could say I felt proprietary, so I kept right on going.

Or, maybe I just wanted to keep Murphy at arm's length and the prospect of walking shoulder-to-shoulder, hip-to-hip, toward the front drive had forced my steps elsewhere.

CANDY APPLE RED 123

"I'm going the long way," I said, my voice disembodied in the dark. The little mushroom lights that glowed along the walkway stopped before the turn to the outbuildings. I could make out the rowboat, but my toe stumbled on one of the jumbled pieces of slate. Murphy's hand shot out to steady me.

"You're going to run into something. C'mon. Let's go this way."

There's something really humiliating about having your ex—the one who broke up with you—wrap his hand around your upper arm and guide you as if you're five years old. I managed about three steps before I eased myself out of his grasp. I wanted to yank my arm free and elbow him in the ribs at the same time, but I managed some restraint.

We walked in silence to my car. Trudged, more accurately. I was feeling angry and uncomfortable. I wanted to lash out, so I said, "Everyone acts like you're the prodigal son, not Bobby. Cotton's always liked you. Heather even wonders if she should be jealous."

"What are you saying?" he demanded.

"Is that what you want? To be Cotton Reynolds' favorite guy?"

"C'mon, Jane, not you, too," he said in disgust.

"Well, are you going back to Santa Fe? Or, are you here to stay?"

A long moment passed and then he grated, "I'm here because Cotton asked me to come back. Because Bobby left his life in shambles."

"You believe he did it, now."

"Yes, Jane," he stated flatly. "And then I come back here and there's this big party going on. Everyone's drinking and socializing and Cotton's talking about selling the house. He thinks he's dying. Maybe he is. That's not what my being here's about."

"Cotton's always liked you," I said.

"Who gives a shit? I wish Bobby would never come back, but I'm not stepping into his shoes. Ever."

Silence fell between us. I swallowed hard. Pain and anger radiated from Murphy. "I don't think Bobby is ever coming back," I said.

"Why?"

"He's been gone a long time. Wouldn't he have shown up by now? How can you disappear for four years?"

"I think it can be done."

"Nah, you'd have to have help," I insisted. "You have to have money. Unless..." He waited, wanting me to continue my thought. I wasn't sure where I was going. "Unless you go off into some wilderness area and live like a mountain man. Even then you'd have to find a way to buy some staples, I think. And Bobby wasn't like that, anyway. He was spoiled."

"He was spoiled," Murphy agreed.

"He wasn't good at independence. He relied on everyone else to keep him afloat."

"You only met him a couple of times, Jane."

"He wasn't hard to read."

"No one guessed what he was going to do."

"Laura and her family pushed him down a path he couldn't travel," I struggled on, the thoughts occurring to me even as I said them. Or maybe they'd always been there, but now talking to Murphy simply crystallized them. "There was no money. Bobby wasn't *good* enough to live on religion alone. He wasn't made that way. He wasn't raised that way. Cotton cut his lifeline and he started drowning."

"Why are you hanging around with Heather? What are you looking for?"

"I'm not hanging around with her. It was just one night."

"You're a goddamn awful liar."

"What do you want me to say, Murphy? I want to figure out what happened to Bobby? Sure, I do. We all want closure, don't we? You do."

"There is no closure," he stated flatly. "Not with murder."

My flesh prickled. He'd stopped defending Bobby at all. Four years after the fact he'd accepted that his best friend had killed his family in cold blood.

"I'm sorry," I said, meaning it.

He nodded. I had a feeling he didn't trust himself to speak. I felt a rush of sympathy, but I gotta be honest, I was glad we'd steered away from what my interest in the Reynolds' affairs might be. I couldn't tell him I was getting paid to rake up the past. He would think me the lowest form of vermin, and though I hated to admit it, I care about what Murphy thinks of me.

We said some murmured good-nights. Silly me, I almost invited him back to my cottage. It really bums me out to know that I still possess stirrings of interest. Not out-and-out desire, mind you. Just little stirrings of interest where Murphy's concerned.

I unlocked my front door, lost in deep thoughts. A muffled little *woof* greeted me and the clickety-click of doggy toenails against hardwood. *Oh, God, I have a dog.*

Binks snuffled my shoes while I groped for a light switch. She panted and blinked when the room suddenly flooded with illumination. I bent down and patted her head a couple of times. She inhaled on a long snort. I took it as a method of greeting. A bit on the crude side, maybe, but a greeting nonetheless.

I checked her bowls. She had water but every kibble was gone. I shot her a sideways glance. She really was built for comfort, not for speed: broad back, four sturdy, but teeny legs.

I headed to bed and she trotted after me. She crawled into her bed which I realized she'd moved from the living room. Beds were for the bedroom even in the dog world, apparently.

"Maybe you're smarter than I thought," I said.

She inhaled on another long snort. I lay awake thinking of Murphy and listening to her loud breathing deep into the night.

Chapter
Nine

I woke to a strange noise beside me, sort of like a strangled yawn. Throwing back the covers I was outraged to find Binky lying on MY bed with her head sharing MY pillow! "Get out!" I yelled, to which she struggled to her feet, shot me a wounded look out of sleep-dazed eyes, then gathered herself for a jump and retreated to her furry bed which she'd pushed into the far corner of the room.

Pissed me off to no end. And that made me feel guilty as hell.

What had seemed almost endearing last night wasn't nearly as such in the cold light of dawn. Or maybe I was just a sourpuss because I knew my brother and his girlfriend were coming over that night and I didn't want to see them.

I staggered into the kitchen. Binks, the little traitor, didn't feel like getting up and joining me at this early hour. I was disappointed to find there was no coffee. What had I expected?

Throwing on my running gear, I dragged the dog out for a morning bathroom break, then I left her back in HER bed, not mine, and went for a run to the Coffee Nook sans dog. By the time I got there I was in a total sweat and breathing hard. I knew I wouldn't see Billy because I was late today. He was long gone. Instead I was treated to a herd of teenaged boys who were desperately, painfully, uncomfortably trying to impress the teenaged girls Julie hires in the summer months. The boys wore baseball caps and one of them had the nerve to bounce a basketball inside the Nook while he flirted. I lamented that Julie wasn't there as she would have nicely shooed them out. I'm not as good at diplomacy because my tolerance level is, well, nil. It's only been a little over a decade since I endured that hellhole known as high school, but my nerves are still raw. It was a terrible, terrible time. These boys' self-consciousness brought the whole thing back in living color. I had to fight to keep from collaring them and booting them out with a swift kick to their collective backsides.

However, the basketball bouncer had to stop. I said politely, "STOP BOUNCING THE BALL."

He jerked around and gave me a startled look. Muttering something, he headed for the door, ball tucked under his arm. His swagger returned at the threshold and he bounced it one more time before he left. The Nook girls tried not to giggle, but it was clear they thought he was beyond cool. His friends parted to let me place an order, all staring at me.

I ignored them and found a place on one of the stools, hoping my breathing would come under control. I'd really pushed it this morning. The day had barely begun and it was going to be a scorcher.

There's a grocery store attached to the Nook. After I'd made a dent in my coffee I carried the cup into the store in search of much needed staples: milk, tuna fish, cheddar cheese, romaine lettuce and bread. By the time I returned the teen group had dispersed and the Nook was empty except for a few retirees. I added a one-pound bag of coffee from the Nook to my purchases.

My purchases left me with the problem of how to get them home. The idea of carrying the bag nearly three miles wasn't a happy one. I was hoping someone I knew would appear and offer me a ride, but the pickings were slim. I asked if I could use the Nook phone and called Dwayne. When he answered I heard a lazy female voice say something in the background.

"Oh, sorry," I said. "You're not alone."

"What do you need?" He yawned.

"Are you still in bed?"

"Mmm-hmmm."

The image of Dwayne having sex filled my mind. I swallowed hard. How long had it been for me? The Pleistocene era? "I need a ride," I said. That sounded so sexual I made a strangled hiccup sound. But Dwayne didn't catch the double entendre.

"Where are you?" he asked, then answered, "The Nook," before I needed to speak.

"I've got groceries."

"I'll be there in ten."

Dwayne is a great guy, I told myself. Really. He was leaving his bedmate to help me out. I was pretty sure I wouldn't be quite as eager to return the favor had Murphy spent the night with me. There are definite flaws in my character. I could obsess about the fact that Dwayne could be a better friend to me than I was to him.

He arrived looking amazingly refreshed and relaxed. The teen girls eyed him smokily as he sauntered in wearing low-cut jeans, a blue shirt he'd obviously just tossed on, the shirttails loose, its buttons only done to somewhere just above his navel. This isn't style in Dwayne's world; it's expediency. He wore the ubiquitous cowboy boots but at least there was no hat. Instead I could see the remnants of bed head, but the faintly curling hair behind his ears was appealing.

"Buying groceries?" He scratched his chin. I could tell he found it hard to believe.

"My brother and his fiancée are coming over tonight. I have to be ready in case they expect me to cook."

"What are you making?"

"Frozen hors d'oeuvres. What do you take me for?" I snapped.

"Don't you have a barbecue, darlin'? You could have steaks."

"She's a vegetarian."

"Oh." He grimaced as he helped me haul out my bags into his truck. This was Dwayne's regular mode of transportation but sometimes he rented nondescript sedans. Surveillance cars. Nothing about them the least bit interesting or memorable.

"So, how'd it go last night?" he asked me.

I was thinking the same thing, wondering about his new "friend." "Kinda weird," I admitted. I caught him up on everything Heather had said about Cotton and my impressions of Craig Cuddahy. I mentioned seeing Murphy but skirted conversation about him.

"Got paid yet?"

"I'm working on it."

"Get your butt down to Marta's office and tell her you're out unless you see the cold hard cash."

"I can handle my own affairs."

"Not very well, apparently," he pointed out.

"I'll get paid."

"Don't be defensive."

"You're putting me on the defensive," I said defensively.

"Just get the money." He turned into my driveway.

I steamed as we grabbed the sacks and headed to my front door. I wanted to snatch the groceries from his arms, but logistically that wasn't going to work. When the door opened Binks darted out, circling Dwayne's boots and snuffling and wagging her curly tail in sheer excitement.

"Hey there," he said, his voice altering to a tenderness that sent my nerves screaming. He headed inside and dropped the groceries on my kitchen counter, Binks trailing after him in delight. Dwayne bent down and roughly rubbed the Pug's ears and back and Binks was wriggling, pawing, snorting and generally living in doggy nirvana.

I immediately resented Dwayne's intrusion. "Dwayne, meet Binks. Binks, Dwayne," I said flatly.

"Great dog," Dwayne said.

"She's all yours."

Dwayne laughed. "You're so full of bullshit." He had the nerve to wink at me as he left. "Type up another report."

"Who's your bedmate?" I blurted, unable to stand it another moment.

Dwayne gave me a classic double take. He seemed perplexed for a moment, then laughed, his teeth white as he grinned like a devil. "I'm sleeping alone, darlin', if it's any of your business."

"Oh, right."

"Does it bother you?"

"Only when I feel like I'm disturbing you, like this morning. Sorry," I added with ill grace as he just kept smiling.

I had this terrible feeling he was going to chuck me under my chin, like a good little girl, but he managed to leave without pissing me off further, except for that shit-eating grin.

As soon as the door shut behind him, Binks' tail unwound in dejection.

"He's not that great," I warned her.

She toddled back to her bed.

I called Jerome Neusmeyer's office and talked to a secretary who was tons more polite than Marta's. She listened to me whine that I really, really, *really* needed to see Mr. Neusmeyer right away. "My mother's unwell. I don't know what to do. If she dies before I get everything right, I'll have a breakdown or something."

"Mr. Neusmeyer's extremely busy this week," she said, "but I could squeeze you in next Tuesday or Wednesday?"

"Oh, really . . ." Disappointment leaked through. "My mother's really failing. She doesn't recognize me." I sent a silent apology to Mom who was healthy as a horse and completely in control of her faculties, at least as much as she'd ever been.

"If there's a cancellation . . ."

"Oh, please call me! I'm really desperate. I don't know what to do."

"Who referred you to us?"

I gritted my teeth. I couldn't say Cotton as he had an appointment coming right up and I didn't want my name to be associated with it in any way. "Heather Reynolds," I said, crossing my fingers over the lie. I hoped this wouldn't get back to Cotton, but if it did, he might not mention it to Heather. Tricky stuff, but I couldn't come up with anything better.

"You know, there may be a spot on Thursday," she said in a crisper tone. "It's extremely tight, but . . ."

"I'll take it," I said, *extremely* satisfied. Bandying Heather's name had apparently worked better than I'd expected. Of course I had no idea what I would say to Neusmeyer when I showed up on Thursday, but hey, necessity is the mother of invention, right?

The doorbell rang while I was struggling over a recipe book. Should I actually try to cook something for Booth and his fiancée? My repertoire was limited, but I didn't feel comfortable going out to some fancy place and facing the bill at the end of the evening. Would Booth expect me to split with him? Would it be halfsies or three-sies? Too complicated.

I wondered if she would like a hearty spinach salad. I could cook up the bacon separately in case she objected.

My head was full of such thoughts when I threw open the front door and saw, with surprise and consternation, that Booth had shown up way early. And he was with his fiancée. And she was tall, thin and African American. Her skin was smooth milk chocolate that was eminently touchable. She stared at me through liquid brown eyes which were slightly cautious. I tried to imagine myself through her eyes. Had I hidden my surprise? How like my twin to neglect to tell me anything about her.

"Hey, Jane," Booth said. "This is Sharona. Sharona, my sister Jane."

"Hello," she said.

"Hello," I managed before turning to Booth with a forced smile. "It's barely four o'clock."

"Are we too early?" Sharona asked, giving Booth a cool look. There was something sleek and imperative about her that worried me.

But Booth was oblivious. "Oh, Jane doesn't care."

"Come in," I said, as there was nothing left but to be gracious. I didn't feel gracious inside, though.

Sharona wore a light gray wool skirt and a silvery silk blouse. Her shoes were expensive-looking black pumps with what looked like stainless steel heels. She wore her hair pulled back tight and her lips were expertly outlined with a deep red lipstick. She looked businesslike and sexual at the same time. I would have melted in her choice of outfit but she was cool, collected and detached. I saw her glance around my place with interest but she kept her thoughts hidden. A lawyer, Booth had mentioned in an aside. Geez Louise.

Booth was in khaki shorts, a dark blue shirt with a muted Hawaiian pattern and leather flip-flops. His dark hair was faintly mussed and there was a definite shadow of beard darkening his strong jaw. You can take the boy out of southern California, but you can't take southern California out of the boy. I wondered what Sharona saw in him. Not that he isn't attractive, but saying they were polar opposites wasn't putting too fine a point on it. Maybe when he was in uniform they got into some quasi-military S&M kinda stuff. Or maybe that was just me being horny, unfulfilled and wishful.

"I don't have any food, or plans made, for dinner. Any suggestions?"

Sharona smoothed her skirt and sat gingerly on my almost threadbare tan couch. Binks chose that moment to tear around the corner from the bedroom and zoom toward Sharona, full tilt. I yelled. At least I think I yelled, but the dog jumped up and squirmed onto Sharona's lap, happy as the proverbial pig in shit. Sharona gasped, froze, and then seemed to take it a bit in stride. She let Binky lick the side of her hand.

Booth said, "What the hell is that?"

"That's Binks. A friend of our mother's—Aunt Eugenie—died, and Mom had promised her she'd make sure her dog was taken care of. I notice that I got the dog, not you."

"What do you call that kind?"

"She's a pug."

"She's fat," Sharona said.

I bristled. Now, there is no question that Sharona was right.

Binky looks like she's never missed a meal in her life. However, it seemed as if Sharona were making a comment on my dog-parenting skills. I rose to the call to arms. "She's slightly over-weight. I'm working on it."

"I'm glad you got her, not me," Booth said.

"That's so helpful."

"We're living in an apartment in the Pearl. There's just no way."

Had I asked him to take the dog? *Had I?*

"She's actually kind of cute, in a really ugly sort of way," said Sharona, and there was just the hint of tenderness in her voice.

"Don't even think it," Booth disabused her swiftly. "No dogs. Jane can take care of this one." He paused. "Who's Aunt Eugenie?"

I filled him in as best I could as we made plans to eat out after all. I was hankering for somewhere cheap, but Booth said Billy Leonard had mentioned a place right on the water: Foster's On The Lake. My protestations that I'd just been there fell on deaf ears.

We were standing at the outdoor bar within the hour, enjoying several cocktails. I was beginning to be a regular and I recognized some of my barfly buddies. If I came night after night, I'd proba-bly see them. The way things were going, by the end of the week I was going to have a chair with a plaque with my name on it.

Manny slipped me an extra strong Mojito and I sucked it down as if it were water. Booth asked me what I'd been up to and I made the mistake of mentioning I was actually working on a case. I guess I was trying to impress him. But when I brought up Tess Bradbury he came unglued.

His fingers gripped my arm. "What are you talking about?"

"Ow." I yanked my arm free. Sharona made a point of pre-tending she didn't notice our sibling rivalry.

"Stay out of that mess," he said, totally serious. "I don't know what you're doing. I don't know what you think you're doing. That was cold-blooded murder, Jane. What is Tess Bradbury looking for? Why is she involving you?"

"Honestly, I think she's trying to save a piece of Cotton's inheritance for Bobby, in case he shows up."

"More likely it's a piece of Cotton's inheritance for Owen," Booth said with a snort. "I don't think Bobby's alive."

"Maybe."

Booth was watching my face. "So, what are you supposed to be doing?"

"I'm just talking to Cotton and Heather and reporting back to her anything that might help her."

"I bet Tess thinks Bobby's dead, too, and she's doing this to find a way to stick Cotton for more money. Not necessarily for Bobby, for herself and Owen."

I was sorry I'd brought it up. I shouldn't have. My excuse is the Mojito went straight to my head. I signaled Manny for another. If Booth was going to make me miserable I might as well get a buzz on.

We had a rather stilted meal. I ordered a Caesar salad, the cheapest thing I could find on the menu. Sharona ordered grilled summer vegetables and a hummus and pita bread appetizer. She teamed this with white wine. Booth had a burger.

I wondered if Owen was part of Tess's motive. He'd been on the periphery of the story, but I hadn't really considered him. He was Bobby's brother, but not Cotton's flesh and blood. But he was Tess's son. And though Tess—and it felt like everyone else— had been more interested in Bobby, the athlete, Owen was a member of the family.

"Why so quiet?" Booth asked me as I chased around my last bit of romaine lettuce.

"Thinking about Owen," I admitted.

"I wonder how he felt about everything," Sharona put in, clearly as aware of the story as the rest of us. She was delicately slicing through julienned strips of red pepper, tomato and onion. I had to admit, it looked pretty good.

I could easily interview some of Owen's classmates if I wanted to know more about him. The Pisces Pub on State Street was the perennial hangout for ex-grads of Lake Chinook's two high schools. There was no money in it for me, but it might provide some enlightenment on the case. For that matter, checking on Owen might gain me more information on Bobby. I knew this avenue of approach wouldn't be what Tess had in mind, not by a long shot, but the investigation had grown a life of its own. I was looking for answers anywhere I could find them, whether Tess paid me for my time or not.

In my periphery I saw Booth's arm move toward Sharona, his hand obscured by the table. He must have grabbed something, her thigh, perhaps, as she shot him a sideways look from the corner of her eyes. Her red lips twitched into a smile. Moments later she turned toward him and bit into a ripe yellow cob of corn. I could see her even white teeth. Booth just gazed at her, his lips slightly parted.

The sexual tension was thick enough to choke on. I think I made a strangled sound.

"It's time for me to go home now," I said.

They didn't waste time trying to talk me out of it.

I called Mom as soon as their taillights blinked out around the corner of my drive, leaving my nose pressed to the window, a bit lonely. Binks seemed to pick up on my feelings and sat beside me, gazing up at me. Mom's answering machine kicked on. I wasn't sure exactly what message to leave. In the end I simply said I had a nice evening with Booth and his fiancée, Sharona, and I thought she would like her a lot. I added that there were no tattoos, facial piercings or Gothic attire and/or hairstyles. Sharona was a criminal defense lawyer which kind of blew my mind. I wondered if there would ever be a time when she and Booth were on opposite sides of the courtroom.

I didn't mention that Sharona was African American. I saw now why Booth hadn't enlightened me, either. It seemed small and prejudiced even to address the issue. It didn't matter anyway. I'd be more concerned with culture shock than race as Sharona seemed more upwardly mobile economically and socially than Booth was. And they were both climbing that ladder a helluva lot faster than I was. I suppose I should worry about these things, but I was more concerned with wondering why my brother should be involved in a healthy sex life while I wasn't.

I woke up the next morning with this same thought in mind. And throughout the next couple of days while I posted more 72-hour notices for Greg, harangued Tess Bradbury for payment to which she grudgingly told me a five-hundred-dollar check was in the mail—not likely, I thought—and generally thought about Cotton, Bobby, Heather, Dwayne and Murphy, not necessarily in that order. Gleefully I related to Dwayne that Tess had paid me. He said he'd believe it when the check cleared.

My mother called back and left a return message on my answering machine. I could tell she was poleaxed by Booth's engagement. She wanted me to call her so we could thrash things over. I reluctantly phoned her back. I mean, why was this my job? I nearly crowed in delight when I got her answering machine again. The gods were looking out for me after all. In as nice a way as I know how I suggested that she call Booth herself if she wanted more information and leave me the hell out of it.

On Thursday I walked the dog early. I tell ya, it's a pain to make certain they've emptied their bladders etc. Never ending. Then I ran through the shower, washed and blow dried my hair, pulled on a pair of silky bright red panties and a short, short black skirt, slid on a white silk blouse, undid the top three buttons, then actually added some makeup to my face. In fact, I added a lot of makeup, darkening my eyes to make them as black and mysterious as I could. I seriously thought about teasing my hair before I slicked it down straight, adopting a bored look. I put on my highest black, strappy heels, definitely CFM material. I was meeting Jerome Neusmeyer and I wanted to be anyone but Jane Kelly.

Billy was at the Coffee Nook when I breezed in. He looked me up and down. "Geez, Louise," he said, more in horror than appreciation.

"I've got a meeting," I said.

"At the Low Brow Lounge?"

"At an estate attorney's office. What you see is meant to distract and confuse. I have questions that need to be answered."

"Oh, Mama," Billy said on a laugh. In fact he kept on laughing right out the door.

Julie said, "I think you look cute," but then Julie's beyond kind.

"I look like a slut," I said, "which is the point."

I have to admit they shook my confidence a bit, so as I drove to downtown Portland and took a ticket for parking in the underground lot of Neusmeyer's building, I was starting to rethink my plan. What did I expect to learn? Who the hell did I think I was?

Neusmeyer had a starched-looking receptionist in a tight brown suit and narrow tortoiseshell glasses. She tried not to eye me too carefully. "May I help you?"

"I have a 9:00 meeting with Mr. Neusmeyer."

"Oh . . ." She glanced at her appointment book. "Miss Kellogg?"

I nodded. Someone once told me that you should use an alias similar to your own name, otherwise you might not answer to it when it's called and give yourself away. Kelly, Kellogg . . . seemed like a good idea. Besides, I like cornflakes. When I remember to keep them on hand.

"I'll let him know you're here." She got up from her chair and turned the corner into a small secondary hallway. The offices weren't huge but they were in an expensive building, one of Portland's notable turn-of-the-century edifices that had been spared the wrecking ball, then updated, renovated and the rents jacked up so here we were. Out the eastern window was a view of the Willamette River and most all of Portland's bridges. I counted the Ross Island, Marquam, Hawthorne, Steele, Burnside, Broadway and a glimpse of the Fremont before I was invited into Jerome's office.

He did not have a view of the water. Out a narrow window I could see west over and into other downtown buildings. Not nearly so commanding, but then Jerome wasn't all that commanding, either. If he topped five foot six, I'd be surprised. I was taller in my stocking feet; in these heels I dwarfed him.

I swear he started to salivate. He definitely was doing one of those suck on your own teeth kinds of things. Since my intention was to act as if Cotton, by Heather's own words, was into affairs and had seen fit to take me as a lover, I took it as a good sign.

I sank down in a chair across from him and crossed my legs. The red undies were there in case I needed them. I couldn't really picture myself pulling a Sharon Stone, *Basic Instinct* kind of peek-a-boo, but one never knew. I wanted Neusmeyer to think I was loose in the worst way.

"Miss Kellogg," he said. "Veronica Kellogg?"

Okay, so I didn't stick with the alias thing all the way and name myself Janice or Jayleen or something. I like the name Veronica. So, sue me. "Call me Ronnie." I leaned forward and offered him a hand.

His gaze shot to the gapping vee of my blouse. Had I possessed a bigger chest he would have gotten quite a view. As it was, a faint shadow between my breasts was about as good as it got. I kicked myself for not adding makeup like they do on TV, enhancing the illusion of depth.

"Ronnie." He savored the word. I hadn't known for certain if Neusmeyer would take the bait, but apparently all the rumors about him were true. My outfit and attitude were spot on. "You gave Heather Reynolds' name as a reference."

I couldn't blame the quizzical note of his tone. After all, would I be Heather's friend? "I'm actually an acquaintance of Cotton's," I said.

"Ah."

"I also said that I was coming to see you about my mother, but well, that was a lie. It's really about Cotton." I recrossed my legs. Nope, no little flash of red. I hadn't worked up the nerve. Neusmeyer's eyes zeroed onto my legs as if magnetized. "Cotton and I have known each other awhile. I'm worried about his health."

Jerome was having trouble bringing his attention back to the matter at hand. "Um, yes . . . ?"

"Cotton's always made it clear that . . . well . . . he loves me." Neusmeyer's gaze shot to my face. "I mean I know he's married to Heather, and he has an ex-wife, but his heart's with me."

"Miss Kellogg—"

"Ronnie, please."

"I'm not certain what you want from me." He dug two fingers under the knot of his tie.

Could I bring up tears? I didn't think so. I sure would've liked to, though. With a catch in my voice, I said, "I've got to be honest. I'm not truly in love with Cotton, but I really care about him as a person. He's such a good man. And he's faced so much tragedy. I don't want to think about him dying, but I can't hide my head in the sand. I'm going to keep living. I'm worried that I'll have wasted a lot of time . . . years . . . Can you assure me his health is better than he's intimated?"

"I'm not his doctor." His eyes darted all over the silk blouse, following the lines of my breasts. I got to my feet, paced to the window, glanced back in anguish over my shoulder.

"I just want to hope that I'm remembered, that's all, in case the worst is realized."

"I can't divulge what's in Cotton's will, if that's what you're asking."

Yeah? He looked like he might give up the code to Fort Knox for one good feel of a breast. I strolled back toward him, sliding a hip on the corner of his desk. Now, I'm no good at seduction if it's for real. I'll start laughing or joking or doing something gauche and stupid. When it matters, I can get all goofy and embarrassed. The man really has to make the move or we can't get out of the starting gate. But playacting? This I could do.

I batted my eyes, at least I hoped I did. His vision never came north of my faint cleavage. "Isn't love hard to believe?" I said in a soft voice. "Just when you think it's impossible, there it is?"

"I thought you didn't love Cotton."

Oh. Right. I barreled on as if he hadn't spoken, "Are you certain you can't tell me if there's anything for little old Ronnie in his will?"

His hand lifted to his face. He rubbed his jaw and I saw the slight tremor. "I don't think you should expect anything . . . Ronnie. I'm sorry."

"What?"

"I don't think I'm giving anything away by letting it be known you're not listed as one of the beneficiaries. I hope you're not too disappointed."

"Disappointed? I'm flabbergasted. And hurt!"

Sensing I was about to move, he grabbed for me. I'm not sure whether he meant to comfort me or if this was merely opportunity. What I did get was a hard squeeze to my right breast, a gasp of pleasure from him, a squeak of surprise from me, and then he had the nerve to rush his palm across my ass when I suddenly jumped to my feet.

"Mr. Neusmeyer . . . !"

He nodded quickly, as if waiting for something. I was kind of nonplussed. What now? He took control, by suddenly clasping my hand in a strong grip. I feared he might actually put it on his willy but he managed to simply hold on.

"It's Heather, isn't it?" I said, upset. In reality, I was a bit shaken up. It's all fun and games, isn't it, till somebody puts their eye out. "That bitch gets everything, doesn't she?"

His gaze was now on my mouth. I tentatively parted my lips. To my utter shock he took the invitation for what it was and suddenly we were in a clinch and he was smashing his lips to mine and thrusting his tongue into my mouth.

Well, good god. I wasn't really prepared, y'know? It was all I could do, and I mean ALL I could do to keep from biting down on that wet, wiggling muscle. Instead I delicately pulled back, and said, "I'm right, aren't I? Nothing for Ronnie, everything for Heather."

He shook his head. I wasn't certain if that was an answer or he was trying to pull himself together. "Or, maybe it's Tim Murphy," I said on a note of discovery. "Cotton acts like he's his new son."

"Ninety-nine times out of a hundred, fathers leave it all to their real sons," Jerome said. "I've seen it and seen it. Wives get something, but sons, they're the ones who matter."

"He's leaving it all to Bobby?"

"Stick with percentages, honey." And then he French-kissed me again and I let him until he clasped my hand again and this time tried to do what I'd suspected earlier. As quickly as I could I murmured a tearful good-bye, thanking him for his kindness. Halfway to the car I gagged a little and shivered. But my true distraction was what he'd intimated: Cotton was leaving everything to Bobby. Bobby, whom he'd supposedly disinherited. Bobby, who'd killed his family and disappeared.

Where was Bobby Reynolds?

Chapter
Ten

On Friday Bobby Reynolds' body was found floating in Lake Chinook. A swimmer encountered something she believed to be a shark in Lake Chinook—fat chance, as it's fresh water, sweetheart—but the scream could be heard a half-mile away. Her hysteria brought in the Lake Patrol and Bobby's dripping remains were hauled from the water.

I learned about the news from Dwayne who called me on my cell phone which was nestled in the side pocket of my board shorts as I jogged toward the Coffee Nook. I did an about-face, ran home and then through the shower. Turning on the television, I caught a local special report where Cotton, Heather and Murphy appeared, white-faced and grim. No one knew anything. The reporter added that, "Tess Bradbury, Bobby's mother, has been notified but she and Bobby Reynolds' half-brother, Owen Bradbury, have declined an interview at this time."

The news hit Lake Chinook with gale force. The downtown area was choked with news reporters, vans, cameras and various and sundry media paraphernalia. A crazed, carnival-like atmosphere took over. People gawked and whispered and sagely nodded. Once again we were treated to pictures of Bobby's family's black-plastic-shrouded bodies and a skimming view of the area of the Tillamook forest where they'd been found. Once again we saw close-up photos of the family. Standing behind his wife, his hand on her shoulder, was Bobby Reynolds, looking the proud patriarch of Aaron, Jenny and baby Kit, swaddled in her mother's arms.

The prevailing attitude about the discovery of Bobby's body was that justice had been served.

I threaded my Volvo through the crowds to Dwayne's cabana. The heat had escalated and we were facing one of the hottest days of the year so far. Dwayne had told me he was going to be working on his dock, so I peered through the open front door. I could see all the way through the cabana to the back deck where Dwayne was diligently working, bent over a moplike tool, wearing disreputable denim cutoffs, a pair of beat-up Topsiders and not much else.

"What do you think?" I asked as I started to step onto the deck.

"Stay where y'are," he ordered and I froze with one foot in the air. He was applying some kind of sealer to the boards. The moplike tool was actually a spreader which slid a shiny liquid across the deck's surface.

Dwayne didn't immediately answer as he was hard at his task. I watched him work from the narrow opening of his sliding glass door. If I'd been in a better frame of mind I might have admired his back muscles, moving smoothly beneath tanned, taut skin. But this was just Dwayne and besides, I had my ever fertile imagination at work, worrying about the shape of Bobby's body after days, weeks, months in the water.

Dwayne worked backwards from the water's edge to the door, slipping out of his shoes, stepping back inside but keeping the applicator outside. He dipped its tip into a bucket full of some strong-smelling liquid. We stood side by side, behind the blockade of his desk, and looked out. One of the Lake Patrol's boats came into Lakewood Bay, its blue light circling atop its crowning metal frame. I craned my neck to look up and behind me. Atop the ridge that defined Millennium Park, people stood in tight groups. Some even lined the railroad tracks which ran between

the cabanas and the short steep cliff where the park and shops
pulled away into Lake Chinook proper.

"Have they said how long the body was in the water?"
Dwayne asked. "I turned off my set."

"At least a week, probably longer."

"No one's talking homicide yet, are they." It wasn't a question.

"Not yet."

"What are the theories?"

Typical of Dwayne to want his information from me when he
was the one who'd first learned of the discovery. "There are a lot
more questions than answers. They think Bobby purposely set it
up to look as if he'd drowned. Did he hitchhike from there? Did
he call someone? They never found any local pay phone records.
He had a cell phone but no calls were made that day or ever after.
Cotton was on the news along with Heather and Murphy. He
looked terrible. I can sure believe he's sick now. This is going to
kill him. Tess isn't taking calls, but she was so sure Bobby was
alive that I know she's undone."

"You ever get your money from her?"

"I told you. The check's in the mail," I said, bristling.

"It's just that it'll be harder to collect now. The question of
Bobby's whereabouts has been answered."

I didn't respond. Mostly because he was right. Partly because
he pissed me off.

"So, what are you going to do?"

"Tess really wanted me to find out who Cotton's beneficiary is.
I think it's probably Bobby." I was reminded of Jerome Neusmeyer's eager hands and tongue and my stomach momentarily
revolted. If Bobby were Cotton's beneficiary then whoever was
next in line would win by default. Unless Cotton rewrote his will.
Which he very well might do. "I put a call into Tess this morning.
Got her answering machine. Told her how sorry I was and asked
her to call me. Guess that's all I can do for now."

Dwayne grunted an acknowledgment. "We'll wait for the
coroner's report."

"You think it's murder, don't you?"

"I don't see how a guy who's managed to evade the authorities for over four years just falls in Lake Chinook and dies."

"It could happen."

"Playing devil's advocate isn't going to get you answers."

"Thanks," I muttered tersely.

Dwayne smiled. It was the kind of knowing smile that suggested I was being a difficult child which pissed me off anew. I left him about a half an hour later, feeling anxious. Hanging around him didn't help as I was alternately too aware of him as a man and irritated with his mentoring, which, between you and me, was way past its pull date.

The second notable occurrence of the day was that the Coma Kid woke up. Everyone committed his name to memory as soon as they learned it from the papers—Jesse Densch. Cheers and happiness abounded though he couldn't recall much of anything except his name and the name of his parakeet which was Buddy.

I watched television all day, keying into every update. Sometime in the afternoon I managed to do some shopping. My first stop was Rite Aid for a new pair of flip-flops. They might not float but they were the right price. Then I made a return trip to the grocery store to buy bread, milk, eggs, cheddar cheese, waffle mix, and a cheap bottle of Chardonnay. I couldn't work up any enthusiasm for the wine. Drinking alone is a problem for me. Instead I poured tap water into a pitcher and put it in the refrigerator to chill, then I fixed myself a cheese sandwich for dinner. This totally captured Binks' attention, so I broke off bits of crust and tossed them for her to catch. She snapped them in her jaws like a crocodile.

Note to self: don't get on the dog's bad side.

The third and last event—and this was the one that really got me—happened as I was getting ready for bed: Murphy dropped by my bungalow, flowers in hand. It was barely nine o'clock and though the heat of the day lay thick in the air, the day's events had left me chilled and peculiarly tired and I'd fallen hard asleep on my sofa. When the doorbell rang Binky launched into a strange barking howl that sounded sort of like *woo-woo-woo*. I was trying to figure out what that meant as I glanced down at my oversized orange T-shirt which says simply: Go Beavs! It's an homage to Oregon State University, sixty miles south in the city of Corvallis, Oregon. I also own a Duck shirt as I'm bi-fan-ial, if that's a word, and root for the University of Oregon as well. But I don't like their colors—yellow and green—so I stick with orange and black.

Peering through the peephole I recognized Murphy in the fading purple light. "Shit." Rapidly finger-combing my hair I wondered if little grains of sleep were stuck in the inner corners of my eyes from my nap. Quickly I scrubbed them with my fists like a child.

Reluctantly, I opened the door. "Hello there," I said with just a trace of question in my voice.

"Catch you at a bad time?"

"It's bad for all of us today."

"You got that right." He brought irises. My favorite. My mind raced. When people are nice to me I don't know what to do. Mostly I think they want something from me.

"Thank you." I shut the door behind him.

He looked like hell, to put it nicely. His jeans were dirty, as if he'd been wiping muddy hands on them. Maybe he'd been part of the rescue team. His hair was slightly mussed, but it was the deeply etched lines bracketing his mouth and the dullness of his eyes that revealed his true state of mind.

"How are you holding up?" I asked, taking the flowers from him.

"Not good."

"I'm sorry about Bobby. And his family. And everything."

"Jane . . ." He swallowed hard.

I stared at him, my heartbeat beginning to speed up. To my shock he suddenly wrapped his arms around me and held tight. From a distance I saw myself, holding out the flowers, my arms stretched out straight and stiff while Murphy drew me to him like a life-giving elixir. I was too surprised to do much else.

"I feel . . . sick," he murmured against the side of my throat.

I shivered from the frisson that raced down my spine. It was my turn to swallow and gently bring my hands around his back.

Binky, whom I'd managed to forget in the heat of the moment, let out a sharp, little bark. I felt Murphy start and he pulled away from me to look down at the dog. The little traitor. I'd just been beginning to enjoy the wonder of Murphy's embrace.

"You have . . . a pug?"

Murphy knew my aversion to pets of all kinds. "She was a gift," I said, scooping Binks up and carrying her to the bathroom where I firmly shut her in.

The moment had passed. I wasn't sure how to feel. My pulse raced light and fast. The depression that had loomed all day hadn't dissipated. It had manifested into something else. Something between us.

"I have some wine," I said through a dry throat.

"Good."

Murphy followed me to the kitchen, his gaze turning toward the bathroom door as Binky began a furious scratching. I figured the paint job was already ruined. Without asking, Murphy let the eager little beast out again. Binks snuffled Murphy's sneakers which were covered with leftover grass from a newly mown lawn. He bent down to scratch behind her ears but she sidestepped him. She's not that easily won.

He said, "Did you hear the Coma Kid woke up?"

"Uh-huh." I thought for a bit. "What's his name again?"

"Jesse something, I think."

"Oh, yeah."

I uncorked my bottle and poured us two glasses of Chardonnay, hoping against hope that Murphy hadn't become a wine connoisseur during our time apart. I possess two wine glasses just for an occasion such as this. One's a little chipped on the edge, and hostess that I am, I kept that one for myself.

"I'm really worried about Cotton," Murphy said as he settled onto one of my two kitchen stools. They sit beneath my counter overhang and like my wine, they're cheap. The stool's legs creaked ominously beneath his weight. "He's not doing well."

"I can imagine. It was a rough day."

"This has put him over the edge. He wasn't well before, but now . . ."

I nodded and sipped the wine. Kinda tart. Spicy. Not especially good, but since we were drinking at my place it was either this or a few shots of vanilla extract. I'm pretty sure I have a bottle of that around somewhere. Doesn't everybody? "There's no more wondering whether Bobby's alive or not. There's no more kidding himself."

Murphy grimaced. "Cotton's always had a soft spot for Bobby, regardless of what he's said. Bobby was his only son. I don't think he believed he could really kill his family."

"No one wants to believe it."

He gave me a straight look. "I had to face facts eventually, Jane. I'm pretty sure you meant that for me."

"Doesn't mean it's easy."

"I hated Bobby for what he did," Murphy bit out intensely. "I didn't want to hate him. It was easier not to believe. It was easier to go away."

"It's over now. At some level, anyway. Maybe this will help Cotton, in some strange way. Give him closure."

He shook his head, teetering a bit on the stool. I prayed it would hold his 6'4" frame. Binks sat nearby, alternately staring up at us and panting.

We drank the entire bottle of wine, saying little of any further import. Two or three glasses in I remembered why I liked Murphy. Or, more truthfully, I forgot what I didn't like about him.

I suddenly wanted to kiss him. To hell with that, I wanted to make out with him like it was a reality show requirement to keep from being kicked off the team/tribe/show. I managed to keep my lust from obvious view. At least I think so. When Murphy moved to the couch, I took the dilapidated rocker—the only other seat in the living room. Binks was torn. She wanted to sleep on the couch by Murphy but apparently felt she needed to show some allegiance to me. She stayed by my chair, flopped on the hardwood.

Time passed and Murphy began to talk about Bobby. It wasn't anything specific, just some memories of childhood that were positive. I think he'd been waiting for the chance, but Bobby's heinous crimes and disappearance had prevented him. Now it came pouring out, all the love of their friendship, all the competitiveness between them, the hurt over betrayals, some minor, some large.

"You know, at first, it was just about Laura. I never forgave him for taking her from me," Murphy said, gulping the last of his wine.

Murphy and Laura had dated first, a high school thing, meaningless, frivolous, but oh, so important at the time. "Weren't you and Laura way over when she hooked up with Bobby?"

"Yeah . . . I guess. There was a lot of time in between. But it didn't feel that way sometimes, y'know?"

"That's merely competition talking."

He looked into the bottom of his now empty wine glass. "You're right. It *was* over."

There was a hint of something in his tone that suggested something else but my own wine consumption was leaving me a little off. "Over, but not *way* over?"

"She was a sweet girl. A woman worth falling in love with."

I buried my nose in my glass. It wasn't meant as an insult to me, but it felt like one anyway. I made a noise of agreement and viciously castigated myself for being jealous of a dead woman.

"I wasn't in love with her. Not in the 'let's get married' way. She was too religious. I couldn't be that way with her or for her. I knew it. I spent most of my time trying to corrupt her, I guess."

"But that was high school."

"I didn't want Bobby to have her. *That's* high school. I didn't want them to get married. I wanted them to break up. I tried to get them to break up."

"That's natural."

"No, it's not. You don't know what I did."

I heard some aggression in his tone. "What did you do?"

"I slept with her some more. A few times. I told Bobby. I made Laura cry."

He looked away, ashamed. "They got married anyway. None of it should have happened."

Seeing the path of his guilt sobered me up as if I'd been thrown into Lake Chinook. "Bobby did not kill his whole family because he was angry at Laura and you."

"I know."

"Do you?" I looked at him hard. "Murphy, Bobby was a hatchery fish. He was made that way. His choices were from a serious lack within himself. It didn't have anything to do with you."

"I wanted to make it up to them. When you and I were together, it was great. We could all hang out as friends."

So, that's what I'd been. The girlfriend to round out the foursome. The balance. Great.

"I loved being with you," he said, grabbing my thoughts before they could follow the path they'd suddenly taken, turning them around. "I loved driving around."

He'd owned a candy apple red Mustang convertible. Not quite vintage. Just old enough to be a tad uncool, just new enough to run. It had come in another shade of red that year, but he'd had it painted in a richer, deeper tone. I followed that car out of southern California. I'd driven around Lake Chinook, the wind tearing through my hair, my thoughts full of love and marriage and tin cans hanging from the Mustang's back bumper as we drove off, into the sunset.

He stared at his empty glass. "Do you have any more wine? I want to get stinking drunk. So that when I wake up tomorrow, I feel like hell."

"You came to the wrong place, I'm afraid."

"Then, I'll be back."

"Where are you going?" He'd risen from the couch with purpose and now I didn't want him to go.

"To the store."

"Are you okay to drive?"

"More than okay, unfortunately. I've had time to sober up. But I'll make up for it. Mind if I sleep on your couch tonight?"

I shook my head.

He returned within half an hour with a half case of wine. I'm no expert on labels but I knew he wouldn't pick the cheapest bottles on the shelf as I was wont to do. I tried to be a host by sharing some more, but honestly, I started feeling dizzy way too soon. I wanted to track his conversation and record these moments. I wanted to remember being with Murphy. I could recall being in that car and kissing in that car and yes, struggling to have sex in that car. And while Murphy drank and mumbled about how he'd betrayed Bobby and Bobby'd betrayed everyone and how he wished it was all the way it used to be and Laura and the kids and Bobby were all still alive, my mind's eye was filled with an image of a bright red car and singing wind and joy.

I don't remember stumbling into bed. I do remember not being able to stay up any longer. I wanted to kiss Murphy goodnight but I knew it wouldn't end there. I chose the safer path and merely up and left him on the sofa, crashing onto my bed, my head full of bright, past images and way too much wine.

I woke at four a.m., mouth dry, every cell screaming: WATER! I stumbled into the kitchen, taking a quick scan of the sofa and finding it empty.

"Shit," I said through my teeth. I grabbed the pitcher of tap water in the refrigerator and thought about drinking out of the side. Good manners prevailed and I managed to pour myself a glass, drinking half down in thirsty, slurpy gulps before I realized my sliding glass door was slightly open.

A jolt swept through me, then a lightening of spirit. I stepped outside into a velvety warm night and found Murphy asleep on my plastic lounge chair. His head was thrown back, his mouth open. His last glass of wine sat beside him on the deck, looking untouched.

I had a chance to view him directly this way through the gray-black darkness. My kitchen light threw a yellow square of illumination across his chest and brought the features of his face into sharp relief. I wondered what I felt for him. Part of me wanted to dismiss him as the past, but isn't there always some irrepressible need to woo the one who dumped you? To make them fall in love with you all over again? To be the one to realize that your feelings really aren't all that deep and that it was over then, and it's over now, and it will always be over? Don't we *need* that?

Moonlight, caught behind clouds, slipped through and played on the smooth water of the bay. I inhaled and exhaled slowly. The trouble was I wanted to jump his bones. I could feel it as if it were a living thing, desperate to feed. Thank God I was still dying of thirst as it kept me from acting like a horny teenager and waking the man up with a kiss. It's annoying to realize that even seeing him sleeping with his mouth open couldn't turn me off. I found it endearing. Made him seem more human. More approach-able. More winnable.

I returned to my water pitcher, gulped some more, and nearly tripped over Binks who'd toddled from her bed and stood blink-ing in the kitchen light.

"Back to bed," I said softly, turning off the light. The dog complied, curling back into her bed and watching me slide be-tween my sheets. I felt her gaze on me, so I leaned over the side of the bed, catching sight of her wide eyes in the ever so faint moonlight sneaking through my shuttered window.

"I didn't kiss him," I said, just to remind her.

I woke at the crack of dawn, scurried through the kitchen and found Murphy still sleeping on the deck lounge chair. Glancing around, I found my pound bag of hazelnut coffee I'd purchased at the Coffee Nook. Hallelujah! Sure, it was girly coffee. No man I know drinks it and expresses joy at the flavor. But it was coffee, for God's sake. It counted.

Pulling out the coffeemaker, my eye fell on the waffle maker. For the briefest of moments I considered trying my hand at breakfast. I'd managed to make myself a passable waffle without benefit of an egg the other morning, now I could do the real deal. In the next second I mentally berated myself. Why was I trying so hard to impress him? We were through and it was okay. *But I can make waffles*, I argued with myself. *I can do that. That's no big deal.*

"Hey . . ."

I spilled grains of coffee across my countertop at the sound of Murphy's voice. Slowly, thoughtfully, I picked them up with a sponge as Murphy entered the kitchen and closed the sliding door behind himself.

"I feel like hell." He rubbed a hand over his face.

"Isn't that what you wanted?"

"Yeah . . . Could I have a glass of water?"

"Sure." I poured him a glass from my refrigerated pitcher. He drank lustily and hormones began to sing through my veins again. I concentrated on the brown liquid pouring through the coffeepot's filter into the glass receptacle.

"Cotton's put me in his will as prime beneficiary," he stated morosely.

The baldness of this brought me up short. "What about Bobby? I mean, his body was just discovered."

"He had it already done. Didn't matter if Bobby was alive or not."

"Wow . . ." I let this process for a moment, then asked, "What about Heather?"

"I told Cotton to leave it all to her. Or Tess or Owen. Anyone but me. I don't want it."

"You talked this over with Cotton?"

"More like he talked to me. Heather's got some idea about it, I think. She's been friendly but tense. I've been staying at the island. I don't want to, but Cotton's been insistent and now . . ." Murphy sank onto a stool, looking upset. "I've gotta get outta here. I've got a ticket back to Santa Fe." He threw me a glance. "Would you come with me?"

"Ha, ha," I laughed, pretending he was joking when I wasn't sure he was. It was a good thing I'd already rewrapped the hazelnut decaf package because I wouldn't have trusted my hands not to spill the whole bag.

"I'm serious."

"You want me to go with you to Santa Fe?"

He nodded.

"Just like that?"

"I can't stay here, Jane."

"Well, I can't go," I said simply.

"Why not?"

I couldn't decide whether I was thrilled or angry. I had a life in Lake Chinook. Without him. Yet he acted as if I'd been just hanging around waiting for him. "You're sure you're the beneficiary?" I asked, sidestepping.

"Cotton met with his attorney, then he talked to me."

Ah, yes. Jerome Neusmeyer.

"I think it would be better if you stayed here," I said carefully. "You need to see this thing through no matter what happens."

He silently stared at me, his chest rising and falling. He was definitely in some kind of emotional crisis. This, too, I found peculiarly attractive. Murphy was always in such fierce control of himself that this faint vulnerability was like an aphrodisiac for me. I liked thinking he might be a bit softer now, which was such a bunch of horseshit when you thought about it. What did I want from the man? *Nothing*, I reminded myself sternly.

"I quit my job in Santa Fe," he said. "Worked freelance investigation for an insurance company there until a few months ago. But I could go back to it. I've got a house there. Small, but functional. I've been thinking about you a lot, and when I saw you at the island, I started thinking a lot of other thoughts."

"Oh?" I poured us two mugs of coffee. Carefully.

"If the Bobby thing hadn't happened . . ." He trailed off, then switched gears. "We were a good team, Jane. If you don't like Santa Fe, we could go back to southern California."

He was waiting for some kind of response. I set his mug down in front of him and cradled mine, distantly aware that I might be burning the pads off my fingers and palms. My hesitation grew into a lengthy pause. Murphy nodded as if I'd slapped him.

"You're saying no," he said to my continued silence.

"You tempt me," I admitted.

"And?"

"But I can't run away. I've got a job here."

He didn't believe me. "And what is that job, exactly? Process serving?"

"Among other things."

He waited for me to elaborate, certain I had nothing left up my sleeve. I hesitated for only a minute, then said, "I'm doing some investigating."

"Investigating?"

"Uh-huh."

"Like private investigating? You mean as a job?"

"That's what I said."

He was perplexed. "You mean right now? Who are you investigating?" He drew a sharp breath as the full import dawned. "*Me?*"

"No!" I half-laughed.

"Cotton? You're investigating Cotton?"

"I'm just looking into some things . . ."

"Don't split hairs, Jane. Someone hired you to investigate Cotton? Why? You mean . . . because of Bobby? Well, who are you working for?" He paused, then came up with the only available answer. "Oh, God. Tess. It's not Heather. She's got too clear of an idea of the finances. It's Tess."

Bull's-eye. I simply didn't respond. Murphy sipped at his coffee, made a face, set the cup down and headed for the door. Binks awoke to say good-bye but Murphy was too pissed to do much more than leave. He hesitated at the door, then came back to where I was standing in the kitchen. He drew me to him and kissed the top of my head, then wordlessly exited.

Murphy's good at leaving me.

Chapter Eleven

Cotton called me within the hour to bawl me out. Murphy is nothing if not efficient and he tattle-taled about as fast as humanly possible. I let Cotton rant on for several long minutes because (a) I felt I deserved it, (b) he sounded so weak, even in his anger, that I seriously worried he might collapse if I put up even the slightest protest, and (c) he needed somewhere to direct his hurt, anger and grief and I was as good a target as anyone.

I said, when he finally ran down, his breath heavy and labored on the other end of the line, "Tess wanted to know where Bobby was. She felt you knew and she asked me to see what I could learn. I'm sorry for the subterfuge. She missed her son."

"Well, she knew where he was!" Cotton growled, then he slammed down the receiver.

I wondered at that. Was he serious, or just furious and irrational? Tess didn't know where Bobby was. That's why she hired me in the first place, wasn't it?

I called Tess and left another message for her. She didn't return my call and by the afternoon, I wondered if she ever would. I was pleasantly surprised to find a check in my mailbox made out to yours truly for a thousand dollars. In a moment of giving, I sent her my neatly typed reports that said absolutely nothing she didn't already know and dropped them in the mail.

I believed our business was finished, and I phoned Dwayne and made a point of letting him know I'd been paid. If I'd been in a better frame of mind, I would have crowed about winning, but the whole Bobby mess had left a deep taint that I didn't want to touch too much more. I drove to the bank and deposited the check, then stopped at the store for more dog food, some sodas and various and sundry canned goods as if I were piling up for the winter. I was glad to be out of the Bobby Reynolds tragedy.

My neighbors the Mooneys pulled into my boat slip and waved at me to come down the path and meet them. I muttered short, pungent profanities beneath my breath as I smiled like a Judas and waved in return. I really can't take their bickering at the best of times, and I wanted to be alone.

However, this was not to be. They waved more frantically for me to come to their boat which makes Dwayne's look like a futuristic model. I stepped down the flagstones with dread. I didn't want company, unless it was Murphy, and I really just didn't want to think too much about anything at all.

"Jane, come with us to Foster's," Arista Mooney said, motioning me into the boat. "This weather won't last forever."

Her husband Lyle nodded at me. He wasn't much of a talker unless Arista got under his skin and then the bickering began. They were both in their late fifties or early sixties. Their children were grown and gone and they had lived in the little house a few down from mine since they'd built it. Not one bit of remodeling or updating had occurred in all the years since, and repairs were a patch of roof here, a mended gate latch there. Trees and flotinia and laurel bushes obscured it from the bay except for steps made out of cinderblock, pounded into the ground. An architectural haven it was not. An expensive waterfront property in need of TLC and lots of bucks it was.

"Did you hear they found that boy's body in the lake?" Arista said. "The one that killed his family?" She shivered. "Get in, hon. Come on. I want one of those Cosmos that Manny serves up. Yumm!" She smacked her lips.

"I can't go. I'm just beat." I made a show of yawning. Besides the Mooneys' company, I just didn't feel like another trip to Foster's, good weather or no.

"Lyle has a gift certificate. Come on, now. We want to take you to dinner. You can't say no!"

This was unprecedented. I glanced at Lyle. His gray hair was hidden under a stained baseball cap but his yellow-collared T-shirt looked natty coupled with a pair of khaki shorts. The white socks with his loafers sort of spoiled the effect, but considering I was wearing my black capris and a white tank that probably needed a serious trip to the washing machine, I had no room to talk.

"My purse is back at the house," I said, hooking a thumb in the direction I'd come.

Binks stepped onto my deck, looked down at us and gave a short, staccato bark.

"Is that a dog?" Arista asked, startled.

"That's Binkster."

"Been chasin' parked cars, has he?" Lyle inserted, chuckling deep in his throat.

"You got a dog?" Arista stared at me as if I'd grown horns.

"A temporary duty."

"My goodness. Is he nice?"

"She's not bad," I said.

"Would she like to go in the boat?" Arista waved at Binks who took that as an invitation and raced down the flagstones to stand beside me, her curly tail a-wag.

I don't know how it happened but I went back for my purse, locked up the cottage and was sitting on the duct-taped white and red tuck-and-roll backseat with Binks on my lap, putt-putting out to the main lake before you could say the cheapskate sold out for free food. I'd managed to bring my cell phone. If I needed rescue I'd call Dwayne. Or maybe, Murphy.

It was evening and the sun burned hot and low in the western sky. Normally I need a jacket or sweater in anticipation of nightfall but today I felt overheated. It seemed as if I would never be cool again. As Lyle thrust the throttle forward and we skimmed across the main lake I turned my face to the resultant breeze. Binks did likewise, her velvety little brown ears flapping backwards.

We arrived at Foster's On The Lake to join an already loud crowd crammed around the outdoor bar. Lyle maneuvered into a boat slip that another boat was waiting for. The captain tooted us in a series of furious bleats. I remember thinking, "We were here first, you idiot!" then wondered at my simmering hostility.

Binks could not go inside so we left her in the boat where she sat on the back gunwale and looked forlorn. People sitting on the patio made sad sounds and commented on how cute she was and couldn't she come inside? Foster looked at them all as if they'd collectively lost their minds.

"That your dog?" he asked me suspiciously.

"She is for now."

"It's a girl?" He looked again at Binks' Ernest Borgnine face.

"Most breeds come in male and female."

"Y'sure?" he responded skeptically, still staring at the pug.

I heard a glass break and turned toward the crowd around the bar, two steps up. Several people backed away from the apparent cause of the incident, and I saw Heather, her eyes sort of starey and moist, gazing down at the shattered wine glass. She looked torn between laughter and tears. I was amazed she'd actually shown up in public, given the events of the week. Cotton was nowhere to be seen, which was expected.

"C'mon, Jane." Arista motioned me to a table under a tilted umbrella whose lime green, plastic-stripped shade sparkled. Lyle grunted an order for bourbon and a Cosmo for his wife. I asked for bottled water.

"I'll be right back," I told them. I went back to Binky and poured water into the tiny cap of my bottle. She lapped at it. We both sat in the boat. I had no time to reflect on the fact that I'd eschewed human companionship for the pug when Heather staggered through the gate, slamming it behind her. Several people hung back, as if they'd been trying to engage her but didn't know quite how. She looked wild and unsettled, her white sundress sporting a wet stain over one breast, possibly the result of her spilled wine. Spying me, she charged like a bull.

"You," she sneered. "Working for Tess!"

"I'm sorry about Bobby," I said.

"Everybody's sorry about Bobby. Except the cops and the Feds and whoever else." She flung her arm wide to encompass the lake and the whole world. "They're all over the island."

I could imagine. After all, Bobby's body had been found in the lake. It stood to reason, didn't it, that he might have been on his father's island?

"Bobby was a killer," Heather said. "I'm not sorry he's gone and I'll tell anybody that."

"A lot of people won't mourn his loss too much."

"I had to get away from the whole damn thing. But Cotton won't leave. This is killing him. He's going to die because of it." Her matter-of-fact manner would have been off-putting if she hadn't been so drunk. "I considered you a friend!" she added, coming back to her first issue. "But you're a *fucking* spy!"

Her scream seemed to echo across the water. Fortunately, music and noise from the bar probably buried the sound for those at Foster's.

Paula Shepherd appeared on the other side of the gate. In a black short skirt and a red tank top, her skin tanned to a toasty brown, she had none of the hesitation of the others. "Heather," she said, all smiles. "Brad's ready to take us back." She winked at another boat. Sure enough, her sidekick, Brad Gilles was at the helm, firing up the engine.

"Fuck you," Heather said, stumbling, climbing into the Mooneys' boat.

Paula didn't even turn a hair. "Are you going home with her, then?"

"I'm not going anywhere."

Paula nodded grimly and returned through the gate, through the patio, then opened another short gate further down where Brad was looking anxious at the wheel. They conferred and

Paula climbed in. I watched them reverse. They took a sweep by our boat and Brad yelled, "You all right, Heather?"

Heather, who'd plopped herself in the seat next to the captain's, closed her eyes as if in pain. "I need another drink. You got anything in this crappy piece of shit."

"Don't think so."

"Figures."

I skipped dinner and drinks with Arista and Lyle to stay in the boat. Arista came looking for me but upon spying Heather in our boat, scurried back to her table. Heather Reynolds was infamous, at least for today.

"You know what I hate the most?" Heather said after a long period of silence. I thought she'd passed out. "All the lies it takes. Everybody asking about Bobby when they know he's a homicidal maniac. Well, I'm glad that part's finished." She slid me a look. "Murphy's really mad at you. If you think you've got something going, think again."

She was beginning to bug me. I was getting over feeling sorry for her in a big hurry. "Cotton lost a son today. I'm glad he's got Murphy with him to offer support."

"Murphy's *not* his son," she reminded me tersely.

"But he thinks of him that way."

"Shit." She staggered up to a pair of wobbly legs and glared down at me. Binks, who'd had her head on my lap, climbed to her stubby legs. She stared right back at Heather. This must have seemed like a call to arms, because Heather jumped back into the fray as if we were in a full-fledged fight. "Murphy doesn't care about you. He doesn't even like you. And Cotton thinks Murphy's a pale imitation of Bobby. He thinks Bobby was everything. Bobby could do no wrong!"

"Well . . . that's been proven not to be the truth."

"Bobby was Mr. Lake Chinook Athlete. Bobby gets everything. Always. Even when he's missing. Even when he's NOT. Cotton's so destroyed now that he knows it's really, really true that Bobby's dead. Now that everybody knows. Now that there's no reason to pretend any longer. Bobby was IT. But it's too late now, isn't it? He's dead. And the dead don't inherit." She glared at me triumphantly.

I wasn't working for Tess any longer, but I couldn't help myself. I said, "Sometimes the wives don't either."

Her face suffused with color. "If Murphy said he's getting the island, he's dead wrong. You can just dream all you want, but it ain't gonna happen. Go be his slut. See what it gets you. You won't get the island!"

With that she climbed over us and onto the dock, teetering her way back to the bar. The crowd quickly moved in, buying her a drink, commiserating, waiting for juicy news.

Arista and Lyle returned to the boat. "What happened?" Arista asked, all agog.

"Heather needed another drink."

"You know her? Oh, my God. She's married to the guy who owns the island. The murderer's dad. What did she say? Do you like her? What's she like?"

I shrugged.

Lyle turned on the ignition and glanced in the direction of the bar. Heather was pressed against the rail, her white wine glass tipping precariously.

"She can't hold her liquor," he said succinctly.

I woke the next morning in a state of mild confusion. It felt as if something momentous had happened. Oh, yes. Bobby Reynolds.

Throwing on my running gear I took Binks out for a quick potty trip, then headed to the Nook. It was still hot. My thoughts were on Heather, but they kept slipping toward Murphy. I had the feeling she was making up some of the stuff. She was mad at me but she was really mad at Bobby. And Murphy, for being the surrogate son.

I grimaced. I didn't blame Murphy for talking to Cotton about my association with Tess. He liked Cotton and wanted to play fair. And even if they were all mad at me, there was nothing to do about it now.

At the Nook I grabbed a cup of coffee and settled myself on a stool. Billy Leonard came in. "How's it going?" I asked.

"Good," he answered.

"How are the hatchery fish?"

"The kids?" He waggled his hand back and forth to indicate so-so. "We got all this shit for college housing. You could go broke."

"You'd give your kids every dime you own," I said.

"Well, sure." He seemed surprised by my observation. This was an understood thing. "Hey, what do you think about that Coma Kid? Doesn't remember anything but his bird."

"Is he still in the hospital?"

"I think he's home. You know my youngest knows his friends pretty well. He said they were on the island."

"Cotton's island?"

"Is there another?"

"Well, how did the accident happen?" I asked. Grant Wemberly had clearly stated that the dogs weren't chasing anyone that night.

Billy shrugged. "I don't know."

"It happened about a week before the benefit," I said aloud, taxing my memory.

"They don't want to get in trouble. You know kids. His friends say he fell off the boat, but my son says the truth is he was running around that island and the dogs came out."

"The dogs weren't out that night."

"Well, then I don't know. The kid came racing around and jumped in the water, but he hit his head on something on the way down. They all hauled him into the boat. He was awake at first, then went out cold. Scared 'em all shitless. They cooked up the story that he hit his head on the boat, but the family called the police."

"So, no one thinks they were on the island except your son says they were."

"Guess so." Billy looked at me. "You think it matters?"

"I'd like to talk to the Coma Kid," I said suddenly.

"He doesn't remember anything."

"Actually, I think I'd like to start with his friends."

"They won't tell you nothin' either, believe me. What do you think's up?"

He regarded me curiously. I lifted my palms in surrender. I wasn't sure what I was fishing for, but anything about the island interested me these days. "Tell your son I'm not interested in getting anyone in trouble. I just want to hear what they have to say."

"Is there money in it for him?" Billy laughed.

"You're hitting me where it hurts, but okay," I said dryly. "A little bit."

"What's the Coma Kid's name again?" Billy asked.

"Beats me. But the parakeet's name is Buddy."

I returned to my routine of process serving and on Thursday Cynthia called me ostensibly to go out for a drink but I think it had more to do with payback for the Woofers incident. She asked me to go with her to First Thursday which is a Portland tradition whereby art galleries mostly around the Pearl District stay open in the evening and the public browses through and around the area, sipping wine or champagne and generally soaking up culture. Cynthia, being the artiste she is, decided the venue as I would normally just stay home alone and either sleep or lament my empty larder or both.

I'd cleaned up for the evening; I'd even combed my hair. In fact, in my black capris and a cowl-necked sleeveless shirt in an ugly shade of mustard that for some reason looks good on me, I was passable. When Cynthia picked me up she gave me a head-to-toe examination. She was in a steel gray jacket and pants with a white form-fitting top tied beneath her breasts in some kind of knot that made her look like a D-cup. Her spiky hair had grown an eensy bit and lay a little smoother against her scalp. Her blue eyes were incisive, however, and when she said, "Next time you're in trouble, remember to call someone else," I could tell it was going to be a while before she forgave me.

"Sorry for not mentioning the dog."

"I'm seriously considering getting my car painted. There are nail marks all along the passenger side."

This conversation may have digressed but we were on the block of the Black Swan gallery and I saw some of Cynthia's watercolors inside. She merely snorted at the sight, as if she were perturbed about something.

As if Tess knew I was outside her gallery, my cell phone started singing and I looked down to see she was the caller. "What does she want?" I murmured aloud. I'd brought Cynthia up-to-date on my exploits in the Bobby Reynolds case, sort of. Her interest was skewed as she was more interested in Tess's gallery than the sordid events of her personal life. Cynthia was nothing if not financially and professionally self-motivated. A true capitalist. At least there were no hidden agendas.

Cynthia's eyes narrowed. "I want that gallery. Tess doesn't know the first thing about art. The higher the price, the more valuable the piece, in her mind."

"Isn't that how a lot of people think?" I asked. Cynthia sure as hell knew how to make me gasp at the amount listed on one of those little white tags. I had to stop myself from screeching, "FOR THIS?" which I was wont to do at the beginning of our relationship. Now, I exhibit more self-control.

"Yes." Cynthia's mouth pursed. "But Tess is in a rare echelon, all by herself. She's crass, Jane. I'm glad you're getting some money out of this deal you're in with her, but the sooner you're done, the better."

"I am done," I said as I clicked on. Luckily, I didn't express this view as Tess's first words were, "Have you learned anything?"

I blinked. "About . . . ?"

"Cotton! Was Bobby living there? Had he been helping him?" Her voice was full of unshed tears.

"I—I really couldn't say."

"I want you to find out. If this is Cotton's fault, I hope he dies!"

She hung up abruptly.

"Well?" Cynthia asked, her attention on a marble sculpture of a penis in the window of the Century Gallery, about three blocks from the Black Swan.

Upon closer inspection I saw it was a palm tree. "I don't know. I don't get why she's still calling me. She blames Bobby's father for everything, which is what mothers do, I guess." I thought about Cotton's assertion that she'd known where Bobby was. I wondered if I dared confront her with that accusation.

Cynthia was cruising through the front door of the gallery. "Tess is a piranha," she said over her shoulder. "Who's the artist of the penis sculpture?" she demanded of the dour-faced, obesely fat gallery owner.

"It's a palm tree." His voice was acid.

"Uh-huh. And I just got off the boat. It's Marcos DeCroix, isn't it?" She leaned into me. "We used to date when he was merely Mark Decker. All men are into their penises, but he was really into his. I must admit, it was pretty nice."

I gave the palm tree a second look while the gallery owner turned on his heel and walked through an arch and disappeared. The palm tree curved a little to the left. I had an unbidden memory of Murphy standing in the shower, dripping wet, doing an impromptu dance whereby he jiggled from side to side, his penis slapping his thighs. He was laughing and happy.

Three days later Bobby's dead family had been found lined up in a row.

"Think how much trouble those things cause," Cynthia said, admiring the sculpture.

I grimaced. Our thoughts were obviously traveling far different paths. All I could currently see was that Bobby Reynolds had begat three children with that thing.

When I got back to the cottage Binks was overjoyed to see me. I checked her water bowl and took her for an evening constitutional. This takes a lot of sniffing of plants and the ground. Her flat nose gets buried in the blades of grass.

When we went back inside, my arms broke out in gooseflesh.

It felt as if someone had been inside my place. I checked my belongings, concentrating so hard on how I'd left things it actually hurt my brain. Nothing seemed disturbed.

I gazed at the dog who gazed right back up at me, head cocked. "Was someone here?"

Binks paused, then looked toward the front door. Low in her throat came this *grrrrr* that sent my pulse into overdrive.

I pulled the shades and rechecked the locks on the doors. A moment later I heard the same noise and realized she was directing her warning to the cover of a magazine that showed a man petting an Irish setter.

So much for the bogeyman.

Still, I rechecked the locks again and I allowed Binks to sleep on my bed.

Chapter
Twelve

Dwayne stopped by the following morning as I was running through a thorough examination of my bungalow. I still hadn't quite gotten over the idea that someone had been there. It seemed to me that the contents of my file on Bobby Reynolds had been shifted around but I couldn't be sure. I had the sneaking suspicion that paranoia was my main enemy.

"Why do you think someone's been here?" Dwayne asked as he handed me the fax of Binkster's medical records. I felt a moment of panic. I'd had the dog for a couple of weeks and I hadn't taken it in for a shot yet. Dogs could contract rabies . . . and other terrible things . . . "You think she's safe?" I asked anxiously.

We both looked at Binks who gazed upward, head cocked as if waiting for me to ask her directly. "Check the dates on the boosters. The dog's fine." Dwayne bent down to Binks, scratching and massaging her ears. She looked as if she might topple off her legs into a flop of ecstacy.

"Maybe no one's been here. I thought my file on Bobby had been touched, but there's nothing in there but newspaper clippings and general knowledge."

"Your imagination running away with you, darlin'?"

"Probably," I admitted reluctantly. I didn't want him to think I was a complete sissy. "These haven't been the most fun-filled last few days."

I was still in my sleeping gear, T-shirt and pajama bottoms. He wore faded denim cutoffs and a gray collarless shirt. I found myself telling him about Heather's scene at Foster's and then about Tess's phone call. I finished with, "She seems to think Bobby was living at Cotton's. She said if Bobby's death is his fault, she hopes he dies."

Dwayne shook his head. "Cotton couldn't harbor Bobby for four years without someone finding out."

"I know. Tess should know that, too."

"Sounds like she was just railing at you."

"Like I can do something about it now." I snorted. "Bobby's definitely dead, so it's all over."

"She's probably pissed 'cause she doesn't have a way to get her hands on the money now."

"True."

"So, you're off this gig. Want some other work?"

"Have you got something?" I wasn't sure I was happy about that or not. "Do I have to get licensed?"

"You're not advertising yourself as a private investigator. You just do research for people. You don't carry a gun."

"God, no."

"Then, don't worry about it yet."

"Are you licensed?"

"Of course." He looked at me as if I were dense, which I was feeling that I was. "You think I want to get the police all over my ass?"

"Well, you just said that I don't need to be."

"Yet, Jane. Yet."

My stomach growled. Last night's meal with Cynthia had been a while. I was feeling ornery and out of sorts. "I wish I felt better about all this. I keep thinking you're wrong about me. I'm not cut out for this stuff."

Dwayne half-smiled. "Well, good God. Could you be closer to this one if you tried?"

He was right. I'd met Bobby. He was Murphy's best friend. The reason I'd been chosen by Tess was because of my relationship with both of them. Marta had just been the tool used to haul me in.

Dwayne told me to stop by his cabana later and I grunted some kind of agreement. Was I through with the Reynolds case? Of course I was. What else was there to do?

I came back from my run to find an ominous black vehicle parked in my driveway. My paranoia over the night before reasserted itself and my already labored breathing turned fast and gulping. There was an official seal on the side of the car, and those red and blue lights in the back window, and one of those bright riot lights by the outside mirror no cop car can be without.

The police. The fuzz. The coppers! What the hell did they want? My heart thumped rapidly. Sure, my brother was a police officer but it didn't stop me from fearing the authorities. Having Officer Friendly come into my third-grade classroom hadn't helped either. By the time I hit high school I knew to avoid the police at all costs. When you're involved with the authorities it's just bad news. I wanted to stay under the radar. Period.

A man stepped from the driver's side as I waited, panting, filled with dread.

"Jane Kelly?" he asked.

Damn. This was no mistake. I nodded cautiously.

He was Hispanic with liquid brown eyes, faintly curling black hair and nut brown skin I would die for. "I'm Tomas Lopez." He pronounced his name Toe-*moss*, stressing the *moss*. I'm sure I would have called him Thomas, if I'd read it somewhere. Otherwise, he had no discernible accent.

"Uh-huh."

"I'm the investigating officer in the Reynolds murders for Clackamas County."

My mouth formed an 'O'. "But the murders took place in Tillamook."

He nodded. "And now a body has turned up in our county."

He smiled faintly, at the irony of it all, I supposed. His teeth were very white and straight. "Mr. Reynolds suggested we talk to you. He seemed to think you might be able to add to our information."

"Cotton told you to talk to me? About Bobby's death?" I felt a shiver of alarm. So Cotton had sicced the authorities on me. Well, thanks a lot.

"This is just a follow-up," he assured me. "He seemed to think you might be able to add to our information."

"Me? No. Hell, no." I paused. "Cotton told you to interview me?" I just couldn't get over it. I was the least likely person to be involved. I barely knew anything!

"He put your name on a list of people whom we might talk to."

"Was I at the top?" I was growing angry which made me feel better. "Am I a 'person of interest'?" I knew what that meant and didn't like it. I felt trapped, submerged, certain they were going to clank the cuffs on me and haul me in for whatever trumped-up charge Cotton wanted to manufacture.

"You're a friend of Tim Murphy's?"

"Not anymore. My brother's a police officer with the Portland police," I added for good measure. "Booth Kelly."

He wrote that down on a little notepad, something to be added to the Jane Kelly file. My mind's eye envisioned a thick manila file with papers stuffed in every which way. My permanent record.

I said, "All I know is that Bobby Reynolds has been missing for four years and that he turned up in Lake Chinook a few days ago."

"You were hired by his mother Tess Bradbury to find him?"

My mouth went dry. I wondered if I needed a lawyer. I have a terrible fear of anyone in uniform. Sharona. She was a criminal defense lawyer, wasn't she? "Yes . . . sort of."

"Why did she think you could find him?"

"Beats me. Truthfully, I felt like I was just taking her money."

"Did she give you a place to start?"

"She just wanted me to talk to Cotton. Find out if he knew anything."

"Your impression was that she didn't know where Bobby was?"

"Absolutely."

"And Cotton?"

I drew a breath, collecting my thoughts. I didn't want to lie to the man. I didn't want to even talk to him. Finally, I said, "Look, I'm just on the periphery, here. I don't think anyone could have hidden Bobby. It would come out. I really think Tess wanted me to learn as much as I could about Cotton's money. He seems to be ill, and I think the vultures are circling. She was hoping for a piece of his estate, but now with Bobby gone . . ." I let that one ride.

"Are you working for her now?"

"No."

He seemed to think that over. I couldn't read his expression. The seconds ticked by and I began to feel antsy and even more anxious.

"What was the cause of death?" I asked. "Drowning?"

Lopez frowned. "You watch the news?"

"Sometimes."

"Bobby Reynolds' body was weighted down with a heavy object. It slipped free and the body floated to the surface."

I gulped. "It wasn't an accident, then."

"Evidence doesn't support it."

Murder . . . homicide . . . I wasn't really surprised but it added a whole new spin on things. "Do his parents know?"

Lopez nodded.

I suddenly needed to sit down. I think I motioned him to follow me inside and then I ran through the door and sank onto the sofa. Binks jumped up beside me, then barked as Tomas Lopez stepped through the door.

"Have a seat," I said in an unnatural voice. I felt odd inside. "Does Murphy know? Tim Murphy?"

"I believe so. Is there anything else you'd like to add?"

I turned my palms up. "I'm in the dark," I said. "No matter what Cotton thinks."

He hesitated a moment, then said, "Mr. Reynolds is upset, and I don't think he's thinking clearly. Call me, if you think you can help." He left a card on the top of the television. "Cute dog."

"Thanks."

I heard his car back out of the driveway but I stayed on the couch. Maybe I should chuck it all. Leave town. Move to Santa Fe with Murphy.

Did I love Murphy? *No.* I couldn't be that stupid about love. Not anymore. I wanted to have sex with Murphy. That was it. There was a big distinction there.

I pulled my cell phone from my board shorts as Binks began furiously pawing at my leg as if she were trying to dig to China. "What?" I asked her, scrolling through my address book. My finger stopped at Murphy.

Binkster gazed up at me. "Bathroom?" I asked wearily. If this kept up, I was going to have to fence the yard and cut one of those rectangular doors into my back door. I was tired of being on her poop schedule.

Except I wasn't keeping the dog.

I hesitated, my finger poised to punch Murphy's number, when the phone suddenly began singing, surprising me into nearly dropping it. Scrambling to hang onto it, I managed to check the caller ID before the third ring. I didn't recognize the number. Cautiously, I answered, "Jane Kelly."

"You still want to meet the Coma Kid?" Billy Leonard asked without preamble.

Did I? Was I still interested in the goings-on of the island? Thoughts of Murphy slipped into my deeper consciousness for which I suspected I should be grateful. I needed a distraction. "Can you swing it?"

"You bet. A friend of his is at my house right now. He's one of the kids in the boat. I'll send him and B.J. over in our boat. You at home?"

"Yep."

"Get ready for company."

* * *

I was still in my running gear when B.J., Billy's youngest son, maneuvered his boat into my boat slip with practiced ease. I have to admire anyone with docking skills as mine are limited at best. I've scared many a sunbather when my boat comes charging toward their docks. Dwayne doesn't let me steer anymore and hey, I'd rather be chauffeured anyway. B.J. cut the engine, the hull gently kissing my dock as he jumped out and lashed the boat to the cleats.

His passenger looked in his late-teens, with blond hair and a skinny torso. He didn't seem all that thrilled to meet me. I invited them to the upper deck. They headed up the flagstones on my heels. I saw the newcomer throw me a quick look from beneath furrowed brows. Once on deck, so to speak, he leaned against the rail, arms crossed, thumbs up, doing his best to make his chest look bigger.

"This is Kurt," B.J. introduced.

"I'm Jane," I said. I would have extended a hand but I got the impression Kurt wasn't willing to give up his pose.

"Uh-huh."

"I understand you and some friends were circling around the island the night your friend was hurt."

"We weren't *circling*." He eyed me warily, looking for the trap.

Semantics. Jesus. "I'm not trying to bust your ass," I said, wondering if I should break into tougher language. Would swearing help? Make me more hip? Ass was good, though. You couldn't turn on the television or radio without someone using it. I made a mental note to adopt ass more. "I just want to know if your friend was on the island. The caretaker there said the dogs weren't out that night, so if he fell in the lake, like he was running from something else . . . maybe . . . ?"

"Why?"

"Why?" I repeated.

"Why d'ya wanna know?"

Excellent question, Sherlock. "I don't know," I admitted honestly. "Was he on the island?"

After a moment, and a shared look between him and B.J., Kurt nodded briefly.

"So . . . did he fall from the island? I know your story was that he hit his head against the boat, but was that strictly true?"

"Strictly . . . no. But if someone asks me, like the cops or something, that's what I'll say."

"That he cracked his head on the boat." Kurt nodded again, and I said, "You don't want to admit your friend was on the island."

"We weren't supposed to be there."

"I'm the last person who's going to care. I just want to know what happened."

Kurt stared at me, then the deck, then B.J., then the deck again. "I don't know, okay? It was an accident."

"Did anybody else go on the island?"

"Just Jesse."

"Jesse. Right," I repeated. "You guys dropped him off."

"Yeah, he was gonna run around it, y'know? Like we always do?" I nodded encouragement. "And so we were all waitin' for the dogs. Like where are they, y'know? They're like always there barking and growling and throwing themselves at the fence. Scare ya shitless. But we always do it. It was Jesse's turn, but he gets over the fence and he won't move. He's about crapping his shorts. He stayed right by the fence. Afraid they'd suddenly gonna jump at him."

"I'd be staying by the fence, too."

Phhhfff. He expelled air through his lips that said I was a wuss. "Well, we all kinda gave him shit, y'know? And so he finally takes off, runnin' kinda slow and worried-like. We pulled away 'cause you don't want to be just hangin' there. The Lake Patrol could come by."

"You pulled away in the boat," I clarified.

"But then we couldn't find him again. He's somewhere back past the swimming pool, or somethin'. Then all of a sudden he's on the other side of the island, by those trees that hang down real low? And he was hanging on one of the branches, but not like over the water, over the land. We started yellin' at him and then he just fell down." Kurt swallowed hard at this point. "It was like slow motion."

"He fell onto the ground?"

Kurt nodded. "We jumped in and swam over and he kinda was lyin' down on his side. Big gash in his head. Lots of blood. Fuck. We brought the boat over as close as we could and hauled him in. He was white as a ghost, but his eyes were open."

"He didn't say anything?"

"No." Something about his answer made me question its veracity.

"That's what you told the police?"

"That's the truth."

I met B.J.'s eyes. He looked away. Kurt added, "Jesse kinda came to for a minute, but he just was muttering. We didn't tell anybody that 'cause he didn't really say anything. We took him to his folks'."

"What day was this?"

"Friday."

"The 17th?"

"I guess."

"Why didn't Jesse come back to where you'd originally let him off?"

"Beats me. Stupid ass. He shoulda. That's where we expected to pick him up."

"Do you think something scared him?"

"You said the dogs weren't there."

"Maybe something else?"

Kurt frowned at me, totally at sea. "Like what?"

B.J. said, "Yeah. Like what?"

I shook my head. I had vague thoughts that didn't have any foundation. I was wondering if Bobby Reynolds had been there that day. Somebody had dropped his body in Lake Chinook, so he must have come off somebody's property. That was about the only way into the lake.

"Is Jesse home from the hospital?"

"Yeah, for a couple days."

"Do you think he'd see me?"

"What for?"

"I've just got some questions about the island."

"Are you writing a book?" Kurt asked suddenly.

My initial instinct was to deny, but I saw that he was kind of excited by the idea. "I'm just taking notes right now," I demurred.

"Cool."

"Would you tell him about me?"

He shrugged an assent, then looked down at Binkster who, fresh from a lengthy nap, was stretching her back legs as she came through the door to the deck. She trotted over to give Kurt a sniff. Kurt patted her then looked up at me with a huge smile. He tickled Binks' ears and cooed at her and she circled between his legs. I get why pedophiles use puppies as a way to lure children to them. Sick brains can still see what works. Binks was my good-will ambassador. I'd just shot up a dozen points in Kurt's biased teen eyes.

"I'll tell him," he said, to which Binks licked the back of his hand.

The television report that night was full of speculation about Bobby Reynolds' murder. I wonder sometimes where these reporters get off. I mean, sheesh. Look closely and it appears they're salivating.

But I learned a few things. The police had searched the island and found nothing to show that Bobby had been killed there. If there had been any physical evidence, however, it could have been washed away by the rain. Not that anyone was saying Cotton or Heather had anything to do with hiding or killing Bobby. Nossirree ... Don't want any lawsuits, thank you very much. The authorities were continuing their investigation into whoever killed Bobby, but were being mum about any leads. There was some discussion about where Bobby could have been

all these years, speculation on the part of the reporters, and quite
a few shots of the island from the bridge, but nothing more concrete than what Tomas Lopez had indicated: Bobby's body had
freed itself from whatever had weighted it down. There was an
abrasion near his temple which appeared to have happened prior
to his body being in the water. More speculation on what that
meant, but from my point of view Bobby had been murdered. It
didn't matter whether he was struck on the head or drowned.
Someone had done it deliberately.

Whoever that someone might be was something to think
about. Cotton? Would he kill his own son? For all the pain he'd
caused, the embarrassment, the incredible disappointment? Or
Heather? To clear out the competition for Cotton's estate? With
Bobby gone would she inherit? Or . . . Tess? My mind shied from
this one. I was no huge fan of Tess but I sensed in her a mother
bear's need to protect her cub. She'd wanted to find Bobby alive.
And yes, possibly to insure her own route to the Reynolds
money. But more probably just because she loved her son. Loved
him fiercely. In an almost scary way, if my impressions were anything to go by. Overmothering did more harm than good, as far as
I could see.

Or was there someone else who would want Bobby dead?
Surely his wife's family hated him for what he'd done. And yes,
they were deeply devout people, but hadn't more wars been
started in the name of religion than any other cause? Wasn't there
something in the Bible about an eye for an eye?

I thought of Murphy suddenly, of his contention that Cotton
wanted to leave everything to him. But Murphy didn't want any
part of the money. That wasn't playacting on his part. He was destroyed over Bobby's death, as he was destroyed about finally realizing Bobby had cold-bloodedly murdered his family. Again, I
was relieved to take Murphy off the list. I'd only added him because I wanted to think I was professional enough to include
people I cared about. Who was I kidding? Professional? My emotions were all over the place when it came to Murphy. I wanted to

just not be attracted to him. How much simpler my life would be!

But back to Bobby Reynolds . . . Was there some other motive, somewhere? Something I was missing?

"Real estate," I said thoughtfully.

Every agent around wanted the island. Craig Cuddahy had gotten into a fistfight with Cotton. Yes, it was over his comments about Bobby and how Cotton needed to move on. But with Cuddahy, real estate was the underlying drive. He wanted to develop the island. Had Bobby somehow gotten in the way of that? Cuddahy had been in town weeks before the benefit. More than enough time for something to happen that would . . . Oh, shit. My mind leaped wildly ahead. Maybe Craig Cuddahy had actually *seen* Bobby, on the island or someplace else. And Cuddahy couldn't have Bobby, the heir apparent, gumming up his plans. No way. Much easier to dispose of Bobby Reynolds once and for all than have the specter of his reappearance hanging over everyone. Then with Bobby disposed of, Cuddahy could put the full court press on Cotton to sell.

I dialed Dwayne's cell as fast as I could, reaching his voice mail. Lucky for me, I didn't just blurt out all my theories—although I really, really wanted to—which later saved me the embarrassment of wishing I could swallow my words. One thing about Dwayne: he hates snap judgments, opinions and theories. "Just do the work" is his motto. I know this about him, but I still want to be his "A" student.

Thwarted, I wrote down my ideas on a scratch pad, circling them in different colors: green for Tess, blue for Heather, yellow for Cotton, red for Murphy, black for the real estate contingency which included Craig Cuddahy, Paula Shepherd and Brad Gilles. Also, Lorraine Bluebell, but only because I wanted to remind myself to call her again. She'd be a perfect source for information on current real estate goings-on in and around Lake Chinook.

I was admiring my color chart when a loose end popped into my head. Owen Bradbury, Bobby's half-brother. How did he fit in? I could go to the Pisces Pub and learn something from his friends. Friday night would be a perfect time.

I gotta say, it's interesting what I can come up with to fill my time. I was off this job. There was no more money in it. My only satisfaction was coming from my insane pleasure in continuing.

What do you want, Jane?

I searched the corners of my own psyche, digging for the source of my interest. A niggling and painful realization surfaced reluctantly in my brain.

You're doing this for Murphy. To make him see how smart you are. To make him want you. To make him not ask—but *beg*—you to come back to Santa Fe with him. To show him how exceptional you are. How much he threw away when he stopped loving, caring or even thinking about you.

I put my color chart away.

Self-realization is a bitch.

Chapter
Thirteen

I went to Bobby's memorial service alone, entering the domed room of the Pegtree Center with an already large group of attendees whose swivel-headed eagerness spoke of desire to gawk rather than show their respects. I'd half-hoped Murphy would call and ask me to join him, but he wasn't over being angry with me. I should know better, but I don't. Under "glutton for punishment," see Jane Kelly's photo.

I'd almost bagged out entirely as I had no wish to stir up Cotton, Heather, Tess or anyone else. But I'd felt that was the chicken's way out, so I'd thrown on my black skirt and a short-sleeved black top out of some kind of polyester material that caused you to sweat as soon as it touched your flesh. But it looked good, so here I was. I'd even managed a pair of strappy black sandals I'd pulled from the back of my closet. They were old enough to give me pause, but they were broken in and the only thing besides my new flip-flops that was reasonable. My appearance, I decided, was okay.

The crowd was large and the room was hot. People fanned themselves with the service programs. I realized with a distinct shock that Cotton wasn't there. I realized with a second shock that Bobby's wife's family was. Laura's mother and father and several of her brothers and sisters were seated on the opposite side of the aisle from the Reynolds/Bradbury contingent. They sat in a clan in silence, their faces collectively turned slightly upward. I couldn't see their expressions from my angle at the back of the room, but I imagined they were imploring the heavens for help and guidance. I glanced at the ceiling myself, feeling suffocated and sad.

Murphy sat next to Heather who was studiously avoiding looking at Tess, who shouldered her way to the first row. Next to Tess was a man in his thirties with light brown hair and broad shoulders. An image of Bobby flitted across my mind before I realized I was probably looking at the back of Owen Bradbury's head. He turned at precisely that moment to say something to his mom and I saw his face in profile. Nope. He didn't look like Bobby . . . well, sort of . . . maybe. As I watched, Tess momentarily rested her head on his shoulder.

The minister led us all in a short prayer. I listened from a self-induced stupor, my gaze touching on Murphy, then over the congregation, then back again. Platitudes about Bobby, about his brief time on earth and how his life was unfinished came at me like waves, breaking over my forced detachment. I glanced at Laura's family and felt a fresh surge of anger toward Bobby that receded as quickly as it rose. Bobby was gone. They were all gone.

The whole thing was over so suddenly that I started. I'd possibly fallen asleep. The somnolence and heat weren't helping. I hurried outside ahead of the crowd into blistering sunshine and headed for my Volvo. No one tried to stop me, but then they were still all saying good-bye and whispering their sympathies. Who was I kidding anyway? I wasn't part of this group. I was *persona non grata*.

"Jane . . ." I recognized the voice and turned to find Murphy, sober and looking more miserable than any human had a right to. He was halfway to my car. "Cotton's in the hospital. Laurel Park. All of this has punched him in the gut. His heart's weak."

And broken, I thought. "I'm sorry."

"He wants to see you."

I stared at him. "Me? Are you kidding? Why?"

"He's not still mad," Murphy assured me. "I'm sorry I told him about you working for Tess. I was angry, but I should have known better."

"Well, I don't know why he wants to see me. I don't want to stir him up. I think it's better if I stay away."

Murphy looked off toward the horizon. "It's not your fault or anyone else's that Bobby's gone. Cotton just flew off the handle because he's upset about everything. He also knows Tess would have done anything for Bobby, so if she hired you it was just to help." His blue gaze turned to me. "If anyone's to blame, it's me. I screwed up, Jane. Just made things worse for you."

"Fuggedaboudit," I said lightly.

"I'll go with you to the hospital."

"Uh, no." That didn't sound like a good idea.

"He's afraid he's dying and he wants to make it right with everybody."

"If I'm going, I'm going by myself."

Murphy shook his head. "I don't want it to be such a task. I'll be with you."

"Is he dying?" I asked.

Murphy hesitated. I got the feeling he didn't want to go there. Finally, he said tersely, "Yes."

"Imminently?"

"I didn't want Bobby dead," Murphy responded, looking around as if for support. "But I thought it would be a relief to Cotton. It's been just the opposite. I really don't know how long he's got."

I didn't want to see Cotton, but if I did, I really didn't want Murphy with me. But reading between the lines I felt like I'd better make tracks to see Cotton Reynolds or it might be too late.

People were surging around us, commiserating. Heather, in a dark blue suit whose short skirt showed off her shapely legs, glanced around anxiously. I could see Murphy was torn. He didn't want to deal with Heather right now, but he didn't feel he could just leave her. I mimed that I would call him later. Murphy nodded. He touched my shoulder gently before moving in Heather's direction. I could feel the extra heat from his fingers long after I was on the road.

I drove directly to Laurel Park Hospital and asked for Cotton Reynolds' room. Might as well get this over with. There was a brief moment of confusion until I corrected myself and asked for Clement Reynolds. The only way I'd pulled that out was because I'd read it in the newspapers recently. I was directed to his floor and I rode up the elevator, half-inclined to just bolt. I'm not good at this stuff. I have an urge to sing or whistle in hospitals and churches that defies explanation.

Cotton's door was slightly ajar and I pushed it inward with trepidation. He lay on a bed with his face turned toward the window. Hearing my approach, he turned my way. Another distinct shock. He looked like he'd aged ten years since the last time I'd seen him.

"Jane Kelly," he greeted me in a hoarse voice.

I nodded. "Murphy said you wanted to see me."

Ill as he was, he caught my pique. "I sicced the police on you."

"Tomas Lopez."

Cotton held up a hand. "Murphy told me you were working for Tess. Probably said some things I shouldn't have. I was mad at Tess, too."

"I saw her at Bobby's memorial service."

A shadow passed over his eyes. "Heather was there."

It wasn't a question, but it sounded like one so I nodded.

"Bobby was my son. And I'm going to miss him."

His voice had grown more raspy with each word and when he fumbled for his plastic cup of water, I quickly handed it to him. It was an effort for him to place the straw between his lips, but he managed to take a few sips before I took the cup away.

"Maybe I should come back another time," I suggested uneasily.

"I want to tell you something."

"Okay." I shifted my weight, growing more uncomfortable by the minute.

"You told me you liked Bobby."

My heart sank. I wasn't sure where this was going, but I'd definitely stretched the truth when I'd blurted that out. "We only met a couple of times."

"Murphy thinks a lot of you."

"Yeah . . . well . . . we're friends," I said lamely.

"I want you to know that Bobby was only missing a little while. I know Tess hired you to find him."

"Bobby was missing for four years," I reminded cautiously.

Cotton looked down at the tops of his hands. Blue veins pushed upward against pale skin. He stared at them as if they held the answers, then fisted them. "Tess knew where Bobby was until a few weeks ago. She gave him money. She kept him going."

"How do you know this?"

"I just know."'

A chill slid down my back at the pointed look he gave me. He'd seen Bobby. I was almost certain of it.

"Tess has funded him since the moment he called her from Tillamook. I think he told her to come get him long before he murdered them. She didn't know why he wanted her to come. She just went. And she picked him up and took him somewhere. I don't know. To a bus, maybe. I don't know when he told her the truth . . . maybe still denies everything. But she's the one who's hidden him."

"This sounds like conjecture." I wasn't sure what I was hearing, but I didn't think it was meant for my ears.

"Up until a few weeks ago there was an intermediary who collected the money and got it to him. I don't know who that was, and I don't know where Bobby was. He never said and I didn't ask."

"You spoke with Bobby?" The hairs on my arms lifted. Dimly I realized this was some kind of deathbed confession whether Cotton died or not. But what was I supposed to do with this information? Go to Tomas Lopez? Viscerally I realized how much I did not want to be involved.

"The police asked me the same thing. I'll tell you what I told them: no." Cotton inhaled deeply several times. His pallor was gray. "But I've talked to Tess a few times. Told her what I know. She's screamed and screamed at me. Thinks I hate Bobby and her. Told me I was a crazy old man. But I know what I know. She loved him almost more than I did, if that's possible."

He closed his eyes on these last words. A lump filled my throat. I said nothing. I glanced behind me, hoping against hope someone was eavesdropping. I didn't want this burden. The room was close and my ears began to hear a distant humming sound. Not a good sign.

"Tess knows how to save money," he said at length, never opening his eyes. "She found ways to get her hands on it when we were married and hide it away. I don't know how much she has, but it's more than enough. It's somewhere outside the banks, outside the government. She didn't use it on that artsy-fartsy gallery. Got loans for that. No, this money was meant for herself. She planned to leave me years before she did it. Then she soaked me good in the divorce." He smiled ruefully. "But I always knew about the money."

"You're saying she used that money for Bobby?"

"Yessirree. She didn't mean to, but after Bobby did what he did . . . ." He trailed off.

"Do you have proof?" I asked, already knowing the answer.

"'Course not. But believe me, I'm not wrong. Bobby lived under an assumed name all this time and Tess funded him. He coulda probably kept it up his whole life, but Bobby got bored." He looked at me through reddened eyes. "I don't think he wanted that small of a life, y'know?"

I wasn't sure I did. "You mean . . . a restricted life?"

"The life of somebody else. Somebody who didn't matter. Just years of living, y'know? Years and years of living and nothing happening."

Mollycoddled. Dwayne's word came back to me. Bobby had been the best athlete, the doted-on son, the heir apparent, the only one who mattered. Would he be able to lead a "small" life, so to speak?

"What happened to him?" I asked softly. "Do you know?"

"Bobby was always no good. You could give him whatever he wanted and he just wanted more. He married that gal to get back at me. I told him she was too religious and that he'd regret it. I warned him, but whatever I said just made him do it all the more." He stirred restlessly. "I never thought he'd do what he did, though. Murphy didn't think so, either."

Why are you telling me this? "Maybe Murphy's the one you should be talking to."

Cotton acted like he didn't hear me. Maybe he didn't. "I went to a lawyer to change my will, but I couldn't make myself."

So, Jerome Neusmeyer had told the truth. I thought about asking, "What are you going to do now?" but there was no need as Cotton, once started, wasn't about to stop.

"He was the disappointment of my life and I couldn't cut him out of my will. What do you think of that?" He didn't wait for an answer. "I told Heather I wasn't going to change my will and she called me all sorts of names. She's mad at the world right now." He grimaced. "Did she wear that blue suit? She's wanted an occasion to wear it for a while now."

"Midnight blue?"

He almost laughed. "That's the one. Don't know why I married her. Was seeing somebody else but it felt like Tess all over again. Thought Heather might give me some fun. Maybe she did, in the beginning."

She married you for your money. The thought must have shown on my face because Cotton said, "I'm not a fool, y'know. But it's not her fault about Bobby. He was spoiled rotten. I never knew how true those words could be. Tess and I just weren't good parents. We never said no, or stop, or you can't. People are stupid who think you don't have to parent your kid. If you don't parent them, they don't grow up."

His voice had softened with each syllable. I had to move closer to his bedside to hear him. A part of me wanted to stop him, but another part knew he needed to get this out. It was weird that he'd chosen me. I wished Murphy could be standing here instead. I probably should have waited for him. But then again maybe he was too close a friend. A confession is easier to a virtual stranger.

"If you want answers, talk to Tess," he said after a long time. His chest rose and fell unevenly, as if it were an effort to breathe.

"I'm not working for her anymore."

"You want to know." He'd started to wheeze.

"I think it's up to the authorities now."

"No!" That came out as a harsh whisper. "They don't give a damn about him. Talk to Tess. She knows him."

I felt like wringing my hands. I didn't want to add to his anguish, but some things needed to be said. "You should know that she intimated you were the one supporting Bobby, not the other way around."

"We both wanted to help him."

I licked my lips. They were dry as sand. "Bobby came to you for help? He was on the island?"

Cotton's eyes met mine. Something flickered in their depths and for a moment I thought he was going to answer me. The blood sang through my ears. I suddenly didn't want to know. Didn't want information that I should tell the authorities.

A nurse whisked into the room before Cotton could decide. "You need to leave, Miss," she stated flatly.

"Not yet . . ." Cotton's voice was nearly inaudible.

"Oh, yes," she said, shooing her hands at me. I held my ground and she glared at me, letting me know I should never have pushed it with one of her patients.

But Cotton clearly didn't want me to go. This was his confession and though I didn't want to be the recipient, it was too late to change the circumstances. "Just a few more minutes?"

"Not a chance. Mr. Reynolds needs rest." She wedged herself between us. She was tall and tough and looked like she might want to arm wrestle me. I was pretty sure I'd lose. She was also in my personal space. I had a mental picture of what we looked like, standing toe-to-toe, Nurse Ratched in white, myself all in black. Yeah. A skirmish here would not look good on my permanent record.

"Go," she ordered.

I gave her a military salute and backed into the hallway, pissed. I nearly bumped into a body which had moved to the doorway. Twisting quickly, an apology forming on my lips, I realized I was staring into the eyes of Laura's father, Bobby's father-in-law.

"Oh, hi," I said lamely. I felt like I'd been caught in some nefarious act.

"Is that Clement Reynolds' room?" he asked politely.

Behind him was Laura's mother. She had soft, liquid brown eyes and doughy skin. Both she and her husband had gray hair and neither was using Grecian Formula 44. She wore a gray dress with black flocking in the shape of tiny rosebuds. He wore a gray suit. Everything was gray.

"Uh, yes," I said.

"Are you a friend of the family?" The tiny voice came from Laura's mother.

"Sort of." I felt completely out of place with them. "I'm a friend of Tim Murphy?"

She blinked. "Oh, yes. Our daughter knew him in high school. She called him by his last name, I think."

"Yes. He goes by Murphy."

"I'm George Monroe and this is my wife, Ruth."

"Jane Kelly."

We shook hands all around. I couldn't have felt more awkward. It seemed as if we were on opposite sides of a battle. I wanted to stand up and shout that I thought Bobby's actions were beyond reprehensible, but instead I stood by with a sickly smile.

"Mr. Reynolds called us," George revealed. "He asked to see us." He sounded nonplussed. I couldn't blame him. "We said we would see him at the memorial service, but we learned he was in the hospital."

Nurse Ratched stepped from the room and scowled at the lot of us. "No visitors."

"Is there a better time to see him? Somewhere we could wait?" Ruth asked.

"Honey, you're going to be waiting a long time. Mr. Reynolds needs a lot of rest. He won't be seeing anyone else today." She made it sound like *or maybe ever.*

"Is there a cafeteria?"

The nurse eyed Ruth impatiently. "First floor. All the way down the hall to your right. But you'd be better off waiting at home."

George touched Ruth's arm and they headed toward the elevator. I didn't immediately leave as the coward in me didn't want to struggle with more small talk. I wondered what Cotton was planning to tell them.

"You're not seeing him, either," Nurse Ratched told me in a singsong voice. She made little walking motions with her index and middle fingers.

I had no intention of bothering Cotton any further, but she was really getting under my skin. I seriously thought about giving her some finger language of my own. Instead I looked at my watch and said, "Time for my assault weapon class," and headed for the elevators.

On the way home I stopped in at Mook's Ice Creamery, a local ice cream parlor and burger joint, and ordered a Burger-Jack, the usual hamburger with avocado and jack cheese. I can tolerate a certain amount of dairy products per day, but the cheese would be my limit. If I wanted ice cream I was going to have to buy some of those lactaid-type pills and personally I find medication just too much trouble sometimes.

I powered through my burger, feeling both sorry for myself and a little bit smug. I was sorry that I now had a moral dilemma of sorts. Basically Cotton had pointed the finger at Tess and blamed her for aiding and abetting her son, a suspected murderer. It was hearsay, as far as I could tell, but the authorities don't give a damn about that. They want information, period. It's up to the lawyers to decide what matters and what doesn't in a criminal case. So, what did that mean about my obligations?

But I was feeling smug because of that very same thing: I had information that others would die for. I could picture the slavering reporters climbing all over one another for the tidbits Cotton had thrown my way. If I wanted to be a minor celebrity, this was my chance.

Then again, Tess had been my client, of sorts, and she still believed we were in business together, no matter what I had told Tomas Lopez. Should I call Lopez? His card was still on my television set.

And why did the idea of telling him make me feel like such a rat?

Because I have a basic distrust of authority. Anyone with the right to tell me what to do just kind of pisses me off. Nurse Ratched, a case in point.

My cell phone started singing. I glanced at the LCD. Murphy. "Damn."

"You went to see Cotton," he said in disbelief as soon as I answered.

"I know you said you wanted to go, but—"

"What the hell are you doing?" His voice rose. "He's sick! And this whole situation is a goddamn circus. All the reporters and police."

"You told me he wanted to see me," I reminded him hotly. "It wasn't the other way around."

"The guy's on his deathbed."

"I don't think I'm the bad guy here!" My own voice started sliding upward.

"I just want to—keep things sane."

"Well, Laura's family was in the hallway, waiting for a chance to talk to him. Nurse Ratched threw me out, but he was okay when I left him."

"Laura's family?"

"Yeah, George and Ruth. Nice people. Cotton had something he wanted to tell them."

"About Bobby?" Murphy was stunned.

". . . About forgiveness, I think," I said, struggling a bit. "Cotton was practically confessing to me that he'd helped Bobby, or that Tess had, or that they both had. I can believe he wants to apologize to the Monroes. I don't know if they've ever really talked. Why would they?"

"They were in the hall?"

"They're probably in the cafeteria now. Why? Do you want to see them? They remember you."

"Shit . . ." He sounded suddenly exhausted.

"Seeing them just makes it all so real," I said.

"It is real. And Jane, it feels like you're trying to prove something at Cotton's expense."

"What do you mean?" His words wounded me in a way I couldn't immediately define.

"Just . . . leave it alone."

I was infuriated. "You told me to go see him," I repeated. I'd be damned if I was going to apologize for doing what he'd told me to do.

"I know, but Cotton's too sick. Heather's on her way to see him."

"Good luck getting past the watchdog."

"She's family."

I didn't want to argue with him further. None of this was my fault and I was good and mad that Murphy was acting like it was. I knew he was feeling the strain, but I didn't like being anybody's scapegoat, no matter what. We hung up in a kind of combative silence. Santa Fe was looking farther and farther away.

I returned home to Binkster who acted as if I were starving her. By her shape, it was pretty clear this was not the case, but I jiggled some doggie kibbles into her bowl and watched her ravenously chomp through them at record pace. I retrieved the bowl before she could make it hop around and gouge my cabinets some more. I probably should tell Ogilvy about the dog's mishap, but I didn't want to get into the fact that I had a pet. I'm sure a new deposit would be slapped on me. Hey, I'd paid the guy my August rent. Maybe I'd bring it up in September.

I spent the rest of the week either debating on what to do or process serving. No serious incidents to report other than my car got keyed. I looked at the mean, little stripe waving along the driver's door and gritted my teeth. I hadn't stopped by Dwayne's for more work because I'd been on the fence about the whole damn job. However, I was about ready to chuck this supposed occupation once and for all.

On Friday I put a call into Tess who didn't pick up. This was about the third time I'd phoned, so I called Marta next, and was delayed by the snotty receptionist just long enough to make me want to rip my hair out. When Marta finally came on the line, she was abrupt, "I haven't talked to Tess in days. I can't reach her. You know where she is?"

"I was going to ask you the same thing. You think she's missing?"

"She's trying to avoid the press." Marta sounded annoyed.

Or maybe the authorities?

I told Marta I'd let her know if I talked to Tess. With time on my hands I decided to check in with Dwayne. Might as well see what he had for me. I left Binks with fresh water and more kibbles that she scarfed down in a snorting rush.

I put on my newly washed black capris, a dark green tank top and my chewed Nikes, then snapped my hair into its ubiquitous ponytail. I didn't know what Dwayne had in store for me but I was going to try to be ready for anything.

Knocking on his front door, I glanced casually at his landscaping. The roadside of the cabana was basically a cement drive surrounded by gravel for extra parking and a strip of earth as dry and bare as a bone. Possibly Dwayne was planning on planting something, but he struck me more as the hammer, nails and wood type rather than a landscaper. In that we were sympatico.

The door flew open and I beheld a nymphet. She was about fourteen with no hips to speak of, a set of budding breasts worn behind an extremely sheer tank top and a pair of teensy, weensy little denim cutoffs that tapered to skinny legs. Her hair was streaky blond, her eyes blue and rimmed with smoky eyeshadow and thick, black mascara, and the scowl on her face could have turned Medusa to stone.

"Uh-huh?" she greeted me, as if I were hugely intruding on her space. I caught the scent of her perfume and realized I'd just met Dwayne's mystery woman.

Either he was a sexual pervert/predator or there was more to the story. Remembering his amusement when I'd demanded to know who his houseguest was, I wondered what the connection was. "Is Dwayne here?"

"No." She folded her arms under her breasts and looked up at me sulkily. She was throwing out all the sexual signals she could think of. The result of too much television, R-rated movies and suggestive magazines, I was sure. She made me instantly tired.

I'm not the most patient person on earth. Through smiling teeth, I asked, "Do you know where he is, and when he'll be back?"

"How do you know him?" she demanded.

"He's a friend."

"Yeah?" A wealth of meaning there.

"Yeah."

I wanted to wring her little neck. It was all I could do not to react to her insolence in the way she probably expected. Instead I simply reminded myself that in a couple of years her hips would grow, her face might break out, her thighs would thicken, and cellulite would find her. She would realize that the junior-high body was a lie.

"Do you mind if I come in and wait?" I asked, then practically shouldered her out of the way.

"Do you work out?" she asked.

Was this a good question, or a bad question? "Why?"

"Your ass is pretty good for someone your age."

Ass. Gee, how sweet. "Thanks."

"Oh," she said, her face lighting with realization. "You're the one Uncle Dwayne was telling me about. You like work with him, or something." I nodded an acknowledgment. "Do you work on cases and stuff? Like . . ." She screwed up her face in concentration. "Murders and suicides and terrorists?"

"Did Uncle Dwayne say where he was going?"

"Oh, just to the store. We're out of nutrition bars. Everything in his refrigerator is gross." She shuddered.

On this I might have agreed. I suspected the inside of Dwayne's refrigerator was scarier than my own, for different reasons. "How long are you visiting here?" I asked, pretending I knew more than I did.

"Oh, God, I was in this stupid acting class this summer. My mom thought it would be so great, but I want to go to Hollywood. These stupid little theater classes are just dumb. Two weeks and all we did was act like morons with these dumb acting games. And then we put on this dumb show. I'm leaving tomorrow."

"Where to?"

"Home. Seattle."

My heart sank. Seattle wasn't near far enough away. Three to four hours depending on how seriously you broke the speed limit on I-5. "It was nice of Uncle Dwayne to have you stay with him."

"Yeah . . . well . . . his boat's really crappy." She lifted a shoulder dismissively toward the back of the house. I could see the tail end of his red and white boat through the opened sliding glass door. "I like those Master Crafts," she said. "With the skiing tower. I want to wake-board. The tower gives you a better angle for jumping over the wakes." Her face clouded. "But Seattle's crappy, too. It's shitty weather there practically all the time. Do you know we have one of the highest suicide rates in the country? How long have you been doing this?"

"Working with Dwayne?" I guessed.

"Uh-huh."

"Just getting started."

"Do you like him?" She eyed me closely. "Do you think he's

sexy? I think he's sexy. I mean he's my uncle and lots older and stuff, but I could see where someone your age would think he's sexy."

It was all I could do not to point out that thirty wasn't exactly geriatric. "He's got a nice ass," I responded.

"Y'think? I'm not sure there's enough of it. I like a little more than that flat cowboy thing."

I was trying to think of a comeback for this when I heard Dwayne's truck rattle into the carport. My little friend skipped toward the door, greeting him with a bright smile and a little swish of her hips. I was gratified to see he barely noticed her. "Oh, so you met Tracy," Dwayne said, hauling a couple bags of groceries inside. I could see he was trying not to break out into a big *hardy, har, har*. He really felt he'd pulled one over on me.

"We've been discussing your ass," I said.

"Oh, yeah?" Dwayne looked surprised, then half-twisted around as if to get a look at it.

"It's the cutest!" Tracy gushed. She made a point of not meeting my eyes.

I wasn't exactly sure what Tracy's game was, but I was getting that radar that said: Alert! Alert! Manipulative female on the premises. There are two kinds of females in my book: the good and the bad. The good are normal, self-aware and I could spend hours in their company. The bad are screwed up, full of insecurity and a really lethal self-doubt that makes them machines of destruction, both to themselves and others. A few moments with the latter and I'm ready to consider a gender change.

It was a bitch that she was Dwayne's niece. She was high-powered trouble.

Tracy started babbling to Dwayne about all the things important to her. I realized she was about to start high school and she seemed to think she had some say about where that might be, Seattle or . . . someplace else. I fervently hoped Lake Chinook wasn't on her list. If so, it would be *hasta la vista* baby to me working for Dwayne. I could see Dwayne tune out. A veil seemed to drop over his eyes.

"What's so funny?" he suddenly asked me.

I wiped the satisfied smile from my face. You can't whine to a man—any man, unless maybe a gay man because he at least understands—about another female, especially if she's related to him, because it'll boomerang back on you. They don't get it. They either don't want to, or they can't. I said earnestly, "I want to talk to you about the Reynolds case."

"What case? Didn't you get paid in full?"

"Yeah. But it's . . . not over."

"The fat lady's sung, Jane."

I really, really, really didn't want to talk about this in front of Tracy. Though she was pretending hard not to listen, she had that tense, avid body language that said she was soaking in every syllable. Luckily, Dwayne seemed to realize this and said, "What time do you have to be back after lunch?"

"I'm not going back. That class is stupid."

"You're going back, darlin'," he said with quiet authority. "It's your last day. Your mom's coming for the performance."

"Performance," she sneered. "We stand around acting like morons. Making noises and jumping around."

"What time?"

"I'm not going Uncle Dwayne! What? Are you deaf?"

Now, Dwayne rarely gets angry. I don't think I've ever seen him be more than mildly irritated. But I could see his temper rise. Though he looked the same, there was a quiet menace building inside him that I wanted to cheer for.

"I'm not going," she said, settling into a whine. "Don't make me," she added tearily.

"I'll drive you," he said, and opened the door for her to step outside and get in his truck.

Tracy thought about defying him. Her body was rigid with fury. My being there wasn't helping the situation, though I have to admit I was enjoying myself thoroughly. If I'd had a beer and some jalapeno chips, I'd be settling down for a damn good time. Who cared about her upcoming performance? This one was four-star.

She flounced out toward Dwayne's truck.

"Nice girl," I said.

"She's a goddamn pain in the ass, and you don't know the half of it." He shook his head as if to rid himself of scary parental-type thoughts and said, "I've got a little thing I want you to do for me."

"A little thing."

"When I come back I'll tell ya all about it. What about the Reynolds gig? You wrapped that up?"

Though I'd managed to keep from blurting out my unsupported theories, I'd told Dwayne about my interview with Cotton and all he'd intimated about Tess and himself and their involvement with Bobby. Dwayne had been noncommital. In fact, at the time I'd wondered if he'd been even listening. Now, I saw what his distraction had been and she was currently in his pickup, leaning on the horn.

"Fuck," he said succinctly, heading outside. I heard his truck thrash to a start and grind gears up the road. Lake Chinook's community center, the Chinook Center for the Performing Arts, (which is lofty in name only) is only a stone's throw from his cabana, so I decided to step onto his newly sealed dock and enjoy a few moments to myself.

I turned my face into a hot little breeze. At least here on the water it wasn't as beastly as it was a few blocks inland. I could use a beer. Or a glass of wine, the glass so chilled it was sweating.

My cell phone broke into my thoughts. It was Murphy. "Cotton died at two o'clock this afternoon," was his terse report.

Chapter Fourteen

Dwayne returned from dropping Tracy at her class but I couldn't hear anything he had to say. Since Murphy's call, my ears were blocked. I could only hear my heartbeat and I was faintly conscious of the sun's heat on my exposed skin.

Dwayne gave me a hard look in the eyes, then hauled me from the dock to his couch where he plopped me down with rather more force than necessary, I felt. Through a distorted lens I watched him slip off my sandals and when he handed me a tumbler with a half-inch of amber liquid swirling in the bottom, I shook my head. He insisted, holding the glass to my lips. I complied, feeling the liquor's scorch all the way down my throat. Sputtering and gasping, I came half out of the chair. Jesus. People drink this stuff for entertainment?

Dwayne's voice returned. "What happened?" he demanded tersely.

I cleared my throat. "Cotton . . . died."

"Drink some more."

"No."

"Drink it all."

I felt a moment of rebellion, but the look in Dwayne's eyes said he was ready for battle. Grudgingly I took another swallow. Tears burned my eyes and the bourbon flamed all the way down to my stomach. Dwayne's piercing examination of me was unnerving. "Stop looking at me," I ordered.

He shook his head. "You got to get a lot tougher."

"*I've* got to get tougher? Bobby's dead, and now Cotton's dead. I think I deserve an emotional moment."

"You told me Cotton was in the hospital and that he made some half-hearted deathbed confession to you."

"Yeah. So?" I was being stubborn but I didn't care.

"You thought he was pretty sick . . . that he might not make it."

"I know that, but it's still a big shock."

"I don't see why," he said maddeningly.

I wanted to retaliate with "you wouldn't" but decided things would only deteriorate from there. "Being sick doesn't mean you're at death's door."

Luckily, Dwayne didn't point out I was arguing against everything I'd already said. "You're getting some color back," he observed.

I did feel better. The medicinal properties of 80 proof. "I've got to talk to Tess," I said. I rose from the chair but my legs were rubbery. Dwayne put a finger at my sternum and gave a teensy push. I sank back as if made of wax. Annoyed, I glared at him.

"I thought you were coming over here for more work."

"I'm too *weak* for this business."

"Why are you talking to Tess?"

"Geez, Dwayne. I don't know. Maybe because her ex-husband just died."

"Is she a personal friend now?"

He had a point but I didn't want to hear it. I wanted to talk to Tess for a variety of reasons, all selfish. This probably wasn't the time for me to call. Wherever she was, she was going to be dealing with the upheaval of Cotton's death, right on the heels of Bobby's.

"Are you still working on that insurance scam?" I asked, trying to put my mind on something else besides the Reynolds.

"Nope, it's finished. Turned over the information I had to the authorities." A faint smile of satisfaction crossed his face. "They're done with their game for good. Headed for jail. The derelicts aren't being tortured anymore. Vicious bastards."

"Good." I was glad he'd helped bring about justice. I really wished I could jump on board wholeheartedly, embracing something else. "What's the little thing you wanted me to do?"

"Are you hungry?" he asked.

I lifted my brows. "You have some food around here?"

He laughed. "No. Let's walk over to the village. I'll fill you in there."

It took a lot for me to get my legs in gear and walk with Dwayne to a little soup and sandwich shop about five blocks from his place and near the new shopping center known as Lakeview Village. The village is a block of two-story buildings centered around a parking structure hidden in its center. The fronts of the stores face the street and the structure is designed to look as if the four corners are four different buildings, the architecture ranging from Swiss chalet to northwest lodge.

Dottie's wasn't actually in the village; it was across the street in a glass and brick facade building from the sixties that is bound to be torn down, rebuilt and house something new. It used to be Dottie's Diner, but it sold out to one of those places where you take a plastic-laminated sheet with a checklist and mark off what you want on your sandwich and/or salad with a wax pen. The new owners shortened the name, and the food's actually better now.

I chose a tuna sandwich with sweet pickles, lettuce, onions and tomatoes. Dwayne was strictly roast beef with lots of horseradish. He had a beer and I worked on a diet cola. More restorative properties. While we munched he quizzed me further about my hospital visit with Cotton. I thought of the last time I'd seen the man and it made it hard to swallow.

Dwayne eyed the quarter of my sandwich I'd left on my plate. "Gonna finish that, darlin'?"

"Yes." I chomped it down just to make a point. I wasn't weak. I was tough. I was not a hatchery fish.

He pushed his plate aside and rested his arms on the table. I could tell he was thinking about what he was going to say which was unusual because with me, Dwayne is blunt to the point of infuriating.

"What?" I asked.

"I've got a situation."

"What kind of situation?"

"My sister Angela sent Tracy here to get her away from a bad crowd."

"How bad a crowd? She just left junior high. My experience is junior-high kids are all mean-spirited bitches, gawky nerds or obsessive jocks hoping to make the high school team. They're all bad."

"There's this older boy who was hanging around the school. He kept waiting around for Tracy when class got out. Started walking her home from school and she got home later and later."

"How much older?"

"Angela was vague on that. Then summer came and Angela thought it might all go away, but she's caught Tracy in some lies."

"Angela hasn't met this kid?"

Dwayne shook his head. "He stays just out of range, just out of sight. But Angela found a couple of joints in Tracy's backpack. Tracy swore it was some other kid's and she'd forgotten about them. Said she'd hidden them for a friend so that he didn't get in trouble, then she forgot about them. She claims she hasn't used the backpack since school. Maybe it's the truth, maybe not."

I thought of Tracy, the way she turned on for male attention. "Where's Tracy's father in all this?"

"A workaholic. He's never paid much attention to her." Dwayne grimaced. "However, my sister's made Tracy her life project. Every class, every opportunity, anything she wants. She's tried to be Tracy's best friend."

"Sounds like Tracy's rebelling."

"Tracy's always been interested in acting. She's been the center of attention all her life and intends to stay that way. So Angela sent her to this acting camp. I figured I could handle her for a couple of weeks." He shrugged. "It's been okay. But I saw a kid the other day, waiting outside the Chinook Center. Tracy came out, took one look at him and started to wave, then she saw me and ignored him. I asked about him, but she said he was just someone from class. He looks older."

I sighed. "Sounds like you want me to scope out the junior-high crowd." I'd expected Dwayne to give me a real job. I know, I know. All I've done is bitch and moan and wring my hands over the idea of becoming an information specialist, but that doesn't mean I don't want to hear how perfect I'd be for the job.

"I want you to go to the performance. See if he shows up."

"And if he does?"

"Try to gauge how much of a threat he is."

"Give me a ballpark on how much older you think he is."

"I didn't really get a good look at him. Eighteen or nineteen. He has Elvis sideburns."

"Ugh." I'm not a fan of facial hair. Watch just one guy leave half his meal within his beard's whorls and coils and it's over forever. "Whatever the case, he's way too old for Tracy." I tried to picture myself lurking in the background while Tracy and this mystery man sought to get together. "What about Angela? Is she going to the performance?"

"That's another problem." It was Dwayne's turn to sigh. "I told her not to freak out but she's just waiting to. She wants this kid arrested, even though, so far, there's no crime."

"But you both think he's followed a fourteen-year-old from Seattle to Lake Chinook."

Dwayne's expression was hard. "That's what Angela says. Anyway, Tracy's too young."

"And he has to know her age because he was hanging around the junior high."

"Yep."

I grimaced, not liking it. And there was the matter of the dope. If not his, then whose? I didn't want to say so, but I thought there was a whole lot more to the story than Tracy was giving out. Yes, she was only fourteen . . . going on thirty.

"Basically what you're telling me is that this is a personal matter," I said, balling up the remains of my sandwich wrap and tossing it in the trash. "You don't have any real work for me. You just want me to quit obsessing about the Reynolds case."

"I'm going to pay you, darlin'."

"Well, of course you are." Like that was ever an issue. "Okay, he's got Elvis sideburns. Anything else?"

"Pants that barely stay on. Attitude."

Sounded like some of my last few dates.

"Angela said she saw piercings. There's bound to be tattoos."

"So, I'll hang around the performance. See if this guy shows. Call you if I do. Anything else?"

"Try to keep my sister from making an ass out of herself. If she spots him, she'll go crazy."

I had a feeling Dwayne had turned this over to me simply because he didn't want to be involved. Who could blame him. *I* didn't want to be involved. But there was money to be earned.

I gave myself an internal check. I was over my shock. I just hadn't wanted to believe Cotton was really gone. It seemed so wrong. But maybe something like this, where I could focus on the fact that this guy was a baddie and needed to be removed from Tracy's life would be a form of therapy for me. No second-guessing. No wondering who was good and who wasn't. "Okay, I'll look for Elvis. I'll call you if I see him."

"If he shows, I'll follow him. I won't be far from the center."

"And when you find out where he goes . . . ?"

"I'm going to have a serious talk with the man." Dwayne faintly stressed the word *talk* and I was glad I wasn't the one he was gunning for.

"I'll do it on one condition: stop razzing me about the Reynolds case. I'm not looking for money on that one. I'm looking for answers."

"I prefer to look for both."

"Dwayne . . ." I warned.

He lifted his hands in surrender. "Go home and put something better on. Believe it or not, the women dress for these arty events."

"I don't have anything better." I wanted to be offended but just didn't have the energy.

"Buy something."

Like, oh, sure. I had disposable income enough to treat myself to a shopping spree. "I'll make sure I look the part."

It was Friday night, hot as Hades and I was wearing an aqua camisole over a black skirt short enough to see France, as they say. I'd twisted my hair into a clip and left a few tendrils down my neck. Sandals? Yes. I'd pulled out my trusty black, strappy ones. The camisole I'd bought a few months ago to go under a black jacket. More of a Cynthia look than a Jane Kelly. The price of it had made me gasp, especially since it was basically a thin piece of lingerie. But hey, it was what was in all the magazines, so I figured I had to pay to be on the cutting edge of fashion. Doesn't mean it didn't hurt.

Binkster watched me dress with a definite lack of interest. If I wasn't in the kitchen, hanging on the refrigerator door, wondering if food might somehow materialize, I wasn't nearly as exciting.

I expected Murphy to call back with more information, but when that didn't happen I phoned him—and ran into his voice mail. I left him a message, saying if he needed anything to call. After I hung up I was kind of pissed with myself. Had I sounded needy? God, I hoped not. We were doing that "are we or aren't we" dance about whether we were "together." I didn't want to screw things up.

I could picture him trying to comfort a wailing Heather, who I suspected was dividing her time between lusty grief and her all-purpose calculator, kept handy to tot up her potential inheritance. My cynical viewpoint couldn't be dislodged. Cotton had known she'd married him for his money. It wasn't anybody's secret.

Despite Dwayne's warning to back off, I tried Tess again to no avail. As I drove myself to the Chinook Center for the Performing Arts—a lofty title for a one-time elementary school with bad heating and the possibility of asbestos inside every acoustic tile—I called Cynthia. I was desperate for information. She answered in a bored tone. I could tell she was driving.

"Have you been to the Black Swan recently?" I asked. "I'm looking for Tess and she's M.I.A."

"I'm pretty sure Tess hasn't been to the gallery." Cynthia turned the radio down so she could pay closer attention. "What's going on?"

"No one seems to be able to turn her up. Maybe she'll surface when she hears about Cotton." I filled Cynthia in on the latest news.

"Death's haunting that family, huh? Wouldn't it be weird if Tess were gone, too?"

Her words stopped me. "Why do you say that?"

"No reason . . . I'd just love to have her gallery. If you find her, feel her out about selling."

"Yeah, right." I calmed down about Tess. She was lying low, that's all.

"I'm serious, Jane."

"Well, after we discuss her son's death and then her ex-husband's, I'll be sure to turn the conversation around to art."

"Just put it out there. That's all I'm saying."

"And if you should hear anything about her? From the people at the gallery? Give me a call."

I wondered about Tomas Lopez. His card was still at my bungalow, on the top of my television set, right where he'd left it. Now that Cotton was gone, should I reveal his theories about Tess to the authorities? My business with Tess was over, at least in my mind, but I felt this loyalty I couldn't quite shake.

The Chinook Center was covered with white lights—like Christmas in August, although it was always dressed this way, so to speak, with flashy bulbs surrounding every window casing, door and eave. I parked in the back lot and headed toward the rear entrance. Dwayne hadn't been kidding about the attire.

These people looked like they were ready to accept an Oscar. As classy as I looked, I was once again underdressed. Sheesh.

I bought a ticket—six dollars—and vowed to write up a report for Dwayne. He'd said clients love hard copy. Well, fine. I was going to bill him with the best of them.

My seat was to the back of the auditorium, one of about two hundred squeezed into a semicircle around a stage that was lower than the audience. I was lucky enough to be only one seat from the aisle. It was amazing there were so many people eager for an amateur performance.

The lights went down and then the acting coach, one Mr. Lemur, who wore a striped tie, let us all know that yes, it was in honor of the lemurs. Laughter and warm looks from the audience. I realized I was in a room full of parents, anticipating the entrance of their little Johnny or Amanda or Brian, budding actors and stars, one and all.

My eyes scanned the audience as the groups came out by age level with Mr. Lemur right in the midst of it, leaping around and clowning it up. The littlest kids sucked their thumbs and looked alarmed. Older ones tried to imitate him. He hammed it up mercilessly. It was the Mr. Lemur Show, folks.

There was an intermission. I headed to the ladies' room, then wandered around, eyeing the sea of soccer/stage moms. I considered which of the women could be Angela, Tracy's mother. I narrowed the list down to three attractive blondes. Dwayne's hair was darker than theirs but he had that sun and country manner that, though I suspected was largely an affectation, definitely worked for him. The three ladies I zeroed in on were athletic and wiry. One had a terrible braying laugh, so I nixed her immediately. Number two seemed sort of silent and brooding. If my pre-teen was as obnoxious as Tracy and was flirting with a nineteen-year-old bad ass, I might be that way myself. The third one seemed distracted. She opened her cell phone and spoke to someone about an upcoming gourmet club dinner. I settled on number two.

We all traipsed back into the auditorium but I hung back.

Maybe Angela was just paranoid and merely thought her sweet, little girl was being wooed by the bogeyman. Maybe there was no supposed Romeo. Tracy's attitude was enough to cause migraines of worry for any parent. I could see where it might be a by-product of parental terror to see danger everywhere.

I couldn't make myself go back inside. I'd had more than my share of amateur hour. Instead I headed into the darkened evening, stepping onto the rear wooden porch where a small group of smokers were stubbing out the last of their cigarettes.

I inhaled the secondhand smoke but tonight it did nothing for me. Just smelled dirty. I walked from beneath the protective overhang to an open side of the entrance and gazed skyward. The last bit of light streaked the horizon and stars were faint in a dark cobalt sky.

I was facing the back parking lot and I don't know how long I stood there. A few minutes, maybe, while my restless mind worried thoughts of Bobby and Cotton and who would inherit and what was really at stake. I wanted to talk to Murphy. Hell, I wanted to see him and wrap myself close to him.

A car door cracked open and the interior light came on. A young man with dark hair and Elvis sideburns stepped from the vehicle and lit a cigarette. From the distance I wasn't completely sure, but if the top of his scraggly head of hair topped five foot six I'd be surprised. I had to be at least an inch taller. Still, his body shape was compact and tough. The vapor lights glinted on his face. I suspected there might be an eyebrow piercing.

Though I was a hundred feet away and shrouded in semi-darkness, I pretended to search for something in my purse. My hand closed around my cell phone and I snatched it up and dialed Dwayne. He answered on the first ring. "Hey there," I said, all bright and chatty. "I've been thinking about our gourmet club." There was silence on the other end. Taking a cue from potential sister number three I went on, "You know, we talked about the fruit torte but I just love, love, love creme brulee. I'm so glad you bought me a torch for my birthday. I love those. Can't wait to carmelize the top of the custard. You might want to help."

Out of the corner of my eye I saw Elvis head up the stairs. He was only about thirty feet from me now, so I wandered to the farthest point of the deck.

"Is he there?" Dwayne asked.

"Uh-huh. Oh, don't say no. You carmelize custard with me and there's no telling what I'll do for you."

"Are you still at the Chinook Center?"

"Stepped outside. I've just got my mind on this dinner we're working on together."

"I'm on my way." He clicked off.

I, however, was kind of into my imaginary meal and my fabulous creme brulee, although in reality if it doesn't say "heat and serve" I'm pretty much a lost cause. "I think I'll serve it with fresh raspberries," I chatted on. "Lucky it's early August so they're still available. And I could really go for some champagne. Maybe I'll bring a bottle."

I turned around, cell phone still at my ear. Elvis hadn't gone inside. He was standing by the door, looking through their glass panels into the reception area of the center. I got a good hard look at him. Yeah, he had the sideburns but my gut feeling was that he wasn't that old. Just an early hair grower. I put him at sixteen. Maybe seventeen.

He turned and stared right at me. I doubled my efforts as Suzie Homemaker. "What's Connie bringing? I'm so glad she didn't choose the entree this time. That baked ziti she brought was so dry I thought I'd choke!"

Down the porch by the handicap ramp was a side door to the auditorium, locked from the outside, used only as another exit after the performances. I saw it crack open and lo and behold, sweet, little Tracy stepped into the night. I averted my head, but she didn't even glance my way. One look at Elvis and she was all over him, tilting her head and looking up at him with her smoky eyes.

"Okay, bye, then," I said in a chirpy voice unlike myself, effectively ending my "call." I gave them my back and moved down the steps, sweating like the proverbial pig. I turned the first corner and tripped, just catching myself. I was damn lucky I didn't twist my ankle or worse. My strappy sandals weren't great surveillance gear, and the sidewalk was a roller coaster of broken cement, pushed up by the roots of a massive Douglas fir. Another quirk of Lake Chinook. Can't cut the trees. The whole damn city is under a wreath of firs but city ordinance only allows homeowners to take one down a year and only if it's not a really big one. The tree police were ever vigilant and nasty. Ogilvy, my landlord, is in constant battle with them. His answer is to "park" his trees, denuding them of all branches right to their tippy-tops. This sounds a lot uglier than it really is. With parked trees you actually get some sunlight. Because of his efforts, I reap the benefits on my back deck. I also contend with far less fir needles than my neighbors whose roofs are carpeted with them.

I braced one hand on the offending tree and listened as hard as I could. Tracy and Elvis were murmuring to each other. I carefully moved toward the edge of the corner, peering through the top leaves of a rhododendron. They were heading toward his car, a dark mid-size with the kind of huge, chrome wheels that look like they could run over an elephant.

I decided if she actually tried to get in the vehicle I was going to run straight at them, screaming. That oughtta put the breaks on for a while. And where was Tracy's mother? Wasn't she supposed to be at the performance? Maybe she was still inside, looking forward to when the oldest group finally got its time on stage. What would she do when Tracy's face wasn't amongst them?

"C'mon, Dwayne," I whispered to myself. Where the hell was he? He only lived a few blocks away.

I was on the balls of my feet. If I had to run, I should really remove the sandals. What to do? My pulse and breathing ran light and fast. I didn't relish the idea of tearing at them like a madwoman, but I couldn't come up with a better idea.

Elvis seemed to be coaxing. Tracy, the little minx, was giggling and twitching her ass some more. Good God. They were dopey teenagers. It was more embarrassing than sinister.

Elvis climbed behind the wheel. Tracy leaned in to him. I saw some smooching. I prayed she wouldn't walk around to the passenger door. *Dear God, don't make me look like a complete idiot . . .*

"Tracy!" a woman's voice shrieked.

My prayers were suddenly answered as woman number one, the brayer, shot from the top of the porch steps, screaming at them in much like the manner that I'd planned to.

"Mom!" Tracy shrieked back in embarrassment. "What are you doing?"

Angela barreled toward them. I braced myself for their collision, but then Dwayne's truck pulled into the lot, parking a few spots down from the group. Angela managed to keep from bowling Tracy over, but she grabbed hard at her arm. Tracy pulled back so fast she stumbled. Elvis was out of the car to catch her which sent Angela into higher-pitched screaming. "Get your hands off her! I've called the police. You're going to be arrested! You . . . pedophile!"

I groaned aloud and glanced toward Dwayne's vehicle. He wasn't getting out of the car.

Elvis said something soft to Tracy and got back in his car, slamming the door. Angela started pounding on his window and Tracy grabbed her mother's arm and yanked as hard as she could.

"You're crazy!" she screamed. "You're fucking crazy!"

"What did you say?" Angela's voice was so high it pierced the air.

"You're *fucking* crazy!"

Dwayne's voice said, "Stop it, both of you," as he slammed his door and strode toward them.

Elvis reversed in a tight little circle and a squeal of wheels. I gauged the distance to my car and started walking fast. Angela reared back. I thought she was going to hit Tracy but I saw she was just stunned with shock. Her face was white, disbelieving, her eyes bulging.

"She . . . she was getting in that boy's car . . ." she choked to Dwayne. "That sick drug addict boy!"

"God, Mom, you're so stupid!"

"Tracy," Dwayne warned.

"You're the one who's stupid!" Angela cried. "Getting in a car with a stranger!"

"Angela." Dwayne tried to get between them.

"He's not a stranger! He was in class with me! We're friends!"

"Don't lie to me."

"I'm not!" Tracy was outraged.

I'd reached the Volvo. I slid in, turned the ignition and pushed the button to lower the window. Angela was attacking Tracy with all her proof. ". . . followed you from Seattle. I'll nail his ass. He won't see sunlight until he's fifty!"

"He lives in Lake Chinook," Tracy declared, infuriated and baffled. "I don't get you!"

I turned the car to follow Elvis. I was beginning to believe something was amiss. Maybe this wasn't the guy from Seattle. Maybe this was just a kid from acting class. But I figured a good information specialist would try to get more information.

I'd just about decided Elvis was okay as I followed him down State Street when he turned the corner and into the lot of the Pisces Pub. My radar went up. Was he twenty-one? I drove past and circled back. I suddenly longed for something else to wear. Elvis had paid next to no attention to me, but my clothes were a dead giveaway. "Shit." I dug furiously through the backseat of my car and found a pair of sweats I hadn't worn in weeks as the weather was simply too hot.

I jumped into them. I'd have to keep the camisole as I had nothing else for a top. Damn. I unclipped my hair and finger-combed it. Looking in the rearview mirror I noticed the "hat ring" the hair clip had left behind. I furiously finger-combed some more and finally slammed out of the car behind my quarry. At the last second I turned back and dug through my glove box, finding the pair of prescription lenses my mother had inadvertently left the last time she'd visited. I've been planning to send them back, I really have. Now, they seemed like a gift. I put them on and nearly fell into the scraggly bank of azaleas outside the Pisces Pub's front walkway.

Note to self: always keep surveillance clothes available. In sweats, aqua camisole, weird hair and glasses, I was about as cool as anyone had a right to be.

As I pushed open the door I called Dwayne. He answered tersely. I could still hear Angela and Tracy going at it. "I followed Elvis to the Pisces Pub."

"What?" That caught his attention.

"More later," I said, then hung up.

I pushed open the door, a heavy oak piece carved with waves and I think what was once a mermaid. But someone had sawed off her bare tits long ago. Probably concerned citizens of Lake Chinook. She looked kind of pissed off. I couldn't blame her.

Loud music and the smell of stale popcorn assaulted me. A bouncer with huge, hairy forearms stepped in front of me. "I.D.," he demanded.

I was kind of flattered he carded me. I handed him my license and he eyed it skeptically. He handed it back to me with a look that said he thought I was up to something. Geez. Maybe this is just my paranoia at work.

He let me pass and I moved through the center room which sported scarred tables and chairs and a rough fir ceiling hung with wagon-wheel chandeliers. The motif had once been the wild west and there were still remnants mixed in with the sea theme. In fact there was a smiling fish statue carved out of wood sitting on the bar. He was standing on his tail and he sported a cowboy hat, bandana, and tiny holster. He'd been stolen once or twice, so now he was bolted onto the bar.

The music was pouring out of the back room which was dark and lined with banquettes covered with black Naugahyde. On weekends the scattered tables are shoved aside to make room for a teensy dance floor. The bands are surprisingly good and this one was running through some music from the sixties. I recognized a stylized version of The Beatles' "Why Don't We Do It In The Road?"

Elvis was inside. I'd bet money he was using fake identification. If I really wanted to be a killjoy I could whisper as much to the bouncer and all hell would break loose. With the fear of identity theft running rampant throughout the land, new laws were clamping down on the poor underage kids just trying to get a beer. If one was eighteen and showed fake I.D., he could be charged with fraud—a felony—and face serious penalties and possibly jail time. With all the real crime out there, it boggles the mind. However, I could see how I could use this information to my advantage. I just wasn't sure whether Elvis was a bad guy or not.

He was standing to one side, snapping his fingers to some beat inside his own head that was about triple speed of the song. I gazed at him over the tops of my mom's eyeglasses and had an epiphany. Disguise, dis-schmize. This kid didn't know me. I was in control here. I should have left the skirt on as I was roasting in the sweatpants.

I shoved the glasses to the top of my head and strode over to him. He looked at me, looked away, looked again, slightly alarmed. I leaned into him. His eyes rolled around as he tried to gaze anywhere but at me. I said, "Let me see your I.D. I know you're not twenty-one."

"The hell I'm not," he blustered, scared.

"I don't even think you're eighteen. But whatever your age, you're too old for a fourteen-year-old, you get me?"

"You're . . . ?" He couldn't form a question.

"C'mon, let's dance."

I grabbed his arm and led him, protesting, onto the postage-stamp-sized floor. There was only one other couple out there.

"I can't dance," he moaned.

"You were supposed to be at the performance arts class. You can dance."

"No, I can't."

"Trust me, making a fool of yourself out here is the least of your worries."

He was shorter than I thought. My gaze hit him right in the middle of his forehead. If I pulled him close to my chest, his face would crush my breasts. I wondered if he would straight-out panic. Probably. "What are you, seventeen?"

He swallowed. I put my hands on his shoulders, strictly the preteen school of dance, and gave him a hard look. He managed to place his hands at my waist. He didn't want to touch me. His fear was palpable.

"Sixteen?" I guessed. He half-jerked away and I knew I'd hit pay dirt. "What the hell are you doing with Tracy?"

"You don't understand," he muttered.

"Are you from Seattle?"

"Seattle?" His eyes met mine straight for the first time. "I'm from here. My stepmom thought I should take this dumb class. She wants me out of the house. I hate it. Tracy's the only good thing about it."

"You never met her before this class?"

"How could I?" he asked miserably.

"Let me see that I.D. How old are you supposed to be?"

"My brother's twenty-one. It's his license. He doesn't know I have it. I've gotta be back in an hour." He threw a harried glance at his wristwatch.

"Why'd you come here?"

"I heard you could get in here. I just wanted a beer."

"Looked like you were trying to talk Tracy into getting in your car. What were you going to do with her? Sneak her in here somehow?"

"I wanted to show her I could get in. That's all." His voice trailed off, barely audible beneath the music. We'd switched to George Michaels' "I Want Your Sex." The band had a nice little theme going.

"Her mother thinks you're bad news."

"She's a friggin' weirdo. Did you see us?"

"I was there."

"Well, shit. A *pedophile*? She's nuts!"

"She thinks you're older than you are. You'd better be able to prove you're not."

That was all it took. He started scrambling for his wallet. I led him over to a more private corner and squinted in the dim light at a copy of an Oregon driver's license for sixteen-year-old Quentin Emerson. He was smiling in the photo which showed the start of his sideburns. Without them, he looked about twelve.

"This your address?" At his nod, I memorized it. "I know where you live."

"Does this mean I can't see Tracy anymore?" He was stricken.

I had a vision of Angela screaming and running at them. "All signs point to yes."

"That just sucks."

I didn't say it, but I thought he was probably lucky to stay away from both of them.

"I'm going," he muttered and headed for the door, shoulders down. I would have followed him but the truth was he wasn't the only one who wanted a beer. I glanced around, wondering if I could sit down somewhere for a few moments and think things through. I wanted to call Dwayne and check in, but if he was still with his relatives chances were he had his hands full. And it was all a tempest in a teapot anyway. Young love. Who knew?

My gaze fell on the farthest banquet which was occupied by a lone man. I did a double take and my heart squeezed. It was Owen Bradbury. He was seated on a section of Naugahyde where there was just enough room for me to sit. I didn't think I was likely to get a better invitation.

Chapter
Fifteen

I made my way over to Owen. The shape of his head still gave me shivery reminders of Bobby, but his eyes were blue, like Tess's. And his hair was a few shades lighter, brown with faint touches of blond.

"I know you," he said on a note of discovery. "I saw you at Bobby's memorial service. I asked my mom who you were and she said you were Murphy's girlfriend."

"'Were' being the operative word," I said. I wished keenly that Murphy would call me back. I figured he was dealing with Heather, but I wanted his company. I wanted to comfort him and be comforted in return. Was that asking so much?

His eyes wandered over my sweatpants. I had to fight not to give some kind of explanation. "What are you doing here?" Owen asked with a slight slur.

The guy was wasted, I realized belatedly. "Looking for a drink. How d'ya get one around here?"

He waved a hand in the general direction of the bar. "They don't come around and serve."

"Ahh . . ." The Pisces Pub was no Foster's On The Lake.

"You can share mine," he suggested, offering up a chilled mug of beer that was half empty.

Now, normally I have aversions to slurping another person's

drink. Especially one belonging to someone I don't know. You can actually hear the germs getting sucked into your system. Even when I'm in a relationship with someone, spending a good portion of my time kissing them, I struggle with sharing their drink.

But tonight I was hot through and through. The air was sweltering and it felt as if steam were running through my veins. Besides, I wanted to ingratiate myself a little. I'd planned on showing up at the Pisces sometime and interviewing some of Owen's friends, but this was even better. And where were those friends, anyway? Owen looked remarkably alone.

I took the proffered mug, fought back my germ phobia and took a swallow. It was still cold. Like heaven, actually. I tried not to gulp the last half down at once. I did manage to leave a little bit for him. Wiping my mouth with the back of my hand, I didn't belch so I figured it was a win.

He squinted at me. "I like a woman who can drink."

"I feel like I'm melting from the inside out."

He nodded. "I feel like dog shit. Don't know if you heard, but my old man died today."

"Cotton?" He surprised me with the "old man" line since they weren't actually related. But then, blood wasn't always what made one a father. "I did hear. From Murphy."

"He wasn't my real dad. He wasn't even much of a stepdad. He was a real piece of work, actually. But he was okay to me, y'know? He was always okay." Owen's jaw tightened. He was fighting emotion. "Fuck," he muttered, holding the mug to his lips and draining the bit I'd left him.

"Let me get us two more," I said.

I went to the bar and ordered a couple of drafts. I wasn't sure what to think of Owen, but he seemed genuinely distraught over Cotton's death. I brought the beers back and we sat side-by-side, drinking in silence. Finally, he asked, "You still on the case?"

"What do you mean?" I responded carefully.

He gave me that "don't con a conner" look. "You were working for Mom, trying to figure out who gets what, where Bobby's

been, who's in on it, the whole nine yards." He thought a moment. "Did you follow me here?"

"No."

"You seem kind of uptight. Like you're pretending to be
someone you're not. Is this how you play private dick?" Another
glance at the sweatpants.

"I'm not working for your mom anymore," I informed him.

"Who are you working for?"

"Right now, no one."

"You want to know what happened to Bobby?" He gazed at
me but he swayed a bit, his eyelids drooping. "I'll tell ya. They
were all in on it. Every last one of 'em. But it was really Colonel
Mustard, in the billiard room, with the wrench. Shhh . . . don't
tell anybody." He nearly fell off the banquette.

"Did you drive here?"

"Yep. Why? You don't think I can drive home?" He half-
laughed. "Well, guess what? You're right! I'm shit-faced. You are
a good detective."

"I've got a car. Let's go to your place."

"Wow . . . I haven't had a woman say that in a long time . . ." He
staggered to his feet. Before we headed out he drained the rest of
his beer. I'd set mine down, barely touched. I would have liked
to have poured it over my head for relief, but I didn't need the
extra alcohol.

Owen threw his arm around me and I guided him outside.
The bouncer watched us warily. We staggered to my car where I
practically dumped him in the passenger seat. "That's my car,"
he said when I slid behind the wheel. He was pointing through
the windshield to a shiny black BMW with spoked rims.

My cell phone chirped. I scrambled through my purse for it.
"Hello?"

"Did you find the kid?" Dwayne asked, sounding out-of-
breath.

"Uh-huh. He wasn't really who we were looking for, though."

"How do you mean?"

"He's sixteen and from Lake Chinook."

Dwayne sighed. "That's what Tracy's been saying."

"How are mom and daughter?" Dwayne's answer was a strangled sound that expressed complete disdain. I shot a glance toward Owen whose chin was resting on his chest. "I'm with
someone right now. Can I call you back?"

That woke him up. "Who ya with?"

"Not what you think."

"You have no idea what I think, darlin'."

"You owe me money." I pulled out of the parking lot.

"Sounds like you've gotten over your shock," he observed.
"Good luck on the home front."

He snorted, drawled, "I think Angela's about to eat her
young," then muttered something I couldn't quite catch. I swear
to God it was "thank you." Cheerily, I told him I'd bill him for
my services.

I drove up Macadam and caught the 405 to Glisan Street. At
23rd I had to rouse him enough to scare an address out of him.
He guided me through the newly chi-chi Pearl District, once
warehouses, now condos, natural food stores and martini bars
amidst clumps of turn-of-the-century Portland homes. It was the
high-rent district, for sure. He was apparently cohabitating with
Tess in her high-rise condo.

"I didn't know you lived with your mom," I said, probing a bit
as Owen, climbing unsteadily from his seat, came around the car
and punched in a code for the gate that led to subterranean parking. As the metal gate slid aside, he sank back in his seat.

"I might not be wonder boy, but I'm still her son."

By wonder boy, I figured he meant Bobby. "I've been trying to
get in touch with Tess, but haven't been able to."

"She's in Texas. Went home after Bobby's body surfaced.
Nothing to stay for."

I absorbed that, glad to hear Cynthia's comment about trouble
for Tess was not true. So, Tess had gone home, so to speak. "Is
she coming back for Cotton's funeral, or memorial service?"

"Only if there's money involved." He snorted.

I parked the car in one of the few spots designated for visitor parking. Owen took his time finding his way from his seat to the elevator. He punched the button for the twelfth floor. The elevator doors opened, whispered shut behind us, then we zoomed upward.

Portland's skyline has been changing in this western corner of the city. High-rise condominiums have sprung up one after another, each trying to outclass the last one. Real estate is out of sight. As Owen pushed open the door, I inhaled on a breath of admiration. Tess's condo was spacious and had a commanding view of the city, her view eastward over downtown and the Willamette River. The lights of the city twinkled. Where the Willamette cut through the center of Portland, it was a pure black ribbon.

The air-conditioning, going full blast, hit me like a welcome arctic wind. I turned my face to it and sighed. Tess must not have given Bobby all her money, I thought. Marta had said she'd made out well in the divorce. She would've had to in order to afford this place and let the air-conditioning run.

Owen cut across the thick, cream carpet and through a swinging door into the kitchen. I could see through a large cutout in the sheet rock which formed an eating bar. I watched him come into my vision and open the left-side door of a stainless-steel refrigerator. I heard the clink of ice.

Straight ahead of me was a fireplace faced in thin strips of taupe, manufactured stone. A white mantel sat atop ornate corbels, capping the firebox like a single eyebrow. Tess had a grouping of crystal birds for decoration. All the furniture was shades of brown, ecru and white. It was devoid of color but reflected Tess's taste impeccably.

I heard more clinking and glanced toward the kitchen. Owen was stirring a pitcher full of either gin or vodka. He poured two drinks, adding several fat, pimento-stuffed olives.

"I don't think I'm ready for a martini," I said. He carefully carried two brimming glasses into the room, ignoring me completely. "I'm serious. I'm driving."

"It's not for you," he said.

He stood in front of the fireplace, held up one of the glasses and gazed skyward. "Bottoms up, Dad," he said, then carefully placed one of the martinis on the mantel, shoving some of the crystal birds out of the way. "Y'know, he loved a good gin martini. Taught me how to do it just right."

I recalled Cotton drinking martinis at the benefit. I stared at the martini on the mantel and thought of the man. I warmed to Owen as he silently sipped his drink.

"He gave my mother more than she deserves. Enough to buy some property in the Pearl. A crappy little house that she demo-ed about eight years ago. She rebuilt, sold the new one, bought two more crappy little houses, did it all over again, then bought this." He gestured around the room.

"She started the Black Swan, too," I put in. If Owen wanted to wax rhapsodic about his family, I was all ears.

"That business sucks. Too much debt. Recently she re-fied this, too. Put her money somewhere else." He slid me a sideways look. "Cotton sure gave her enough, but it ain't here."

"You sure she's not a smart saver?" I suggested lightly.

"My mother?" He threw back the rest of the martini. "Come on. I know what you're thinking."

"What am I thinking?"

"You think the money went to Bobby. Maybe you're right." Since I hadn't said anything, and I didn't appear to need to, I kept my mouth shut. Owen was in the mood to talk and who was I to stop him? "Mom's got enough to keep going, but not in the manner to which she's accustomed. That's why she hired you. To find out who inherits what. But now that Dad's gone, it won't be a secret much longer."

"Cotton did intimate that your mom was funding Bobby these last four years," I admitted.

"Why wouldn't she?" He shrugged. "She did everything else for him."

"She thought Cotton had a hand in it."

"You know what I think?" Owen suddenly said. "I think Bobby finally slipped his leash. She had him stashed away somewhere for four years and he just couldn't stand it anymore. So, he left. And maybe he went to Cotton. He always needed money. Why wouldn't he try to tap out the old man?"

"So, where was he?"

"Who the hell cares? He's dead now. Somebody made sure of that."

A long pause ensued. I checked my watch. I wanted to get home and let my dog out and think. But I also didn't want to lose a golden opportunity to learn more. "You lived here long?"

"Nah . . . I'm just staying for a while. I'm unemployed at the moment," he added, smiling faintly. "Y'see, Dad was all about teaching Bobby how to invest money. How to make your money make more money. He was always lecturing Bobby and his friends, like your pal, Murphy. Everybody. Any friend of Bobby's was a friend of Dad's. And he told 'em what to do. Told 'em, and told 'em. It was a joke. They never listened."

He gazed at the martini on the mantel. "But I did. Dad hardly knew I was there. And when I graduated high school I asked him for a loan. Wanted to buy some real estate. So, he helped me out." Owen nodded. "Bobby went off to college and dropped out, and went back, and dropped out, and got Laura pregnant and got married and then had a couple of more kids and then killed them all. But I bought a place on the east side. Sellwood area. Fixed it up and sold it to Cotton!" He chuckled. "I helped my mom with her projects. And I kept making some money and it kind of snowballed and now I own a decrepit apartment complex in First Addition. I'm going to fix it up next year."

I was totally blown away. Owen, not Bobby, had become Cotton's protege. Owen had learned from his stepfather. The First Edition neighborhood of Lake Chinook was tiny cabins near the center of town which were being revitalized at an alarming rate, at least for the other homeowners in the area. It was one of the fastest-growing areas in Lake Chinook and the house

prices were steadily rising. If Owen owned an apartment building there, he was well on his way to making his own small fortune.

"It's all about real estate," he said.

It's all about real estate. The words sank into my brain. It was
the theme of the whole sordid mess, I thought. Money and real
estate.

"Bobby never got it," I said, thinking aloud.

"He never got nothin' if it didn't have to do with sports and
flash. He was all front, no back." Owen laughed. "Dad used to
say, 'Big hat, no cattle.' 'Course he never meant it about Bobby,
but it was true."

"What do you think really happened?"

"To Bobby?" I nodded. Owen considered for a long moment.
"I need another drink. You want anything?"

"No, thanks," I said regretfully. I would have loved a drink,
something cold and refreshing. But I didn't feel like leaving the
Volvo and calling a cab, so it meant alcohol abstinence, more's the
pity.

While Owen fixed himself another martini I walked toward
the bookcase that ran along the south wall. It was painted white
and the books and objets d'art filling its shelves were arranged by
design. Bobby wasn't the only one who was all about flash. The
books were all classics, leather bound, the titles gold embossed,
but I doubted Tess had ever read anything from any of them. I
saw Shakespeare and Dickens and poetry by Emily Dickinson,
Robert Frost and William Butler Yeats, to name just a few. They
seemed out of place in this white, cold room. There were biogra-
phies mixed in as well, past presidents and emperors and famous
industrialists.

One name was out of place. A small book tucked against two
others with similar gold-colored spines. *Audrey Hepburn.* Well,
okay, maybe Tess had read *one* book, or at least part of one, I
thought meanly. I slid it from its spot and noticed the book jacket
was tucked inside the front cover. Unfolding it, I gazed at a photo
of Audrey wearing a pink scarf around her head and a pair of

round, black sunglasses. Too weird. There was writing inside the
jacket. It was an address in Hepburn, Oregon, which was way
east in the dry part of the state, towards the Idaho border.

"She's never read a book in her life," Owen said, startling me.
I dropped the book to the carpet. When I picked it up again, I
slid the book jacket inside the pocket of my purse.

My phone rang. Sliding it from my purse, I checked the number: Murphy. "I'd better go," I said. The phone kept ringing.

"You going to answer that?"

I clicked the red 'off' button. "I'll call them back."

"I don't even know your name."

"Jane Kelly."

"Come back any time, Jane Kelly. 'Course I probably won't be
here. Mom'll lose this place unless Dad left her a hefty chunk of
his estate. But I might fix up a couple of those apartments into an
owner's unit and move back to Lake Chinook. You live there,
right?"

"Don't forget your car's at Pisces," I deflected.

I was out the door before he could turn the tables and start
grilling me.

"Are you hungry?" Murphy asked as soon as my cell phone
connected with his. I was driving fast toward the I-5 freeway,
south.

"Starving."

"I'll meet you at your place."

"There's nothing there."

"I'll bring pizza."

"Pepperoni," I said.

My mouth watered at the thought of pepperoni pizza. It was
after ten and there was hardly a place open for food consumption,
although I imagined some frozen jalapeno peppers or fish sticks
might still be available at the Pisces Pub.

I realized as I drew close to my exit that I was grinning like an
idiot. Murphy wanted to see me. My wish had been granted.

"You're a glutton for punishment," I reminded myself aloud. But even scolding myself couldn't stop me from being happy.

Murphy's SUV was parked in my driveway. I walked to his car and looked in the window. No sign of him. Stumped, I glanced around, then headed to my front door. He had to be around somewhere. Maybe he'd opened the gate to the backyard.

But I had to let the dog out, so I threaded my key in the front door lock. Before I could twist the knob, the door opened inward. I gasped in shock. "Murphy?"

Binkster wriggled around my legs, half-jumping, trying to lick my hands. I bent down to her automatically, as Murphy said, "The pizza's on the kitchen bar."

I could smell it, the scent pulling me inside. Binky whimpered in expectation. "How did you get in?"

"You've got a window in the back that doesn't quite latch. I hauled myself inside." When I didn't make a beeline for the food, he asked. "Should I have waited?"

I realized then how tired he looked. His eyes were dark-rimmed, sunken. Cotton's death had dealt a blow. "No big deal. I just thought someone had been in my place a while ago, but I didn't see how. Now, I guess I know."

Murphy said, "Test a few windows on some of these old cottages and there's a good chance one'll give."

I nodded. I'd all but decided no one had actually entered my bungalow uninvited. Now I didn't feel safe. I walked through the bungalow and opened the back door to let Binks out. She stood in the kitchen, torn, needing to relieve herself but unwilling to leave the prospect of food. I went outside with her and she finally capitulated, running down the steps, sniffing around the yard, nose to the ground, then taking care of business in record time and racing back to me.

"How's Heather?" I asked Murphy as I sat on the stool next to him. Murphy flipped open the pizza box. Hot pepperoni and little orange bubbles of oil mixing with melted cheese greeted me. I had a momentary rational thought and popped a lactaid pill before I dug in. I didn't want anything slowing me down while I ate. And I didn't want any regrets later. Binks put one paw on my leg, so I quickly filled her bowl with crunchies. She stared at the hard, little brown kernels, then looked at me askance. I ignored her.

"Not as broken up as I would have expected, or maybe just hoped," Murphy admitted. "It's like she's moved into phase two. Cotton's dead and now we must all go on." He grabbed a slice of pizza and bit into it almost viciously.

For my part, I propped my arms on the counter and gave myself up to the pizza. It was heavenly. Juice ran down to my elbows and onto the Formica. I closed my eyes and munched.

We ate in companionable silence, punctuated by some moaning by the Binkster. I finally broke down and gave her a little piece of crust which she gobbled up quickly and stared at me for more.

"Who do you think killed Bobby?" I asked.

Murphy gave me a look. "What brought that on?"

"I think whoever killed Bobby basically killed Cotton. Once Cotton knew his son was gone, he gave up. He knew Heather married him for his money and whatever he'd once gotten out of that relationship was over. Everybody wanted a piece of his fortune. The real estate agents were panting over the island. The only person Cotton seemed to really care about is you. Maybe Owen."

Murphy dropped the remainder of his pizza crust back in the box. There were two slices left. "You're still in the thick of it, aren't you? You're still working for Tess!"

"Nope. She's off in Texas."

"Texas?" he demanded.

I gave him a quick rundown of my conversation with Owen. My eyes strayed to my purse where the book jacket was carefully folded. "She left after she knew Bobby was dead. I think she was helping him. Owen said he thought Bobby slipped his leash. Maybe Tess figured he'd gone to his father and she wanted me to learn what I could about Cotton—his health and whether he could be hiding Bobby."

"He wasn't hiding Bobby." Murphy was adamant.

"Maybe he was," I argued. I thought of Hepburn, Oregon. I've never been there and I'm sure it's a nice town, but it would be nowheresville for someone like Bobby Reynolds. "Maybe Bobby thought it was time to get out of Podunk, U.S.A. and start living again," I suggested. "Maybe he never felt remorse for killing his family. Maybe he turned to dear old dad and—"

"Goddammit, Jane!" Murphy exploded. "You're such an amateur!"

My mouth dropped open. I'd expected him to be like Dwayne; someone I could bounce ideas off. But he was way too close to the situation, I realized belatedly. Still, that didn't give him the right to call me names. Amateur? I never claimed to be anything but! "I asked you what you thought," I reminded a bit tensely. "I was just telling you what I thought. How do you know Cotton wasn't hiding Bobby?"

"The man's been dead a matter of hours and you're maligning him."

"Come on, Murphy. I'm theorizing. Somebody helped Bobby. He didn't stay hidden for four years alone. And he got to Lake Chinook somehow. And he met with *someone* because *someone* killed him."

Murphy seemed to want to say something more, but he held it inside. Swallowing hard, he exhaled on a long sigh. "You know what I want? I want to get through the next couple of days. I want to be here for Cotton's memorial service. I want to be there when they pour his ashes into Lake Chinook. Then I want to leave. For good. I don't want to think about Bobby or Cotton or anybody involved ever again."

He rose abruptly, nearly knocking over the stool, and strode into the living room. Binkster watched him and I followed after him. Whatever I'd hoped for with Murphy didn't look like it was going to materialize. He'd called me to get away from it all, but I'd jumped in with both feet. Maybe he was right. Maybe I was obsessing about this case. Maybe I should take a tip from him and just forget the whole thing. What was it to me, anyway?

He was standing by my television set. In his hands was a business card. Tomas Lopez's. He looked up from it and stared at me as if I'd sprouted horns and a tail. "What is this?" he asked, but his expression said he'd already leapt to his own conclusions.

"He stopped by," I said, indicating the card. "Cotton sicced him on me when he learned I was working for Tess."

"What did you tell him? Your *theories?*"

I bristled at his tone. "I didn't tell him anything."

"Why have you got his card?"

"He wanted me to get in touch if I learned anything. I may be an amateur but I guess Lopez figured he'd take whatever help he could get." If Murphy chose to look at this thing rationally he would realize that it was *him* telling Cotton about *me* that had set the whole thing in motion.

"It's like you have this gruesome fascination with this tragedy."

Now that was just plain unfair. "I was dragged into this by Marta Cornell and Tess Bradbury." *And the offer of cold hard cash.* "And then you told me Cotton wanted to talk to me. I can't seem to give it up even when I try."

Murphy set the card back down on the television. His whole body radiated anger. I remembered a couple of doozy fights we'd had when we were together. We'd ended up in bed, having some of the best sex of our lives.

"What are you trying to do, Jane?"

"Honestly? I don't really know."

"Jerome Neusmeyer is going to read Cotton's will on Monday."

"Well, goody. Hope Tess makes it back in time."

I was good and angry. It had been one very long day.

Murphy had a hand on the front door handle. "For what it's worth, I think you're right about Tess. I think she knew where Bobby was, and I think she sent him money. But if that's ever proven, she'll go to jail."

"I know."

"Cotton wouldn't want that."

"Are you telling me to back off?"

"In simple English: yes."

"What about the will? Who inherits? Think that has any bearing on any of this?"

"I don't give a damn. I just don't want it to be me."

So, that was what was really bugging him. "You'll know on Monday."

"And then I'm out of here, Jane." He gave me a long look, the kind of smoldering gaze that tended to curl my toes. "I'm starting my life over. I know we've circled around it, but I'm serious about Santa Fe. I want you to come with me."

I was still nursing my anger. Still . . . "I don't know, Murphy."

"I haven't forgotten . . . how we were."

We stared at each other. My gaze seemed to move from his eyes, to his mouth, to his chest, to his jaw, then back to his mouth. I hadn't forgotten either. It had been a long, dry four years.

Something in the air pressure changed. I flashed on moments with Murphy: the sight of our limbs tangled together, rumpled bed sheets and laughter caught in the back of our throats. I saw his finger tracing the curve of my calf. My mouth was dry. My heart lurched.

"Jane . . ."

I don't remember crossing the distance between us. It wasn't like those commercials where we were running in slow motion and finally embraced. One second we were ten feet across the room, the next we were all over each other, the next we were ripping off clothes as we stumbled toward my bedroom. Binkster tried to get underfoot and we slammed the bedroom door in her flat, little face. Maybe it was rude, but who needs anyone watching you in the throes of passion, be it human or fuzzy little beast?

I'm never sure about protocol during sex. Should we take it slow, say soft, sensual things to each other? That wasn't what was happening. It was pure animal. Too much time had passed.

We stopped for a moment to take a breath. I was in my sweatpants, bare from the waist up, breathing hard. Murphy's shirt was off, his eyes slitted as he examined my heaving chest. It's not huge, but it's adequate, and it certainly seemed to be doing the trick tonight. He reached out a hand and cupped one breast. My skin shivered involuntarily.

"I've missed you . . ." he murmured.

Ditto, Bucko.

And then we were all mouths and hands and clinging limbs. I wanted to cry with joy and relief.

My last thought before falling into exhausted sleep was thank God my brother wasn't the only one having *great* sex.

Chapter Sixteen

I woke up with a smile on my face. Murphy was lying on his side, his back to me. I thought about wrapping my arm around him but felt shy. Ridiculous, I know, but true nevertheless.

My slight movement caught his attention and he turned over on his back. I realized he was wide awake and looked like he had been a while.

"Good morning," I said. "What's your name again?"

He cracked a smile and reached for a strand of my tangled hair. Turning, he gazed down at me with affection. "Your hair's a mess."

"You have no idea what it's been through."

"It gives you that 'freshly fucked' look."

"I take offense to that."

"No, you don't."

We grinned at each other like idiots. The moment spun out. I was hoping for another trip to the moon, but Murphy's cell phone rang, shattering the moment. He'd left it on my bedside table. I'd thought it looked cute, side-by-side with my own cell phone. Glancing at the caller ID, he muttered, "Damn. It's Heather."

"She's an early caller."

"She's been in a state since Cotton died. I left her at the house last night with Craig Cuddahy."

My ears pricked. I tried not to sound interested when I asked, "He's been staying here a while, at the Shoreline, right?"

"He thinks Heather's inheriting the island. Maybe she is." He closed his eyes a moment, gathering strength, then he climbed out of bed. Dwayne wasn't the only one with a nice ass, I thought happily.

"Mind if I take a shower here?"

"Go for it."

I thought about jumping up and joining him but was distracted by my own cell phone chiming away. I glanced at the LCD. "Out of Area" and a phone number. Mom. Guiltily, I thought about not answering. She'd left a few more messages on my answering machine and now had resorted to my cell phone, a last resort as she seemed to think cell phones were futuristic devices that might signal circling UFOs, calling them down from outer space.

"Hey, Mom," I answered.

"Well, there you are. I've been trying to reach you. Haven't you got my messages?"

"I haven't been around."

"Where have you been?"

"Working. Process serving and stuff. Lots to do."

She got to the point of her conversation. "Your brother's engaged!"

"I know. I left you a message to that effect."

"I don't know anything about her."

"I told you she's a criminal defense lawyer."

"Where's she from? Who are her parents? What do they do?"

"Mom, I don't know. You'll have to ask Booth."

"I've asked him! He just fobs me off. I'm coming up there. I need to meet her."

Coming up there? I listened to the shower run. "You should let Booth know. They've both got tight schedules."

"Jane, is it all right if I stay with you? I have a feeling he and . . . Sharona . . . are living together. Booth didn't say so, but . . ."

Santa Fe was looking better and better. "When are you planning to come?"

"Is it a problem?" She sounded distressed.

"No. I was just—asking."

"I don't know. I'll call you next week, okay?"

I was getting that stifled feeling. Not now. Not while Murphy was here. Wearily, I said, "Fine. You can meet the dog."

"What dog?"

"Aunt Eugenie's dog." My voice was tight. "The one you had delivered here?"

"Oh." My mother half-laughed. "God, I'm just a mess. Your brother's thrown me for a loop. No word from him hardly in months and then bam! He's getting married. Where did he meet her?"

The shower ceased. "I don't know. I'll figure it out. Let's talk later, okay? I've got to get going."

"I'll call you next week," she reiterated and I murmured a quick good-bye and hung up. Geez, Louise. A visit from Mom! Love her to death, but it was going to be inconvenient. Binkster and I would end up on the couch, and it would be a tight fit. Not to mention the entertaining I would have to do. But at least Mom would get her eyes on Sharona and all deception would be over.

Murphy strolled out of the bathroom, a green towel slung around his slim hips. Binky eyed him with interest. She padded into the kitchen and stood by her bowl while I threw on a robe and watched Murphy pull on his clothes. He had a similar build to Dwayne, lean and tall and muscular. But Dwayne had longish, brown-blond hair and a drawl and Murphy was dark hair, blue eyes and dimples. But the dimples didn't make him approachable. There was a deep reserve about him that I still struggled to breach, even after a night of lovemaking. Of spectacular lovemaking, make no mistake. The earth pretty much moved, at least on my part.

He kissed me on my cheek, murmured something about calling later, then headed out the door. I looked down at Binks who'd pressed her chin against my leg, looking up at me with those begging, doggy eyes. If I relocated to New Mexico with Murphy who would take care of her? Booth? Dwayne? Mom . . . ?

"Want to move to Santa Fe?" I tentatively invited.

She ran to her bowl, misinterpreting completely.

I showered, dressed in denim shorts, a white tank top and my Nikes without socks, and was locking my door, after having placed a small piece of wood in my unlatched window to keep my place safe—kind of like locking the barn door after the horse escapes—when my cell phone rang. "Out of Area" again, but this time with no number. "Hello?" I said, unlocking the Volvo.

"Hi, Jane, it's Tess."

I leaned against the car. "Well, well. Did you get my messages? All ten of them?" I felt snarky. I wondered if she'd talked to Owen this morning.

"I'm sorry if I put you out," she snarked right back. "You don't know what it's been like, losing Bobby. I feel like I've died myself."

"What about Cotton?"

"I'm sorry about him, too, of course. It's one tragedy after another." Her voice really seemed to lack the emotion one might have expected.

I decided I didn't have any more time to waste on this job. Jumping feet first into the fray, I said conversationally, "I think you were right: Cotton did see Bobby at the end. That's what you wanted to know, isn't it? That's why I was hired. That, and to learn what I could about Cotton's will."

"It's a mute point, now, isn't it?"

That would be *moot*, Tess, I thought. "Maybe," I agreed. "But it's worth discussing a little. I mean, that's what you paid me for, right?"

"I don't understand your attitude," she said frostily.

"Bear with me, Tess. The way I see it, Bobby came to Cotton and they had some kind of reckoning. Good or bad, I don't know. And then something happened and Bobby . . . was murdered."

"Someone killed him," she said. "And it makes me furious! I can't think about it! How dare they take him from me! He was my son and I want whoever killed him to be found. I want them to hurt and suffer! They took him from me and I don't forgive."

Now there was some real emotion, but I found it hard to feel sorry for her. She was in this up to her bleached-blond eyebrows. "Are you coming back for the reading of the will?"

"I don't know." She struggled to pull herself together. "I just don't care. Maybe."

"If Cotton left everything to Bobby, doesn't it revert back to you?" I was really hazy on this kind of stuff, but with Bobby having wiped out his nuclear family, I thought Tess must be next in line.

"Cotton didn't leave his estate to Bobby." Her voice was firm. "He told me he was changing his will. He went to see his lawyer to change things."

"You talked to Cotton?"

"One quick conversation. He wanted me to know he'd cut Bobby out. All that talk about how much he loved him and in the end it didn't matter. My guess is he left it all to Murphy. Or Heather . . ." She said her name as if it tasted bad. "I don't know if I even care. I just had to come home to Houston for a while because I feel so godawful."

"Tess, I met with Cotton right before he died. I think you should know that he intimated you were taking care of Bobby all these years. You told me you thought Cotton was taking care of him."

"I never said any such thing!"

"Well, yes, you did." I hadn't forgotten our meeting in Marta's office even if she conveniently had. "But I'm not the only person Cotton spoke to. The Monroes came to see him."

"What?" She was startled.

"They were waiting outside his hospital room when I left. Either Cotton wanted to talk to them, or they wanted to talk to him."

"Did they talk to him?" she asked urgently.

"I didn't stay long enough to find out. But maybe Cotton told them what he told me. Or, maybe he told someone else."

"I haven't done anything wrong!"

"That's good, because I had a feeling you had Bobby holed up in Hepburn."

She drew in a breath. "Hepburn?"

"You helped him get there. You gave him money. Cash, that you'd gotten from Cotton before you were divorced. Maybe more cash since you mortgaged your business and your condo. But Bobby got tired of being a nobody out in the boonies. He came back and hit up his father for money, a new identity, I don't know what. Cotton loved him, wanted to help him, but couldn't bring himself in the end to be an accessory after the fact. He cut Bobby loose."

"I really don't understand how you can say all these things," she said weakly.

"I saw the address, Tess. Hepburn, Oregon. I think you chose it for Bobby. I think he was desperate and you decided to keep him somewhere far enough away, yet close enough, too. Hepburn's a six- or seven-hour drive from Portland. Not right around the corner, but doable."

She tried to laugh, but I'd hit her in the gut. "What a wild story."

"You've got a fascination with Audrey Hepburn," I went on. "That's why you came in disguise to get a peek at me that day at the Coffee Nook. Maybe you took out a map of Oregon and your eye fell on Hepburn. Maybe it's just circumstance. But you couldn't do this alone. You needed a liaison, a go-between. Probably a rancher. Maybe someone you knew in Texas who was willing to relocate?" The idea zinged from the blue and hit a bull's-eye as Tess made choking sounds. "You got him to buy some piece of property and you plunked Bobby down into the middle of nowhere. Did he become one of the farmers out there? I hear the area's known for its watermelons."

Tess pulled herself together with an effort. "I didn't pay you good money to come up with a bunch of inflammatory theories that are nothing less than slander!"

"You paid me to get close to Cotton and find out if he knew

anything about Bobby," I answered. "I did that. And you wanted to know about his estate. On Monday, we'll all know."

"Well, that's just fine. You just go ahead and rant and rave and see who listens to you. You don't know anything about me or my family. And don't help me any further, Jane Kelly!"

"Not a problem, Tess. We're done."

From the moment I hung up with Tess, a weight was lifted from my shoulders. I immediately wondered why I'd bucked Dwayne all this time. Why had I followed up on the Reynolds/Bradbury debacle? What had I expected to learn? What was the point?

I drove toward the Coffee Nook. Halfway there my cell phone rang again. I was about to chuck the damn thing out the window when I realized it was Murphy this time. "Hello there," I greeted him, trying to keep the sickening, bubbling happiness coursing through me from sounding in my voice.

"Breakfast?" he asked.

"Sure."

"Let's head to La Mer."

"You buying?" I asked.

"As if you'd spring for a meal that expensive."

"Touche."

My smile was huge. Love is such a silly thing. I turned the Volvo around and headed back the way I'd come as La Mer was in my neck of the woods, up on a hill with a peek-a-boo view of the lake far below.

I was slightly surprised he'd picked one of Lake Chinook's more upscale restaurants. I generally avoided La Mer for two reasons: (1) I couldn't afford it, and (2) it attracted the snobbiest of the city's inhabitants and consequently the waitstaff looked down their collective noses at anyone they deemed short of the mark. But it did have a large brick patio that was ringed by trees. In spring and fall the patio was covered with black-and-silver-striped awnings which were rolled back in the summer. In winter a sliding wall of glass cut the patio from the rest of the restaurant, keeping it warm inside while patrons could still enjoy the view. La Mer was definitely a haunt of Lake Chinook's rich, famous and infamous. Foster's On The Lake was where everyone went on the east end of the lake; La Mer was the west end favorite. I brave the terrible prices at Foster's during the summer months because it's on the water. I steer clear of La Mer as a rule, always.

I had to stop back by my place and scrounge for something better to wear. I kept the white T-shirt but found a pastel blue loose skirt which drifted around my legs as I walked, and traded in my Nikes for my new flip-flops. These flip-flops were a step up from my old ones; they had little gem-like doohickeys on their plastic straps that looked as if they were dangling by a thread. I was bound to ruin them before sundown.

I hurried back to my car and raced to the restaurant. Luckily, there's enough parking nearby La Mer for me to usually find a spot. I found one not too far away and hurried past the black-vested valets standing outside the front door. I hate that shit. Where do they think they are? Downtown L.A.?

I headed inside and through the main dining room to the patio. Murphy was there ahead of me, standing by the maitre d' stand. He was dressed in a khaki shirt, chocolate chinos and leather sandals. He looked exactly like the California boy he'd once been. Yes, he was an Oregon transplant, but I'd met him in Santa Monica and that's how I always thought of him. These days I was more "Oregon" than he was.

He was trying to wrangle us a table near the edge of the patio. One that would offer us a view. The maitre d', who looked as if she sucked lemons on a daily basis, melted at his charm. Murphy didn't turn it on often, but when he did he slayed 'em right and left.

We were seated near one of the broad leaf maple trees which ringed the patio. Beyond them was a dense forest of Douglas firs that sloped down from the restaurant to the lake. I could see glimmering slices of green water far below. The sun filtered through the branches. It was such a lovely morning. Thinking about the delicious breakfasts La Mer served, my mouth started watering on its own. I could count on one hand the amount of times I'd eaten here. This was a treat worth savoring.

I heard the scrape of chairs behind me, but I was deep into scanning the menu. Maybe I could have a mimosa. Orange juice and champagne to brighten the palate.

"Tim Murphy!" a female voice crowed in delight.

I turned to see Paula Shepherd with her sidekick, Brad. I groaned inwardly. As they approached our table Murphy gazed at them with a serious lack of enthusiasm.

"I'm so sorry about Cotton," Paula said, her eyes assessing Murphy, trying to get a read on his emotions, her mouth a tight, false smile. Brad shook Murphy's hand and murmured condolences.

It was all totally awkward. Paula and Brad were finished with breakfast and we were waiting to be served. They stood beside our table, doing a dance with the waitstaff to keep out of the way as waiters and busboys filled water glasses and took orders, rushing around the patio.

I found myself wanting to say, "Get to the point," because it was clear they had something on their minds. Finally, Paula said, "We were talking to Heather yesterday and expressed our interest in the property. I guess that's no surprise. She wasn't sure it was hers and suggested maybe you might inherit it. If that's the case, I just want to say how much Brad and I could do for you." She nodded while she spoke, as if this would assure Murphy of her good intentions. Her red lacquered nails lifted a card from a side pocket of her purse as she talked. Lightly, she dropped it on the table, next to Murphy's knife. She kept a nail on the card a second or two longer. I shot Murphy a look across the table. He was silent but his face was suffused with dark red. I had to restrain myself from pushing my chair back to get out of harm's way.

Murphy slowly stood up, but something in his bearing caused Paula and Brad to step back. Maybe they were more perceptive than I gave them credit for. With quiet fury, Murphy gritted, "Get the hell away from me."

"I understand how you feel," Paula soothed. "Just wanted to say hello."

"Don't talk to me again."

"Maybe this isn't the right time." Her smile was fixed on her face, but her eyes darted around. She smiled at someone across the way.

"Get . . . out . . ."

They made good-bye noises and scooted away. Murphy sat back down. Several long moments passed. The waiter stopped by and I ordered a veggie omelet, orange juice and coffee. It kinda felt like my chance for a mimosa had passed. Murphy could barely bring himself to order. With an effort, he ordered eggs benedict, one of the house specialties.

"Who the hell are these people?" he finally demanded as we were halfway through our meals. I had a mouthful of omelet. Little bits of broccoli caught in my throat as I tried to answer. I reached for the water and gulped. Murphy didn't even notice my distress. "They're vultures," he bit out. "They're picking the bones and Cotton's body is practically still warm."

That image kind of put me off my food. I pushed my plate away and tried to think past it, cradling my coffee mug in both hands. "Wasn't Cotton cremated?" Which reminded me that I didn't know what to think about tossing his ashes in Lake Chinook.

"You know what I meant."

I nodded. I didn't want to think about any of it anyway. My brain was singing a little tune about Santa Fe. Love was making me giddy . . . or lust . . . or maybe just hope. I didn't know and didn't care.

My cell phone rang again. I made annoyed sounds as I examined the caller. It was Dwayne. I shut the thing off without answering. "Who was that?" Murphy asked.

"Dwayne. I'll call him later."

"What's the story with the two of you?"

I was surprised. "No story. He just wants me to work with him."

Murphy frowned down at what was left of his meal. "I have no right to ask. I just got the impression you were . . . more."

"How'd you get that impression?" I asked, mildly horrified. "Dwayne and I are friends. Period." I probably said this with more force than necessary, but I really wanted to be clear on the issue. Call it guilt over my semi-attraction to Dwayne.

"He's the reason you kept pushing about Cotton and Bobby after you stopped working for Tess."

I couldn't let Dwayne take credit for that one. "Uh, no. Actually, that was just me. Dwayne's been telling me to give it up for weeks."

Murphy's brows lifted in surprise. "Dwayne hasn't been pulling your strings?"

"Hell, no." I took offense. "Dwayne wants me to work with him but believe me, it's all about collecting the fee. If I'm not making any money, he doesn't want me on the case, whatever it is."

"Guess I'll have to rethink things."

"Guess you will."

He shook his head as if to clear everything out. In the slanting sunlight he again looked tired. He caught me staring at him and said, "I've never wanted anything to be over so much. Except before, with Bobby, when the shit hit the fan. I just wanted to run away that time."

"You did run away."

"Yeah, and I want to again. Right after the reading of the will. What a crock. I hate this kind of ceremony."

"Is it really okay to toss Cotton's ashes in the lake? I mean, isn't there a law or something about that? I know they sprinkle ashes in the ocean, but in our lake? That seems—wrong."

He half-smiled. "Heather doesn't give a rat's ass. She wants to get Monday over almost as much as I do." He glanced up. "You're coming to the house for the reading?"

"Uh, no . . . I hadn't planned to. I don't think I'm really invited." I had a picture of Jerome Neusmeyer seeing "Ronnie" again and didn't think I wanted the fallout from that.

"I want you there," he said. "The will's read, we scatter the ashes and then it's over." He reached across the table and clasped one of my hands. I realized how cold my skin was. "It's all happened kind of fast. You're thinking about Santa Fe, though. Aren't you?"

"Thinking about it."

"Good." He smiled.

I left Murphy at the restaurant. He gallantly paid the bill even though I got a peek at the amount and emitted a squawk of shock. I got a second shock when he asked, "Mind if I move to your place?" as we walked to our cars. "I've had about as much of Heather and the island and the whole goddamned circus as I can stand."

Honest to God, I had a moment of pure fear. A roommate? I mean, yes, Santa Fe was on the table, but *now?*

"My door—or more precisely, my window—is always open," I invited graciously. "Although my mother's threatening to visit."

"When?"

"This week."

"Better call her off. We'll be gone by then."

He pulled me to him and kissed me hard on the lips before leaving. My heart was jumping all over the place as I climbed into the Volvo. I tried to concentrate on tasks at hand, like that I needed to fix my window. Maybe Murphy could do it. Dwayne was handy with those kinds of tasks, but I was avoiding him. I didn't want him to spoil what I had going with Murphy and I knew Dwayne would, if only for the reason that he was losing his only student.

But I needed to check in with him. I pulled my phone out of my purse. He hadn't left a message. Reluctantly, I punched out his number. He answered on the third ring, sounding disgruntled. "What's eating you?" I asked.

"Tracy and Angela. They just left to go back to Seattle. I'm thinking about getting drunk. Wanna join?"

I examined the height of the sun. "It's barely noon."

"Jesus. Those women. That kid wasn't the one from Seattle, as you well know. Angela's a nut bag. If she doesn't let up, Tracy'll do everything she's accused her of. It's out there, just waiting for her. I tried to tell my sister as much and she went crazy all over me. God. Couldn't get them out fast enough."

"Nice of you to try to help."

"A waste of time and energy." He snorted. "You did good work, though."

The praise got me. "You owe me money," I responded. I had a vision of me telling Dwayne I was leaving for Santa Fe and the coward in me decided now was not the time.

"Come by and I'll pay you. I might even have something more substantial for you. Like a real investigation."

"What kind of investigation?"

"Messy divorce. Sex. The guy works for a company with a private plane and I think he and the flight attendant are clocking the hours in the Mile-High Club. The wife wants his balls. I think I could get you on the plane."

"Sounds like fun," I said without enthusiasm. I was afraid to face him. Afraid what I might say and what that scene might be.

"What's up?" he asked. He was like a bloodhound, sniffing the air.

"Later, Dwayne." I hung up, pissed off to no end. Why was I feeling so shitty? I wasn't. I was walking on air. I was on the threshold of new beginnings. If Dwayne wanted an information specialist, he was going to have to look elsewhere. If Tess wanted more information on Cotton and his money, she was going to have to come to the will reading. If Owen wanted to get drunk and mourn Cotton's death, he was going to have to find a different listener. And if Heather and Paula Shepherd and sidekick Brad and Craig Cuddahy wanted to cut up the island and serve it into little pieces, it didn't matter to me.

It's all about real estate.

I said, succinctly, "I don't fucking care."

* * *

When I got home I had a little bit of time on my hands, so I did a quick inventory of my belongings. Not too many. Could I move to Santa Fe? *Would* I move to Santa Fe?

Stepping onto the back deck, I turned my face up to a faint breeze. A passing boat caught my eye, heading toward the main lake. It was the Mooneys. They waved at me energetically. I lifted a hand, wondering how much I would miss my bungalow.

Binky sat at my side and panted. She looked up at me. "Want some water?" I asked.

She toddled back inside ahead of me and waited at her bowl. I poured her some water and examined the shiny, empty bottom of her food dish. "The way you eat, it's a wonder you haven't gained ten pounds." She stopped lapping at her water and cocked her head.

I shook my head. I was getting way too used to this dog.

The day wore on. I thought about calling my mother, or Booth, or Cynthia, or Dwayne, but I couldn't find the energy. I was filled with the kind of low-level dread that accompanies every icky task that must be faced. My friends and family were not going to jump for joy if I told them I was back with Murphy, sort of, and we were planning on moving to New Mexico together.

When my cell phone rang around six p.m. I snatched it up eagerly. From feeling harangued earlier in the day, now I felt abandoned. I worried for a moment that it was Mom, ready to tell me she'd booked a flight, but the caller I.D. wasn't a number I recognized. "Hello. Jane Kelly."

There was breathing on the other end. Not exactly heavy breathing, but breathing nonetheless. Maybe I was getting an obscene call. Quickly I tried to come up with a sharp, witty response to some lewd suggestion he might make. All that came to mind was: "You coming, or just breathing hard." It wouldn't be a bad start but I thought it best to wait till he made his move.

"Hi ... uh ... it's Jesse."

An obscene caller with a name ... hmmm ... The voice was male but it sounded young. Maybe jailbait young. Just my luck

to get an underage pervert. He probably had a soccer mom eavesdropping on the other line. "Well, Jesse, how can I help you?"

"Kurt gave me your number."

"Okay . . ." I felt a faint stirring of memory.

His voice had grown softer. So soft, in fact, that I was straining
to hear. "He said you wanted to talk to me."

Kurt . . . The lightbulb went off. The Coma Kid. "Yes! That's
right. I told him I wanted to talk to you."

Silence.

"You there?" I asked.

"I don't really have anything to say."

It sounded as if he were looking around, moving his mouth
away from the receiver and then back again. His nervousness
came across the wire to me and I found myself looking over my
shoulder.

"Yes, Jesse. I was interested in that night, when you fell from
the island?"

"I already talked to the police." He was skittish, barely audible. I knew he was already sorry he'd called me. "I don't remember anything. I already told 'em."

"I know. I was just wondering if there was anything else. Some
little thing maybe? The dogs weren't chasing you but you fell.
How did that happen?"

"I don't remember."

He was lying. I heard it flat out. For a moment I forgot my
newfound resolve to let the whole thing lie and I asked, "Do you
mind if I stop by and see you?"

"I . . . think I'd better go . . ."

Desperate, I blurted out, "How's Buddy?"

"You know Buddy?" he responded, surprised.

I knew it was all he could only remember in the beginning,
the name of his pet parakeet. But it sounded to me like he was
recalling a lot more now. At least he knew his own name—some
of the rest of us had a hard time remembering it.

"I know he's a parakeet."

"A budgie. Yeah." He seemed to roll that over. "You know

where I live?" He reeled off the address and directions, as if the faster he spoke, the less real it would be. I memorized and visualized and scrabbled around at my desk for pen and paper. Jesse could change his mind in a heartbeat.

"I could be there, in say, twenty minutes?"

"O—kay." The hesitancy was back.

"Looking forward to meeting Buddy," I said with enthusiasm, then hung up before I overplayed my hand. It was scary how these young kids could be bowled over by animals.

Note to self: Don't get overly stupid about your dog.

"Guard the place," I told Binkster, and she watched me go with wide, solemn eyes.

Chapter
Seventeen

Jesse's house, a daylight-basement on stilts in serious need of new paint, lay on the south side of Lake Chinook, perched on a hill. Its window side faced northeast and they might have had a view of the Willamette River except for the thick grove of Douglas firs which canopied their backyard and obscured everything from sight.

I carefully worked my way up the asphalt drive. Tree roots had buckled the left side and the ground sloped away toward a ravine. A rusting Chevrolet was parked on the right. I moved carefully as fir needles made the incline slick. Nobody seemed that interested in maintenance.

A woman cracked open the door. She looked to be somewhere in her forties with hair dyed jet black and blue eyes clogged with eye makeup. She gave me a head-to-toe once-over, but good. "I'm here to see Jesse," I said with a smile.

She swung the door wider and left without a word. Sheesh. So what was I supposed to do? Gingerly, I stepped into the room, closing the door behind me. She could have really stood to open the drapes. It was a beautiful evening beyond these dark, shadowy shapes. I inhaled dust. Not much going in the way of housekeeping, either.

"Jesse!" she suddenly hollered from somewhere out of sight, causing me to jump. "There's someone here for you!"

A few moments later Jesse appeared. He wore a baseball cap, but I could see hair to his shoulder on one side, a buzz cut on the other. Apparently his head wound had been shaved and treated. In some circles, his hairstyle could be the height of fashion.

He wore khaki shorts that covered his knees and a blue T-shirt advertising wakeboards. "Hi," I greeted him, holding out my hand. "I'm Jane."

Uncomfortably, he shook my hand. "I guess you know who I am." He seemed to wake up to his duties as a host and gestured toward the couch. I perched on the end of it. He sank into an overstuffed chair opposite me and I saw the *poof* of dust rise into the air.

Yeah, like I had any room to complain about housekeeping. Still, I couldn't quell the little cough that fought its way up my throat. "Do I get to meet Buddy?" I asked, trying to break the ice.

Jesse perked up. "Ya wanna? He's in my room. C'mon back." He leaped up and I followed him down a narrow hallway to another dimly lit room. But here Jesse threw back the curtains and I was treated to the disaster of an unmade bed, athletic gear and clothes strewn over the floor and a cage near the window which smelled sourly of bird.

"He's molting some," Jesse told me.

No kidding. Buddy had once been blue and white. Now he was a splotch of ragged feathers which he dug at ferociously with his beak, his little head bent to his task. Tiny pebbly black, green and white bird poop littered the bottom of his cage.

I hardly knew what to do next. For the life of me I couldn't dredge up the fire of interest I'd once had concerning the Coma Kid. I'd thought he might know something. Maybe he'd even seen something the night he was on the island. Something to do with Bobby Reynolds. Now, I wondered if I hadn't been overly zealous in my "investigation." I'd wanted to crack a case that the authorities were still working on. Call it beginner's overeagerness.

Jesse was studiously watching Buddy gnaw at his little body. Not sure what to do, I studied Buddy, too.

Eventually, Jesse cleared his throat. "I know that old guy who owned the island died, so I guess it doesn't matter anymore, really."

His voice was a decibel or two below comfortable hearing. I leaned into him. "What doesn't matter?"

He swallowed hard. "Y'know, I saw him. The one in the paper. The killer guy."

The hair on my arms lifted in spite of myself. "You *saw* him?"

"I didn't really remember, but then I kinda did," he said quickly, the words tumbling out. "I'm not sure. I don't want to say. It's weird, y'know? Like a dream? But I'm pretty sure it happened."

I felt myself go cold. So, Bobby had been on the island. Hearing it from this boy's lips made it real. I felt less elated than I would have expected having my theory proved true. "What did you see?" I asked.

"I was coming around the path. It was dark and I was looking for the dogs, y'know? My buddies left me." He still sounded upset.

"They were circling the island. Trying to keep from drawing attention to themselves."

"So, I was scared, y'know? Running kinda light and fast. And I came around this curve. The path kinda jogs inward there? It's right by that garage building? Runs along the back of it. But you step out into this grass where there's no trees, if you're not careful."

I visualized the garage. I could almost pinpoint where he meant. "Go on."

"There were two guys there. One of 'em was the guy who killed his family."

"You're sure?"

His eyes were huge, scared. "Yeah. I could only see one of 'em. *Him.*"

"But they were both men?"

He nodded. "I heard their voices. They were shouting at each other."

I took a breath. "Do you remember what they said?"

"No. I was about to shit my shorts. They were just yelling and I turned around and sorta slipped. Then one of 'em yelled louder. At first I thought it was at me! I was running away, but careful like, 'cause I didn't want to make a sound." Jesse shivered involuntarily.

"What was he yelling?"

"He was really mad. I mean, like really mad."

"Bobby?"

"Uh-uh. The other one. He said ..." Jesse screwed up his face, thinking hard. If he were milking the moment for drama, he was sure doing one hell of a job. I wanted to reach down his throat and pull the words out. "I think he said ... *the area's mine* ..." He shook his head. "I don't know. I remember wondering if the area was his. Like he owned it? Or maybe he used to own it and was really mad that he didn't now? It kinda creeped me out. *The area's mine.* That's pretty close. Made the hair stand up on my head. Like my scalp lifted, y'know? The killer guy stepped away from him and I just kept running."

"You didn't ever see the other guy?"

"Uh-uh. I wanted out of there. I just took off as fast as I could. Got to the fence and jumped over, but then I fell. Smacked my head, I guess." He reached up and gently touched the shaved side of his scalp below his hat.

"Do you think you'd recognize his voice again, if you heard it?"

"Hell, no! He was just yelling. I could never pick it out. Uh-uh! I wouldn't. No way!" Terror filled his eyes. "I'm just telling you this 'cause Kurt said you were okay. You have a dog and you wouldn't turn me in. But I won't tell anybody else, and if you tell 'em I told you, I'll say you're lying. I will!"

"Relax. I'm not really investigating this case. I don't know if what you saw means anything anyway."

"I mean it."

"I know you do."

Jesse pressed the knuckles of one hand to his lips, his eyes on Buddy again. After a long moment, he said, "They say the killer guy was murdered. Do you think . . . it happened that night?"

I thought it was a damn good bet, but I said offhand, "I don't think anyone knows. Probably not."

"You think they killed him 'cause he killed his family?"

I shook my head and shrugged. I thought it sounded a lot like they killed him over the island. I didn't say so to Jesse, but I thought the terms of Cotton's will just became a hell of a lot more interesting.

I didn't go into the main salon where Jerome Neusmeyer was presenting the last will and testament of Clement Reynolds, but I did go to the island because Murphy insisted. I wore a black skirt, this one a little longer than the one I'd had on Friday, and a dark lavender blouse that I absolutely detested as it had way too many frills and was a misguided gift from my mother so I hadn't been able to throw it out. Yet.

I stood near the pool and gazed beyond to the green waters of the lake. Trolling near the property was the cleanup barge, a watercraft operated by mostly teenagers for a summer job which cleared debris from the lake. Idly, I watched it move out of sight along the bank. Other people would be joining us in about an hour, post will-reading. Then we could all watch as Heather poured Cotton Reynolds into Lake Chinook.

I thought about the last time I'd seen Cotton on the island. Then, he'd been trying to convince me that Bobby was the one and only, the good son, innocent of all charges. Later, on his deathbed as it turned out, he'd taken a different tack entirely.

Murphy had moved in with me Saturday night. He'd displaced The Binkster who, before his arrival, had slowly inched her way from her bed and into mine. I'd stopped shooing her out, but Murphy's arrival had shoved her into the living room where she whined piteously. Luckily, a little carnal knowledge between

Murphy and myself had kept me from caring too much. Hey, how bad was the sofa really, anyway?

Tess had managed to show up for this occasion. She was in a dark blue suit with a narrow skirt and short jacket. Her blond hair had been cut and coiffed and her nails done a faint shade of puce. She looked as hard and brittle as glass. I'd steered clear of Neusmeyer so I hadn't been able to speak to her. It was just as well. One look my way and her blue eyes narrowed. We really didn't have a lot left to say to each other.

Murphy couldn't understand my aversion to being with the others while the will was read, but I held firm. I'd slicked my hair into a very tight, librarian-type bun, sprayed the hell out of it, then placed a pair of sunglasses firmly on my nose. I didn't think Neusmeyer would tumble to whom I was, given the old lady, feminine blouse and sensible shoes, but I didn't want to take the chance. I really did not want to have to make half-assed explanations should the issue of Ronnie come up and ruin the solemn tenor of the day.

There were several surprise attendees. A woman who reminded me a lot of Tess came in at the last moment, dabbing her eyes with an embroidered hankie. She wore a black sheath and a hat with a net. Very forties. Very chic. I learned from Murphy's surprised intake of breath that she was Dolly Smathers, Cotton's paramour after his divorce from Tess. A woman hated equally by both Tess and Heather. Upon seeing her, both Tess and Heather stiffened like mannequins.

The other surprise beneficiaries appeared to be George and Ruth Monroe. The lot of them were ensconced inside the house, listening to their bequeathments.

I strolled over to the garage and looked around. The grounds were groomed and trimmed, the patio swept. Grant Wemberly in action. I walked in the direction Jesse had indicated and found the little jog of the trail. I stood on that jog and looked toward the house and garage, the angle I believed Jesse had been positioned. My view was obscured by Douglas firs, naturally, but I could see slices of grounds and house between the trees. If

Bobby and his combatant were standing away from the garage, Jesse would have been able to see and hear most of what was happening. If they were standing closer to the garage, which I expected our mystery man had been, it would have been more difficult.

I'd been wrestling with the idea that I should tell someone what Jesse had told me. But who? Dwayne? I had yet to stop by and see him, mainly because I was so involved with Murphy. Murphy? Nah . . . He was focused on getting through this ordeal today and I didn't want to muddy the waters with information that would probably only depress or anger him. Tomas Lopez? I shied away from going to the authorities, especially since Jesse had said in no uncertain terms that he wouldn't back me up. Booth? Now, Booth was a possibility. He was an officer of the law, but he was also my brother. Hypothetically, I could give him what I'd learned and he might be able to make a judgment call on it that we could both live with. However, Booth was unpredictable. More than once when I'd brought him a problem, he'd gone all "big brother" on me and made me sorry I'd ever said anything to him.

So, to date, I was sitting on that information. I had a theory I applied to: *the area is mine.* After all, it was all about real estate, wasn't it? Real estate agents had been circling the island all summer, waiting for a chance to pounce. Paula Shepherd and her sidekick, Brad, were especially obnoxious. However, it was Craig Cuddahy where I'd put my money. He was the developer. He was the one who wanted to subdivide. He was the one who'd gone a few rounds with Cotton over it. I wasn't sure what Paula's plan was, but Craig seemed the more likely suspect. He wanted the island. He'd stayed around all summer in the hopes of gaining it. I believed he would make a deal with the devil to gain control of it.

Or maybe just a deal with whomever inherited it.

Which meant that Craig Cuddahy had faced off with Bobby Reynolds. Had snarled at him that the area was his. Had . . . killed him?

I grimaced, trying to picture that. I already knew Cuddahy was quick with his fists, but even Heather had said that was after Cotton took a poke at him first. So, what had happened? Had he knocked Bobby unconscious, taken him out in a boat and then sunk him? To gain control of the property? How? He couldn't have expected Cotton to die. I mean, sure, we all heard he was ill, but death is coy. It isn't something that can be predicted with any accuracy. I did not for a minute believe Cotton had been murdered by Craig Cuddahy or anyone else.

So, how had Cuddahy felt the island was his? Why would he murder Bobby for it?

Something was off here. A piece missing. I felt like I was close to the answer but it was eluding me, just out of reach.

I walked back to the garage and scanned the area, trying to picture the scene as it had been that night. If Bobby were standing farther from the garage, more toward the grounds and patio, then Craig would have been hidden from Jesse's view. My gaze traveled over the rhododendrons, now bereft of flowers, and the hydrangeas, still in luscious full bloom. I frowned. Something looked different from when I was here before.

I cast my mind back to that unexpected meeting with Grant Wemberly the day of the benefit. Grant had alluded that rogue animals—read Bobby Reynolds, for that—should be put down once and for all. Did *Grant* feel this property was his? Would he take out Bobby to simply be rid of a really bad egg? To make it easier for Cotton to move on?

Or, to die?

Who *was* inheriting the island?

I sat down on a bench next to the pool and decided I would know soon enough. Other mourners began gathering and we made a quiet group.

Twenty minutes later, people began emerging from the main house. Murphy brought up the rear. I stood and waited for him. I wondered how long I could keep from blurting out the question.

Murphy saw me and headed my way. Jerome Neusmeyer was listening hard to something Heather was saying, ogling the front of her decolletage. Heather was in dark gray, but it was sexy as hell. She had another big flower, this one dusky yellow and real, a rose, pinned on the lapel of her bolero. The bolero buttoned beneath her breasts, enhancing their perky appearance. Neusmeyer was lost in them, so I was safe.

Murphy's face was pinched. "What happened?" I asked.

"Cotton wrote the will after Bobby's death. Tess, Owen and Dolly each got cash settlements. So did the Monroes, who looked shell-shocked by the amount. He left me his cars, remembering that Mustang I used to have."

I nodded. I had my own vivid memories of that convertible.

His gaze traveled to the garage, his mouth twisting with emotion. "Heather got the island."

"Heather?"

"All his property. He has a rental house in Sellwood."

"Oh, that's right. He bought it from Owen."

"Heather'll sell to Cuddahy." Murphy was darkly positive. "She practically squealed with delight when she heard." I gazed at him in disbelief. "Oh, she didn't make a sound, but that look on her face. She was bursting."

I glanced over at her. Her body language said she was happy. Her face was wreathed in smiles, but when she saw me looking she sobered immediately.

"She's bending Neusmeyer's ear about it now," Murphy went on. "She wants to unload the property as soon as possible. It's the last thing Cotton would have wanted."

"Then he shouldn't have left it to her."

"Who was he going to leave it to, then?" Murphy demanded. "There wasn't anyone else."

There was you, I thought. But then immediately I reminded myself that Murphy would have wanted neither the money nor the burden from the property. Cotton knew that.

There wasn't a lot of time for further conversation as our small group banded together near the water's edge. I kept an eye on the silver urn which contained Cotton's remains. I had this fear the wind might throw the ashes back on me. Sorry, I just didn't think I could take that. To protect myself, I stood a little to the right and behind Murphy. Jerome Neusmeyer glanced around, his gaze briefly touching on me, but I kept my vision straight ahead, hidden behind my shades, and his glance passed over me.

Heather stood up and after a cold glance thrown in first Tess's, then Dolly's, direction, she began a stilted little speech. Her goggly blue eyes teared over. I glanced at Tess whose mouth was a grim line, then at Dolly, whose mouth appeared just as grim but who kept dabbing at her eyes. A frisky little breeze played havoc with our hemlines and just for a moment Heather's black skirt flipped skyward, revealing a very naughty black lace thong.

Owen coughed into his fist. I felt a new kinship with him. Murphy's hand held mine and squeezed. Heather smoothed her skirt, gave Murphy and myself the old fish eye, then continued on. With Owen's help, she then tipped the silver urn upside down over Lake Chinook. Bits of ash rode on the breeze. I held my breath, but the bulk of Cotton floated on, then sank into the water.

I vowed solemnly to myself, *I will never swim in Lake Chinook again.*

"I'm going to miss you, Daddy," Heather said, a little throb in her voice.

I gotta be honest. It kind of choked me up.

I thought Murphy was going to crush the bones in my hand, but he finally relented, practically whirling me around in his haste to get away. I was all for it. We were halfway up the slate pathway to the house when we encountered a late arrival.

Craig Cuddahy, an appropriately sober expression on his countenance, greeted Murphy and me with appropriately sober words of regret. Murphy let go of me for a moment, getting ready for God knew what. Cuddahy took the opportunity to give Murphy's hand the double-clasp, which I guess declared he really meant what he said.

"Cotton was one of a kind," Craig said.

"Yes, he was." Murphy was coiled with tension.

I slipped my arm through Murphy's, gently nudging him. Now was really not the time for this. But Murphy held firm.

With Murphy glaring daggers at him, Cuddahy shifted his weight from one foot to the other. He glanced around for reinforcements. Heather was still in her role as grieving widow and didn't notice. But Owen was bearing down on us as if he had something to say.

He did. "What the hell are you doing here?" he demanded of Cuddahy. "Get your tail between your legs and vamoose before I call the dogs on you."

I nervously glanced toward the garage which I realized belatedly had been remarkably silent today.

"Heather asked me to come," he answered, clearing his throat.

"Well, you're getting told by Owen to leave," Owen said.

There was something kind of scary about Owen. Grief had made him reckless. He had this "I don't have any reason not to kill you" attitude. And then there was that resemblance to Bobby. I was glad I wasn't standing in Craig's shoes.

Murphy's narrowed eyes switched to Owen. Owen caught his glance and silently stuck out his hand. They shook peremptorily. Something between them. A kind of brotherhood forged by the loss of Owen's half-brother, Murphy's best friend.

And they both loved and respected Cotton.

"You're a jackal, Cuddahy. Go pick someone else's bones until we've all left. Then you want to see Heather? Have at her."

"I'll wait outside the gate."

"Wait in the next county," Owen suggested.

Craig tried to look past us, hoping for Heather's rescue. She was in a tense, private conversation with Dolly Smathers and her attention was riveted. She looked, in fact, about to fall over. Dolly actually put out a hand to steady her. I would have given a lot to know what they were talking about.

In the far distance I saw the cleaning barge heading back in the direction of its mother dock, the Lake Corporation's marina and offices. In the near distance we were being approached by

Tess whose gaze was ice when it touched on me. Jerome Neusmeyer was hurrying toward us, checking his watch.

"We've gotta go," I told Murphy.

Owen's eyes were on me. "Thanks for driving me home the other night."

"No problem."

"I was going to stop by and thank you personally. You're renting from Ogilvy, aren't you?"

I must have looked alarmed at his knowledge, but he shrugged it off. "I've been trying to acquire a bunch of his properties, but Ogilvy's something else. Can't get him to sell."

With Tess glaring at me and Neusmeyer getting too close, I tugged more urgently on Murphy's arm. Abruptly, he turned and we walked quickly to his SUV which was parked beside Owen's BMW. We didn't say much on the ride home. I was lost in thought and I guess Murphy was, too.

As I unlocked my door I got that same feeling that someone had been in my place. But no . . . it was just the unfamiliarity of seeing all Murphy's things scattered around.

He brushed past me to one of his bags, tossed casually on my couch.

"Guess we'll have to find room in one of my closets," I said. "I wonder if—" My thought died on the vine.

Murphy had pulled a Ziploc baggie from the interior of his sports bag. Inside was a steely blue handgun.

Chapter Eighteen

Murphy kept digging in his bag as if nothing strange had just occurred. At my sudden silence he looked up.

"What's with the gun?" I asked.

He glanced at it. "I had it shipped here from Santa Fe."

"Why do you have a gun at all? You said you weren't in private investigation anymore."

"I said I wasn't much," he corrected. "I thought I wanted out. I'm sick of all that's happened here. It's too close." He gestured around himself to encompass all of Lake Chinook. "But I've got a thriving business in Santa Fe. We could work together, you and me. Actually, Jane, you're not half bad."

"You called me an amateur." For some reason this wasn't quite my ideal vision of our life together in Santa Fe. Private investigation equaled Lake Chinook and Dwayne. Love, hearts and roses equaled Santa Fe and Murphy.

"I didn't say you were perfect, I said you weren't half bad."

"Why did you bring the gun at all?"

"I wanted to have it nearby, just in case."

Just in case what? I asked slowly, "When Cotton called you to come to Lake Chinook, did he give you a reason? I mean, besides just coming for a visit?"

"What are you getting at?"

"Just the timing, I guess. I mean, Bobby showed up about the same time. I thought . . ."

"That Cotton was upset that Bobby was back and he wanted me to do something about it for him?" Murphy straightened.

Well . . . yeah . . . that was kind of where I was headed.

"For God's sake, Jane. Give it a rest!"

I shrugged sheepishly. "Sorry."

We stared at each other for a couple of seconds, then he shook his head and finished reorganizing his bag. He placed the gun, still in its baggie, on the television set.

I changed the subject. "Did you look at the cars Cotton left you?"

"No, I'll go later. The dogs were there. Tranquilized, because they've been acting strange ever since Cotton died. They know something's wrong. I don't know what Heather will do with them."

I suddenly worried for the Dobermans. "What about Grant Wemberly?"

Murphy gave me a long look. "How do you know Grant?"

"I only met him once. The day of the benefit. He seemed to care about the dogs quite a bit. Maybe Heather will give them to him." I paused. "He's going to be out of a job if Heather sells."

"He's already out of a job. Quit the day Cotton died."

"Quit?" I was surprised.

"All I know is, we're not taking the dogs to Santa Fe. No animals at all."

"*None?*" My eyes searched for The Binkster who was flopped on her little bed, eyes closed, breathing regularly, except for the occasional snort or two.

Murphy's gaze followed mine. "You're seriously attached to that dog? I thought it was just a temporary situation."

"It is." My heart felt weighted with lead. "The gal who brought her to me, Megan Adair, is a bartender at the Crock in downtown Portland. I've got her number. She said if I needed to find Binky a new home I could call her."

Murphy grunted. "Good idea." He kissed me on the cheek. "I'll see ya later. I've got something to take care of."

If I'd been myself I might have asked what. As it was, all I could do was stare at the fawn-and-black creature lying so peacefully unaware on her fuzzy bed.

Tuesday morning I gave myself a punishing run to the Coffee Nook. I stepped inside, gasping for air. The day was hot and muggy. Odd weather for the West Coast, but it happens from time to time. I was dripping in sweat and had to head to the bathroom and hold a towel to my face for several minutes. This cannot be good for you.

I was feeling, well, weird. Murphy came back from wherever he went and we went to Dottie's for a sandwich. I picked at mine, roast turkey on sourdough. Murphy seemed off his feed, too, eating only half of his corned beef on rye.

It was as if Murphy had a new lease on life. He chatted up the waitress in a way I found faintly annoying, then made plans for us to get moving, so to speak. He wanted me to call Ogilvy and cancel my bungalow. I told him that my rent was paid till September first, but Murphy wasn't waiting that long. He pointed out that it was already the middle of August. A perfect time to leave. People would be wanting to get their kids in school, so they'd want the cottage by the first.

I couldn't sleep the whole night. I lay in a frozen position, not wanting to bother Murphy, staring at the ceiling. I'd gotten ready for my run while he was still asleep. His gun still lay on my television set, right next to Lopez's card. Shivering, I'd let myself outside into air as thick as molasses. Well, at least it felt that way to me. I fought my way to the Nook but it about killed me.

Billy Leonard was on his stool when I returned, red-faced but at least every pore wasn't leaking fluid, from the bathroom. I sat down next to him.

"You ran here? In this weather?" he asked, incredulous.

"Yep."

He looked at me like, "it's your funeral," but left it for the moment. "Hey, B.J. says you talked to the Coma Kid. Learn anything?"

"Not really. I'm through working on the Reynolds case."

"Yeah? The kid didn't help you?"

I debated on telling Billy what Jesse had said about seeing Bobby, but I didn't. I'd put in a call to Booth last night, wanting to hash things over with him, but his voice mail picked up. He was probably working. Now, I was wishing I hadn't called at all.

"B.J. and his buddy Kurt were on the lake last night and they ran into some friends who run the cleanup barge? You know the one."

"I saw it yesterday."

"They were working around the island and hauled up pieces of roof slate. Said it must've fallen in sometime in the last few weeks 'cause they clean around the island on a schedule. They keep tabs on that island. It's like a fascination for teenagers." He chuckled. "We used to try to steal beer when I was a teen. Out of the refrigerators people keep in their boathouses. Nobody used to lock anything."

"The paths are slate. And the house and garage roofs are slate. I saw an extra pile of roof slate by the garage."

"Somebody just off-loaded some into the water?"

"The regular maintenance man quit last week after Cotton died. Maybe the new people tossed them into the water."

"Don't let the City of Lake Chinook and the Lake Corp. know. You know how much they fine developers for stirring up the water? A small fortune. You can hardly afford to build anything anymore. And don't even think about taking down a tree." He left some money on the counter, said good-bye to Julie and me, and headed out the door.

To my surprise and delight the door opened again and Lorraine Bluebell sailed inside. She wore a black skirt and a short-sleeved white blouse with gold buttons marching down its front. Her purse was about as big a monster as I'd ever seen. Black and white with a gold clasp and a little gold chain looping across the front.

"Jane!" she called, equally glad to see me.

"I've been thinking about you," I said. "You know, the island belongs to Heather now."

"Does it?" She nodded as if she weren't surprised. "A shame about Cotton."

"I think she's selling to Craig Cuddahy."

"Humph." Lorraine shook her head. The swatch of white hair across her bangs matched her outfit. "Don't count Paula Shepherd out. She's a barracuda."

"From what I understand, it's practically a done deal."

"Well, then, I'm sorry. I would like to keep the island as one property."

We chatted further and then she got her double vanilla latte and headed out. I realized I felt the exact same way. I wanted the island to remain one piece.

But then why did I care? I was leaving Lake Chinook for Santa Fe.

My own inner ambivalence bothered me. Deciding to do something positive, I pulled my cell phone from the zippered pocket of my running shorts and put through a call to Dwayne. It took him six rings to answer.

"What? Did I get you out of bed?"

"Nah, I was on another call. More business. So, are you coming in with me or not, darlin'? Business is getting out of control."

This is why I'd put off this call. "I'd have to say . . . or not."

"What?" he asked, unable to hide his surprise.

I counted to three in my head. "I'm moving to Santa Fe with Murphy."

"Bullshit!"

"I am," I insisted.

"Jane . . ." His drawl was bitten off, as there weren't words for what he wanted to say.

"Forget whatever you're going to say," I said tersely. "My mind's made up. Murphy wants me to throw in with him down there. He's doing investigative work in Santa Fe. I thought he'd gotten out of it but apparently not."

"You're going to just leave?" He couldn't believe it.

"That's what I'm saying." I hesitated. "You wouldn't want to take care of my dog for me. For a while."

"*Your* dog?"

"Murphy doesn't want any animals."

"Darlin'," Dwayne said, switching to serious Southern charm mode. "If a man doesn't want your dog, he's tellin' you somethin' about himself. Somethin' you need to hear."

"I don't see you jumping up to take the dog."

"I'm not dragging you off to Santa Fe."

"Fine. Someone else can take Binks. I'll figure it out." I clicked off in a huff. It bugs me when Dwayne pulls that "I know better" shit. Especially when it's the truth.

Because I was pissed at myself, I made myself run all the way back home, too.

Murphy was at the computer when I let myself inside the cottage. I could hardly speak. My legs were shaking and there simply wasn't enough oxygen in the world to fill my burning lungs. Binky came out and licked one of my sweaty legs. She backed away. Great. Even the dog could tell how disgusting I was. I stripped off my clothes and jumped in the shower, lowering the water temperature to lukewarm and turning my face to the spray, standing there for what felt like an eternity.

Murphy opened the bathroom door a crack. "You gotta get a new computer, Jane. You can hardly get on the Internet with this dinosaur."

"Why do you need the Internet?" I called.

"To get us some airline tickets." He closed the door behind him.

Suddenly energized, I shut off the shower, grabbed a towel, wrapped it around me and practically skidded across the hardwood floor to where he was standing in the bedroom, tucking his wallet into the back pocket of his pants.

"Airline tickets? What about our cars?"

"Mine's a rental." He gave me a look. "I figured you'd sell the Volvo."

My heart. I pressed a hand to it. "What . . . what about the cars that Cotton gave you? You said you got cars."

"I checked them out. I've got to sell them. They're ancient monsters. Cadillacs from the days when Caddys were a mile long and a mile-and-a-half wide. One is, however, a red color. Not exactly candy apple, but close."

"You want to fly to Santa Fe? What about all my things?"

"We'll ship them." He gazed at me closely. "You're having second thoughts."

"Right the first time, Bucko."

He nodded, finally hearing me. "I've got to go, Jane. I'm pushing you hard because I just can't do Lake Chinook a second longer."

"I get that." He'd said it enough times. "But I've got to slow down."

My cell phone rang. I wouldn't have answered it, but Murphy dug my cell out of my zippered pocket and handed it to me. It was Booth. "It's my brother," I said.

"Take it. I'm going to call the airlines. See ya later."

He was out the door before I could argue. Reluctantly, I pushed talk. "Hey, Booth."

"Mom just called. She said she's coming up here this week. She said she's staying with you."

"She wants to meet Sharona."

"Does it have to be now?" He sighed. "I just got your message. You wanted to discuss something?"

I couldn't talk to him wearing only a towel, one that kept slipping from my hands. "Let me call you right back."

"Make it quick. I'm on my way to work."

I toweled myself off with inner fury, threw on my tan capris, a white T-shirt and my beloved Nikes. I brushed my hair hard until it lay straight and wet against my head, the tips touching my shoulders. I glanced in my refrigerator. Not—one—goddamn—thing—worth—eating. Couldn't Murphy have at least stocked the fridge?

I slammed the door, swept up the receiver for my landline—why run up my cell bill if I didn't have to?—and phoned Booth. He answered immediately and suddenly I had nothing to say.

But Booth had lots to say, about how he didn't think he was

ready to have Mom come, about how wonderful Sharona was, and finally a hint about how I should get my life together.

I was bugged. Why were all these decisions being thrust on me now? I'd been happy, hadn't I? Hanging around Lake Chinook, making friends, process serving? Was that so bad?

"So, what's up, Jane?" Booth asked. It was the opening I'd been waiting for.

In fits and starts, I told him everything I knew about the Reynolds investigation. I needed a new perspective. I needed someone to bounce ideas off. For better or worse, this time it was Booth.

There was a moment of silence when I finished. I might have thought he'd hung up on me but I could just hear his measured breathing. He said, quietly, "You think this Craig—what's his last name?"

"Cuddahy."

"You think Craig Cuddahy got in a heated argument with Bobby Reynolds over the island property and subsequently killed him?"

I opened my mouth, closed it, opened it again and said, "Maybe."

"What's the investigator's name? Lopez?"

"Yes."

"Call him up, Jane. Tell him what you just told me."

He sounded so serious that I almost laughed. Almost. "Booth, half of it's theory. And I won't get any backup. Jesse, the Coma Kid, said he will not corroborate anything he told me and—"

"Doesn't matter." He cut me cold. "Hand it over to Lopez. Let him break the kid."

"I feel a certain responsibility to Jesse," I said heatedly.

"Tough. I don't know if you're right about this, Jane. I don't even care. I want you out of it. Pass along whatever you even *think* you know. Let the professionals figure it out."

"Okay."

Though I acquiesced, he heard the recalcitrance in my voice. "Do it, Jane."

I have really got to improve my lying. "Didn't I say I would?"

"You're not up to this. Sorry, if that bursts your bubble. But you're not. And stop listening to Dwayne Durbin. He's going to get you hurt or killed."

"Thanks for the vote of confidence. I'll put it in a memo to the staff."

"Damn it," he said through his teeth.

"I'll talk to Lopez, Booth, okay? I've been meaning to anyway." I hung up as quickly as I could as he started to launch into a dozen more reasons why I should stop trying to be something I'm not. Trust Booth to set my teeth on edge. I was *really* tired of people telling me what I ought to do.

And I was going to talk to Lopez. I was. I just wasn't going to do it right yet.

I visited Greg Hayden and picked up some more 72-hour notices. The heat bore down on me until my tongue felt like it was hanging out like Binkster's. I managed to post two with minor difficulty. One man called me a fucking bitch, but hey, he was probably hot, too. I told him, "Have a nice day." He threw a dirt clod at me as I headed to my car but missed by a mile.

By four o'clock I was done. I drove to Foster's On The Lake. I wanted a drink, preferably alcoholic, but a bucket of ice water tossed over my head would suffice in a pinch. The only person at the outdoor bar was Manny and his shirt was sticking to him.

I climbed onto a stool. "Have you ever had everyone you know give you advice you never want to hear?"

"Frequently." He placed a cocktail napkin in front of me and waited.

"Something really, really cold."

To my chagrin he poured me a concoction made from blue curacao. My nemesis. It was bright blue and beautiful and spoke of Scandinavian fjords but I knew it would taste godawful. "Oh, Manny." I sighed. "Give me something I can drink."

"Try it, Jane."

Well, hell. I picked up the martini glass, silently saluted him, then touched my tongue to the lighter fluid within. I sampled the flavor. Not bad. I took a swallow. Drinkable. "I used to make blue curacao drinks at Sting Ray's, but I never could make one that anyone would order twice."

"What do you think?" He nodded toward my glass.

Light refracted in blue prisms against my skin. "I think you've got sugar or Hpnotiq or something in there to make it less terrible." I took another swallow. "Something that doesn't corrupt the color."

"So?"

"It's okay." I thought about it as I kept sipping. "I actually could drink two."

Manny smiled. "High praise, indeed."

I didn't have to order a second because Manny slid one across the bar as soon as my first one was drained. I was already feeling lightheaded, so I took a long, long time over it, and Manny put some salt bread and hummus nearby, so I dug into that, too. I had a feeling it might all be free which cheered me up a lot.

I supposed I should go home to Murphy. But then, he could always reach me on my cell phone.

Slowly people began arriving. The temperature had to be in the nineties, so only the brave and foolish were outside their own air-conditioned splendor. I was twiddling with one of the little parasol umbrellas Manny sometimes sticks in chunks of pineapple when a boat came screaming up to the dock. I swear everyone on Foster's deck inhaled in shock and braced themselves. I know I did.

But the engine was cut at the last second and Cotton's boat, captained by his lovely widow, bumped hard enough into the dock to give us all a little sway. Everyone at the bar kept her in their sights. And it was worth the viewing.

Heather climbed out of the boat, wearing a hot pink bikini with a sheer white overshirt and a pink and red wraparound flowered skirt. The wraparound had unwrapped, however, and we were all treated to her tanned, bare legs as she staggered through the gate into the patio. Her skirt fell back like a bridal train.

Foster himself came out to view the new arrival, a frown on his face. I slid off my stool and walked over to him. "Give her a drink. I'll take her back in my car," I said.

"You're awful chummy with the widow."

"My new best friend."

Of course, chances were Heather would scream and rail at me. She seemed to vacillate on her opinion of me at any given time. I wondered what had her in such a state. When she removed her sunglasses her eyes were red and any makeup they'd previously worn was rubbed off. As if realizing it, she sniffed and put her shades back on. Her nose was also a hot pink shade and it wasn't from the sun.

Foster took me at my word, letting Heather order a Mojito. He pointed his finger at me which meant I was the designated driver and babysitter. While she sucked down the first drink I moseyed over to her table.

"You," she growled, shaking the ice cubes in her glass then lifting it to her lips, sticking her tongue inside to catch a few more drops. The mint leaf on top nearly went up her nose.

"This is just an observation, but maybe you shouldn't be driving right now."

"So, turn me in." She waved an arm around. "Go ahead. Screw me like everyone else."

I joined her at her table. She snapped her fingers for service. The waiter looked a little askance as her intoxication level was obvious. He went back and conferred with Jeff Foster who reluctantly nodded an okay, giving me the evil eye at the same time. It irked me that he didn't believe I had things under control.

"I understand you're selling the island to Craig Cuddahy."

"Yeah? Well, you understand wrong. Catch up, girl. That's yesterday's news."

I gazed at her in perplexity. "I heard it was practically inked."

"*You* didn't talk to Dolly Smathers. *You* don't know jack shit about what you're talking about." The waiter delivered her drink and Heather gulped at it.

"What's Dolly got to do with it?"

"Dolly Smathers, bitch extraordinaire, has turned herself into a matriarch of Lake Chinook society. *That's* what she's got to do with it. Didn't you know? Dolly's vice president of the Hysterical Society. Isn't that unbelievable? A slut like her? I guess being Cotton's whore put her on somebody's A-list! And guess what? Now Cotton's house is on the List of Historical Homes. Courtesy of Dolly Smathers who just happened to blab all about it to that group of tight-assed snobs. And you know what that means? It means I can't fucking subdivide, that's what it means! It's got to be one parcel. The whole damn thing!"

Heather drained her glass and thumped it back on the table. I searched in my purse for my car keys. "You want to create a scene, or do you just want to get drunk?"

"I just wanna get drunk," she muttered.

"Then let me take you back to the island."

"Fuck that," she said, but when I paid the bill—only her drinks as Manny shook his head when I tried to pay for mine, thank the gods of free booze—Heather capitulated. Although it practically killed me to fork over the money; Foster's *rapes* you on the price of drinks, it won me enough brownie points to get Heather to leave with me, weaving her way through the restaurant on her long tan legs, causing quite a stir among the male patrons.

Did this blow my theory on Craig Cuddahy? I didn't think so. How would he have known about this turn of events? He'd been charging after the island like a Poloma bull for weeks. Had he killed Bobby over something that wasn't ever going to happen? Wouldn't that be irony in its purest form?

Halfway to the island Heather started to cry. Big, gulping sobs. "I'm gonna miss him!" she wailed. "And it's all that fucker Bobby's fault. I wish he'd died years ago!"

"Cotton was ill," I reminded her.

"Well, he got ill-er after Bobby showed up." She wiped ignominiously at her running nose. "Did you know that? Did you know he came to the island? I saw him. Cotton didn't want me to. He tried to hide Bobby. I think he was scared shitless I'd go to the police. I would've, too, if I coulda got away with it without Cotton knowing. That shiftless no-account. Whined to Cotton about needing money. I would've kicked him in the balls. Murdering bastard!"

"Where was Bobby staying?"

"Not with us! Cotton gave him money. All these secret calls, like I'm too dumb to notice? Gimme a break."

I love it when drunk people start talking. Note to self: use alcohol as an investigative tool. "But he did come to the island," I pointed out as if it were fact.

"I saw him once. About a week before the benefit. I just came unglued. Cotton tried to tell me I'd seen wrong, but I told him he'd better get rid of him and quick. I thought the benefit was important." She snorted. "If I'd known what those fat, pink-assed old ladies were cooking up, I woulda pushed 'em in the lake!"

"Cotton changed his will after he saw Bobby?"

"Yeah, he finally got it! That Bobby was a total loser. He kept trying to act like he was so great. Talking, talking, talking about Bobby! Wonderful Bobby!"

"What changed his mind?"

"Oh, who cares. Bobby did." She swiped her nose again. "It was never enough, you know? More money . . . more money . . . more money . . . I caught the tail end of enough calls to know. Still, it wasn't until after the benefit that Cotton finally woke up. Murphy coming to town helped. Cotton called him up and told him Bobby was here. Murphy came right up from Santa Fe."

My hands tightened on the wheel. "Murphy knew Bobby was here?"

"Ya think it was just coincidence he showed up this summer? Cotton told him Bobby was here. That's what got him here."

"You overheard this?" If Murphy had lied to me, I wanted to be absolutely certain.

She waved that away. "All I heard was money, money, money. Poor Bobby needs money. Poor, poor Bobby. Killed his family and now can't get a break."

She was just talking. I set aside my concern about Murphy and said instead, "So, if Bobby hadn't died, he would've inherited. That's the way the will was originally written. Neusmeyer practically said the son always inherits."

"I guess so."

"So, it would have all been Bobby's."

Heather squinted at me as I turned onto the bridge that led to the island. "What are you saying?"

"I'm just trying to get it straight."

"Wait a minute . . . wait . . . just . . . one . . . minute." She waved a finger at me and glared. "You think I woulda got screwed if Bobby was still alive. You think I wouldn't'a got a red cent."

"Possibly. I'm just thinking out loud."

"*You* think it was in my best interest that Bobby died! Well, I'm not the only one. What about Owen? What about Tess? What about those goddamned blue-haired bitches of the Hysterical Society, like *Dolly Smathers*? They got what they wanted, didn't they?"

But they would've got that regardless. Heather, Owen, Tess and the Monroes were the ones who'd gained by Bobby predeceasing Cotton.

"Oh, shit," Heather said, lifting her head as I drove through the island's open gates. "That's Craig's car. What's he doing here?"

I really didn't want to see Craig Cuddahy. The idea made me tired. "You've still got a really valuable piece of property," I pointed out. "Maybe he still wants to buy."

She laughed at me. "Forget it. I'll have to contact Paula Whatever-her-face. She's the one who'll find a buyer for this piece of crap. I mean, really, who wants their own island?"

I could think of a lot of people. Most just didn't have the money to maintain it.

Craig was waiting outside the front door. Seeing me brought a look of consternation to his face. We were equally underwhelmed to see each other again. "I thought we were going to talk about our problem," he said meaningfully to Heather.

"Oh, that's right. I was supposed to meet you." She lifted a shoulder and laughed without humor. "I forgot. I took the boat to Foster's."

Cuddahy pursed his lips. "You're lucky you didn't get arrested."

I gave him a hard look. Like he had any room to talk when it came to alcohol consumption. I suppose I should have been more cautious around him. After all, I still sort of believed he may have murdered Bobby Reynolds. But there was something about Cuddahy that simply didn't scare me. I wasn't a threat to him, at least from his current perception. The truth was, I was having a hell of a time keeping him as my primary suspect.

He ignored me, and although he was gentleman enough to let me walk through ahead of him, he practically trod on the back of my Nikes in his urgency to get to Heather. She went straight to the bar and pulled out a half gallon of Skyy Vodka. He followed after her toward the kitchen but I hung back.

"They can't do this," I heard him say in a low angry voice.

Heather gave a little bark of laughter. "They fucked us, Craig. We're fucked."

I went outside to the backyard. In this case I was glad, actually, that the Historical Society had stepped in. I hated to think what this island would have become if Heather and Craig had gotten their way. It lightened my heart to think it would remain a private residence with its sweeping grounds and circular trail.

Long shadows cast by the towering firs were striping the lawn. I walked toward the lake, stopping above the pool, wondering who in the world would buy such an expensive piece of property. Somebody. But Heather was right: it didn't sound like it was going to be Craig Cuddahy.

I strolled back toward the house, near the garage. As I neared it, the Dobermans started growling and barking in a regular fury. They'd been weird since Cotton's death, according to Murphy. Unweird Dobermans were bad enough. I moved away quickly, but my eye caught on something. I slowly turned back, looking hard, searching for what it was. Finally it dawned on me that it was what *wasn't* there. The roof slate. The untidy pile I'd noticed the day of the benefit. Billy had said the kids from the barge had picked it up, so someone had dropped the pile into Lake Chinook.

I retraced my footsteps to the house where Heather and Craig's voices were raised with the consumption of alcohol. Heather sounded teary; Craig sounded enraged. "I'll sue 'em," he said. "I'll stop 'em. It's your property. You can do with it what you want."

"It won't work," she sobbed.

"Hey!" I called into the house. "Who's your new caretaker? Is he here?"

"I don't have one!" Heather wailed anew at this fresh insult. "Grant left and everything's just gone to hell!"

"Someone's cleaning the grounds," I said.

"Not since Grant," she sniffed. "I gotta figure something out."

"I'll sue 'em," Craig muttered fiercely.

I thought I heard a motor. I walked to the edge of the island, catty-corner from the house and garage. There were boats on the water but none close enough to explain what I heard. I strolled back, lost in thought.

In the center of the backyard stood Betty and Benny. I stopped short. My heart leapt. *How the hell had they gotten out?*

They stood shoulder-to-shoulder, their sharp eyes watching me. My breathing grew shallow. I felt slightly dizzy with fear. A low whine issued from the larger one's throat. Betty? Grant had said she was the leader. They'd chased me once and lost. I didn't see how that could happen again. They were between me and my car, between me and the gate.

I kept my arms down. "Hey there, Betty," I said soothingly, but my voice shook a little.

There was only way out: toward the lake. I would have to jog left and run for all I was worth, leap the fence but hang on, otherwise I'd be dropping the long way into the lake.

I silently cursed myself for the punishment of running this morning. I was tired. I couldn't do this. But adrenalin was singing through my veins. I balanced on the balls of my feet.

A door slammed inside the house. Benny glanced over. A split second later, Betty looked and I was gone. I tore to my left. The dogs set up a fearful growling howl as they charged after me. I ran blind. Past the spot where Jesse had stood. Down the path. I swear I could hear their jaws clacking behind me.

The fence lay just ahead. Betty and Benny were slipping up close behind me. I crashed through underbrush. My hands were reaching, reaching. Instead of the fence I snagged a lowered branch, jerking my legs up high beneath me. The dogs leapt and snapped. I saw teeth and slaver. I cried out, scrabbling, hanging on for dear life, my legs churning, practically running over the fence. The top rail scraped my leg but I was over. I hung onto the branch. The dogs threw themselves at the fence. The chain link shook and jangled. I clung to my branch. My lungs burned. My arm muscles ached.

I looked below me and it was a long way down to earth, rock and water. I held on with everything I had. I screamed for help.

The fingers of my left hand slipped. I prayed for more strength. I found religion in a big way.

The dogs stopped barking. They sat on the opposite side of the fence and watched me. I swear Betty was smiling.

My left hand gave completely. I watched my right fingers lose their grip.

Then I was falling, falling.

I closed my eyes and thought, *I should've told Lopez.*

Chapter
Nineteen

Don't let anyone tell you that shock isn't a wonderful thing because it is. Some might argue, claiming that shock is a sneaky killer, as dangerous as the injury or event that brought it on. I'm here to tell you, as a drug, it's the best. No pain. Not a whole lot of clear thinking. A feeling of cold, yes, but hey, better than the screaming pain you just *know* you're going to feel later.

I was semiconscious. Above me, in the darkening evening, I could make out the fir limbs gently swaying. It was still hot. The air pressed on my face. But the rest of my body was cool and growing cooler. I was lying on rocks and needle-covered dirt. My right leg dangled into the water leaving my Nike underwater. My right shin wet nearly to the knee.

If I'd been able to think, I would have asked myself a whole lot of questions, but that would come later. For the moment, I lay in a strange stupor. Whatever my future fate, I was damn glad the dogs hadn't got me. I think I hate Betty.

There was noise above me. The sound of shouts and running feet. At some point I saw Grant Wemberly's face swimming above me. He gazed down at me in concern. I was glad. That must mean I wasn't one of the no good ones who needed to be put down. I was worth saving.

I wanted to ask him what he was doing on the island. He'd

quit, hadn't he? I certainly remembered something about that. But I was just glad to see him. I tried on a smile but it felt funny and fat. I'm not sure the muscles in my mouth worked.

Suddenly, the Lake Patrol was there. A carnival of flashing yellow lights, humming motors, more shouts, and a frothy wake that slapped further up my leg. They hauled out a Gurney. I was intrigued. A water rescue.

I was bundled up, gently heaved onto the Gurney which sent spikes of pain running crazily throughout my body. The pain seemed localized somewhere around my right shoulder and arm and ominously in my lower back. I didn't want to think about that, so I just didn't.

I really thought I was a quiet patient. I was fairly certain I hadn't voiced my wishes. This turned out to be entirely false. I later learned that I told them Dwayne Durbin's cell phone number over and over again. I was polite about it, I guess, but insistent.

So, when I was wheeled into Laurel Park Hospital Emergency Room, I was surprised to see Dwayne already there. I swear to God he looked haggard. I tried to say something witty, but his response was a terse, "She needs water," to the EMTs who regarded Dwayne as if he were a nuisance.

Actually, I could use some water, I thought.

The Emergency Room was abuzz with activity. Apparently I wasn't the only one who'd met with an accident on this miserably hot day. The uncommon humidity had sent large crowds of people to their boats on Lake Chinook and the Willamette River. There was also partying involved. Some alcohol-fueled incidents which included reckless driving, fistfights and one attempted homicide.

Accident victims, family members and police filled the area. I had to wait to be examined. I started feeling weepy. When Dwayne said, "You're a tough nut, darlin'. You're gonna be A-okay," it just did me in. I sniffled and Dwayne found me a tissue which he dabbed at my eyes as my right arm was pretty much useless and my left seemed wrapped under a tight blanket.

I hate to be a whiner, but when they finally came to examine me, it was a little bit rough. I mean, sheesh, hard fingers probed my flesh until I literally screamed. Dwayne frowned and listened to their talk. I basically closed my ears. We went through X-ray and then there was a long wait. I faced the indignity of being moved to the hall as other, more pressing cases, were whisked into the cubicles. From somewhere down the hall a man was moaning loudly.

My ol' buddy "shock" became my enemy. My teeth chattered and my body quivered.

"Can you sit up, Miss Kelly?"

I stared into the eyes of an intern whom I doubted was legal to drink alcohol. Dr. Kitsworth. Like, oh, sure, this kid knew what he was doing. "I'd have to say 'no'."

"Why don't you give it a try?"

It took everything I had but I managed, with Dr. Kitsworth's help, to prop myself into a sitting position. I might have slipped sideways but Dwayne held me up with a strong hand.

"Breathe in." I tried but my lower back seized up and I gasped in pain. "Bruised kidney," Kitsworth informed me. "You've strained your right shoulder and arm. Might be some damage to your rotator cuff. Ask your orthopedic."

Like I have one of those. "Bruised kidney?" I asked tentatively.

"Expect to see blood in your urine. You need to see an internist as well."

I felt faint.

He scribbled furiously and handed some papers to Dwayne. "You're ready to go."

They transferred me to a wheelchair. I waited patiently. I wondered idly if that's why we're called "patients." Dwayne finished up and wheeled me outside.

The bad news was: Dwayne had come in his truck. He helped me inside as best he could but all I did was whimper. Still, it was a relief to be out of the hospital with injuries that would heal. I hadn't even rated a real room. Something to cheer about.

"Did I see Grant Wemberly?" I asked, wondering if I'd dreamed it in the same way Jesse had felt he was dreaming.

"Uh-huh. He called 911."

"Really." I thought that over. "They took me out by boat."

"Darlin', on that side of the island, you're way down the cliff. It was the easiest way."

"Who let the dogs out?"

Yes, the song with the same title flitted across my mind but I wasn't in the mood for distractions. Dwayne, however, grinned briefly. I swear to God, if he broke out into song I was going to kill him . . . later . . . when I was better.

"I don't know yet. I'll fill ya in when I do."

He helped me into the bungalow. "Oh, Dwayne, Binky needs to be let out. Could you take her to the backyard?"

"You need a doggie door."

"You need to build it for me."

"I thought you were moving to Santa Fe."

Which is when I suddenly realized I hadn't thought once about Murphy. I hadn't called him for help, nor warned him of my accident. This gave me pause. In my hour of need, I'd sent for Dwayne. I didn't want to think what that could mean.

Murphy wasn't at the bungalow when Dwayne half-carried me inside. And his gun was not on the television any longer. I sank onto the sofa with relief. Binks ran over and stood on her hind legs, reaching a front paw out to dig at me.

"Now, leave her alone." Dwayne picked her up and they went out the back door.

I must've drifted off because suddenly Murphy was standing over me. His face was pale. "Jane," he said, looking stunned.

"I'm okay," I said.

"What happened? Who did this?"

"I don't know."

I closed my eyes. Vaguely I heard Dwayne and Binks come back into the room. Through squinted eyes I witnessed the two men square off. I would have smiled if I'd remembered how.

Those sneaky hospital folks must've given me a pain killer of some kind, as I was not tracking as I should.

"Hey . . ." I said. Murphy and Dwayne looked my way.

And I fell asleep.

Being injured and unconscious is kind of like being thrown a surprise party. You open your eyes and the room's full of people staring at you, waiting for your reaction. I don't like surprise parties and I didn't like waking to the crowd in my living room. I reacted with shock and dismay to the realization that Murphy and Dwayne had been joined by Booth and Sharona.

They'd been talking in low tones. I could tell Murphy wanted Dwayne out of the room and Dwayne was ignoring him completely. Booth was frowning. Sharona stood with her arms crossed, poised for battle. Whatever was wrong, you'd want her on your team, I decided.

"Hey," I said weakly.

The phone rang. Dwayne picked it up, beating Murphy out because he was closest. "Hello," he greeted the caller, his gaze on Murphy. His eyes swept my way, "Yeah, darlin', she's going to live." He listened. "She'll call you later. Yeah . . . good . . ." "Cynthia," he told me after he hung up. "I called her on the way to the hospital to pick you up."

"What time is it?" I asked.

"Late," Murphy said, eyeing the others.

Booth wasn't intimidated. "Jane, I need to talk to you."

"Now?" I asked, closing my eyes again.

"How about tomorrow?" he suggested.

"Tomorrow would be good," I murmured, closing my eyes. I felt Binks' hot breath on my cheek. She licked me on the mouth and nose.

Sometime in the night Murphy helped me to the bed. He tried to leave the door cracked but Binkster kept coming inside the bedroom, so he firmly shut her in the living room. I vaguely heard them fighting over the couch.

I woke early, my nerve ends screaming. I must've grunted in pain because I heard Murphy roll off the couch. He looked in on me. "How are you doing?"

"I hurt all over," I said grouchily.

He nodded. "I'll make coffee."

I stared at the ceiling. I wondered if being an invalid entitled me to order others to go grocery shopping for me. I think it does.

Murphy brought me a cup of coffee. I couldn't drink it in bed. I also had to pee, and I was afraid of what that might be like. I staggered out to the couch. Binky wagged her tail at me. She was on a pile of blankets on the floor. Seeing me gingerly perch on the sofa's edge, she jumped up beside me, taking it as an invitation.

"That damn dog won't leave you alone," Murphy observed.

I grunted again. I didn't know how to say I was more comfortable with her company than his.

"Why don't you lie down?"

"I'm planning a trip to the bathroom. Don't rush me."

Struggling upright again, I crab-stepped my way to the toilet. It was a painful trip, but not unbearable which made me feel better about what was going on with my injured kidney. If there was blood in my urine I wouldn't know. So, sue me. I didn't look.

I spent the morning napping. Dwayne stopped in at one point. I didn't open my eyes, but when he came close to me I recognized him by his smell. He leaned in and said, "I'm going to go get your car."

"Thanks."

Murphy said, somewhere behind Dwayne, "I've got some things to take care of, Jane. Booth'll be here soon."

"Go." I was glad I was going to be alone. I mean, puhleeze . . .

Booth and Sharona showed up about noon. I was sitting up by that point, propped by my bedroom pillows. Binks greeted the newcomers with a wagging tail, then jumped up on the couch beside me. She rested her chin on my thigh.

"She's so cute," Sharona said.

"Cute?" Booth swung around to stare at his fiancée.

Sharona lifted a dismissive shoulder. "Well, she is."

My heart lurched as I realized that here might be someone who would take the dog.

Booth didn't waste anymore time. "You didn't talk to Lopez," he accused.

"I'm going to. I just haven't yet."

"Don't worry. I've taken care of it."

My gaze flew to his. "What?"

"When Dwayne called me from the hospital, I phoned Lopez and told him what I knew."

"You told him about Jesse?" I straightened up involuntarily, felt a jab of pain, and forced myself to relax. But I was pissed.

"I told him everything that you told me. He's coming here to talk to you. Somebody caused your accident, Jane."

"When's he coming?"

"Anytime. I'm glad you're alone. You need to talk to Lopez without Murphy and Dwayne hanging around."

"Damn it, Booth! I don't need this."

"Yes, you do. And when Lopez gets here, tell him everything you told me. And anything else you're holding back. I think you're in danger. You need to be more careful."

"I'm too tired and I'm too weak to have some kind of interview now!"

"You just don't want to. And since when is Murphy your roommate?"

I clammed up. I wasn't talking to Booth about my personal life. I wished they would both just leave me alone. It worried me that Tomas Lopez was on his way over.

"I could make something for lunch," Sharona offered. "Are you hungry for anything?"

Murphy had forced some toast down me this morning. I shook my head, but Sharona was on a mission. She went into the kitchen and started rummaging through my cupboards. She said, "There's a waffle maker on the counter, and there's some mix. You need milk and eggs, though. You can't make waffles without milk and eggs."

Wanna bet?

"I'll go to the store," she said, all business. I smiled to myself. Yes, being an invalid meant minions forage for you. Things were looking up.

When Booth and I were alone, he drew a chair up to the couch. Absently, he scratched Binkster's ears. The dog stretched her front legs over my thighs, kicking out her back ones. She heaved a happy sigh and let Booth have his way with her.

"How are you feeling, really?" he asked.

"Shitty. My arm and shoulder are killing me. I already injured them a few weeks ago and I think I just made it worse. I also bruised my kidney."

"What's your medical insurance like?"

Barely existent. "The cheapest I could find."

He snorted and shook his head. "In your 'business,' you need some serious coverage, Jane."

"Yeah, I suppose so."

The front bell rang. Booth went to the door and admitted Tomas Lopez. He looked taller and grimmer today. I smiled weakly.

"So, you had an accident," Lopez said, taking over the chair that Booth offered him. He pulled out a small notepad and pen. "Your brother told me you were doing some private investigating on the island and that's how you were injured."

I shot Booth a look. He folded his arms over his chest, impervious. He looks a lot like me, Booth does. Same light brown hair. Same shape and hazel color of eyes. I kinda thought I might be looking at a mirror image of my own face: stubborn, determined and basically pissed.

"Where do you want me to start?" I said, giving in.

"Wherever you want."

I thought about everything that had happened. I have to admit, the idea of passing the baton to Lopez, so to speak, kind of bothered me. But then I thought about falling from the tree limb and I began my story. I started way back, from the time a girl from California followed a guy from Oregon back to his hometown of Lake Chinook. About the guy's best friend who turned out to be not only a hatchery fish, but a family annihilator as well. About how the girl got dumped by said boyfriend and stayed on in Lake Chinook, process serving and toying with the idea of becoming an information specialist. About how the boy returned to Lake Chinook just when the missing family annihilator reappeared.

"Reappeared?" Lopez questioned, his dark eyes on me.

I had to tell him about what Jesse, the Coma Kid, saw the night of his accident: Bobby Reynolds, in the flesh. Then I went on from that to my impressions about the rest of the Reynolds/Bradbury family: Cotton, Tess and Owen. I brought up visiting Cotton in the hospital and how Cotton had fingered Tess, and how Tess had fingered Cotton right back. I took a sidebar to mention the address I'd found in the book at Tess's condo and what I thought it meant. I couldn't tell by Lopez's expression if he thought I was brilliant or nuts. I then revealed how Cotton had suffered a change of heart about his wonderful son, Bobby. I added that I felt the whole thing was all about real estate. That Craig Cuddahy seemed to have a strong motive for killing Bobby, since he had no idea the Historical Society was going to throw a wrench into his plans. I told him Cuddahy's comment was that "the area is mine."

Booth interjected at this point. "But Cuddahy couldn't know Cotton Reynolds was going to die. And he couldn't know who would inherit after Bobby died unless someone told him."

"I'm just saying what I thought," I reminded him with an edge.

Lopez nodded. "That's what I'm looking for. The events that happened and your impressions." He couldn't help chiding, "It's what I asked for earlier."

I decided not to take offense, though I wanted to.

"Let me know if you're getting tired," Lopez added, more kindly.

Getting tired? He clearly wasn't on the drugs I was. But once started, I wanted to get it all out.

Sharona returned and took her parcels into the kitchen. I heard her messing around and tried to pump up a desire for waffles. One of the few times in my life I wasn't that hungry.

I continued, "Jesse heard a male voice yelling at Bobby, so it wasn't a woman."

"Could it have been Cotton?" Lopez asked.

The thought blew me away. "No . . . no . . ."

"If he said 'the area is mine,' wouldn't that stand to reason?"

"Well, yes . . ."

"Is that what he said? Or, was it a corruption of something else?"

"What do you mean?"

Lopez was patient. "Did Jesse actually hear 'the area is mine' or was it something he tried to make sound like that?"

"Jesse said the man yelled 'the area is mine.' " I hesitated. "Or maybe 'the area *was* mine.' "

Lopez left it for the moment. "At the benefit, Cotton was trying to convince you that Bobby was a great guy. This was about a week after the confrontation Jesse overheard on the island? But then, Cotton altered his will. Bobby's body was discovered, weighted down with slate."

"Slate?"

"We dredged up some pieces. They were in Phantom's Cove, approximately where the body floated loose. We think it's what the killer used to hold the body down. A section of it may have been the murder weapon, as Bobby died from his head wound." He frowned down at the notes he was taking. "The slate matches the roof slate from the Reynolds' property. We believe it came from somewhere on the island. We haven't made that detail public."

I was silent. The slate was the murder weapon. And it had weighted Bobby's body down.

"You've thought of something?" Lopez queried, reading my face.

Booth was leaning forward as well as Lopez. He gave me a look that warned, "Don't hold back!"

"There was a pile of slate by the garage. Roof slate, I think. It was just some rubble, really. But then later I saw that it had been cleaned up, and I heard the salvage barge had picked up pieces near the island. It just seemed odd that someone had thrown the pieces into the lake."

"You think someone was trying to disguise where the slate came from?"

"There's no escaping the fact that the slate is on the roof," I said. "But I think, whoever tossed the pieces in the water didn't want to advertise that there were extra pieces at hand? Easily grabbed in the heat of an argument?" I was guessing, groping my way through. Mainly I was thinking about what I would do if I were in a situation where I wanted to cover my tracks.

Lopez nodded. He scribbled on his notepad. I felt like a fraud. Like a tattletale. But Booth was giving me the evil eye, so I spilled my guts. As he'd said, let Lopez figure it out. I was done.

I could smell the waffles. My stomach wasn't ready, however. It was a tight ball. *Stress*, I thought. Great. I was hurt and stressed out, too.

Lopez got to his feet and exchanged handshakes with Booth. Booth asked Lopez if he would like to stay and have something to eat but Lopez declined. I just wanted them all to leave. Disappear. Evaporate. Vamoose. I watched the door close behind Lopez at the same moment Sharona appeared from the kitchen and announced the food was ready.

There was a big discussion about where I was going to eat: the kitchen counter, or on a table scooted up to the sofa. I didn't have the heart to say I wasn't hungry, so I let them slide the scarred end table in front of me, then place on it a plate heaping with waffles, butter and syrup. It looked wonderful, but . . .

"I just can't eat," I said regretfully.

Sharona peered at me. "You need rest."

"All I've done is sleep."

Booth frowned. "They gave you pills, Jane. Do you need another?"

"I don't think so."

"I'll put the waffles on a plate and save them in the fridge," said Sharona, doing just that.

"Should I tell Mom you've been in an accident?"

"No!" I croaked. "But call her. Tell her this week isn't working for me. Don't make me do it."

I could tell he didn't want to. Booth likes me to be the one to run interference between him and our mother. She's the one person he can't seem to get around, so he goes into avoidance mode whenever possible.

Sharona returned, touching Booth's arm. "We'll give you some peace and quiet, Jane."

"Thanks." I was liking her better and better.

She glanced at Binkster. "Don't give the dog any of the waffles."

Okay, maybe I didn't like her *that* well.

Booth said, "I don't think we should leave."

"I'll be fine," I assured. "Murphy'll be back soon."

He disagreed. "We can stay till he gets here."

"No . . ." I wanted to scream from frustration.

"Come on, Booth." Sharona's voice brooked no argument.

Okay. I did like her. Booth looked ready to argue some more but Sharona won out. As soon as they were out of sight I slid back down, pushing a reluctant Binkster to the end of the sofa. We both curled up and slept.

I was dreaming. I stood at the edge of a park and there were children playing in a sandbox nearby. Off camera, someone was yelling, ". . . area was mine . . . !" Beside me was Tomas Lopez. Neither of us could see who was yelling. One of the children, a boy, poured a bucket of sand over his sister's head. "I think he said *was*," Lopez pointed out to me, as if we were involved in a friendly debate on the subject. I listened as hard as I could but my ears couldn't pick out the words. The man was still yelling, but it was as if the sound had been put on super-slow play. "I don't get it," I said to Lopez. He said, "It's a misdirection . . ."

A sound penetrated my brain and I dragged myself up from the depths of sleep. Murphy was tiptoeing inside the bungalow.

The soft scent of roses perfumed the air. I opened an eye. He was carrying a huge bouquet of scarlet roses, the heads of the flowers bobbing in his arms. Seeing I was awake, he said, "I'll put these in water."

He'd barely left the room when I heard a light rap on the front door. I wondered how sick people ever got well. I didn't even have that many friends.

"Come in," I called, wondering if I should be more circumspect about allowing just anyone through the door. But it was Dwayne. "Hey," I greeted him, relieved. I glanced toward the kitchen and Dwayne did the same. Murphy appeared in the doorway at that moment. I could tell he wanted Dwayne to skedaddle, but he kept the thought to himself. Instead, after an awkward moment, he came up with something to do. Mumbling that he'd be back later, he headed out the door.

Dwayne stepped to the window, twitched the curtain back, watched him leave. We both heard the engine of his SUV rumble to life. "Don't want to add strife to your life, but I don't like him much."

"That's because he's taking me away from all of this." I smiled and it felt more natural.

"No, darlin', I just don't like him." He sat on the chair pulled closest to me. As much as Dwayne pisses me off, I feel satisfied and safe with him around. This was the feeling I wished I had with Booth, but until he gave up "big-brothering" me, it was not to be.

"Your car's outside. I left the truck near the island. Figured I'd walk back and pick it up."

"Murphy could take you."

Dwayne merely gave me a look. "I would have been here sooner, but the widow caught hold of me. I ended up driving your car to Foster's so she could pick up her boat. She was distraught about you. Sort of. She was a little fuzzy about what went on last night."

"I drove her home from Foster's. She and Craig Cuddahy were drinking vodka when I took my stroll around the grounds."

"Well, neither of them let the dogs out. It was the caretaker. Wemberly. He didn't know anyone was outside. It was a shock to him when the dogs started howling and chasing you."

"What was he doing there?"

"Picking up some things he'd left behind. Wemberly was also worrying about the dogs because the widow sure ain't thinking about 'em. He was at the house when I got there today. He was waiting to hear how you were. Blames himself."

"What did you tell him?" I was sort of deflated. Like everyone else, I'd thought this was some grand plan to eliminate Jane Kelly once and for all.

"I told him you were beat up but it was going to be okay."

"I feel kind of stupid now. I just spilled my guts to Tomas Lopez. I gave him every piece of information and half-assed theory I could come up with."

Dwayne shrugged. "It's his case. Let him figure it out. Besides, you weren't getting paid."

"No, I know . . ." I reassessed. "It's funny. Now that I know it was truly an accident, I should feel safer than I do."

"Hey, you're hurt. Makes you feel vulnerable. I don't like Murphy, but at least he's looking out for you."

"Thanks, Dwayne."

He smiled at me. "Don't go to Santa Fe. Date him if you have to. But don't go."

"I'll think about it," I said, meaning it.

Dwayne patted Binks on the head. She'd been so relaxed her tail had unfurled but now it wound up tight again and she looked at him with bright eyes. We both heard the hum of an approaching engine. Dwayne pulled the curtain aside again and said, "Your protector has returned." He sketched a good-bye to me and headed out the door. A half beat later Murphy let himself inside. As if they were involved in some elaborate dance, he took up position at the window and watched while Dwayne got his truck started and throbbed out of the drive.

"How are you feeling?" Murphy asked.

"How do I look?"

"Kind of beaten up."

I'd tried not to look while I was in the bathroom but I'd gotten a quick glimpse in the mirror before I could avert my eyes. The left side of my face was scratched and my chin was fat and starting to discolor. I looked like I'd been in a fight.

"Well, I feel worse than I look," I said, just as my cell phone rang.

It was a private number. "Hello?"

"Jane? It's Tomas Lopez. I've been following up on some of the leads you gave me."

"Already?"

"A couple of things are easy to figure out, if you have the means. I thought you should know that Craig Cuddahy was not on the island that night."

"You're sure?"

"Cuddahy was on a flight from Phoenix to Portland from nine p.m. until eleven. Jesse was taken to the hospital at ten-thirty. If there was a man confronting Bobby Reynolds as Jesse said, then he's someone else."

Chapter
Twenty

It took me another two days before I felt like really stirring around. Everyone said it was so fast. I was so lucky. Well, I didn't feel either fast or lucky. I felt irritated and annoyed. Everyone said grouchiness was a sign of improvement. That really pissed me off.

Murphy was the only one who seemed to think I was taking my sweet time, but then he was chomping at the bit to get the hell out of Dodge. For my part, I simply did not know how to feel. I wasn't up to planning a move out of state. I could tell Murphy wanted some sign that I was ready to go, but it just wasn't in me.

On Friday evening Cynthia stopped by. She examined Murphy's roses which had passed their zenith of beauty. She brought me a bouquet of long stemmed glass flowers: roses, irises, and snapdragons. I was overwhelmed and worried about the cost.

"They're on sale at the Black Swan," she said.

"I'm afraid to think about the price."

She gave me a crooked smile. "Well, since it looks like it's my gallery, I figured I could splurge."

"You bought the gallery?"

"I'm in the process. Your friend Tess has apparently moved

back to Texas permanently. I made her an offer. She turned me down flat. I made her another offer and said that was it, and she accepted. She likes to think she's driving a hard bargain." Cynthia's smile deepened. "So many people do."

"Tess isn't exactly a friend of mine. Certainly not anymore."

"Your ex-client, then." She gazed critically at my face. "Glad to see you're going to live. And playing house with Mr. Murphy, too. Finally getting some good sex?"

"I was."

"Where is the man?"

"Tying up every loose end he ever had in Lake Chinook. He wants me to move to Santa Fe with him."

That caught her attention. "*Are* you?"

I lifted my palms.

Cynthia could only stay a few minutes, but I assured her I would let her know my decision as soon as I'd made it for certain. After she left I removed Murphy's dying flowers from the only vase I possessed, cleaned it out, then arranged the glass flowers inside. I really liked them. If I'd had a mantel, I would have set them on it, but as it was my beat-up end table would have to suffice.

Bored, I wandered around the bungalow. Murphy had purchased a new computer, ostensibly for me—a laptop. It was so quiet, it worried me. He spent half his time on the Internet. He'd managed to find buyers for the four vintage Cadillacs Cotton had given him, and he was wrapping things up at the speed of light. A last few items were scattered across the kitchen counters. His smallest bag was there and I unzipped it and peeked inside, only to be faced with the gun again. I rezipped the bag. He was going to have to ship the damn thing back.

I walked out my back door and rested my elbows on the deck rail. The evening was warm. It was still light out, but growing darker. I watched a boat slowly pass by, its lights switched on as it cruised along. Slightly depressed, I walked around the house, passing between the cottage, the shed and the detached garage where Ogilvy stored God knew what. I'd argued with the man long and hard about letting me use the garage, but Ogilvy liked to play the deaf card when it suited him. He was old enough to be hard of hearing, but I knew it was a ploy.

I was itching to get in my Volvo and go somewhere. I wasn't leaving my car. And I wasn't leaving Binkster, either.

Standing in front of the cottage now, I glanced back. Binky was on a chair under the window, her nose pressed to the glass. She watched me as I stood in the middle of my driveway, gazing back at the house, memorizing it. I hate to admit it, because I don't like getting all sappy, but I loved my cottage. Okay, strictly speaking it was Ogilvy's, but I'd put my stamp on it.

I didn't want to leave.

Kicking a rock out of the way, I walked back toward the garage which lay on the east side of the cottage. From the west side there was no getting to the backyard, as the access was cut off by an overbearing laurel hedge. But a dirt path cutting through volunteer tufts of crabgrass gave access on the east side. I retraced my steps but stopped about halfway toward the deck.

The dusty ground in front of the garage bore the tire tracks of a car that wasn't mine. Nor was it any of my recent visitors. None of us ever parked off the asphalt that led from the road to the front of the cottage. My usual spot, where the Volvo sat currently waiting, was the parking pad which was perpendicular to the dirt drive that led to the garage.

But there were a clear set of tracks in the dust. I thought hard. Murphy didn't park there. Neither did Dwayne. I'd seen Cynthia's car in the driveway, and I didn't believe Lopez would have pulled up so far.

I walked back down the asphalt toward the main road and looked back. A maple tree, bent over as if it were bowing, obscured that section of my property from anyone casually driving by. You had to look hard anyway, down my long drive, to see anything. A car parked in front of the old garage would never be seen.

Back inside the house, I called Dwayne on my cell. "There are tire tracks at my house that I don't recognize," I said when he answered.

"You've had a lot of people there lately," he pointed out.

"Come and take a look."

My perfunctory manner seemed to penetrate. He said he'd be over in fifteen minutes. I'm sure he thought I was being paranoid, but I didn't care. And besides, he'd been kind of over-protective lately anyway. This would give him something to think about.

As soon as he arrived, I showed him the tracks. He took one quick look and decreed, "High-performance tires."

"How do you know?"

"Angela drives a BMW with high-performance tires. Left marks like these."

"You're kind of observant, aren't you?"

"Comes with the job, darlin'."

I looked at the tread again. "I don't know anyone with high-performance tires. None of my friends, anyway." In my mind's eye, I suddenly saw Owen's black BMW parked behind the Pisces Pub, then beside Murphy's SUV at the island. His shiny, spoked rims had been wrapped with a black strip of rubber, not the full-size width of regular tires, but the narrow band that signified high-performance tires.

"I know whose they are," I said and gave Dwayne the details.

"Leave it alone for now," he urged me, but I said no. Against his wishes, I called Owen and asked him to meet me at the Pisces Pub. Dwayne had made me promise I would call him immediately on his cell if there was any trouble. He didn't like it, but he would be standing by.

Murphy returned as I was dressing to meet Owen. It was a workout for me to pull on real clothes after lounging around in my sweats the past few days, but I had to look semi-presentable. I managed to pull on my black capris and a red, button-up blouse. No moving that left arm much. I tried to cover the scratches on my face with makeup, but it was pretty much a losing proposition. The ivory-to-light beige coverup hid the healing scabs and green-purple bruising but the bumpy skin under the makeup made it appear as if I were hiding some hideous disease. Ah, well, my flip-flops still possessed their little gems, so I looked as good as anyone could expect.

"Where are you going?" Murphy asked, looking concerned, as he followed me outside.

I gave him a brief recap as I unlocked the Volvo. I was really going to have to get that scratch fixed. Assholes who key cars should have to pay.

To my surprise, I hit a hot button with Murphy. "Are you ever going to give this up?" he demanded harshly.

I narrowed my eyes at him. I was getting sick and tired of all the obstruction I had to deal with. "I'm just going to talk to Owen. I'd like an explanation."

"All I want to do is get out of this town," Murphy muttered.

That did it. "You think I don't know that?" I shot back. "You think I haven't heard you glomping around here, griping and moaning, as if Lake Chinook is the scene of all the tragedy in the world?"

He was surprised that I talked back to him. I hardly ever talk back to him. Maybe to everyone else, but not really to Murphy. He stared at me as if I were a stranger. Maybe I was. He sure as hell felt like a stranger to me.

He said with an effort, "This is where it all started."

"I *know* this is where it started. I know it shattered your illusions about your best friend. I know, Murphy." My voice was calmer, but I wasn't. "Yet, you don't want me to even whisper the words: *family annihilator*. Bobby Reynolds murdered his family. He killed them one by one."

Murphy jerked as if I'd physically touched him.

"And the repercussions probably shortened his father's life. Cotton's in an early grave because of Bobby."

"And you won't give it up," Murphy stated grimly.

"Not when I'm involved, whether I want to be or not. Owen came to my place and I want to know why. And who's responsible for Bobby's death? That's what I want to know. Who knocked Bobby out with a piece of slate, rowed him out to Phantom's Cove and tossed his body overboard?"

"Why do you say rowed? Is that what Lopez told you?"

"I'm guessing, okay?" I said, frustrated. Couldn't he just let me rant? Just this once? "Nobody took the powerboat. Somebody would have noticed that. The rowboat was right by the garage, easy to grab. There's no road to Phantom's Cove, only steep trails and stairways from private homes. Only one way to get there: by water. And now that we know Bobby was on the island, it stands to reason. Lopez will keep digging till he learns the truth."

I climbed into my car. Murphy stood in the shadows. I shut my door, switched on the ignition, then rolled my window down. I stared through the gloom at him.

"You're not coming to Santa Fe." It wasn't a question.

I opened my mouth to say something assuring. *I love you ... I want to be with you ...* But all I could manage was, "Not till I'm finished."

I threw the Volvo into reverse and backed away, my headlights holding him in their lights as he watched me leave.

The mermaid on the door of the Pisces Pub looked a little worse for wear this evening. Someone had tossed a drink on her and it was dripping down her scales. I didn't get carded at the door, but it was a different bouncer tonight. He took one bored look at me and went back to a discussion with one of the barmaids—the ones who do not come around and take your order. Their function is still a mystery to me.

I tucked my hand inside my purse and fingered my cell phone. I wanted to know just where it was in case I needed to call Dwayne. It was comforting to know that with just a press of a button he'd be on his way.

I beat Owen there. Glancing around, I saw the only private spot was where two bar stools, tucked around the corner of the bar, were squeezed up to the wall. The glass shelves which made up the wall behind the bar itself, stuck out about a foot, kind of blocking the view of the stools. It might be tough to order a drink from this angle, but the area suited me just fine tonight.

Owen arrived ten minutes later, looking harried. He ran a hand through his hair, a curiously sensual gesture, and glanced around the room for me. His gaze passed over me twice before I lifted a hand and caught his eye. Maybe I was looking worse than I thought.

"Your invitation—or should I say ultimatum—sounded urgent," he said.

"I just wanted to make sure you came tonight."

"Why? Is this about Bobby? Do you know who killed him?" he asked quickly.

I hesitated, thinking through several gambits before deciding to play it straight. It seemed the quickest way to get answers. "Owen, this is about how you came to my house, let yourself in uninvited, and then left. What were you looking for?"

"I didn't let myself in," he answered instantly, so fast I almost missed the other implications.

"But you came to my house." He hesitated a moment, thinking fast. "Don't make up a lie," I warned.

"Yes, I came to your house," he admitted reluctantly.

"And you parked in front of the garage."

His lips tightened. "All right, I thought you were home. I just kind of wanted to block you in. I didn't want you to leave until I talked to you."

"I don't park in the garage."

"Well, if I'd known that, I wouldn't have bothered." He signaled to the bartender who nodded but didn't make any move to take his order. "It didn't matter anyway, because you weren't there." He turned my way, frowning at me. I could tell he was assessing me. "Turned out that was the night of your accident. I didn't know it at the time. So, I figured I'd talk to you later. How're you doing, by the way? The coverup's not working all that well."

"Thanks."

He heard the irony and smiled faintly. "You can *never* get a beer around this place."

"What is it you wanted to talk to me about?" I wasn't sure I was completely buying his story, but I was willing to go with it.

"The book jacket."

My brows furrowed. "Book jacket? You mean . . . ?"

"The book jacket you took from my mother's condo," he said patiently. "She wants it back."

"It won't help her. I already told Lopez about the address and what I'm sure it means."

"According to my mother's lawyer, since you *stole* that item, it cannot be used as evidence by the police. The prosecution will have to prove they learned of that address some other way. This way it's 'fruit from the poisonous tree,' or something like that. Can't be used in a court of law."

"Tess has engaged a criminal defense attorney?"

He nodded. "She thought it might be a good idea."

The bartender brought us both a beer. I'd stopped taking my meds a few days earlier, but I decided not to risk alcohol on my bruised kidney (which I'm happy to report seems to be working just fine now, thank you very much).

As Owen drank lustily from his glass mug, I said, "So, if it's meaningless, why does she want it back?"

"It's hers. She doesn't want you to have it."

"And you didn't break into my cottage to steal it back?"

"Swear to God."

I watched him finish his beer, checking my bullshit meter to see how much I believed him. Curiously, I did think he was telling the truth.

"Did you help her hide Bobby all those years?" I asked.

"Nope. And I'm not saying she did, either," he added quickly.

"Duly noted."

"After what Bobby did, I wouldn't lift a finger for him except to call the police." Owen was clear on that. "I kind of thought

Mom might know where he was . . . but I wouldn't be able to swear to it. It's all over now, anyway. I don't want her to go to jail."

"She broke the law," was all I said by way of answer.

"That remains to be proven."

Owen slid me a sideways look. "So, why were you so all-fired eager to see me tonight? What did you think I'd done, besides break into your place?"

"I just wanted to know what you were looking for."

"You thought I had something to do with Bobby's death," he guessed. "You're still working on that."

"Only as an exercise in futility."

He smiled. "You don't know whether I'm guilty of something or not." He twisted his beer mug around on the bar. "Well, I didn't kill Bobby."

I was beginning to believe him. "Glad to hear it. I was having a hell of a time ascribing a motive to you."

"What about plain old jealousy?"

"I guess."

"What happened to Cuddahy? I thought you were zeroing in on him."

"Who told you that? Murphy?"

Owen nodded.

"Cuddahy's got an iron-clad alibi for the night Bobby fought with his killer."

"The night Bobby fought with his killer," Owen repeated. He made it sound like the title of a movie. "What night was that?"

"Bobby was seen on the island by the kid who ended up in a coma for a while. The kid heard someone yelling at Bobby. The kid ran away, but it's pretty clear Bobby and another man got in a fight. Bobby was hit over the head with a piece of slate and dumped in the lake."

Owen stared at me. Maybe Lopez would have preferred I kept the information to myself, but I wanted to see Owen's face when I laid it all out. He was surprised, but more than that, he was interested. "Who did it, Jane?" he asked, and I realized all at once that he didn't know, that he was waiting for me to tell him.

"I don't have the answer," I said, discombobulated.

"Oh, come on."

"No, I'm serious."

"You did think it was me," he said on a note of discovery. "You really did." He gave a little bark of laughter. "If it's not Cuddahy, and it's not me, who is it?"

I slid off my stool. The sixty-four-thousand-dollar question. "Someone else, I guess. Someone the authorities are going to have to find."

"You're throwing in the investigative towel?"

"I'm seriously thinking about it."

I called Dwayne on my drive home and said, "Owen stopped by to collect Tess's book jacket with the Hepburn address inside. I wasn't home because I was being chased by Betty and Benny and taking a trip to Laurel Park Hospital."

"That's all it was?"

"I think so." I filled him in on my conversation with Owen and my impressions.

Dwayne listened hard. "So, you've dropped the real estate motive?"

"Yes, but I don't think it's jealousy, either."

"Maybe we've made it too complicated. Misdirected ourselves."

I was gratified that Dwayne included himself, though it wasn't exactly true as he'd been warning me against staying involved for weeks.

The jaunt to the Pisces Pub had taken its toll. My tail felt like it was dragging. When I drove into my drive, I saw Murphy's rented SUV. It was heartening to see, as a part of me had expected him to chuck it all in and take off. It's what he wanted to do. He'd just been waiting for me.

But when I walked inside, greeting an eager Binkster with pets and smoochy sounds (yes, I've now become officially stupid

about this dog) I was met by a sober-faced Murphy whose bags
were stacked near the front door and who was wearing a light-
weight jacket even though the temperature was still in the high
eighties.

"You're leaving," I said.

"I came to the conclusion a few hours ago that you're hanging
onto this investigation as a means to keep from coming to Santa
Fe. There's no reason for me to stay any longer."

"Wait." Perversely, now that he was really going, I wanted to
slow him down somehow.

"For what, Jane?"

I didn't answer. I brushed past him to the kitchen. I wanted a
means to stop him. Desperately I glanced around, searching for
something to delay his departure until I had a chance to talk to
him. I pulled open the refrigerator door and saw milk, eggs and
four-day-old waffles.

"I'm starving," I lied. "Sharona made me waffles the other
day, but I couldn't eat them. I want some now. Breakfast dinner.
Nothing sounds better."

"I've got a flight scheduled. I'll catch something on the
plane."

"Are you kidding? Pretzels and Coke, maybe. Haven't you got
a few minutes?" I cringed at the begging note in my voice.

I thought he was just going to take off. He was grim, determined and out of patience. But he came back into the kitchen.
Hurriedly, I plugged in the waffle maker and grabbed the mix,
milk and eggs.

I was chattering. I wouldn't have been able to tell you about
what. My lack of culinary skills got touched on. A joke about how
I was going to have to expand my repertoire past waffles. "Do
you know Phil Knight, Mr. Nike himself, used a waffle iron back
in the good old days when he was just starting to make running
shoes? That's how he got the soles to have those little designs.
Better traction, I guess."

Murphy stood near the back door, at one end of my galley

kitchen. I faced the counter, whipping up the batter, waiting for the waffle iron to heat. Something was off, but I couldn't quite put my finger on it. Binkster hung by my feet but her gaze was fixed on Murphy.

"Aren't you baking in that jacket?" I asked.

He shook his head. "What did Owen say?"

"Oh. Those were his tire tracks, but his visit really wasn't anything sinister."

"I could have told you. I know Owen."

"You were friends with him, too."

"Not really. He was just around." Murphy stared off into space. "The guy's a born wheeler and dealer."

"So I've learned."

"You've learned a lot," he said.

"No, I was way off, Murphy. I thought it was all about real estate. I've tried to force square pegs into round holes. It seemed to me it was about money and property, but I was . . . misdirected." Something clicked in my brain. My dream. Tomas Lopez said the same thing, and then Dwayne had, too. Misdirection. "I don't know what it's about, " I said. And then something else fell into place, a second click in my brain. A realization that had been there but I'd ignored. "Yes, I do! It's about retribution for Bobby killing his family. It has to be! Somebody served him up the justice they felt he deserved."

"The waffle iron's hot," Murphy observed.

I poured the batter distractedly then picked up a spatula. "Lopez asked if the man's voice could have been Cotton's. I dismissed that. I didn't want it to be Cotton. I couldn't believe he would kill his own son. But then Bobby killed Cotton's grandchildren, baby Kit and Jenny and . . ."

There was a long, weighty pause. I looked at Murphy. He stood like a statue. "What's wrong?"

He suddenly came toward me and wrapped his arms around me. I still had the spatula in one hand and was so surprised that I just stood there, my arms sticking out on either side of him, one hand holding the spatula, the other reaching forward as if ready to offer a handshake. Awkwardly I patted his back with my free hand. "Murph?"

He pulled away almost immediately and went back to stand in his earlier position. "His name was Aaron."

"Oh . . . right. Aaron."

"I have their pictures from the newspaper. It's hard to look at those photos and think about what Bobby did."

Murphy's face was white. He was staring at the ground. He'd shoved his hands inside the pockets of his jacket. Binkster growled, low in her throat, staring back at him.

I gazed at the dog, almost amused. "What's with you?"

"She doesn't like me," Murphy said in a strangled voice.

"Binks likes everybody."

"Not me."

I didn't answer.

"You really think Cotton killed Bobby?" The words seemed ripped from Murphy.

"I just said I didn't want to believe it," I answered slowly, trying to make sense of the strangeness that had come over the room. There was something in the air. Something off-kilter. "But 'the area is mine' . . . who would say that?"

"I've got to go, Jane," he said abruptly. Binks' eyes were fixated on Murphy's right pocket.

"She thinks you have food," I said. But Binkster's stance was aggressive. The little roll of ruff on the back of her neck was electrified. Murphy shifted. I realized with a distinct shock that he held his gun in his pocket. I'd felt its hardness when he hugged me but hadn't registered what it was. "You've got your gun," I said, stupid with disbelief. "You've got your gun in your hand. You can't take a gun on the plane."

Murphy's eyes were glued to the dog. He pulled the gun from his pocket and looked at it, as if deciding what to do. My pulse skyrocketed.

"What . . . *what?*" I asked.

Binkster quivered. Then suddenly, she charged Murphy. She

moved like a shot. I couldn't take it in. Murphy, surprised himself, automatically aimed the gun on her.

"*Stop!*"

Binkster sank her teeth into Murphy's calf. Murphy yelped. His finger tightened on the trigger.

"Stop! Goddamn it! *Stop!* Hurt her and I'll knock your *fucking* head off!"

My left arm grabbed the waffle iron. I slammed it against the side of his head with the force and fury of a mother bear.

Blast! The bullet ripped through my cabinet, sending shrapnel splinters zinging everywhere. I shielded my eyes.

Murphy went down like lead. The waffle iron bumped away. I scooped up my dog, shaking all over. Binks growled and scrambled to go after Murphy some more, but I held her tight, stunned. I was shocked at myself, shocked at the dog, shocked at Murphy.

Murphy lifted a hand to his face in disbelief. I could smell batter and cooked flesh. Little, angry red square blisters formed on his cheek. Superficial wounds. He looked up at me. With the emotion I'd felt when he threatened Binks' life, he was lucky I hadn't killed him.

"Why?" I asked, my voice shaking. "*Why?*"

His gaze was tortured. "Because . . . *Aaron was mine . . .*"

Epilogue

A week later Dwayne took me to Foster's On The Lake and bought dinner and drinks. He said he was celebrating the fact that I'd finally gotten off the fence and joined with Durbin Investigations, his unofficial business name. He told me I was going to have to apply for an investigator's license. He also told me I should apply for a gun license. I have yet to do either.

I'm ashamed to say that when Murphy hit me with the fact that Aaron was his, it took me a few minutes to assimilate. I just couldn't process. I'd like to say I was right on it. The path to the answer was finally clear to me. Hallelujah! I see all!

Unfortunately, I was way off. Maybe, in a teensy, dark corner of my heart I'd worried that Murphy wasn't playing fair and square. He'd told me too many almost lies for me to completely trust him, though I'd sure as hell tried to.

As soon as he was down, he started to talk. It just came pouring out. A flood of relief that he could finally confess.

Bobby had taken up with Laura on the heels of her relationship with Murphy. Apparently, she didn't tell anyone she was pregnant. Maybe she didn't know. Either way, Bobby seized the opportunity to steal her from Murphy. When he offered marriage, she accepted. Somewhere in the years that followed Laura, or Bobby, confessed the truth about Aaron to Murphy. Bobby had told Cotton already. His motive remained a mystery. Maybe he'd hoped his father wouldn't care so much about Bobby's best friend. Maybe he wanted to sever Cotton's grandfatherly interest in Aaron. Either way, it didn't work. Cotton loved Murphy like a son and when Bobby showed up on Cotton's doorstep, the first thing Cotton did was call Murphy. Heather had been right on that and Murphy had lied.

I wasn't completely off, as it turned out. Tess had been taking care of Bobby financially, but he'd grown bored and restless and headed like a homing pigeon back to Lake Chinook. Cotton was overwhelmed to see his son again, but Bobby's actions could not be denied, forgotten or forgiven. And when Bobby seemed to express little or no remorse, Cotton placed the S.O.S. to Murphy.

For his part, Murphy was torn, desperately hating Bobby for what he'd done, desperately wanting to see him again, to learn anything about why Bobby had killed his family. He planned to beat the hell out of Bobby when they came face-to-face. He wanted answers. He wanted to understand. He wanted some kind of revenge.

But there were no answers to be had. When Murphy saw Bobby he was swept by more sadness than rage. The question I'd asked Murphy—"Why? *Why?*"—had no answer from Bobby when Murphy posed it to his best friend. Maybe Bobby just couldn't respond. And truly, there had never been any answer that could've explained killing his family. Nevertheless, Murphy pressed until Bobby grew furious. Murphy didn't understand. Nobody understood! The whole world was against him. It wasn't his fault! They *drove* him to it!

Murphy couldn't fathom it. Bobby, the boy who'd had everything, the hatchery fish, was blaming *them*?

Heated words became enraged fury. Jesse Densch happened to be running around the island at Bobby and Murphy's final face-off. What Jesse didn't see was that Bobby held a gun on Murphy—the weapon Murphy bagged and removed from the scene. But looking down the barrel of his best friend's gun, Murphy's rage exploded. He yelled at him, "Aaron was mine!"

and slammed him in the head with a piece of slate. Whereas my waffle iron blow merely knocked Murphy down, Murphy's slate hit Bobby in the temple and killed him.

It happened fast. Murphy was shattered. He had a moment to choose: go to the authorities or hide the body. Making his choice, he rowed Bobby to Phantom's Cove, the site of some of my most treasured moments with Murphy. Well, believe me, I don't feel the same way now.

Then I showed up at the benefit, all gung-ho about being a private investigator. Did Murphy decide to suddenly invite me to Santa Fe because it would derail me? Or did he actually care?

That question hasn't been answered. I choose not to think about it too much. I did, however, suggest Sharona to be Murphy's criminal defense attorney. His actions were in self-defense, but then there's that tricky issue of sinking the body. . . .

I have faith Sharona will do well for him.

Of course, Cotton suspected what had transpired between Bobby and Murphy, but at some level, I think he believed justice may have been served. Ill as he was, however, the events served to end his life.

I was seated at the table, lost in thought. Late August and it was still hot. Dwayne leaned into me. "What would you like, darlin'?"

"How about a Sparkling Cyanide?"

"That's a drink?"

"Blue curacao and some other stuff. Cyan means blue."

Dwayne gave me a look that said, "remember who you're talking to." "People who ingest cyanide choke from a lack of oxygen, and darlin'," he drawled, "when you don't get your oxygen, you turn blue and die. That's why it's *cyan*ide."

Jeff Foster leaned in to our table. "I'm not naming any drink around here cyanide."

"Be adventuresome, Foster," I suggested.

"And you're not getting any more free ones. I had a talk with Manny."

I glanced over at Manny as Foster walked away. He grinned at me and winked. I was still safe.

I'd kind of gone into a mild depression after Murphy's confession. It was really a blow to my ego to realize everything I'd built my dreams on was false. But the good news was I didn't have to leave Lake Chinook.

Tess remains at large somewhere in Texas. It's a big state, but maybe not big enough to escape the long arm of the law. Tomas Lopez isn't a guy who's going to just let it be. But since Tess has already lawyered-up herself, maybe she'll come out with a light sentence.

And Heather has apparently listed the island with Paula Shepherd and Brad Gilles. I understand Owen is interested in purchasing it. I wish him all the luck, but even with his apartment building in First Addition, I'm not sure he can swing it.

Misty, the sassy waitress who Heather thought Cotton had his eye on, took our order. Since Dwayne was buying I picked the prime rib. It was the most expensive item on the menu.

"Knock yourself out," Dwayne told me, amused.

I think I love him.

No. I'm not even sure I like him. Well, okay, I'm mildly attracted but I'm *not going there*.

I glanced over to Dwayne's boat. We brought the Binkster along. I could tell even from the distance she was whining. I'd like to say it was because she wanted to be with me, but I imagine it was the smell of the barbecue. It still amazes me how she read Murphy that day. Honestly, I didn't think she was capable of it.

Murphy had broken into my place. I'd apparently worried him right from the get-go. To get me to stop thinking the break-in had been related to Bobby's death, he'd told me about the unlatched window. I still worry that I'm not cut out for this business, but then I remind myself that love makes you stupid. I'd fallen in love with a guy who dazzled me with a white smile and a red convertible, but I hadn't known that guy at all.

Note to self: no more falling in love.

When Booth learned about my run-in with Murphy, he was nearly as shocked as I was. He'd known Murphy a long while as well. I'm happy to report, though, that it seems like he's finally accepted that I'm working with Dwayne. We Kellys may be bull-headed, but once in a while we know when to give up. He's been as good as his word about the medical insurance: I'm scheduled to meet with an agent from my new company next week. Who knows? I may even find I have an internist and orthopedist available.

Mom is arriving on Monday. Booth and I have kept my exploits to myself, for the time being.

Misty brought my blue martini on a silver platter. It looked divine. Dwayne shuddered and lifted his beer. His tastes are far more pedestrian than my own. But I can't complain. He called a friend of his who knows a guy who paints cars. The Volvo is scheduled to get rid of its scratch.

A lady at the next table over, clad in an expensive taupe suit and carrying a Louis Vuitton bag, leaned toward me. "Do you mind my asking?" she whispered, pointing to my drink. "What is that?"

"Sparkling Cyanide."

"Oh, goodie." She broke into smiles and looked around. Foster was at another table, making sure his guests were all happy and satisfied. Catching the woman's signal, he came to her table.

"I'll have what she's having," she said. "Sparkling Cyanide!"

I lifted my glass to Foster in a salute.